MORE PRAISE FOR

Magic City

"*Magic City* is one of those fine novels that one reads not because right makes might, because good does not triumph, but the book is read because we need to remind ourselves of the sad failure to safely, thoroughly, integrate America's human community." —*Flagstaff Review*

"As in *Voodoo Dreams*, Rhodes calls upon her talent for summoning up the literary device called magical realism." —*Mesa Tribune*

"A combination of history, mystical happenings and murder makes this a thrilling read." —*Newton* [Massachusetts] *Tab*

"With precise detail and fully drawn characters, Jewell Parker Rhodes has created a novel that brings us closer to the truth about our country and ourselves. These are the truths we should be seeking. This is the place to find them."

—Susan Straight, author of *I Been in Sorrow's Kitchen and Licked Out All the Pots* and *The Gettin Place*

"In *Magic City*, Jewell Parker Rhodes has made a tragic American story come vividly to life and has made these people—black and white and red, rich and poor, educated and illiterate—all achingly human. Rhodes must be commended for bringing such an important story front and center, and for making it as instructive and as moving as it is horrific."

—Randall Kenan, author of *Let the Dead Bury Their Dead* and *A Visitation of Spirits*

"Jewell Parker Rhodes's *Magic City* takes an ugly chapter of American history and turns it into a human tale of vulnerable people with imperfect motives and skewed vision, people who interact in dire ways with monumental consequences. . . . I could not, would not put this book down, not even after its last searing sentence."

—Julianne Malveaux, author of *Sex, Lies, and Stereotypes*

"We've seen Jewell Parker Rhodes use magic before to explore the meanings of, and urge drama from, history, and her approach here to the evocative and outrageous events of 1921 shows us that magic can cut two ways. Rhodes writes about our common human plight with a powerful dramatist's voice; she has created with *Magic City* a clear open window on a rueful day."

—Ron Carlson, author of *Plan B for the Middle Class*

"*Magic City* is a victory against amnesia. One will remember Tulsa, 1921! This book captures the literary magic of a woman who is fast becoming a bright and shining star. Not even Houdini could create more wonder."

—E. Ethelbert Miller, editor of *In Search of Color Everywhere: A Collection of African-American Poetry*

Magic City

Jewell Parker Rhodes

HarperPerennial
A Division of HarperCollins*Publishers*

Grateful acknowledgment is made to Warner Bros. Publications U.S. Inc. for permission to reprint lyrics from "I Want to Be Happy" by Vincent Youmans and Irving Caesar. Copyright © renewed 1924 by WB Music Corp. (ASCAP) & Irving Caesar Music Corp. (ASCAP).

A hardcover edition of this book was published in 1997 by HarperCollins Publishers.

HarperCollins books may be purchased for educational, business, or sales promotional use. For information please write: Special Markets Department, HarperCollins Publishers, Inc., 10 East 53rd Street, New York, NY 10022.

First HarperPerennial edition published 1998.

Designed by Liane Fuji

The Library of Congress has catalogued the hardcover edition as follows:

Rhodes, Jewell Parker.
Magic City : a novel / by Jewell Parker Rhodes — 1st ed.
p. cm.
ISBN 0-06-018732-8
1. Afro-American men—Oklahoma—Tulsa—Fiction.
PS3568.H63 M34 1997
813'.54—dc21 97-4271

ISBN 0-06-092907-3 (pbk.)

00 01 02 ❖/RRD 10 9 8 7 6 5 4 3 2

To Kelly and Evan
Live your best dreams

Tulsa is the "Magic City."
Young, prosperous,
New oil spewing from the ground.
A dream land,
The most modern city in the West.

—*Dunn's Western Travel Guide,* 1920

Go down, Moses
Way down in Egyptland
Tell old Pharaoh,
Let my people go.

—Negro Spiritual

Magic City

1

Sunday, May 29, 1921

Joe Samuels had decided to quit dreaming. Decided to stop dreaming of leaving Tulsa, of discovering new horizons streaked with magic. Yet here he was lying by the tracks, his head to the ground, listening to the rumblings of the 9:45 preparing to leave, trailing Pullman cars and flat cars loaded with cotton and crude.

Weary, disoriented, Joe needed sleep. He wanted to ride the rails over the Rockies to the Pacific in a sleeper car, cozy, dreamless in an upper bunk. He didn't want to dream of dying. Three nights in a row, he'd had the same dream. A dream that he sensed was something more than a dream—a haunting, a premonition, an evil worked by the Devil.

The train whistle squealed: two short bursts, one long. The conductor called, "All aboard." Joe fought the urge to dash forward, jump aboard, and settle in the converted boxcar for Negroes. He'd be thrown off without a ticket. He could hide wedged between animals or crates. But without cash, he'd starve wherever he ended. He'd be forced to wire his father. Forced to admit he couldn't make it on his own.

Joe felt the ground vibrating beneath his fingertips. Steam hissed.

The train lurched, picking up speed—its headlight glaring, glinting against the steel rails—moving, groaning, journeying on. *Then gone. Leaving no trace, no murmur.* Only stillness, quiet rails, and humid heat.

Despair washed over him. Joe did and didn't want to be in Tulsa.

He loved Deep Greenwood, the Negro section of Tulsa. Church women testified how Greenwood had risen miraculously out of the dust, how ex-slaves had built a town of telephone poles, electric lights, and a Booker T. Washington High School.

"In America, there's no better place than Greenwood to be a Negro," his father always said. "No better place to be a Samuels." Property and wealth. Joe, the youngest son. Born a bit too brown for his mother's taste; too lazy for his father's. But always, in Greenwood, he was the banker's son.

In Tulsa, he was just another nigger. A two-bit shoeshine.

Joe imagined himself riding the rails to the ocean. Then he'd leap, manacled, off the Golden Gate Bridge, just like Houdini had. He'd surface, hands freed, to champagne and cheering.

In a year of shining shoes, Joe had saved two hundred dollars. Another year, he'd have four hundred. Another year, his father might understand why he wanted to go. Might even wish him well. In another year, Joe might be able to say good-bye to his sister Hildy. To Lying Man. His brother's grave. He might understand why, in a place he loved so much, he felt like he was dying.

He was afraid of going home to bed, of being haunted by his nightmare. He'd give up all his imaginings, his longing to leave Tulsa, if only his nightmare would stop. He'd vow never to dream again. He'd be grateful for living in Tulsa.

Lifting his head, Joe thought he heard Lying Man's harmonica:

How long the train's been gone?
Baby, how long? How long?

Reluctant, Joe stood, humming the tune. Negro curfew was ten o'clock. He passed the ticket window. The clerk hollered, "Best hurry home, boy. Else you'll catch it."

"Yes, sir."

"Boy!" the ruddy man leaned out the window. Joe held his breath. The clerk's bald head caught the light. "Do that trick again."

"Yes, mister." Retracing his steps, Joe pulled a coin from his pocket. It flipped in and out between his knuckles, picking up speed, a thin ribbon of silver diving, weaving in and out across his dark fingers, until it disappeared.

"I'll be damned."

The station clock read 9:55.

Joe murmured, "Got to hurry, mister," and turned onto First Street. Glancing in the windows of the Pig's Ear Diner, he saw deputies still drinking coffee. He ought to make it.

A crowd was leaving the Opera House: women draped in silk and fox stoles; men, in top hats and tails. Joe avoided them, studying the pavement's cracks—he was still in Tulsa, not Greenwood.

Walking briskly, Joe turned into Courthouse Square. It was faster cutting across the park. Bluegrass cushioned his feet; oaks arched overhead. On the left was the Ambrose Building, where he worked, and the Henly Hotel. On the right was the Courthouse and the city's pride—a seven-story, steel and brick "inescapable" jail. Joe bet it couldn't hold Houdini. They could handcuff Houdini, lock and chain him in a darkened cell, and he'd still escape.

He headed northeast for another mile. Greenwood and Archer divided Tulsa like a cross. Bawdy houses, juke joints, and gambling dens flourished in back alleys.

Joe stepped onto the northeast curb; he was safe. Home. In Deep Greenwood. But he didn't feel any ease. He turned onto Elgin where, in daylight, children tossed balls, skinned their knees, and climbed trees. Atop the hill, in front of him, he could see Mt. Zion's steeple outlined against the sky. Street lamps cast gnarled shadows. Joe hesitated, feeling dread as he remembered his nightmare. *His home, the entire street bursting into flames.*

"Evening, Joe," voices called from the enclosed porches. Shrill and bass voices blended with evening sounds: trilling crickets, a hiccuping baby, frenzied moths batting at screens. Joe couldn't see faces. He didn't need to, for he knew everyone, who lived where.

"Fine evening."

"Yes, Mrs. Jackson."

"A bit late, aren't you, Joe?" asked Abe, a sweeper at McNulty's Baseball Park.

"Visiting a girl?" asked Miss Wright, his third-grade teacher, now blind as a newborn.

"No, Miss Wright."

Joe exhaled, feeling his spirits lift. Deep Greenwood. Tulsa's darker cousin. A black small town within the white city.

What was it that salesman had said? Joe had been buffing the final polish when the freckle-faced man, pleased with his day's sales of aluminum pots, dish rags, and lye, crowed to his companion, "I'd live in Greenwood myself, if there weren't so many niggers."

Joe slipped through the back door of his house, tiptoed through the parlor.

He wouldn't dream. "Everything is a matter of will," Houdini had said. He'd read it in a magazine. Staring at Houdini's eyes, brows arched, pinpricks of light trapped in his irises, Joe had felt magic stir inside him. He could be more than Tulsa's nigger, more than the banker's son.

A light was on in the kitchen. Hildy was probably reading her Bible and making biscuits. He climbed the stairs to his attic bedroom, stripped his clothes, and crawled into bed.

Handcuffs held him. Not regulation cuffs but metal of some private design with double bolts and a strange inflexible spring. Joe could feel fear tricking him, causing his heart to contract, telling him it couldn't be done—that he couldn't escape.

"Who do you think you are?"

Joe bit the thin skin inside his mouth, tasting blood, feeling pain rush behind his eyes. It was all a matter of will. Pain lessened fear. All he had to do was let himself relax, detach himself from the panic of feeling cold metal twisting his arms back in their sockets. The trick was to feel the steel's special grace. Not to be afraid of stillness, of wrists trapped in polished bands. He stretched his fingers, long and dark, arcing them as though he were about to sound a chord on ivory keys. Then, he sighed, clasping his palms (fingers alternating) in a gentle embrace.

"Who do you think you are?"

His street was deserted. Shutters closed; screen doors locked. No one could save him.

The sun scorched his neck as he tried to force back sweat running from beneath his arms, along his bare waist, and down to his penis, which hung limp, as shriveled as the bulls' balls hauled from the slaughter.

It was all in how you relaxed. Just as he tried to relax now—to detach himself from the band of white-robed ghosts circling him, humming disjointed campfire tunes, sparking high-pitched laughter while drinking from bottles of rye. Joe noted how their pointed leather boots kicked up dust, dirtying the edges of their gowns. Cowboys still, every one.

"Nigger, who do you think you are?"

Joe blinked. He was as bare and vulnerable as the day he was born.

"Who do you think you are?"

Joseph Samuels born of Douglass and Ruth. An uncherished son.

A hood covered the man's face. When a breeze lifted the cotton, Joe could see blunted roots from the man's morning shave. He smelled a licorice-scented pomade. But it was the eyes—Harry Houdini eyes—wide, focused, and gray, staring deep into his soul that unnerved him.

"Who do you think you are, boy?"

Joe longed to disappear magically, to confound everyone and have them pay due reverence. He was extraordinary, special. But, today, he'd settle for a simple escape from metal.

Joe unclasped his fingers. It was time for the Houdini flair—time to undo galvanized steel and shame these white men. Yet his hands and wrists began swelling, pressing against the metal cuffs. His fingers became stumps, unable to bend and disengage the clasp. He felt his panic rising again.

"Who do you think you are?"

"Nobody."

The ghosts multiplied, fertile as high-plains rabbits. Wind whipped their robes, making them look like white-water foam rushing toward him.

His hands and wrists were engorged—metal cut into his expanding skin. Blood pooled on caked soil. A squat ghost threw the contents of a bucket at him. At first, the wet splashing against his skin, into the dank crevices of his arms and legs, felt good. Then the smell drew up his nose: gasoline.

The man with the Houdini eyes struck a match on his boot.

Joe started screaming. It was all a matter of will.

The flame was tossed. "Burn your black ass in hell."

A roar rose from the crowd, circling in to see the spectacle.

Joe began screaming as waves of thick smoke washed over him, as flames peeled back his skin, consuming his swollen hands, leaving charred bone dangling in the cuffs.

Sparks leaped from his skin, clinging to porch steps, the rooftops of Greenwood, before bursting into showering flames while he screeched hopelessly and helplessly, "Water."

"That's right. You better get your black self out of bed. You think you can sleep all day?"

Sheets wet and tangled from his dreaming, Joe Samuels woke to a bright morning.

"Damn you, Hildy. You crazy?" Joe was trembling, sitting upright, gasping from the cold water thrown onto his face. "You think I'm drunk?"

"You were drunk with dreaming. What's the difference?" Hildy set the pitcher by its basin. "I'm not going to make breakfast twice today."

"The way you cook I don't need to eat."

"Then don't." She turned toward the steep stairs.

"Hildy, I'm sorry," Joe called.

He heard: "*Who do you think you are*?" Eyes squeezed, he gripped the metal bedpost, feeling bile rise in his throat.

"Joe?"

"I'm all right." His chin grazed his chest. "I'm all right."

"Should I call the doctor?"

"No. I'll be all right." Joe managed a grin. "Couldn't you have used warm water?"

Hildy smiled, hands deep in her apron, her hair tucked beneath a lace cap. Joe was struck by how much his sister looked like a servant. Thick, black-soled shoes. Rough hands. At least she wasn't useless, Joe thought. She didn't spend her days, like Emmaline, dressing for one social after the next. Father said they could afford servants: "Maids, cooks. Any number you want." But Hildy wouldn't have it, and Joe figured maybe she was the smart one—buttering toast, serving coffee instead of sitting, brooding at the family meals.

"You're in enough hot water already," Hildy murmured. "Father's not particularly happy this morning. I thought a little water was better than his fist."

Joe stood, his mind already racing toward the daily confrontation with his father.

Hildy threw a towel at him. "Show some shame, little brother. Nobody needs to see your naked self."

Joe shrugged, wrapping the striped towel about his waist. "Nothing new to see. You're the one who changed my diapers. Even taught me how to stand and aim."

Hildy blushed and, for the second time, Joe found himself saying, "I'm sorry." He hadn't meant to disrespect Hildy. He was certain Hildy was the only one at home who loved him.

Joe moved toward the dormer window, peering through the chintz curtains his mother had purchased from a Sears catalog. Ten years ago, his father had built the "tallest black man's house" and Joe had claimed the attic as his bedroom. He had a crow's-eye view of the city and, as a boy, it'd been his glorious kingdom. Growing up, Mr. Jackson had slipped him pennies; Miss Lu, slices of peach pie. Abe had a special chair for him on his porch. Everyone seemed to understand (especially during the war) his need to dawdle after school, to hear tall tales, to delay going home. Lying Man would spin him in the barber's chair until he was too dizzy to feel anything other than happiness.

Joe stared at the horizon: a flock of crows, perched along rooftops, pecked at the shingles.

Joe shivered, feeling he'd failed. He was no Houdini. Dread was sniffing at his heels and he didn't know why. He only knew his restless longing and the shattering nightmare of the last few days.

He saw Hildy's reflection in the window. Her eyes were brown and wide, looking ready to leap from her face. As a child, he used to bat his fists at her eyes, shudder with glee at seeing himself locked in her irises. Now he couldn't see himself at all.

"What were you dreaming?"

Joe licked his lips. "Doesn't matter. Nothing matters in this house."

"You think you're old enough to be cynical?"

"Let it go, Hildy." His hand swiped the air, hitting the sloped ceiling. "I'm not myself. Let it go."

"Dreams matter, Joe. Father says they shape a man's life. Steer him on the right course."

"Sure, as long as it's *his* dream—the damn bank. Samuels & Son."

Abruptly, Joe turned, demanding, "And which son, Hildy? Which son?"

"He only has one, Joe. One son."

"You mean *now,* don't you, Hildy? He only has one son *now.*"

Hildy frowned. "That's right, Joe. One son."

"One alive, one dead."

"Yes," she said, stepping into the alcove, her hands outstretched.

After Henry was buried, Father had forbidden the family to speak of him.

"Fathers always have dreams for their sons," said Hildy, carefully. "Dreaming they'll . . . *you'll* be like him. *Want* to be like him. Follow in his footsteps. Is Father's dream so terrible?"

"I don't see him having no dreams for you."

Hildy sighed. "It's not the same, little brother."

"Because you're a woman?"

"It doesn't matter about me, Joe. I've made my choices. I'm talking about you."

"You *are* a woman, you know."

Caught in the attic dormer, his back bent against the angled ceiling, Joe could smell gardenias wafting from Hildy's throat. He was surprised she wore perfume, surprised she was really quite pretty. Corkscrew strands lingered on her temple and throat. Though she tried to hide it, Hildy had a good figure. Full breasts. Strong legs.

Lack of air, the tight space was making Joe lightheaded. If he gripped his sister's waist, his fingers would touch.

"Hildy," he whispered. "Hildy." He wanted to see the real Hildy, to see in the flesh the girl who had placed gardenia water along a vein in her throat. She was only thirty-four.

"Damn it, Hildy." He slammed his fist into the sloped ceiling. "Dressing like an old woman. How'd you ever expect a man to want you?" Then, he moaned, "Jesus, I'm sorry, Hildy. I'm sorry. I don't know what's wrong with me."

"Joe, what's the matter? What's wrong?"

He swallowed, wincing against the sunlight.

"You're going on eighteen," murmured Hildy. "Two days time, the world will recognize you as a man."

Will Father? Joe thought.

"But it's lonely, isn't it? Do you have someone, Joe?"

There was Myra, a "Choctaw special," brown to his black, who he paid two dollars each week. But he didn't love her. Not like Hildy meant.

"I know, little brother. Believe me, I do. Loneliness can almost kill you."

Hildy touched his arm. Joe flinched. She stepped closer. "Sssh. I'm here." Her arms slipped round his waist and Hildy molded herself against his chest, pressing his back into the beams.

Joe wanted to cry. "We all need comfort," Hildy crooned.

Joe held tight, curved about his sister's slim form, smelling sweet gardenias. "I have such dreams, Hildy. Terrible dreams."

She tried to rock him. In the glass reflection, the two of them looked mournful, cramped together in a jutting alcove with a view of rooftops. Joe trembled, hearing Hildy's coo of "little brother, little brother."

"Hil-dy! Hil-dy!" Father was hollering from below stairs. "Folks down here want to eat."

"I'm coming," she shouted without shifting her gaze from Joe. "You'll be all right?"

"Sure," he said, the word choking deep, so only the vowel rose.

"Let's talk tonight. Do you hear me, Joe?" She stroked his hair. "You're feeling your way toward manhood. It's a hard thing. Living's a hard thing. Listen to your dreams, Joe."

"Hildy—" He couldn't say more. *His dream was rising vividly and he was scared.* He was awake—he *knew* he was awake, but he could *smell* gasoline, *see* the white-gowned figures stalking him, *hear* the taunting refrain: *"Who do you think you are?"*

"I'm nobody."

"Don't you ever say that," Hildy insisted. "Don't ever say that."

Joe buried his hands in his armpits, afraid they were swelling. He didn't want his sister to see his monstrous hands. He closed his eyes.

Hildy cupped his face and gently kissed him. "Come on down, you'll be late for breakfast."

He didn't move.

"You coming down?"

"Sure," he said.

Hildy tucked a strand of hair into her cap, smoothed her dress, and with a flick of her wrist untied and retied her apron. She was at the top of the stairs, her foot poised to step, when she said flatly, "Watch out for Father."

"I will." He listened to the staccato of her feet, descending.

Joe stared at his hands. They were normal size. He began moving his fingers as though he were ten and still playing scales. Some of his tension left him. He opened the trunk at the edge of his bed. Handcuffs, coils of rope, padlocks, and decks of cards layered atop each other.

Buried beneath twine and metal were a dozen pictures of Houdini carefully cut from magazines. Joe reverently stared at his photographs: Houdini at rest, Houdini handcuffed, Houdini chained upside down. Houdini's intense, gray eyes were always prominent. Eyes which seemed to dare anyone to be as competent, as brave and as willful as he was.

Joe turned toward the mirror, his eyes were rimmed red, his skin ashen. He inhaled and, for a moment, felt strong, invincible inside his body. *I can escape anything.*

He blinked, something flashed in the mirror. He spun around but the room was empty.

He turned back to the mirror.

In his reflection, his eyes were receding into his skull. Charred flesh peeled from his fingertips. Joe closed his eyes. *How could he escape a dream?*

2

Monday, May 30, 1921

Mary Keane had spent nearly an hour at the kitchen window, watching, waiting for Dell to be gone. Now she moved hurriedly, knowing the jersey would curse her, if she could. The sun was creeping out of the ground, but she was just now milking because Dell had been slow to rise from his pallet in the barn, dress, and begin his chores. He'd been slow to step into the starlit yard, surveying the land like he owned it, stretching his back like some red-tailed fox as if he knew she was at the window, her head tucked behind blue curtains.

"Damn." What good was a hired hand if he slept late? Pa might as well have hired a colored.

Mary pushed against the barn door, scurrying forward to light a lamp. The barn was already hot, humid from the musk of animals and urine-soaked straw. Sadie whinnied, eager to escape and run riot in the back field. "Hush." Mary pulled a pockmarked apple from her pocket, fed it to the mare, then settled a pail beneath the restless, sad-eyed cow.

Sweat itched her skin. Mary forced herself not to turn and stare at the northeast corner, the farthest stall, where Dell slept. Last month she'd stumbled into the barn too early. In the darkness, his flickering lamp had beckoned. She'd seen Dell bare chested, flat on his back, staring at the rafters. Inching forward, she'd held her breath. Dell's body overwhelmed the makeshift bedroom: his arms, tucked high beneath his head; his chest, arched and smooth. She'd always admired Dell moving, lifting, hauling. But utterly still, he was beautiful, powerful, bathed in lamplight and shadows. His head had slowly turned and Mary glimpsed something she'd never seen in any man's eyes—desire for her. Silent, she'd turned and walked out of the barn. She'd been careful to avoid him ever since.

Mary bit the inside of her lip. "Fool," she muttered, squatting on the stool, her brow pressed against the cow's brown side. A shuddering low escaped the animal as Mary's hands tugged the loose teats and milk flowed, steaming, into the pail.

It didn't make sense for Dell to desire her. A too big, too bony girl. Not a damn delicate thing about her. Thick, brown hair. Eyes wide apart; lips too thin. Her prime, if she'd ever had one, was gone.

Last harvest, out of nowhere, Dell had walked onto Pa's farm, knocking at the kitchen door, asking for work in exchange for food and a bed in the barn. She'd somehow known not to trust a man who'd stepped out of the horizon like God had just thrown him down, blown life into dust, answering Pa's prayer.

She must've imagined Dell's desire. No call for a man like him to want her. Big, handsome men wanted small, pretty girls. But she couldn't help having dreams.

She knew an ugly man would marry a plain girl if she doted upon him enough. Mary refused to dote on anybody. Yet, since Dell had arrived, loneliness haunted her even more. Worse than missing her brother Jody during the war, this new loneliness was insistent like a fever, causing her breasts to ache, her womb to feel sore—reminding her she'd never been kissed, never been held, never been told she was desirable. Let alone loved.

Mary stared at her hands: nails clipped, rough, capable. She was proud of her hands. Sweaty, reddened from milking. Her hands did things, made things. They could cut cloth, snap a chicken's neck, operate an elevator, but they couldn't make a man love her. They couldn't ease desire in the dark. She shivered, wiping her sweaty palms on her lap. She stroked the cow's spine, cooing as the dumb animal flattened its twisted ears. She was shamed by her own touching, her need to touch. Shamed because all her life she'd counted only on herself. Now all she could think of was babies and a man caressing her.

"Mary."

Startled, she turned, nearly upsetting the pail. The jersey skittered, side-stepping, pressing her against the wall. She slapped its flank.

"Damnit, Dell, you scared me."

Dell leaned against the door, his arms dangling, head cocked. Sunlight and dust glimmered behind him. Mary felt she'd conjured him up, gone truly crazy—wished for him, and, magically, he'd appeared. He was dressed carelessly, his shirt half-buttoned, his pants, beltless, streaked with dried mud. His eyes were blue like robins' eggs, blue like a cloudless sky. Blue enough to see right through her.

"What do you want?" She dried her hands, keeping her eyes focused on the ground, the cow. On anything except Dell.

Dell drew the latch closed and smiled. "I came to keep you company, Mary."

"I'm done milking," she said curtly, lifting the pail. "Breakfast be ready in an hour." She skirted past him, her knee hitting the bucket, splattering milk.

"Sit with me. Talk." Dell caressed her back as she passed.

"Don't touch me." Mary turned, furious at herself for trembling. "You're supposed to be working. Plowing. Laying down the new crop. You're paid for it."

"Sure," Dell shrugged. "Meals." His head tilted. "A soft bed."

Flushed, Mary looked toward his pallet—straw banked beneath gray flannel. "Pa never claimed to be rich. We pay what we can."

"I'm not complaining, Mary." Dell stepped toward her. "Are you complaining?"

Mary meant to march straight to the house, but Dell's gaze held her. He lightly cupped her face. "I've been thinking of you, Mary," Dell whispered. "Thinking how we'd be a good pair."

Mary felt lightheaded. She'd never been this close to a man. She could feel Dell's breath on her face, smell soap on his skin. She swore she could hear his heartbeat, see the pulse, the rush of blood beneath his temples. Her fingers traced his cheek, the curve of his chin. She closed her eyes against his desire. Dell couldn't want her. Nobody had ever wanted her.

"Damn you," she said fiercely, turning, stumbling over the pail. Dell caught her from behind, his arms crossed beneath her breasts, his torso pressed into her back. Warm milk soaked the straw.

"You like me some." His lips caressed her neck. "I know you like me some." Mary moaned and, for a minute, she stopped struggling, letting herself feel his hands roaming over her breasts, her belly, through her hair. Dell had fine hands: scarred, callused palms and fingertips.

How many times had she dreamed this? Dreamed of his hands stroking her? Dreamed of herself pressed against his chest?

"Mary."

She felt his heat, his body hard against hers. Pa had told her to keep her legs shut. But he never explained what to do with the ache of wanting somebody to want you. Her mother, who might've explained, had died birthing Jody.

"Ma—ry. Ma—ry," the sound swelled, filling the cavernous barn. *She was on a precipice, lost at the edge before dreaming.*

She faced Dell. "If you don't mean this, leave me alone."

"I mean it."

Mary shuddered.

"Lay with me, Mary."

She shook her head. "I can't."

"Then let me hold you. Just hold you." His voice was plaintive, pleading. Gripping her shoulders, Dell held her slightly apart, "Come. Feel how soft a hired hand's bed is."

The packed earth floor shifted beneath her feet. Mary fought an urge to run.

"You believe in dreams, don't you, Mary?"

The cow was lowing again. Sadie whinnied, kicked her stall.

"I've been dreaming of you," said Dell.

A slight breeze blew through the planks. The lamp dimmed. Dell's hands spanned her waist, making her feel small, delicate. She shivered as he lowered his head, kissing where her breasts swelled above her bodice.

"Mary." His hands clasped hers. "Mary." *She hadn't known her name could sound so lovely.* Walking backward, whispering, "Mary, Mary,

Mary," Dell tugged her toward his bedding, to the L-shaped corner where he lived. His spare shirts and pants, his silver-buckled belt hung neatly on a row of nails. "Mary."

He pulled her to her knees, feathering her face with kisses.

Emotions rocked her. *She'd slipped inside her dreams and felt shielded from loneliness, soothed from the ache of being unloved.*

Dell began unbuttoning the front of her dress.

"Don't."

His fingers undid another button.

"Don't, Dell." What a fearful, old hen she was—scared of Dell's desire, scared of getting pregnant, scared of her own passion. If she gave herself to a man, she'd be giving him everything. She wanted Dell more than anything. But he hadn't said he loved her. He couldn't really love her.

"I can't."

Dell's fingers kept moving, releasing the last button. His hand slipped inside her slip, stroking her breast. She shoved him. "Stop it, Dell. I can't."

Dell sprawled on his back, his face streaked by light poking through rotting wood. He tucked his hands beneath his head, studying her.

Fingers trembling, Mary buttoned her dress. But, then, she couldn't move. Folding her legs beneath her, her thigh brushed his hip. The contact burned. She felt foolish saying no to the only man who'd ever wanted her. Despite Pa's warnings, no boy had ever tried to lift her dress. With each passing year, she'd grown more invisible to men.

Mary clasped her hands. Her dress stuck to her skin. Dell's space was like a burrow, hidden from the barn's door, angled diagonally across from the animals' stalls.

"I'll be late for work," she said, staring at her hands, telling herself she had to get up, get out.

"What do you work for?" Dell's fingers stroked her knee.

"Money. Same as you." She exhaled. "Started during the war. Didn't stop when Jody came back."

"Crippled Jody."

"Don't," she said angrily. "Don't ever say that."

Dell laid his head in her lap. He brushed her hair forward, gently stroking the strands over the rise of her breasts.

Mary blushed guiltily, thinking how strange that if Jody hadn't lost a leg, Pa wouldn't have hired Dell, and she wouldn't be here dreaming of being loved. Oil men said Tulsa was a "magic city." A boom town. But her family had always been poor. All the wells Pa had dug came up dry. The only magic she'd ever known was here, right now—a handsome man seeming to want her.

She felt overwhelmed by the heat and weight of Dell's head pressed against her legs, by his mouth turned inward, lightly pressuring her belly.

She touched his hair, marveling at the blond silk.

Dell pulled her head down toward his; her back curved like a bow. "Kiss me, Mary."

His eyes were darker now, midnight blue. She was scared again. She plucked threads in her hem.

"I have to go to work." Still she didn't move. Didn't leave. A man had never treated her as if she were pretty. She jabbered, "Last week a man gave me two dollars. Can you believe it? I closed the elevator cage. Shifted the levers. Took him to the fourth floor. And he gave me two beautiful, green dollars."

Dell sat up. "He must have wanted something else," he said flatly.

Mary blushed again. "Naw. Just had money to burn. Oil rich."

"You shouldn't have taken it."

"I'm gonna buy me a scarf. Silk. Twist it around my neck. My waist, maybe. Like in the magazines. It'll be pretty. Soft. Might even make me beautiful."

"You're pretty enough for me," Dell said fiercely, clasping her neck.

She gripped his hand. "Really?"

"You're beautiful." He pressed her backward, onto the blanket.

"It's all right if I keep two dollars, isn't it?" she said breathless. "Pa needn't know. It's all right to keep a little bit back. Isn't it?"

Dell straddled her, his knees locked against her thighs. "Yes." He kissed her deeply.

Mary clung, returning his kiss with all the passion nobody had ever claimed. Dell's touch felt like sweet grace. A young man who lost his leg in the war got plenty of sympathy. An old maid got none. She hadn't planned on not marrying, on not loving and being loved.

Dell was murmuring into her hair. Mary didn't care what he was saying. Whatever it was, the answer was yes. Yes, because Dell's touch was filling her with wonder.

"The two of us could make something of this farm, Mary." His breath tickled her ear. "If we cleared those back acres, we could double the crop. Maybe get a tractor. Build onto the house."

"Not mine," she murmured, feeling desire overwhelm her.

"We could work the land together. Imagine it." He kneaded her thighs, nibbled at her breasts through cotton. "Make a good future. Feet up on the porch in the evenings. Maybe have kids."

"The farm's Jody's when Pa dies."

"Me and you, Mary." His hands hitched her skirt, his body rocked, rubbing hard against hers. Mary felt herself drowning, losing herself in a wealth of feeling. Trembling, she pulled back. "Stop, Dell."

Elbows locked, he looked down at her.

"Dell?" His eyes didn't quite meet hers. Bewildered, she called softly, "Dell?"

He was staring through her, his fingers digging into her arms. "Nobody's going to marry Jody. Nobody. What woman would want a one-legged man? A cripple. Your Pa and me, we've already agreed."

"What'd you agree?"

"You and me, Mary. Our kids will inherit the farm."

The ground was hard. Beneath the blankets and straw, stones scratched at her back. Mary stared at the knotty wood, the frayed clothes hanging neatly on nails. The half-filled hayloft, crisscrossing beams scabbed with dung. Dell's face was ugly. There wasn't any magic.

"I have things to do."

"No, you don't, Mary."

"I have to get breakfast. Go to work."

"No breakfast. No working in town. I'll take care of you."

"Liar." She struggled to get up. "You don't care about me. All you want is the farm."

"Mary. Sweet Mary." Dell's torso collapsed, his arms pinioned hers, his mouth touched her ear.

"Let me go, Dell."

"I'm a desperate man, Mary. Don't you know that?"

She didn't know anything about him. Not even his last name. Or where he'd come from. Dell's weight was suffocating. She couldn't move. This was her luck, her punishment for thinking a man might really want her.

"Stay with me today. Forget about work."

"Pa's counting on the money."

He squeezed her buttocks. "You like taking fat men up two floors? Having them watch your backside? Thinking you're loose?"

Dell was becoming aroused. "You take niggers up too, don't you, Mary? No decent woman would risk it."

"Stop it, Dell." She flailed her legs helplessly. "Mr. Bates makes coloreds take the stairs. Only place they go is the washroom. On the fourteenth floor. 'Specially for coloreds."

"But you walk by them shoeshines in the lobby everyday. How can you stand them looking at you? Thinking about you."

"Those boys don't look at me."

He bit her throat, sucking her skin into his mouth. "Marry me."

She felt like crying. "*Marry me.*" This was what she'd been taught to wait for—*Marry me*—this was what a good woman wanted to hear.

"Let me go, Dell. Let me go."

"Marry me." He guided her hand down to his crotch. "Feel what you do to me, Mary." She tried to pull her hand back, but he held it. "I know you can love me, Mary."

"Stop it, Dell. Stop it."

His hands pinched her nipples; he tugged her panties, his knee spread her legs.

"Stop it."

She scratched him; Dell slapped her. She cried out—her head bounced against dirt.

"You don't know what's good for you, Mary."

"No, Dell."

"You don't even know your own mind."

He sounded like Pa, dogged, grating in his certainty.

"You think you're better than me?"

"No. I'm not better than anyone."

Holding her hands in one fist, he reached back, grabbing his silver-trimmed belt off the nail.

"Dell, don't." He was going to beat her like Pa did. The buckle caught the lamp's glow and it glittered, the silver showering rainbows.

Mary fought—bucking, trying to free herself as he bound her hands in the leather. She felt cold silver cutting deeply into her wrists.

"Dell, please, let go my hands. Let go." Tears drained into straw. She felt helpless, like Jody must've felt when they'd tied him down and sawed. "Please, Dell." Hysteria choked her throat. "Let me go."

"Not 'til I'm done." He jerked her backward, stretching her arms over head, and caught the buckle on a nail. "Scream, Mary. Your Pa and brother might be heading back for breakfast."

The silver buckle reflected her tangled hair, the shadow of Dell bending over her.

Dell unbuttoned his pants. "Go on, scream, Mary. I want you to. Your Pa will make you marry me."

She wouldn't scream. She kicked; he caught her legs.

"It doesn't have to be this way."

"I'm not a whore, Dell."

"Look where you are, Mary. Look around. It ain't much. But it's a man's bed." He leaned close, their lips almost touching. "I didn't drag you, now did I? Scream, Mary."

He rammed inside her and she swallowed a wail. The narrowness of the pain surprised her, then it began spiraling outward, cramping her abdomen. She bit her tongue, tasting blood. *Lie still. Don't scream.*

"I didn't know you were a virgin, Mary." He entered her again. "Got to be a grown woman sometime."

When she'd started bleeding at thirteen, Pa had handed her worn sheets, telling her, "You're grown now. Don't let any man touch you. Your body's meant for a husband's use. Seeds are meant to bear fruit." He watched her burying her bloodied rags behind the shed, admonishing, "Whores like doing it. Good women don't."

"Mary." Dell was thrusting deep, his mouth slack.

Blood speckled her pubic hair. What would life have been like if her mother had lived?

Like a revelation, she saw her mother, her lips pursed, eyes shut, lying beneath Pa's bucking abdomen.

"Ma," she whispered. Probably, Pa had made her mother feel guilty for every season she didn't harvest a son for his land. What good was a woman anyhow?

"Ma," she whispered again, trying to comfort herself.

She felt herself hurtling to some abyss, turning into a speck of nothing—no heart, no feeling, no body. A good woman who really wasn't a woman at all. Just some hole for Dell to plow into, just as Pa plowed his fields, littering seeds which never grew strong enough or big enough.

The final thrust and she swallowed all her sounds. *No whimpers. No wails.* Dell's semen exploded inside her; his fluid mixed with her blood, draining down between her legs into straw.

Through the planks, she could tell the sun was well out of the ground. Pa would curse her for fixing breakfast late.

Dell laid his head on her breast and tucked a hand beneath her buttocks. "This is your fault, Mary. But don't it feel good? You'll marry me, won't you, Mary?"

Strands of his hair touched her lips.

"Yes, I'll marry you," she said. Right and proper.

She was deep in the abyss. *When she closed her eyes, she thought she saw an angel, a woman with wings.*

3

Dread followed Joe down the staircase. First, there were the attic steps, rugged and plain. At the second-floor landing, the quality improved. Pine became buffed oak and the stairs curved, spiraling for a grand entrance, down to the half-opened doors of the dining room.

Nothing had changed. A huge table for ten. His family sitting in the same high-backed chairs. The same gaping mouths, the same forks scraping on china. Everybody focused on his father.

On the left, spreading a biscuit with honey, sat Emmaline. She'd been a twelve-year-old skipping off to school while Joe was still squalling, sucking on a bottle. Emmaline had never liked him.

On the right sat his mother swallowing poached eggs, glancing furtively at his newspaper-reading father, Douglass. Beside her was Tyler, his father's father, gumming grits in a cushioned wheelchair. Joe had never heard anyone call him Grandfather, Father, or even Pa—just Tyler. Tyler—stricken dumb by a stroke last year. Arthritis curled his hands into claws.

Yet, today, watching from the room's threshold, Tyler seemed special. Head rolled back, eyes closed, Joe knew Tyler was dreaming. Dreaming something bigger than a banker's family chawing on breakfast. Something bigger than his own son, who sat at the table's head, dominating his family with indifference and silence.

Joe patted the pair of handcuffs he'd slipped inside his jacket's lining. Inhaling, he slipped on the mask of contented son. "Good morning, good morning. How are you all this fine morning?" He kissed Mother's powdered cheek.

"You took your time coming down," said Emmaline, licking her lips.

"Don't have to be to work until two. Might as well enjoy the bed's soothing grace. You might feel better, Emmaline, if you let yourself sleep in."

"I feel fine," said Emmaline, bristling.

"Good. Then you can stop worrying about me."

Hildy pushed through the kitchen door carrying a platter of bacon.

"Hey, Hildy." Joe snatched a slice, closed his palm, then opened it. The bacon had disappeared.

"How'd you do that?" Emmaline demanded. "Tell me how you did it."

"One less bacon for you," said Hildy. "Don't be complaining if you're hungry later."

"You wound me, Sis." Joe reached behind Hildy's ear, pulling out the vanished bacon, which he popped into his mouth.

"Tell me how you did it, Joe."

"My secret, Emmaline. Yours to find out. Isn't that right, Tyler?" Joe asked, slipping into the chair beside him. Usually he sat on the left, beside Emmaline. But, today, inexplicably, he felt safer beside Tyler. In Henry's old space.

Hildy filled his glass with water.

"You too good to be sitting next to me?" asked Emmaline. "Seventeen years and on this day, you move to a new chair. You too good to sit by me?"

"Emmy, let it go." He reached for his napkin.

"My name is Emmaline."

"Emmy. Emmaline. What's the difference?"

"You lack the sensitivity to understand."

"Fine. Then I can call you Emmy."

Emmaline's lips puckered. "Turning eighteen doesn't make you grown, Joe. You're no different than any other Negro. Crazy and inconsiderate."

"Hush," said Mother. "I will not have arguing at my table. Joe, you know I don't like heathen games in my house."

Joe marveled how his mother lost not a bite or chew.

Emmaline smirked.

His father turned to the stock pages.

"What do you want for your birthday, Joe?" Mother was smiling. "I thought maybe you'd like one of those new phonographs. Can you imagine? You can hear symphonies. Piano concertos. We could have a small party. We'd be the only Negro family that has a phonograph. Would you like that, Joe? Would you want a house filled with music?" Hands plucking delicately at her lace collar, her voice still rich with Louisianian cadences, Joe glimpsed the pale, proper beauty who'd won his father thirty years ago.

"I want . . . I want . . . " *What did he want?* He flexed his fingers and a rose appeared. "I want you to have this, Mother."

"Joe, stop it." Her lips pouted. "I want you to stop this mumbo-jumbo. I'll not have a devil's carnival. Not in my house."

"Who've I hurt, Mother?"

"You've hurt me." She slapped his hand. "I don't want a grown son engaging in magic. The Devil's game."

Hildy placed a plate in front of him.

Emmaline twittered, picking up the yellow rose. "You could get a good price for a dozen, Joe. That'd be a fine trick."

"Shut up, Emmy." Joe stared at his plate. Four soft yolks, luminous with grease, lay beside a mountain of grits. Bacon, thick and rind-edged, crisscrossed at the top, jam-stuffed biscuits leaning off the plate's edge. A growing boy's breakfast. The same breakfast he'd eaten for years, but now it seemed disgusting in its lavishness. Joe pushed away his chair.

"You will not leave this table until I give permission." His father's voice cut deep.

Mother and Emmaline, startled, fell silent. Hildy edged closer to Joe.

"May I leave?" Standing, Joe clutched the back of his chair.

"No." Father lifted his eyes from the newsprint. Joe knew this was the moment his father had been waiting for. Father's eyes pinioned him like the preserved butterflies—Red Admirals, *taenaris macrops*, and a Blue Morpho from South America—he kept in a glass case beside his ledgers.

Joe stared back.

Father was awash in a back draft of sunlight. Joe could see his blunt frame, broad shoulders squeezed into a gentleman's suit, hands flexing, hands that were capable of spanning anything—a woman's waist, a sow, a usurious deal with no mercy for a man undone by gambling.

"Hildy, make some toast," Father said, setting aside his paper, his eyes never leaving his son.

Everything about his father had to be outsized, garish—this house, the heavy sterling, even the chandelier swaying above. Needing toast when there were lard biscuits, demanding Hildy light the stove and cook bread beneath the broiler (careful not to let it burn), all to make a point to his son—that there was more. Always more. *I earned it. I paid for it. And you, like everyone else, will eat it.*

"Father, Joe's not feeling well," said Hildy.

Joe quickly glanced around the table. His mother was twisting her napkin, Emmaline's mouth puckered like a beached fish. Even Tyler was restless, bobbing his head, his eyes shifting between him and his father.

"I'm all right, Hildy."

Lips pursed, Hildy glared at Father, then pushed through the kitchen door, causing it to flap furiously on its hinge.

"Sit down, Joe."

Joe sat and lifted his fork, thinking of metal, thinking he had the dexterity to escape anything. Houdini did it—escaped jails, straitjackets, a thousand metal bands. It was all in the hands. Strong, flexible.

"How's work?"

"Fine, Father."

"It must take real skill to know which rag best buffs a leather shoe."

Joe studied his breakfast.

"You don't do anything any ignorant nigger couldn't do."

"But I do it better. I have all the advantages."

"Don't smart mouth me."

"He could go back to school," said Mother.

"Booker T. won't have him," said Emmaline. "Mr. George didn't like being handcuffed to his desk."

"I can make them take him." Father folded his paper. "The school owes me. I loaned them money for a furnace. Mr. George and that skinny ass principal will do what I say."

"The school hasn't been built that could hold me," laughed Joe.

His father slapped the table. "Do not smart mouth me."

"I like shining shoes," Joe said stubbornly, feeling a new recklessness. "I get to see my face looking back at me in the shiny leather. All you get to see is money. I get to say 'Good morning,' to everybody. All you get to say is 'Foreclose.'" He finger-stirred the ice in his glass. "Like you did to those Indians on Easton."

"Indians are worse than niggers." Father stabbed his fork into grits.

"The piano, Joe," lamented Mother, her voice rising to the center of the room. "You were so good at the piano. Why can't you play the piano?"

At ten, Mother had introduced him to beauty, teaching him piano and the delicacy of Mozart. Chopin. Beauty wrung from his fingertips. While his mother had praised the sound, Joe had reveled in the motion, in the dexterity of his fingers.

"The boy might have been all right if you hadn't interfered. We never needed a piano. I never should've bought it. Joe needs business sense. Not your damn piano."

Joe looked at his hands, imagining how they moved in a simple coin press. He was good with coins, but not the way his father wanted.

"You don't deserve to sit in that chair."

A shudder passed round the table.

"That's it, isn't it, Father? I'm sitting in Henry's old place."

"Joe," Mother cautioned.

"He was a son. Proud to be my son. If he was alive, he'd be working in the bank with me."

"How do you know?"

"What do you mean?"

"I mean how do you know that? Did you ever ask him?"

His father was dumbstruck, caught off-guard by Joe's rebellion. The newspaper fluttered to the floor.

"I'll work, Father," said Emmaline.

Joe cocked his head, surprised by Emmaline's boldness.

"I can help you, Father. I know I can." Emmaline was pressing her chest against the table's edge, stretching toward her father.

"What do you know about anything, Emmaline? You've been in my house, how many years, and can't find a man? I didn't raise you to hang on, eating my food, sleeping in my house. At least Hildy makes herself useful. What's wrong with you, that you can't find a man?"

"Douglass!" said Mother.

"You never like any man I pick."

"Not if you pick men like Gabe. Back from the war three years and won't get a job."

"He's sick. Can't you see that?" Emmaline glared.

"I can see you're all a trial to me." Father folded his hands. "I can see you expect a man to work all his days building something, and once it's built, you drain it like worthless sap. A house full of women."

"Oh, leave them alone." Joe stood, overturning his glass.

"You," Father shouted. "You're not worth my name. Shining shoes like some buffoon. Playing magic tricks."

"I like shining shoes," Joe said stubbornly.

"Shine mine then. I raised my sons to be better than shining white men's shoes."

"I'm the only son you have left. And this son . . . *this* son likes shining shoes just fine. I like it fine."

"You're a fool."

The two of them were standing now and Joe knew his father was furious enough to plow through platters of eggs, biscuits, toppling crystal and juice, and smack his face. His father was breathing hard, a wheeze beginning in his chest.

Astonished, Joe realized he'd grown as big as his father. He realized, too, there were things a man didn't have to take.

Joe remembered Henry arguing with Father the summer he'd gone to war. *Just thirteen, Joe had been sleeping, but near daybreak, voices woke him. He'd stumbled down the stairs, fearful of discovery, fearful of Father's strident voice turning upon him, and glimpsed Henry weaving from room to room, opening and shutting doors, screaming, "I need more gin." Father had dogged his heels, bellowing, "Ingrate," until Henry turned, arms flailing, roaring, "I don't have to take this." Then Henry opened the front door, stepped into the morning mist, and was gone.*

"You're an important man, Father," Joe said softly. "But I like my work. I got it on my own. I didn't have to ask you or anybody."

"You're going to throw away all my advantages."

"That's right. 'Cause they're *yours*."

"You don't deserve them."

"Didn't think I did."

"Others would kill for what I'm offering. It's more than my father gave me. An illiterate ex-slave still working the land."

Tyler flapped his jaw, trying for sounds.

"I took that land and made something of it. Built a bank. Grew money instead of wheat."

Tyler's mouth was wide open.

"I gave my sons a chance to make something of themselves. Carry on the business." Father's breath came in short bursts.

"Is that why Henry enlisted?" *Joe remembered Henry returning sober, splendid in a private's uniform.* "Your money wasn't good enough for Henry."

"Who do you think you are?"

Joe staggered, thrown back into his dream. Eyes closed, he gripped the table for balance.

The kitchen door swung open. Hildy, holding a plate stacked with toast, stopped, arrested. "Joe?"

He was bare, hands bound, close to dying. He was nobody. His father had told him so.

"Joe?"

Sounds assailed him: He could hear the asthma shuddering through his father's lungs; his mother's soft wail, "Don't fight. Lord, have mercy. Please, don't fight"; Emmaline muttering, "I could work at the bank. I could." *A roar off in the distance—the whoosh of gasoline lit with a spark.*

"Joe?"

Pale and wild-eyed, he looked at Hildy, then at Tyler.

Tyler's hands, no longer gnarled, ruthlessly gripped Joe's forearm. Tyler was trying to speak. Saliva ran down his chin.

"Joe!" Father doubled over, wheezing.

Joe shivered and began to walk out—one step in front of the other, hearing his father's wheezing snapping at his heels, his mother calling, "Come back, Joe. Get your father to the sofa."

Left foot, right. He couldn't stop. Out of the house.

"Joe," Hildy called.

His pace quickened. He was running full out.

"Joe!"

The sun seemed to be growing brighter, flooding the porch. Off in the distance, he swore he heard the rush of water. He ran, but he didn't think he could outrun his dread.

4

Mary wondered if she was going crazy. Her head flickered with pictures. She needed to keep moving—stirring grits, setting the table, mixing meal. She didn't have time to wash or cry.

"Ma," she whispered. Ma—buried; good and gone.

She had to make it through her morning chores. Then she'd escape to town and her elevator where with her fingertips, she'd make the steel-rimmed cage soar. For now, it was best not to feel anything. Best to still the scream bubbling inside. Best to keep moving.

"Ma," she murmured. She was a fool to be remembering her mother's lavender-scented hands stroking her back. A fool to be thinking she could still hear lilting lullabies and murmurs of "Love you." She was too old to be crying for her Ma. Too old to be needing a woman to talk to about her shame.

"Ma."

Laying strips of bacon in the pan, she remembered well what she tried hard to forget:

Her ma standing in the kitchen, her abdomen contracting in visible waves. Slow and easy, at first; then, erratic and punishing. Ma reassured her: "It took days to birth you." Newly seven, she stood at her mother's side, braids down her back, making preserves, snipping off stems, pressing mounds of blackberries into boiling syrup. The big-bellied pot cackled over the fire.

Mary cracked two eggs deftly into the batter, tossing the shells into the sink.

Ma's hands, stained with black juice, guided hers. Strong, lean-fingered hands stroked her hair, tickled her sides. Her mother hummed softly through her belly's unproductive heaves, through the rising scent of berry juice. Mary's terror grew as sun flooded the kitchen, glinting like flames. The curtains fluttered like bird's wings.

Mary paused; the curtains hung limp. She tossed more wood into the stove.

Ma tilted her head, as if hearing a sound from far off. Blood drained down Ma's legs, catching them both by surprise. Ma collapsed on the linoleum, her legs hitched, thrusting the baby out of her. Newborn Jody slipped out of her body, skittering in a pool of blood; Ma's yellow skirt turned red. Mary began screaming. The boiling juice caked in the pan. Ma gripped her hand, insisting, "Hush." She made Mary promise to mother Jody.

Mary wiped down the counter.

Ma lay flat on the kitchen floor, hair fanning, arms grasping her flattened belly, whispering to Mary. Whispering, "Hush. Don't scream. Don't blame Pa or the baby. It's God's will." Jody slept, wrapped in kitchen towels. "Hush. Don't scream."

Pressing her legs together, Mary flipped another meal cake. "*Hush. Don't scream.*" The grease cackled and gurgled. Dell's semen leaked through her underwear, sticking between her thighs. Mary stopped moving and stared at the linoleum. *She could see her mother lying dead beside the sleeping child.*

"Hurry up, Mary. Man's got to eat."

She was startled by Pa's grating voice. He and Jody washed their hands—dirt clogging the sink—talking about the harvest, the tilling that needed finishing in the north field.

The curtains ruffled. She smelled an acrid burning, heard the wail of a baby being born.

Spooning another cake into the pan, Mary turned the fire high. She felt weighted before the stove.

Jody stole behind her, squeezing her shoulders, "You all right?"

Hands trembling, her wrists bruised, Mary smoothed her apron. "I'm all right."

"You sure?"

"I'm hungry, Mary." Pa tapped his fingers on the table ledge.

"Sorry, Pa." She scooted past Jody and slid two yellow cakes onto Pa's plate.

"Syrup," he said.

She pulled the molasses down from the cabinet.

"Milk."

She poured a small glass. Most of the morning's milk had spilled in the barn.

Mary moved away from the table, whispering fiercely, "Nothing's wrong, Jody. Sit down and eat. Nothing's wrong." She smacked more meal into the pan and a spray of oil licked her fingers. She stared at the rising blisters; then lowered the flame, scooping more batter into the sizzling pan.

Mary listened to the scrape, the shuffle of wood as Jody maneuvered his body into a chair. Damn him. Why was Jody so woebegone? He was the one who'd left her to go to war.

"*Don't blame Pa or Jody.*" But she did.

She slapped the spoon. So eager to get off the farm, Jody had enlisted and been gone after a quick good-bye. For two years she'd heard nothing. She'd listened to Pa whine, watched the fields lay fallow, and when there was nothing to eat, she'd gone to work to replace Jody's lost labor. Two years. Not a letter from Jody. Nothing to ease her worry that he'd be shipped home in a box. Until, one day, an uneven scrawl on thin paper arrived: "I'm coming home."

Carrying cigarettes and meringue pie, she'd met him at the train station.

He'd moved slowly—one pant leg pinned up, his crutch tap-tapping the platform.

Now Jody looked like somebody had cut off his other leg, all because she hadn't told him: "I'm *not* all right." Yet he was the one who had left her.

Mary was sorry for everything. Sorry Pa couldn't love a one-legged son any more than he could love a wife who couldn't bear a dozen sons. She was sorrier still for wanting Dell, for wanting someone, just once, to ease her loneliness. She squinted as sunlight rimmed the window.

"Dell's late. Must've had problems with the fencing. Did you see him, Mary?"

"No, Pa."

Mary pressed a quick kiss on Jody's cheek. She slid two cakes onto his plate, turned back to her small stove to fry bacon as Dell stepped inside the door.

"You're late," said Pa.

Dell shrugged. "Got some griddle cakes for me, Mary?"

Her knees buckled. Dell was handsome again; his hair newly wet; his silver-buckle casting rainbows.

Dell sat across from Jody, to the left of Pa like a second son. Mary wanted to smack him. Poor Jody. A good harvest outweighed a brave veteran any day.

Keep moving. A scream constricted in her throat. Mary's hands fluttered nervously. She wanted to be buried with her mother's bones. All the men she'd ever known had taken from her: Dell by plowing into her, Jody by skipping off to war without a care for her, and Pa, his hand out on Fridays, collecting the dollars she'd earned working the elevator.

"Father, we are thankful for Your bounty." Pa nodded, then the three of them, sitting on the lilac cushions she'd embroidered, began chawing like desperate bulls. Nobody said, "Thank you." No, "Fine breakfast, Mary." Just hands moving toward mouths; jaws chomping food; throats gulping milk. Between bites, Dell had a wide, fat smile.

She heard Ma whispering, "Hush."

Mary looked out the window at the settling dust, the lopsided barn, the crow sitting atop Pa's scarecrow. Life would've been different if there'd been oil. Every farmer but Pa seemed to have a small derrick, a black stream buying bits of comfort. Sometimes she dreamed of living in the city; her life transformed by a colored girl bringing tea, serving her sandwiches without crusts. On Main Street, she'd purchase gloves with tiny pearl buttons and a golden-edged mirror. She'd stroll Courthouse Square wearing a blue dress, felt shoes, and a straw hat. When she got restless, she'd ride in a shiny motor car across the plains to Chicago, New York, Boston.

If there'd been oil, Pa wouldn't need to swap his daughter for two good legs. Wouldn't need her to betray his own son. If there'd been oil, a man might've decided she was worth loving.

Suds crept up her arms. Mary tightened her legs, dreaming of someone touching her with grace.

"I'll take real good care of her. Provide and the like."

Behind her, she heard Pa's jubilant, "Yes," as Dell spoke confidently about leaving the barn for her bedroom and fixing the attic for children. "Nothing much will change. I can keep plowing. Mary can fix meals, be with kin when children come."

Mary stopped cleaning. Children, she thought. Water drained from her hands, pooling at her feet. Bubbles floated out the window. Her mouth puckered. A fly swept by her ear and she stared out the window, studying the mound near the shed where she'd buried countless years of bloodied rags. Each month, tossing in the week's rags, shoveling dirt, she'd mourned—not just the lost babies—but all the touching, kissing she dreamed flowered between a man and woman before making life.

Dell was right. Nothing would change. There wasn't any magic in the world. His touch would sharpen another kind of loneliness. She'd cook, clean, launder, sew; when the sky filled with stars, he'd take her without asking and make her crazed, mourning for an honest loving he couldn't give.

"*Hush.*"

Mary pressed her damp hands against her mouth, quelling a gurgling scream. The only comfort she'd ever found was in her own hands. Doing work that needed doing. Holding herself when loneliness haunted. Dell was a poor excuse to betray Jody.

She could see herself pressing linens between Ma's thighs trying to stop the bleeding. Red saliva drooled from Ma's mouth.

She was alone now. Had always been and would always be—alone. Marriage wouldn't change anything.

She stumbled, upsetting the bacon grease. She hit her hip against the stove. "*Hush. Don't scream.*" A howl swirled in her belly. The men were still eating, swallowing milk, mouthing words she couldn't hear.

Her tongue nearly severed, Ma hadn't screamed.

Mary clamped shut her ears. But the howl inside her, foreign and insistent, kept spiraling. Choking her air. As the scream swept into her throat, she pressed her fingers to her lips, thinking, hearing, "*Hush,*" willing herself to silence.

Calmed, she stared at her hands. Strong, yet not strong enough to stop Dell. She stared at him. "I won't do it. I won't marry you."

"You promised," said Dell, his voice hardening.

"He's all right with me," said Pa, lifting a hand to stop her.

"He's not all right with me." Mary headed for the stairs.

"Maybe she wants to be asked," said Jody, sarcastically. "Asking would be more graceful."

"I did ask," said Dell.

"I changed my mind." Her hand on the rail, Mary began climbing the stairs. Dell grabbed her waist.

Mary flailed. "Leave me be."

"Mary," Dell whispered, turning her, his arms encircling, stroking her back. "I'd treat you good. Real good." His hair curled like an angel's.

Mary felt sorry for them both. Dell wanted the farm; she wanted someone to love. Her body was betraying her, yielding, tipping her off-balance.

"I know you care for me, Mary."

"Take him, girl," said Pa. "You want to spend your life alone?"

Pa's blue-veined hand clutched hers. Mary leaned over the railing, searching Pa's weathered face, trying to glimpse the man her mother had loved.

"Take him, Mary."

She was trembling.

"I'll do right by you," said Pa. "Fair dowry. Unless Jody marries, and looks like he won't, your sons would own the farm."

"Pa," she murmured.

"Take him, girl."

"Marriage ain't like mating animals," said Jody, angrily. "Mary should be the one to decide. She'll be the one sleeping with Dell."

"That's right," said Dell. "It'll be me she's pleasing."

"Shut up," said Mary.

"Just being blunt, Mary." Dell spread his palms, grinning slyly. "Aren't we old enough to be blunt?"

Mary stepped backward, her foot scraping against the stairs. She wanted to run. Moon-faced, the men pressed forward, expecting her to make things right. She was being trapped as surely as Dell had trapped her in the barn.

"Take him, Mary," said Pa.

"You don't know anything about him."

"A man's got to care about his line."

"You're mine, Mary," said Dell. "You were meant to be mine."

"Don't do it, Mary," said Jody. "You don't have to marry him."

"Mary, Mary," Dell crooned, reaching, tugging her apron's hem.

She covered her ears. "Stop it, stop it. All of you, stop it."

She stumbled farther up the stairs. Dell caught her, his lips burying against her neck. She fought down her screams.

Dell bent before her, his hands touching her knees. "Mary. I want a family. I want you. That's something, isn't it, Mary?"

"Mary." Dell's face was a sweet roundness, hale and pink-toned from the sun. Not gray-faced like Jody. Dell had never been to war. Where'd he hide himself? What other farm girl kept him warm and protected until Armistice? Maybe she'd been older, plainer than her. Or maybe she'd had full-limbed brothers and a father who couldn't be seduced by taut muscles lifting bales of hay.

"Take him, Mary. It's the best way."

Mary looked up. Hovering, strained, his eyes sharp, she realized Pa was afraid. He wasn't young anymore, wasn't rich. He wanted grandsons to carry on his line, hearty like Dell, not crippled like Jody.

"Mary." His voice low, Dell's hands cupped her face, "I could do you good. You know that, don't you, Mary?" He lightly brushed her breast; her face wet, she buried her head in the crook of Dell's chest and arm. If he said, "I love you," maybe she could do it.

His buckle glittered like diamonds. She drew back, remembering how Dell had trapped her hands, held her helpless as he rammed into her. She slapped him. Dell slapped her back.

"Idiot girl. Nobody else wants you," said Pa.

Cane upraised, Jody cautioned, "That's enough, Pa. Dell, leave her be. Mary knows her own mind."

Dell rested his head against the wall, his eyes closed. Pa hit the rail with his fist. Jody almost smiled; he was still the heir, someone to be reckoned with.

It was over, Mary thought. Done. Dell could leave. They'd scrape by as best they could. Pa would die having his bit of land worked by a woman and a one-legged man.

Without opening his eyes, Dell said, "She's already given me a husband's privileges."

Pa crowed in triumph, "You'll have to marry him."

Mary flinched, stunned to see Jody looking up at her with hatred.

"I won't," she vowed.

"Then you'll leave this house," Pa shouted, his hand slapping the wall. "Without money. Without clothes." Slap. He scuttled up the steps. "Without food. Don't return until you're willing to marry Dell."

"I don't need Dell. Or you," she screamed back. "Nobody. I'm moving to town."

"You'll come back on your hands and knees."

"I won't. I make my own money." She did, too, her fingertips pressing levers, making the cage sway.

"You're ungrateful, disobedient, just like your mother."

"Don't you talk about her. Don't you dare."

"I done promised the boy your hand," yelled Pa.

"You marry him," she said, moving past him on the stairs, focusing on the top. One step, two.

Pa thundered, "Working in town has ruined you."

"Dell's ruined me," she hollered. She untied her apron, letting it float down the stairs. Another step. Another. Up she went, undoing buttons, lifting her dress overhead, spilling it over the banister. She reached the landing, stripping her slip and stained underpants. In her bedroom, she pulled her gray uniform over her head. Reflected in the vanity mirror, she saw Jody studying her body. She tugged and the dress slid down. It had a lace-trimmed bodice, white cuffs, and a pocket with *Mary* embroidered on it.

"This is mine. I paid for it." She sat on the bed, slipping on black pumps. "These too. I'm not going to marry Dell. I'm marrying nobody." She whipped clothes out of a drawer, looking for a purple satchel buried deep. "Here it is." She undid the drawstring, shaking out a vial of lilac perfume, a few bills, and red lipstick. She puckered her mouth and painted it. Dabbed perfume on her neck.

She counted eight dollars and stuffed them into her uniform pocket. She stepped back and looked at herself in the mirror.

"You look like a whore," said Jody.

"That's what Pa says I am."

"You can tell you ain't got underpants on."

"Really?" She twisted and stared at her backside. "Naw. You just saw me without them. No one else would know."

"I tell you you look like a whore," Jody said softly, vehement. "Like one of them women in France, ready to do anything with anybody. Not caring about color. Women eager to show themselves off—to white or nigger. Acting like men were all the same or something."

Mary was astonished. It was the most Jody had ever said about the war.

She touched her brother's hair. Both of them had been lonely children—were lonely still, filling space in Pa's house.

Jody laid his head on her breast. She cradled him as she had those first weeks, home from the war, a summer of nightmares, hollering for his lost leg. They'd never talked about his dreams come sunrise. Never mentioned sweat dampened sheets or his struggling with the memory of an ether cup clamped over his nose and mouth.

"I won't help Pa steal the farm from you, Jody. I wanted to say yes to Dell. Part of me still wants to. Pa's always talking about the Devil leading us to sin. About temptation. Dell tempts me." Mary smoothed her dress over her hips. "But I know there's no good in him, Jody. He doesn't love me."

She slid her hand under her mattress. Buried beneath it was a pin locket, a portrait of her mother smiling. She wanted pleasure, laughter. Is that what her mother had wanted?

All these years, she'd been waiting for love to come to the farm. Maybe she'd find it in town. She needn't be so prim and proper. Maybe she'd smile more, stroll through Courthouse Square. Maybe she'd dance on Decoration Day. Maybe she'd see the man who gave her two dollars. Maybe they'd talk.

Mary walked out of the room, her heels clicking.

Jody shadowed her steps down the staircase.

At the landing, Mary spun on the tips of her toes. "I'm going to work."

"You're going to town to be a whore," called Pa. She didn't flinch when he threw his Bible at her. Didn't flinch when Dell stood on the porch next to the dog, patting him gently while insisting fiercely, "You'll be back. You'll be missing me."

She smiled gaily and said, echoing Pa, "I'm going to town to be a whore."

When she got to the gate, she looked back at the three men. Pa had come down off the steps. She could tell he was damning her. His face blotched, his words were an angry gibberish. Dell stood tall, handsome on the porch, looking like he already owned the farm. The sun was barely up. Jody was in the background, caught by the doorway's shadow.

Mary waved at her brother, then turned, her heels scraping on gravel, kicking dust onto her skirt. She didn't wait to see if her brother waved back.

5

Joe leaped from the porch, his gait stretching until he was running swiftly down the alleys, between row houses and backyard vegetable gardens. He kept hearing: "*Who do you think you are?*" and he thought his heart would burst as he raced in the morning sun. Someone hailed him from a window and he pressed forward, afraid to stop and have anyone guess his fear—his fear that he'd always be afraid, that he'd never be a real man. Joe was ashamed he'd abandoned his gasping father, ignored his mother's call.

He steered left, away from the stirring neighborhood and moved toward Lena's River, a basin where drunks, whores, and ailing Indians lived in scattered, clapboard shacks and swapped tales about Lena who one moonlit night, lay face down in the stream and let herself drown in a foot of water. Some seasons the creek crested, displacing the squatters. Other times, it ran dry, exposing odd white stones, tree roots, and clay. Across the creek were lush acres studded with derricks—Ambrose Oil. As long as Joe stayed on the Greenwood side of Lena's River, he was safe, Father had warned.

Breathing hard, Joe maneuvered down the rocky embankment. Granite tore at his skin. He remembered playing here with his brother. Henry, ten years older than he, used to bring him every summer's day to Lena's River. When he'd been barely walking, Henry would carry him down the embankment and all day, they'd build dirt forts, float navies, and search out pebbles for cannon fire. As Joe's limbs grew sturdier, Henry had taught him how to chase lizards, skip rocks and dig, like breathless prospectors, for Lena's bones. Then Henry had stopped coming. Joe never lost the habit. He'd grown up counting the summers his brother didn't come. He'd turned eight, nine, ten. Each summer day, from June to September, sunup to sundown, Joe waited—waited for his brother to bring ropes of licorice, bottle caps, cats' eyes, or nick his thumb and smear blood across their brows, swearing, "Brothers. Always."

Eleven, twelve, thirteen. He'd grown resentful. Occasionally, Henry surprised him. He'd unexpectedly appear, staggering, smelling of gin and roses. Joe always forgave him. And if the light was strong enough, Joe would step inside Henry's shadow, zigzagging along the rocks, and pray for magic which could join him to his handsome, laughing, older brother. *Always.* Like Lena's ghost and the riverbed.

Joe's foot slipped and he fell flat on his back, his arms and legs spread-eagled. Pain shot through his spine. He tried to relax. He focused on each breath moving through his body. He missed his brother terribly. The sun warmed him. Rocks pressed like knives into his back.

"Clumsy this morning?"

Joe squinted. He couldn't see the face—a dark circle haloed by sun, but he knew the buttery voice. "Henry?"

"Like hell."

Joe's eyes widened. *He thought he'd heard Henry.*

"You're gonna need to move better than this if you expect to do magic. Box escapes and all that shit." It was Gabe's grating voice. "You can't even walk."

"Shut up, Gabe," Joe said, suddenly angry. "Don't mess with me."

"Baby brother has shocked me this morning."

"I'm not your brother."

"True," said Gabe, sliding down in a shower of rocks. "But I'm the closest thing you have. Can't bring a dead man back to life."

Joe shut his eyes.

"Want to talk?" asked Gabe.

"No." Joe peered at Gabe. He still wore khaki pants and shirt. He had black, metal-tipped boots but no socks. Despite the heat, Gabe wore his trench coat and deep in the inside pocket, Joe knew, Gabe packed his Army .45. His clothes were frayed but clean.

Joe remembered his brother writing that Gabe had made corporal. Henry had been so proud of his friend. What would Henry think now?—the war long over and Gabe, still in uniform, living like a friendless dog, away from town and his folks. Joe wondered: How did he keep clean? Keep his shoes shined, his pants pressed? How did he eat?

"Do I pass inspection?"

Joe flushed. "Just wondering who shined your shoes."

Gabe slowly smiled and Joe felt his mood lightening. There was a gentleness about Gabe. Joe watched him deftly draw the knife beneath his nail and flick away imaginary dirt. Henry, in his last letter, had said Gabe could be vicious too. "Fight with the best of them." When Gabe had come home with Henry's coffin, he wore a medal on his chest.

"What was it like?" Joe asked. "The war."

"Blood-thirsty this morning."

"No, I mean it."

"I mean it too." Gabe looked away, then got up wordlessly.

"Hey, man, wait up." Joe was following, breathless. "Hey, Gabe, don't be mad."

Joe knew Gabe didn't talk about the war. But this morning he felt impatient, angry that four years had passed and Gabe still had nothing to say. Joe didn't really care about the war—he only cared that he'd been too young to go, cared that his brother died in the Argonne while he'd been in Tulsa. He was still trying to circle in on some truth.

"Gabe? Come on, man."

Gabe headed toward his shack, his knife sheathed, his hands deep in his pockets.

"Come on, man." Joe slipped and caught himself, scraping his hands on the rocks. "Shit. Don't you sweat? Slow down, man. Damn you, Gabe."

Other than "He's dead," Gabe had had nothing to say about anything. The government letter had read:

> PFC Henry Martin Samuels died heroically in an enemy engagement. Burial should be with full military honors.

But it hadn't been because Henry was a Negro. Gabe had to get permission from Sheriff Clay just to play taps.

> Be advised: Coffin should remain sealed.

Gabe had folded the flag expertly and handed it to Joe's weeping mother. The coffin was lowered. His sisters—Emmaline and Hildy—fluttered like wing-clipped birds. His father posed like a general and Tyler, trapped in his wheelchair, wailed and sang hymns.

Afterward, Gabe had gone to live near the dried creek. He'd built a one room shack, asking nobody for nothing.

Joe crossed the threshold and stopped. The shack was dark but neat. It held a cot, a desk with an oil lamp and unlined paper filled with a wide, open scrawl. A spent fire still glowed in the hearth. Joe felt lightheaded. Other than the draw on the fireplace, there wasn't any circulation. Planks were nailed across the windows. Anything could happen here—no one need ever know.

"Emmaline defended you this morning," Joe said.

"I don't need her."

"You used to."

Gabe shrugged. "I needed a lot of things before the war."

Joe stared at Gabe, his arms limp, his shoulders rounded like somebody had battered his spine. "I don't understand you, man."

Smiling, Gabe shrugged slightly, his palms upturned.

Joe was reminded of his brother. At thirteen, Joe had discovered Henry was going to war. For weeks, he'd badgered his brother, "Why do you have to go?" Henry had given him an odd smile, shrugged, palms upraised. Joe remembered the train station:

Hundreds of people—Negro and white—milling about, waving, shouting, murmuring, "Good-bye." Men and women kissed. Children cried. The sky was pink and cloudless.

Everyone in the family, except Father, came to say good-bye. But Henry was nowhere to be seen. As the conductor shouted, "All aboard," Joe had the wild idea Henry had deserted. When he caught sight of his brother lurching out of a cab, his head thrown back in laughter, Joe shouted, "Why do you have to go?"

Gabe shadowed Henry, helping him to stand as he shook hands with Tyler and hugged his adoring sisters and mother. Both men reeked of gin. Henry kept boasting, "We've been to bed but didn't sleep. Ain't that right, Gabe? Been servicing our country. Servicing all the women."

Gabe shook him, muttering "Shut up." But Henry didn't care about offending his family. Emmaline glared at Gabe.

When the whistle shrilled, Gabe turned Henry toward the train. Watching them, Gabe's hand on the small of Henry's back, Joe felt rage. Felt the difference between being thirteen and twenty-two. Gabe acted more like Henry's brother than he.

He yelled, "Why do you have to go?"

Gabe and Henry vanished inside the rear car overflowing with Negro servicemen, eager and anxious for war.

The train began moving, vibrating the platform. Chug. The final: "All aboard." Steel clacking. Chug. Chug. The psst of steam. Joe cried, feeling abandoned.

Through windows, he saw his brother running down the coach aisles. Joe started running too, tasting steam, trying to catch the moving train.

Henry stood on the steps between cars, shouting.

"What? Henry! What?"

Henry's face contorted, sound bellowing out of him. But Joe couldn't hear his words.

His brother slouched against the rail.

Joe kept running: his lungs aching, gasping for air. He was almost there. Almost. Almost able to reach the rail and hurl himself aboard the train.

His brother's mouth moved and Joe caught snatches of sound beneath the roar of steam, the clank of metal. Vowels floated back to him. The train gushed steam again. His brother disappeared in the mist.

"Hen—ry!" Knees buckling, falling, pressing against the pain in his side, Joe knew his brother wouldn't return.

"Henry was a good soldier," said Gabe.

Gabe's fingers pressed against Joe's shoulders. Joe knew he was supposed to feel comfort. But he didn't. He felt hot and ill again.

"How'd he die?

"Like a man. He went down hand-to-hand." Gabe sunk into his chair. "Hand-to-hand."

"You were there?"

"Yes."

"You *saw* him die?"

Gabe nodded. Pain furrowed across his forehead. He closed his eyes and swallowed. "He told me to look out for you. Help you find Lena's bones. Told me to kiss his mother."

"Why didn't you tell us?"

"Tell you what? Tell you I saw him die?" Gabe sprang from the chair, pummeling his fingers into Joe's chest. "Tell you I saw blood spilling out his mouth like dirty water. Saw him trying to squeeze his intestines back inside. He was screaming my name. Hollering for his momma. Is that what you wanted me to tell you? Should I tell you I felt his spirit sifting through my hands? Felt his slippery insides? Felt his soul?"

Joe's back pressed against the plaster wall. He felt sick, horrified.

"Is that what I should tell you?" Gabe's fingers poked deep in Joe's abdomen.

"Don't do that, man."

"Don't do what? This." Gabe poked again. "This. This."

Joe shoved him.

Gabe pushed against Joe's chest so hard he couldn't breathe.

Joe punched him.

Gabe staggered, then lunged and the two fell to the floor in a fierce grip, rolling on the dirt. Joe flailed wildly.

"That's right. Hand-to-hand. That's right."

Joe didn't understand why they were fighting. Gabe was on Joe's back, pinning his arms, pummeling his face into the dirt like they were old enemies instead of friends, nearly brothers. Joe roared, using his legs as leverage to topple Gabe. Straddling him, Joe struck Gabe's face, beating back the smile, the mocking gaze, the guttural encouragement, "That's right. Hand-to-hand."

It was crazy—all of it—his dreams, his brother dead. A spray of blood washed across his face. *When had Gabe stopped fighting?* Gabe's nose was draining red and his left eye was swelling, discoloring. Joe's hands were bruised and bleeding. Forcing back his anger, fists still clenched, Joe rolled off Gabe's chest.

Gabe got up and found a clean rag and held it to his nose, head thrown back. "You fight mean, little brother. I thought that magic shit had made you soft."

"How'd he die, Gabe? I want to know everything. How'd he get hit? Where? How'd it happen?"

Gabe looked at him, arrested. "What could I possibly tell you that you don't already know? I thought you knew everything. How to do magic. How to beat back the white man."

"Stop it, Gabe."

Gabe cocked his head and squatted, the bloody rag dangling between his legs. Joe faced him, cross-legged, on the dirt.

"You know all about me, don't you?" asked Gabe.

Puzzled, Joe heard a soft threat behind the words. "No," he said carefully. "But I think I can guess."

"Do tell."

"I'm your friend, Gabe."

Gabe waved his hand, dismissive. "What do you know?" he asked softly.

Joe felt small again. He didn't want to be fighting Gabe. "I already figured Henry was hurt bad. That's why the closed coffin. I figured you told them government people to write that, knowing how vain Henry was about his looks. How upset Mother would be."

Gabe had his knife out, digging a hole. Joe looked at the small well Gabe was making—sloping and deep in the center.

"I know war must be bad. Terrible things must happen. All you needed was to tell Mother Henry was calling for her. That's all. But you never said a word. We—I wanted to know it wasn't a lie."

Joe swallowed, staring at the triangle of dirt between Gabe's legs. "I was only fourteen. I kept expecting the coffin to open and I was mad 'cause it wouldn't. I was mad at you. Mad you had nothing to say. You wouldn't even praise Henry. So I figured it was all a lie. Someone else in the coffin. Henry wasn't dead. There was some trick like Houdini's boxes. All I had to do was open the coffin, find the magic key—" He shook his head. "I tried it when folks were asleep. I went down to the viewing room and tried to pry open the coffin. Prove to everybody that Henry had disappeared. He wasn't dead."

Joe remembered the haunting sounds of wood beneath his feet, moths beating at the window, and his own ragged breath. He'd stared at the gleaming coffin until dawn. He'd sworn he'd find a way to bring his brother back—some magic, some trick. He'd make his brother reappear.

Joe looked up, realizing Gabe was staring at him.

"I've grown up now. I realize Henry's dead. I ain't crazy. But we all would've believed it better if you'd been the one to tell us, Gabe. A government letter don't mean nothing."

Joe let his head thump against the wall. "No one speaks of Henry anymore. Father won't allow it. It's like he never was."

Joe feared he'd always be less than his brother packed in a coffin under an avalanche of dirt. He needed a man's recognition to find his place in the world. Houdini helped. Staring at his eyes could make Joe believe in anything, believe in himself. He could never see himself in his father's eyes. He simply disappeared. Joe looked but he couldn't find his reflection in Gabe's blood swelling eye.

"Your eye looks pretty bad. We should go to town, have Lying Man look at it."

Gabe said nothing.

"Come on, man. I'll even buy you a haircut." Trying to coax a smile out of Gabe, Joe made a quarter appear.

"Rustle me up a dollar. A quarter won't buy shit."

Joe dodged out the door, relieved to be out of Gabe's shack.

Gabe followed; he picked his way carefully, deciding a split second beforehand where he was going to step. He walked with his hand in his pockets, his fingers closed on his gun.

Joe paused at a small crest and watched an eagle swoop across the sky.

Without looking at him, Gabe murmured, "Now if you could make me disappear, I'd buy that. I'd climb in any damn box you want."

"Yeah, that's the best trick of all. Disappear. Escape. That's what makes Houdini special. He escapes. He broke out of Murderer's Row in D.C. He unlocked all the prisoners and then locked them in different cells."

"You believe that?"

"It's true. He's an escape artist. Don't you ever want to escape, Gabe? Houdini does easier tricks, but he's better when he's escaping. He can will himself out of any jail. He has the power in his hands, his body. Makes you believe he's got other kinds of powers too."

Gabe looked at him, searchingly.

"Houdini's trying to reach the dead."

"What?"

"I read about it." The eagle screeched again.

Gabe clutched Joe's shirt. "Three years, Henry's been dead. Time to let it go, Joe. I loved him. You loved him. Let it go at that. Let him stay dead."

How did he explain his dreams? His dread?

Gabe's hands dropped to his sides. "The dead don't come back, Joe. Henry's not coming back. He wouldn't want to. Ain't nothing for a black man in Tulsa. Even when your daddy owns the bank."

Gabe fell silent for a moment. He crushed a stone with his boot.

"He decomposed, Joe," Gabe said softly. "Three weeks by boat, another by train. Nothing much of Henry was left. Do you see?"

Joe saw: *Henry's face pockmarked with rot, his skull and cheek bones glimmering white. No, the dead couldn't come back. Shouldn't come back.*

6

The closer Mary got to town, the worse she felt. Sweat pooled on her neck. Her feet hurt. Her narrow skirt made it difficult to walk. Normally she would've packed her uniform and changed in town, but her other comfortable clothes belonged to Pa. She worried Mr. Bates would say she wasn't presentable. Her first day working he'd told her to scrub her nails, buy lipstick. Another girl had complained she smelled manure on Mary's shoes.

The road to town followed the Arkansas River. Mary saw dragonflies flitting about in the cattails at the edge of the muddy water. The water, glistening with oil, smelled of rotting leaves. On the opposite bank a herd of cattle had come to drink. Oil rigs, pumping furiously, dotted the field behind the cattle and Mary wondered how long the Andersons would keep ranching, now oil was coming in. She'd heard Mrs. Anderson had bought a dozen silk dresses from Seville's.

Mary stepped in a rut; her heel snapped, and she fell backward on the dusty road, the air knocked out of her. Her hand scraped on the rocks. "Damn. Damn all to hell. Damn Dell."

Nothing was fair. She was dirty, her skin tacky from Dell's rutting. Sun chapped her lips and dulled her lipstick. Burrs stuck in her hair. Her lilac perfume couldn't compete with the road, spotted with manure from horse-drawn wagons and grease from rich men's Model Ts.

Mary lay on her back, exhausted, feeling the intense sun. Nothing seemed to matter. She could lie here all day and dry up like an oversized prune. Right now, she wouldn't mind if Pa or Dell or Jody came along. They'd just pick her off the ground and take her back to a lifetime of barn and kitchen duties. But that wasn't Pa's way. He'd wait until she crawled back, desperate. Dell would be too arrogant to come. Jody might want to, but wouldn't disobey Pa.

"Damn. Damn everything to hell." Not a soul seemed to be traveling down this road except her. All right. She'd just lie here and die. Like Lena.

Mary didn't know if Lena had been an Indian or a colored, but she knew Lena had been pretty and had let herself drown. Somebody would've cared about Lena because she had been beautiful. Even now folks talked about her. Everybody had their own explanation for why a lovely girl let herself die. *Her man had left her. She couldn't have babies. A prettier girl had stolen her man.*

Dying somehow made Lena lovelier. Folks who claimed they'd seen her ghost said she was stark, raving beautiful.

Nobody would care about Mary Keane. She could lie here and starve. Some coyote could gnaw her bones. There wouldn't be any legend. Pa, at the funeral, would call her dumb.

Mary gave a big hiccuping cry. Pictures of Dell raping her snuck into her mind. She balled her hands into fists and punched her head, trying to batter out the memory. She sat up, squealing. Red ants crawled on her arms. "Damn. Double damn."

She squinted in the sunlight, looking back where she'd traveled. She patted the money in her pocket. She was more frightened than she'd ever been in her life. Where would she live? How would she eat?

A roadster with a bleating horn swerved, showering dirt and small rocks. A goggle-eyed man cursed.

"Damn you too. Damn you all to hell." If she'd been pretty, the car would've stopped.

She fell back, waiting for a car or a horse's hooves to run over her.

Then she heard a sweet voice call, "Rise."

"Ma?" She picked herself up. Nothing around but empty road. Nothing to do but walk.

She tried to move with new confidence—she tried to sway and glide like she'd seen pretty women do. Pretty women with golden hair and pink cheeks. The heelless shoe kept tripping her.

"Rise," she told herself. She was glad she didn't have a mirror. She could feel terror settling on her face. She walked. Mincing steps. Gimpy-legged like Jody.

She started singing:

"I want to be happy.
I want to be happy.
But I won't be happy
'Til I make you happy, too."

A man in her elevator last week had been singing the song as they rode up. He'd laughed and spoken into the air, "It's stuck in my head." Then, he'd looked directly at her, his hair and beard luminous white, making his albino face even paler. He'd said, "*No, No, Nanette.* I saw it in New York." He'd smiled, inviting her laughter.

She hadn't had the slightest idea of what he was talking about. He didn't sound like a Tulsan, no twangy drawl; instead, his voice was lilting, high pitched. Such a curious man, she'd thought, making herself stop staring at his skin. He'd tipped her a quarter and exited into the lobby. Then he'd turned back, his hand stopping the elevator door, and confided, "You should've seen the dancers. They tapped like angels."

The sun grew bigger on the horizon. She hummed. She'd buy a silk scarf, maybe feathers for a hat. She'd even go to the cinema.

"I want to be happy.
I want to be happy.
But I won't be happy
'Til I make you happy, too."

Swatting flies, trudging the long, dry road, Mary kept singing until she grew hoarse.

* * *

Mary's head hurt. She'd gotten to town too early; she didn't start work till noon. At first, she thought she'd arrived in the wrong place. Red streamers decorated lamp poles, flags adorned shops, and coloreds were building a stage in the center of Courthouse Square. Then she remembered Decoration Day. Tomorrow, ex-soldiers were going to march.

For a while, Mary stared in the Ladies' Emporium window, but the display of jewelry, boots with tiny buttons, perfume flagons, and beaded dresses paralyzed her. Fashionable, well-cared-for women entered the store whispering, turning to stare at her ghostly face through the window. Embarrassed, she limped back and forth along Main, nearly a hundred times. Drenched in sweat, she lost track of time, feeling confused by the busy street with its motorcars, newspaper hawkers, clerks, and office workers, flowing around her, muttering, cursing, "Excuse me. Watch your way!"

The albino man stood before her. His fingers were stained and he had a grease-streaked apron tied about his neck and waist. He looked at her inquiringly; his smile, kind. Though he wore no hat, he pretended to tip one to her.

Mary smiled. He'd sung the odd song in her elevator.

"I thought you needed help," he said. A wide matron jostled them.

The man drew Mary closer to the building. Again he spoke, gently supporting her arm, "May I help you, miss?"

Mary shivered, feeling both hot and cold. She stared at his lips, expecting a song.

"My name is Allen. Allen Thornton. I'd like to help, if I may. May I help you? Miss Mary, isn't it?"

She touched the embroidery on her breast pocket.

"A lovely name—Mary."

Allen's eyes were the lightest blue with a thick fringe of white lash. His brows were nearly invisible; pale skin shone through.

She stumbled.

Allen's arm wrapped about her waist. "Are you all right?"

Her fingers traced his. She'd never met a man with such gentle fingers. Though the tips were dirty, there weren't any calluses.

She opened her mouth like a baby bird.

Allen bowed his head, trying to catch her words.

Mary liked the way his ear curled, soft and pink. A bit of hair was in his inner ear. "I . . . I . . . " *There was no one else in the world but the two of them.* "I—"

"Yes? Yes?"

"I want to be happy."

Allen peered at her. His hand closed over hers. "Yes, my dear. I understand."

Tremors swept through Mary's body. The sidewalk felt like water; horns blared. The press of bodies bumping about her, the grocer hammering a melon display, and the sun glimmering in shop windows overwhelmed her. Two coloreds on ladders struggled to hoist a banner. Far off, she heard a train's whistle and the clang of a firemen's truck.

She felt lost. "I'm *not* all right. I'm *not* all right." Her legs buckled.

Allen lifted her as firmly and gently as he would a child. "Dear, dear Mary."

Mary tightened her arms about his neck. She closed her eyes against matrons' shocked glances, ignored the giggling girls they passed.

Allen walked determinedly and Mary relished the feel of being carried, gently bouncing, her head stable against the sweaty slope of his neck.

"We'll go to my shop," he said. "I'll fix you a fine cup of coffee." Then she heard his thin tenor:

"I want to be happy.
I want to be happy.
But I won't be happy,
'Til I make you happy, too."

She felt she'd slipped inside a dream, swept along, floating above the sidewalk—people, store windows, flags, bright streamers blurring. Allen began the verse again.

Heads turned, mouths opened in amazement, a Packard came to a halt.

Letting her mind drift, Mary hummed the tune with Allen Thornton.

7

The barbershop bell jangled as Joe and Gabe walked through the door. Joe thought it was strange: nobody getting shaved; the shears, still. Over a dozen men sat silent, torsos pressed forward, listening to Lying Man, owner of the four-chair shop. Lyman was nicknamed Lying Man because in fifty years, he'd never lied. He could tell hard truths better than any preacher.

Joe cocked his head, listening to Lying Man's cadences.

"These folks were trying to organize workers. Oil gushing out of the ground every day, and these boys, mainly white, wanting to know why only certain folks held land, built refineries, decided who got jobs. One of 'em, named David Reubens, would even strip his pants, show his chicken legs and drawers, then tug his pants back on—demanding, wanting to know if any man did it any different. Was any different. David would scratch his head, curious why there wasn't no justice. He'd say: 'We're supposed to be equal in America. Things supposed to be fair.'

"I could've told him there wasn't any fairness."

"Amen," "Yes, sir," "Un-hunh," floated out of the listeners' mouths. Lying Man was testifying.

Joe and Gabe waited just inside the door.

"I told David every plantation only has one master. Always been that way. One master, then lots of poor whites to do the dirty work and lots of blacks to do what was beyond dirty. But this Jew kid believed he could make things better. He'd come into town ready to organize. Called himself a 'friend of Negroes.' Maybe he was too.

"Folks called him a Red, a Bolshevik. Other choice words too. He was seventeen like you, Joe."

Joe cocked his head.

"Yep, weren't any older than you, Joe. Tulsa don't like unions. Never has." Lying Man whistled air through his teeth. "His parents moved from Chicago and made him a farm boy. They weren't any good at it. Nearly starved every season. David wanted to do carpentry. Instead he learned all the different ways a bossman had of saying no. In the city, he was 'poor white trash.' But no trash in David. He was as sweet and righteous as any prophet.

"Y'all know I like my music?"

Everybody knew Lying Man lived for the blues. "David could play harmonica like you wouldn't believe." Everyone was entranced by Lying Man. Herb and Ernie didn't touch their checkers. Nate didn't wipe the lather off his chin. Joe stared at Lying Man, pot-bellied, surrounded by pomades and cans of tobacco, his razor slicing the air.

"David even wore a white hat. Said his mam had given it to him. He truly believed in unions. But he'd no more sense than a babe.

"If he'd been a Negro, he would've been told, 'Don't be disrespectful . . . don't antagonize whites with money. Don't think you're better than anyone else. Certainly don't believe you're equal, unless you're ready to die.'"

The men nodded their heads. Nate pounded a fist against his thigh. Gabe rocked, his arms crisscrossed over his chest. Lying Man gazed solemnly at each man in the room.

Joe wasn't fooled. Lying Man was talking to him. Telling him something Lying Man felt he needed to know.

"David thought he was as good as the white man who owned the feed store, slaughtered the pigs, sold the ham, and *still* had oil gushing in his back field. I tried to teach him. But they bombed his house. Klansmen thinking about Jews killing Christ, worried about Reds overrunning the country.

"It was a Sunday morning. David's folks died in their beds." Lying Man set his razor on the counter. "I didn't have no power to do a damn thing.

"David came to me. He wanted to play his harmonica. Here. In the barber's chair. He talked about wood, building houses and schools. He stayed for almost an hour, harmonica wailing, playing the saddest blues.

"When the men came for him, I thought they'd come for me too. But they didn't pay me no mind. I don't think they even saw me." Lying Man closed his eyes, ashamed of how helpless he'd been when David was dragged from the barbershop. "But I had power enough to watch him die. I owed him that. Owed him a witness.

"Lots of folk watched. But I witnessed it. Do you understand? I ain't told nobody. The time's not been right. But I'm telling you."

Lying Man looked first at Gabe, then at sallow-faced Billy, Chalmers, then Nate. Joe realized they'd all fought in the 369th with Henry.

In the grip of some power, Lying Man tottered forward, clasping Joe's wrists. "But I'm telling you now, Joe. I woke up this morning knowing I was supposed to testify. I never told anyone this story but I knew I was supposed to tell it today. I dreamt it."

Terrified, his dread returning, Joe tried to pull away. Lying Man held tight.

"They hauled David to Martin's field. Seems like everybody white was there. Women with picnic lunches. Children too."

He went on relentless: "They handcuffed David and chained his legs so he couldn't escape. They broke every bone in his arms and legs. Steel-toed boots. Baseball bats. They took their time over his hands. One of the carpenters, non-union, mind you, used a hammer. Then they lynched him. Didn't quite snap his neck though. They wanted him alive when he burned. Didn't take long for David to die. Bursting into flame in the bright light of day. Everybody packed up. Singing songs. Swapping recipes. Talking about what work needed to get done tomorrow. They left his bones and ash for the dogs."

Lying Man paused. The men pitched forward, waiting for his final words.

"If they'd do that to a white man, think what they'd do to you."

"Lawd, Lawd," Ernie exhaled. "Lawd, Lawd."

Joe saw himself burning inside Lying Man's irises. "Naw," Joe breathed. He jerked his hands and turned to escape. The copper bell jangled.

Joe saw his dead brother leaning against the lamppost outside, beckoning.

Stunned, Joe stepped back into the shop, shutting the door. He would've slid to the floor if Lying Man hadn't grabbed him.

"It's all right. Gonna be all right," Lying Man whispered, steadying him.

Joe thought he was crazy. *Clear as day he'd seen Henry, just like he'd never gone to war. Never died.*

"You all right, Joe?" asked Gabe.

"Stand for me. You've got to stand," said Lying Man.

"I can stand." Joe peered out the window, but Henry was nowhere to be seen. His brow touched the glass.

Ernie cleared his throat, pounded his pipe on his checkerboard. "Joe and Gabe! Y'all some sorry looking folk."

"Fell down in an outhouse, did you?" asked rheumy-eyed Herb.

"I had a cousin did that once. Never found him since."

"Ernie, if you was my cousin," said Herb, "I'd choose the outhouse too."

The barbershop exploded in laughter. Lying Man went back to shaving Nate.

Joe was caught off-guard by the change. The story was over. Men were playing cards again, reading magazines, trading jokes. Hair was being trimmed. Everything was normal. Like nothing had happened. He swallowed. "Me and Gabe, we were fighting."

"Gabe? You mean to tell me this boy whipped you," demanded Ernie.

"Ain't a boy no more," said Gabe. "Couple days, Joe be eighteen."

"Go on. You lie," said Sandy, another old man.

"Henry's baby brother?"

"In that case, give this man a drink," said Sandy. "Tater, get a red cherry pop. I'll buy." Tater, feeble-minded, quit sweeping loose hairs and shuffled back to the cooler.

"Bet he be wanting a different kind of cherry to celebrate," said Chalmers, a veteran who clerked in the dry goods store. The men laughed uproariously.

Joe turned back to the window.

"I got black cherry," hollered Tater from the back.

"Best kind," said Ernie. "Sure 'nough. You know what they say. The blacker the berry—"

"The sweeter the juice," laughed Herb.

Joe slid his palms across the bay window. During the war, he'd spent his Saturdays in the barbershop. Heat would spill from the window while he listened to the old men's playful banter:

> *"Remember when Charles' cow thought it was a bull? Silly animal was humping everything."*
>
> *"Remember when Wylie got the clap? His wife hit him with her frying pan. Knocked him cold for two days."*
>
> *"Remember Henry sweet talking that gal with the big legs?"*
>
> *"Ramona, was it?"*
>
> *"Heard she was waiting for Henry to come home from the war. Says she's going to marry him."*
>
> *"Yeah, but did he ask her or just pop her cherry?"*
>
> *"Henry could charm anybody."*
>
> *"Even them Germans."*
>
> *"Tight-legged virgins."*
>
> *Joe would feel peace inhaling licorice-scented pomades while he stared at the ceiling fans whirring, slicing the thick air, dreaming of tricks and illusions.*

He hadn't had nightmares then.

Joe stared down the avenue searching for his brother. He was disgusted with himself. Something magical had happened and he'd been too stunned to walk out the door. What if he'd shaken his brother's hand? What would've happened then?

"Joe? Joe? You hear me calling you? You're a dreamer, boy," said Lying Man, applying more lather to Nate's face. "It's not your usual day for visiting. You got a date this evening?"

"Naw." *Had Lying Man seen Henry too?* "I brung Gabe. Wanted you to fix his eye."

"What happened to your magic?" called Sandy, dealing poker and puffing on a Lucky Strike. "Fix Gabe's face yourself. Wave your arms, say mumbo-jumbo. Ain't your magic tricks any good?"

Joe touched the deck of cards, pulling out five aces. "My magic beats your cheating any day."

"Got you, Sandy. Got you good," said his partner, Cool Jack.

"How'd that get there? How'd that get there?"

The men laughed again. Sandy gulped his morning brew—coffee doused with whiskey, then shook his head, marveling at the five aces.

"Gabe needs some stitches," said Joe.

"Doc can handle it."

"I want you to do it," said Gabe, moving across the room. Folks knew Lying Man was better than Doc for fixing ailments.

Lying Man nodded. "I'll be done in a minute." Expertly, he flicked his razor.

Joe and Gabe sat, resting their backs against the wall. Except for the blotched eye, Joe thought Gabe looked relaxed, almost happy. Joe envied Gabe's certainty: "Dead don't come back." He flexed his trembling fingers. "*Who do you think you are, boy?*"

His magic tricks weren't enough. He needed to *be* Houdini, *be* someone greater than he was.

"Give you a shave too, Gabe," said Lying Man, his arm swooping, flicking lather. "I ain't shaved that mean neck of yours since you marched off to war. You and Henry both came. Gave me a two-bit tip."

Joe felt Gabe tense.

Lying Man washed his razor in the sink.

"Ain't seen you in awhile, Gabe," said Nate, rising, wiping the red-striped towel across his neck. "Not since Henry's funeral."

Nate worked at Thompson's. Single-handed, he could haul and S-hook a dead steer. Nate tossed the red-striped towel in the sink. "What you been doing, Gabe? Messing with someone's woman?"

Gabe didn't move.

"No *savoir faire.* Isn't that what we learned in France?" asked Nate. "You had *savoir faire* in France. I remember. Saw you *savoir faire* this black-headed gal many a time."

There was silence in the crowded, overheated shop. Inexplicably, hate had oozed into the room, and the fan seemed to be stirring it, spreading it to the corners.

"Wish I'd been with you," said Joe. "I bet France was something to look at."

"So was Gabe's girl." Nate never blinked.

"Nate, don't be starting nothing," said Lying Man.

"I'm not starting anything. It was Gabe who introduced the white girls. Me and Henry just followed. Isn't that so, Gabe?"

"Shut up, Nate," said Gabe.

"You had yourself a white woman?" broke in Sandy, his voice awestruck. The players laid down their cards. Joe stared at Gabe. Gabe's eyes were shut, but Joe saw sweat draining beneath Gabe's collar. The fan kept its lazy spin. Tater kept sweeping tufts of hair across the floor.

"Damn," said Sandy. "I thought you boys went there to kill Germans. White women? You boys sure had it good in France. White pussy."

"Good? You don't know nothing," said Nate. "How many niggers came home in boxes? A thousand, two? Three thousand? White men were glad about the war. It makes sense, don't it? Let us die. One way or the other. Give us guns and hope we die. And like fools we begged the bossman generals to let us man the front lines.

"Tell 'em, Gabe. Wasn't it so?" Nate waited for a response. He grabbed Gabe's lapels, shouting, "Gabe, I'm talking to you. Wasn't it so?" He shoved Gabe, then turned, pacing. "Nobody minds sending Negro men off to die. You should've seen how well some of us died. We did it good. Henry was the best. Until he got blown to pieces."

"What do you mean blown to pieces?" demanded Joe. "You saw my brother die?"

"Settle down, Nate," said Lying Man. "There's no war in here."

"You saw him?"

Nate ignored Joe. "White man celebrating Decoration Day tomorrow. Fried chicken, fireworks. Did they invite any Negroes? Anyone want to decorate me? Tell 'em, Gabe. Tell 'em what we lived through for America. Tell 'em."

Gabe opened his eyes. Weariness, palpable like dirt, shone on his face.

"Only compensation was white pussy. Tell 'em, Gabe."

The barbershop men were expectant, breathless. The ceiling fan slowed, the wall clock stilled. All of them could be murdered for such talk about white women. Nate and Gabe, their breath quickening, their skin flush, had their own private war.

Gabe said, "I don't recollect."

Nate smiled sweetly. "Tell 'em, Gabe, about the pussy you had. Tell 'em how good Francine was."

Gabe charged out of his seat.

The checkerboard overturned, cards fluttered to the floor. Herb, Ernie, and the others cleared the shop. The fighting was brutal, fierce. Gabe swung his fist. Nate dodged, battering Gabe's puffed eye.

"Stop!" hollered Lying Man. "You're ruining my shop."

Gabe double punched and Nate stumbled back, gasping. Nate seized Lying Man's razor and sliced Gabe's coat. The second slice nicked Gabe's arm.

"Francine was good, wasn't she?" murmured Nate.

Gabe cursed, "I'll kill you, Nate."

Joe readied his handcuffs, looking for a chance.

Nate's fist reared and Joe rushed forward, grabbing his wrist, clicking on the metal cuff. Startled, Nate paused, and in that second, Gabe hit him full in the face while Joe snapped the free cuff to the barber's chair. The razor clanged to the floor, glinting, reflecting sun on the chairs.

Blood draining from his nose and mouth, Nate howled, "Let go. Let go my hand."

"Do it your own self," said Joe. "You're the brave man who fought in the war."

"Give me the key." Nate sputtered blood. "The fucking key."

"I don't have one."

Nate lunged, the cuff snapped him back.

Joe laughed. The sound rumbled bitter and deep inside him.

Gabe thumped Joe on his back. "You would've been a good soldier, Joe. Henry would've been proud of you."

Joe shoved Gabe, snarling, "How'd Henry really die? Hand-to-hand or blown to bits? You were supposed to look after him, Gabe. What happened to him? What happened to you?"

"Tell 'em," said Nate.

Gabe clenched his jaw, but held his silence.

"I want to know how my brother died."

Nate looked away. "Died in the war, Joe. That's all."

Joe picked up the bloody razor and held it to the light. The ceiling fan whirled. He was panting, feeling like he'd been running forever. "I wish I'd never woken up this morning."

Joe stared at Lying Man's palm, the pink crisscrossing lines, the callused thumb.

"What's wrong, Joe?" Lying Man asked softly. "What's wrong?"

Joe walked to the window, pressed against it, trying to soak up the sun's heat and merge with the glass. He looked up and down Greenwood Avenue at faces and landmarks he'd known forever. Mrs. Regan, with her mustached chin, was carrying a bolt of red cloth. Ed, long faced, with eyes like a pup's, was climbing into his wagon, hauling feed from Reye's General Store. Ramona was across the street pinching plums at the grocer's. The Dream Time Cinema had a new picture; Bill Johnson was pasting up a billboard of a starry-eyed woman facing the horizon.

The war in France had changed Greenwood. The men were different. Gabe. Nate. Chalmers. Even Lying Man. And Joe knew he was different too.

Looking through the glass, he saw Greenwood as a withering photograph. Behind the brightly painted buildings and brightly dressed people were shadows of frustration, pain. Deep Greenwood. The black city within the white. He should've left yesterday, been far away, riding the rails.

"Everything's wrong," Joe answered Lying Man. He tossed the razor at the mirror, reached for the door knob.

"Joe. Get these damn cuffs off."

Joe pulled a lock pick from his pocket. It should've been easy. But it took three tries before the cuffs released from Nate's wrist and the chair's leather arm. Joe plunked the cuffs into his pocket.

"You've got a nice touch," said Nate, blood sluggishly draining over his lips. "We could've used you to defuse mines."

"Yeah," said Joe, dazed, hands shaking. The copper bell rang as he opened the door. Joe looked back. "You were wrong, Gabe. Dead do come back."

Joe reeled down the street, feeling the ground trembling beneath him. Feeling oil trapped in the soil, ready to gush and burn. Knowing Lying Man was at the window, watching, Joe lifted his hand and waved. He glanced left and right, paying attention to shadows, the darkness behind the brightly lit town.

Nate slumped in the barber's chair. "Don't be telling folks this story, Lying Man. If folks knew Joe locked me to a chair, I couldn't show my face. Hear?"

"I hear." Lying Man craned his head, watching Joe weave like a drunkard down the sidewalk. He murmured, "That boy needs watching over."

"That's what I'm doing," said Gabe, digging his nails in the window frame.

"Then you better high tail it." Lying Man patted the pocket holding Gabe's revolver. "Keep it handy."

Gabe nodded. The copper bell shook.

"Gabe, don't you let any harm come to that boy," he yelled.

Gabe strode quickly, his trench coat flapping as he set off after Joe.

8

Allen Thornton didn't know what to do about Mary. He knew she was troubled, but he hadn't the slightest idea of what was wrong or how to fix her heartache. He spent his days and nights repairing timepieces. He pried open the most delicate mechanisms, miraculously taming minute and second hands. Yet, with people, he felt awkward. He preferred actors—dancing, singing men and women—whose problems were solved by act three. Then, too, his lack of pigment never assured his social welcome. It was easier to retreat to his bench, magnifier pressed to his eye, peering at clutters of wire and springs.

Mary had brought a new sense of urgency into his shop. He'd thrown open his shutters, made strong coffee, and watched her tug her hem repeatedly and fold her dirty, work-scarred hands. The bruises on her wrists made him ache.

He'd handed her his best cup; it'd slipped through her fingers. Porcelain slivers had showered her feet. She'd cried and when he finished sweeping up the pieces, he'd asked, "Are you afraid of me, Mary?"

She'd shaken her head no and he'd left it at that. But he'd felt a release, a lightening of tension and he'd stared dumbly at his prized clocks, smiling at the thought of her in his back room, straightening her hair, washing her hands and face.

Now Allen supported Mary as they walked toward the Ambrose Building.

"I think you should rest, Mary. Tell them you're sick." She was limping sadly because a shoe was broken. He admired her: brown eyes fixed straight ahead, her lips firmly pressed. She was terrified but bent on not showing it.

"Watch out, Mary," Allen urged as she almost tripped over a box of goods set out for the post. "I don't think you should be working today. Let me tell your manager—Mr. Bates, is it?—you're sick. You don't look well."

"I need to take care of myself, Mr. Thornton."

"Allen." He supported her elbow.

"Al's better." She smiled. "I do thank you, Al."

They were in front of the gray-stoned Ambrose Building. It was the most impressive structure in Tulsa, with gold-caged elevators and elevator girls with their names stitched on their breast pocket. Like *Mary.* Allen didn't want to let her go.

"Excuse me." A Negro boy brushed past him, pushing through the revolving glass doors.

"Sorry." Allen stepped aside, thinking it peculiar that handcuffs swung, like a pendulum, from the Negro's back pocket. Through the spinning glass, Allen could see flashes of the slim, dark figure striding confidently into the marble lobby. The doors slowed their rotation. The young Negro was lost from sight.

Allen shrugged. "I'm in the way here, I guess." He drew Mary aside, studying her face. When he'd carried her in his arms, he realized how lonely he'd been. He couldn't remember the last time he'd been alone with a woman.

"My hand," Mary murmured.

"What?"

"Please, let go my hand."

"Oh, I'm sorry. I didn't hurt you, did I?"

"No."

Her lower lip was trembling and Allen, embarrassed, withdrew. "I enjoyed your company. Good day to you, Miss—" He didn't know her last name. "Miss Mary."

He turned abruptly, walking quickly, cursing himself for losing time when he had Bailey's pocket watch to repair. He shouldn't waste his mornings caring for frightened girls.

Mary.

His steps slowed. He should've invited her to dinner. Or perhaps to the cinema. A show with lots of dancing. She hadn't been afraid of him—a slightly thick-headed, white-haired man. Maybe she'd felt sorry for him? He was beyond pale, stoop-shouldered from bending, squinting at wires and springs. He saw himself reflected in a hotel window. At forty-two, he'd had years of women lowering their eyes, angling their bodies away from him. No, he wasn't handsome. Nor rich enough to overcome his oddness.

The only time he really lived was during his yearly visit to New York to see hoofers, vaudevillians, and magicians. The train carried him away to a few weeks respite from being Allen Thornton, repairer of timepieces. Albino.

When he'd seen Mary through his shop window, he'd recognized her at once as the elevator operator. She'd never flinched from him like other women. Twice he'd ridden the elevator just to see her. Sometimes he'd glance sidelong at her legs, the curve of her neck, her short brown hair. Seeing her limping peg-legged, retracing the same block, he'd felt an urge to rescue her. And he had. Like the hero in *No, No, Nanette.* He'd felt infused with life. *Mary.* He didn't know where she lived. He'd taken a hold of life. Him, Allen Thornton.

Mary. Allen stopped, seeing the town anew. Office buildings, hotels, and emporiums rose against the blue skyline. The Grecian-columned courthouse was flanked by a square of lush lawn and elegant oaks. Sophisticated, bowler-hatted gentlemen and elaborately clothed ladies departed the Henly. For the first time, it occurred to him that Tulsa was a stage set ready to come to life. Mary had removed the scrim; experience was now fresh, heartfelt.

He turned back around, almost running. He wouldn't lose her. Tulsa was awash in sunshine; it would stay that way, if Mary were beside him. He rushed through the Ambrose door, spinning full circle twice. Breathless, almost slipping, he stepped into the cool, dignified lobby. He didn't see her.

"Mary." He called as loudly as he dared. "Mary." His heart was racing; he thought how unjust it would be if she disappeared.

He saw Mary in the elevator waiting for passengers.

"Mary!" She didn't look up. He started running between the finely dressed gentlemen, the oil men, the lawyers, the gentrified farmers. He passed the shoeshine stand. A Negro was tapping his foot against a box of paste and dye.

A small crowd of men, arguing heatedly, blocked the path to Mary's elevator.

For a second, Allen saw Mary, her hand on the release bar, ready to shut the interior gilded doors. "Wait." She had a passenger. The Negro boy who'd brushed past him earlier was in the elevator. Odd, Allen thought. Negroes took the stairs.

"Mary, wait." How glorious it would be—a splendid finale, the two of them ascending in the elevator. He was almost there.

Mary released the lever: The exterior doors, heavy and impenetrable, started to close. "Mary!"

Men behind Allen started buzzing, "Look at that. Did you see that?"

"A nigger. Riding the elevator."

"I'll be damned."

Allen couldn't see Mary. It was as though she were off-stage and the Negro, smiling, impressive, had moved center stage as the outer doors, like heavy velvet, squeezed shut.

The pulleys lurched into motion.

The lobby seemed suddenly crowded as men, heads uplifted, stood before the elevator doors, watching the arrow move from *L* to *2* to *3*. The tenor of the lobby changed. Like a timepiece wound too tight, like the darkening of lights before the villain's arrival. *4, 5, 6.*

Allen surveyed the uplifted faces: jowled, angular faces. Some had broad cheekbones, others barely had chins. Eyes, blue and brown. Thick-haired men, balding men, some with sandy-colored curls. Lips stretched thin, some puffed, lips gleaming with saliva from their tongues. All of their faces, white as the moon—all of them marking the slow course of the elevator rising. *8, 9.*

Aside, to the far right, the shoeshine was muttering, "He could've peed in the alley, Gabe. Damn fool." A Negro in a battered army coat said something Allen didn't catch.

10, 11. Washrooms for whites were on every floor; "coloreds only" was on the fourteenth. *12.* No *13.* Allen exhaled. He'd been holding his breath. The Negro boy would get off. Mary would come down. He'd convince her to quit work for the day and have dinner. He smiled. A small tempest—Tulsans getting riled because a Negro took an elevator to relieve himself.

14. The arrow hadn't moved. *14.*

"What's she doing? Waiting for the nigger to piss?" Several men laughed.

Allen wanted to curse at them. He pressed the call button. "Come on down, Mary," he whispered. "Come on down." He pressed his ear against the metal doors; he heard nothing. Then he heard the clang of the gilded gates shutting. "She's coming down," he shouted to no one. "She's coming down." The pulleys whined into action again. *12.* He smiled. *11, 10.* He pressed the call button repeatedly, hoping to hurry the descent. *9, 8, 7.* The elevator stopped. *6.*

A woman screamed.

"Mary," Allen shouted. Fear gripped him. He pounded on the doors. "Mary."

A horrifying wail spiraled down the shaft. He remembered once making such a sound when he'd seen Reubens' charred remains. "Mary." He slammed his fist on the elevator doors, repeatedly pressing the call button, shouting, "Mary, Mary," counterpointing the keening above.

"Stairs. Somebody take the stairs."

Yes, thought Allen, but before he turned, the elevator groaned into motion. The wail had ceased and the lobby was quiet, all heads upturned, listening anxiously for sounds.

A man whispered, "She ain't dead, is she?"

4, 3, 2, L. The engine and pulleys stilled.

Allen was clawing, trying to open the elevator doors. Fingertips bruised and pinched, he cracked the door. The boy's back was to him. He was leaning over Mary, who lay sprawled on the floor. Grunting, Allen shoved the door wide.

"What have you done, nigger?" Outraged, Allen grabbed him. "What the hell have you done?"

"Sir, she—"

Allen saw the change: the split second in which the boy registered terror.

The crowd surged forward. "Nigger, you're supposed to take the stairs."

"Get away from that white woman."

Allen almost toppled from the press of bodies, the hands clawing at the Negro. He couldn't see faces. Only legs and feet jostling forward and, in the far corner, a pair of handcuffs which had fallen from the Negro's pocket.

Then he heard a great roar followed by a powerful thrusting of hands, feet. Maddened, emboldened, the Negro boy fought his way outside the elevator. Startled, the crowd in the lobby parted before the fury. "Joe," he heard someone shout. "Joe!"

The Negro ran, dodging hands, veering left, right, heading for the revolving doors.

"He's escaping. Get him," someone bellowed, mobilizing the well-dressed men. They were after him, sliding across the wide marble lobby, a raucous crowd tracking down a single man.

Allen didn't think the boy would make it. At the last minute, the Negro in the army coat came from nowhere and threw himself into the oncoming crowd. Seconds. He slowed the crowd by seconds. Some kicked and punched him. Others tripped over him. It was enough. The escaping Negro was out the door. The glass was spinning. The crowd's bulk didn't fit through the revolving door. More delay. A few precious seconds.

Allen felt like cheering, thinking the Negro just might make it—just might escape. Immediately, he felt guilty. He bent his mouth to Mary's ear.

"Mary. It's Al," he whispered. She stirred and Allen forgot about the drama outside the Ambrose Building, on the streets of Tulsa.

He concentrated on awakening his beauty with a kiss.

9

Joe spun blindly through the revolving glass door, stumbled, and fell onto the sidewalk, rolling into the legs of a man carrying a suitcase. The suitcase skittered into the gutter, popped open, spilling shirts, ties, a shaving kit, and postcards. Joe lay face down on the pavement, blood dripping from his lip. He could hear the slap-slap of the revolving door, see cards of Tulsa's skyscrapers, oil rigs, gingerbread homes, and herding cowboys, fluttering to the ground. Joe knew he was as good as dead.

"Son of a bitch." The man was bending over him, shaking his fist, cursing, "Nigger, look what you've done."

They'd take him now. He was good as dead. His legs felt weighted; he was sinking. "*Run, Joe, run.*" Was it his voice or Henry's?

"Look what you done, nigger." Stubby hands grabbed his collar.

"*You gotta run, Joe. Escape.*"

He might be as good as dead, but they had to catch him first.

"Who do you think you are, nigger?"

Scrambling up, Joe shoved the irate man and ran. Ran as if the devil was tracking him—ran, breathless, his heart racing, his mouth soured by fear. "Henry!" he called, thinking he might sight his brother. "Henry!"

He reached an alleyway just as an angry crowd exploded from the Ambrose. "Nigger took him a white woman!"

Joe nearly tripped as he skated around the corner into the alley.

"Catch him."

"There he goes!"

Joe ran harder, dodging a delivery van coming up the alley, seeing the driver's surprised expression, just managing to slip between the van and the building's brick wall. The van's brakes squealed as he flew down another alley.

A song started running through his head:

Run, nigger, run
The paterrollers come.
Run, nigger, run.
The paterrollers come.

Before his stroke, Tyler would circle the garden, singing: "*Run, nigger, run. The paterrollers come.*" Generations of slaves had escaped from the white man. Running from patrols of men and dogs. Tyler had done it—run through cotton fields, swamps, just like Joe was running. His shadow stretched like tar; clouds glowed yellow. Joe remembered celebrating Juneteenth, marching behind Tyler in the yard, chanting, "*Run, nigger, run. Run, nigger, run.*" Just ten, his voice mimicked Tyler's bass:

Dis nigger run, he run his best,
Stuck his head in a hornet's nest,
Jumped de fence and run fru de paster;
white man run, but nigger run faster.

Father had stripped his pants and beat him with his belt.

Joe exited the alley onto Main, drawing stares from pedestrians as he ran past the courthouse. He ran in the street, outpacing a carriage and its horse. He skirted round cars. Dodged produce trucks. Let himself fly.

"Over there. He's over there. Near the courthouse."

Joe looked back, seeing shadows of men pointing, hearing a steady pounding, feeling tremors beneath his feet. A car horn blared. "Damn nigger. Get out the way."

He cut across Courthouse Square leaping over a bench, frightening a Negro woman feeding crackers to a white baby. He flew over the grass, smacking his hand against the oak trunks, darting left, right. He ran past fashionable women, avoiding any men. Even old men resting their joints on benches. The wind carried voices: "What's that nigger doing running?"

He'd been taught to fear this moment. Never be a colored boy hunted. Never have cause to run from a white man.

"You are Joseph David Samuels," Father hollered between belt swings. "No paterrollers here." Slap. "You are . . ." Slap. "Joseph David Samuels." Slap. Slap. Welts grew on his back.

Joseph David Samuels. Like his brother was Henry Martin Samuels. They were supposed to be safe. Safe because they weren't ordinary colored boys. They were Douglass Abraham Samuels' sons.

Joe laughed harshly, his breath exploding in bursts. His side ached. What would Father think now? His brother dead, killed by pale-faced Germans, and him running for his life.

Suddenly Joe wasn't afraid. Being hunted, running like Tyler had, like so many others had from slavery, released him from his dread.

Joe stumbled, his hand scraped the ground. "Run," he told himself. "Run."

Maybe Henry had felt this too, the sheer exhilaration of knowing there was nothing left to dread. Joe felt free.

He cut left at the Square's edge, heading northeast, away from the business district, toward Greenwood. He breathed, deep and even. He could feel the pain in his side easing. He could do this. *Relax. Breathe like Houdini.* He felt powerful, strong.

He'd escaped the Ambrose Building, outrun the crowd. He'd escape from Tulsa. Nothing bound him now. Not even his father.

His gait stretched. Inhale. Exhale. His arms swung free and easy. He was the center of a blur of motion. He left the main roads, avoiding Greenwood and Archer, cutting across the railroad tracks, down Tulsa's back alleys. He was heading home.

Sweat dusted his neck and back.

He wanted to tell Tyler he'd heard the paterrollers. He'd heard: "*Run, nigger, run.*" And he'd done it. He'd done it good. He'd outrun the paterrollers. He'd outraced them all.

The sky was burnt orange. Day was nearly done. He ran skillfully, dodging clotheslines, vaulting fences, his breath roaring like surf in his ears.

10

"Let me through. Coming through." Sheriff Clay elbowed his way inside the crowded elevator. The external doors were solid but the interior resembled a gaudy cage. Ambrose, the building's owner, called his elevator girls canaries. Clay had always thought him crazy.

Bates, the building's manager, thick-jowled, gut shaking like jelly, tapped his nails incessantly against the bars. Clay guessed Bates was already worried about losing his job.

A brown-haired girl lay flat on the cage floor. Another girl, *Louise* embroidered on her pocket, was trying to use smelling salts but a white-haired man blocked her, not budging from his position, hunched over the unconscious girl.

Several men—too old to chase the colored—lingered just outside the steel doors. Heads cocked, they were peering at the girl on the floor. Clay realized they were staring at the girl's crotch. Her gray skirt was hitched to her thighs. Pushing to the front, Clay saw what the men were seeing—wisps of hair, pink thighs. Underpants gone.

Clay flushed. He said, more harshly than he intended, "Is she dead?"

Shocked, the man turned, his brows pinching upward. "No."

Recognizing Allen Thornton, Clay muttered, "Damn." His luck—a colored on the run and Albino Allen hovering over the woman like she was some baby bird. Allen didn't know anything about how Tulsa worked.

Clay shook his head. Ambrose would have a fit. He was probably already strutting like a peacock, screaming about his reputation and honor. Everybody knew Ambrose plowed a different prostitute every night. Nonetheless, Ambrose and his oil men friends hand picked the railroad and school boards, even the county sheriff. Ambrose paid him to keep the peace.

Clay bent, laying his jacket over the woman's legs. *Mary,* her pocket said.

"Does anybody know what happened?"

"They were alone in the elevator," said Bates, his face pained as if "alone" explained everything. A colored man, a white woman. Together. In Tulsa.

"So no one knows what happened," said Clay, irked by Bates.

"Just the nigger and her."

"Shit," muttered Clay, wondering how he'd ended up here. Clay's job was to harass loiterers, keep the town respectable by jailing drunks and any coloreds who weren't shining shoes or cleaning houses in Tulsa. And, as he was often reminded, to look the other way when the KKK did its haul. The worst had been the lynching of David Reubens. Ambrose told him to take a day off. To his shame, he'd gone hunting in the hills.

"Can't this wait?" asked Allen. "She needs care."

Clay remembered Allen coming to the jail after Reubens' lynching and cursing him. Overturning chairs, Allen had bellowed repeatedly, "I demand justice. You know damn well who did it." Clay had his deputies throw him out and he'd listened to them scuffling, battering Allen in the back alley, before letting him go. He hadn't forgiven himself for that either.

"You know her?"

"Yes." Allen crouched back on his heels.

"Bring her 'round," said Clay.

Louise, flashing a triumphant glance at Allen, pressed the vial under Mary's nose.

Mary woke up howling. Everyone fell back; the sound redoubled in the tight space. Louise retreated, pressing her salts to her bosom. Bates slammed his fist into his palm. The howl crescendoed, flying out through the lobby. Clay gritted his teeth. He remembered such screams from the war, remembered himself howling like a fiend when a man's head landed in his lap.

An old man murmured, "Nigger better run. Better run good."

"Hush." Mary gulped air. "Hush." She covered her mouth with her hands.

"Mary—" Allen reached for her.

"Let go. Let go my hands." She scooted backward, her hands striking the air, her eyes wide and staring. "Please. Please let me go."

"Mary—" Allen's arms snaked around her.

"Let go," she screamed. "Let me go." She clung to the bars, sobbing.

"Let her go," said Clay.

Allen flinched. "She's upset, can't you see that? She thinks I'm—"

"I'd feel the same way if a colored touched me," said Louise. "Wouldn't trust any man."

Arms across her abdomen, her brow touching her knees, Mary whimpered, "Ma. Please, Ma."

Clay felt sorry for her. There were scratches on Mary's legs and hands. Bruises on her wrists. *Bring the nigger in. Case solved. Simple.* Mud speckled her hem. Tangled hair curtained her face. Her shoe was missing its heel. Clay knew nothing was simple. He stooped low.

Allen was cooing, "Mary, Mary." She wrestled away her hands. "Let go my hands. I'm not beautiful. I'm not."

"It's a damn shame," said Louise.

Mary sobbed harder. Clay reached forward and slapped her.

Allen swore. "There's no need to hit her. She's been through enough."

"She's hysterical," said Clay. "I need her to talk."

Mary hiccuped, "Hush."

"I'll take care of her," said Allen.

Ignoring him, Clay moved close to Mary. "There's a boy running for his life. Can you tell me anything?"

"He touched you, didn't he? Took your panties and touched you," said one of the old men.

Mary bit her lip.

"I need you to answer me, ma'am."

"A proper woman don't talk about such things," said Louise, pulling at her collar.

Clay studied Mary. She must be in shock, he thought. She looked at him strangely, lines furrowing her plain face.

"We've never had anything like this before," said Bates. "Niggers always take the stairs. He should've been on the stairs."

"How long were they together?" asked Clay, looking up at Bates.

"Long enough," said Bates.

"Two minutes. Maybe four," said Allen. "Not long enough—"

"Yes?"

Allen shook his head.

Whimpering, Mary collapsed against Allen. Clay thought it curious that Allen buried his face in the girl's hair. Kissed her dull strands. Clay shrugged. He didn't care who aroused Allen's interests, even a vacant-eyed girl. Everybody had their tastes: Ambrose for big-bosomed girls; his friend, Gainey, wanted them black. Colored men supposedly liked them light-skinned or white.

Clay could see Miss Louise's toes, Bates' perfectly shined shoes, Mary's bruised knees. The elevator was hot. Airless. Maybe six by four, if that. Clay looked up. A minichandelier dangling from the apex cast slivers of light.

Why take a woman here? A cage within a box. The chute was lined with mirrors. When the "bird cage" rose, everyone got to see themselves behind gilded bars. Ambrose's fancy. Images multiplied like fun house mirrors. A white man would be mad to rape a girl here. A colored would have to be desperate to die.

Clay stood. "I can think of smarter places for a rape."

"Nigger's got to pay," said Bates.

"Are you telling me my job?"

"You're wasting time." Bates squinted. "Ambrose won't like it."

"The girl hasn't accused anybody."

"We all saw it, didn't we?" Bates said, his hand sweeping, taking in the nodding, elderly men who on ordinary days rode the elevator to offices where they bartered oil rights, managed trust accounts, and discussed wills.

"What did you see?" asked Clay, softly. "I mean, that you can testify to? Can you see past events? Can you see through steel?" He stared the men down. Glances shifted, feet shuffled. Funny fools, salivating at the thought of sex. "I'm in charge of this investigation."

Bates peered at him like an old pig. "Ambrose is going to be upset."

"I know."

"Nigger's got to pay," said Bates, stubbornly. The old men nodded.

Clay ached behind his eyes. He yearned for bourbon. *Bring the nigger in. Case closed.* "Who we talking about?"

"Joe. One of our shoeshines," Bates replied. "Douglass Samuels' son."

"The banker?" Clay couldn't hide his surprise. "What's a banker's son doing shining shoes?"

"Just because a nigger has money, don't mean he's got sense. He's like any other nigger. Wanted a white woman. He deserves hanging." Others murmured agreement. "Niggers been too riled since the war."

Bates slowly smiled and it was this, more than anything, that made Clay want to hit him. Cowards like Bates never made it to the war. But they liked the notion of blood flowing. Bates wore klansmen robes, keeping alive a war against coloreds, reds, unionizers, and anyone else Ambrose might dislike.

"I can haul your ass to jail, Bates. Inciting a riot."

"I can say what I damn well please. Got as much right as the next."

Clay grabbed Bates' collar, feeling his sharp intake of breath, his Adam's apple bobbing. "The boy'd have to be crazy to try anything here. In an office building. Not just any building. Ambrose's."

"Niggers ain't smart. Wanted a feel, a taste. Joe gave me trouble all the time. Talking back to customers."

"Something's not right," said Clay, letting go of Bates.

"Right, hell—things ain't been right since the war. Niggers thinking this is France. Thinking they can do what they want."

"They're always looking at us," Louise whispered. Her words stopped them dead.

Clay pinched the flesh between his eyes. Shit. *Case closed.* Joe Samuels didn't have a chance.

Allen lifted Mary up; her head bobbled, her jaw opened, and her tongue pressed forward in a wordless "ah."

"She's coming with me," Allen said, daring anyone to stop him. He pushed past Clay and Bates.

"A nigger's done felt her up. Raped her he did. Took a white woman," proclaimed an old man tapping his cane, his voice echoing in the high-ceilinged lobby.

Bates clutched Clay's arm. "Nigger's on the run. Knows he's guilty."

"Maybe," said Clay, pulling free of Bates.

"What are you going to do, Sheriff?"

"I'll be bringing him in. For questioning, at least."

Clay saw Louise's reflection preening, her fingers patting the curve of her hips. "Go home, Louise," Clay said. "You've been a great help." She looked at him quizzically then scooted past.

"Joe gave me trouble all the time," Bates complained. "Talking back. Doing bad shines. Didn't know his place."

Ignoring Bates, Clay scooped up his jacket.

Clay sighted Allen at the revolving door, trying to spin through without putting Mary down.

"Allen," he called out. "What's her name?" He could ask Bates but he wanted to find out whether Allen knew it. "What's her name? Her people's name. Mary—what?"

"Go to hell, Clay," Allen called back, maneuvering his and Mary's bodies sideways through the revolving glass.

Clay chuckled. Then turned, "You still here, Bates?"

He listened to Bates' soles slapping on marble, watched the old men shuffling across the floor. Louise clutched herself dramatically, giving a sidelong glance to two colored men watching the drama from the lobby's far side.

Bates hollered, "Louise, get on now." He shooed the shoeshines like they were pesky flies.

Clay stared into the elevator and at himself, reflected in the mirrored wall behind the cage. He didn't look any different. Weak chin. Hair longer than was considered genteel. Eyes cloudy from too much drink. Limbs soft since the war. A perfect specimen for a rich man's sheriff.

He stepped inside the elevator's belly, stretching his arms to steady himself against the bars. He'd better get moving. He'd have to find Samuels before the mob did.

He studied the parquet floor. He didn't see panties. No cotton or lace like he'd seen on dead whores. In France, the women wore silk. He felt aroused remembering Mary's open legs. He didn't like to think of any man, colored or white, taking advantage of a woman.

He saw a glint of silver. He stooped and lifted a pair of handcuffs. Professional. Maybe even from his own jail. He heard a step behind him, and without thinking, he stuffed the cuffs into his pocket. "I thought I told you—"

It wasn't Bates. Clay saw a dark man, rail thin, his pants stained with polish. "Shine, Sheriff?"

The man was sizing him up, measuring him like they were equals. Adversaries.

Clay snapped, "Did you think I wouldn't get to you? I'm conducting this investigation. I would've gotten to you in my own good time."

The man angled his head disbelievingly.

"What's your name?" Clay asked.

The man stared back balefully.

"I'm looking to help. See that justice is done. Where'd he go? Joe Samuels, is it? Tell me where he went." Except for a nerve quivering beneath his eye, Clay thought the man had become stone. "Come on. Help the boy out."

The man advanced. Clay's hand went instinctively to his gun.

"Joe's been working here for over a year," the man hissed. "You come in once a week. Half that time, Joe's given you a shine. Gave you one last week. Remember what he looks like, Sheriff? Tall? Short? Light or dark brown? You remember anything about him? Joe even told you a joke. Remember? You said it was the best joke you ever heard."

Clay struggled to raise an image. Other than Joe being colored, Clay couldn't remember a damn thing.

"I didn't think so." The man set his jaw. "You're no different than any other white man."

"So, I forgot. I can't remember every colored I meet. Where's he now? Where's Joe now?"

"You ever take the stairs to pee, Sheriff? Thirteen floors?" The man spat. "Nickel for a shine, Sheriff. That's all I tell men like you." He turned, walking away.

"Damn." Clay rubbed his brow, feeling a raging ache starting. He should've stayed in bed this morning, drunk himself silly. His only hope was that the boy escaped Tulsa altogether. If Joe was never found, Clay wouldn't have to decide what to do with him.

11

"Tyler, Tyler!" Joe bounded up the stairs, two, three at a time. The staircase seemed to curve forever. "Tyler!" His side hurt.

"Joe, what are you doing home?"

The clipped voice stopped his momentum. Joe spun around, teetering, his hand gripping the banister. "Hello, Hildy," he gasped, seeing his sister at the bottom of the steps.

"Tyler's sleeping. What are you doing home? What's happened?"

"The most wonderful thing." Joe collapsed against the railing, sweat trickling from his forehead.

"What?" she nervously wiped her flour-smeared hands onto her apron. "Tell me."

"I escaped."

"What are you talking about? Escaped?" Her brows arched. "Joe?" Hildy moved quickly up the steps. "You're hurt. You need a plaster for your cheek." Delicately, she touched his skin. "Joe, is somebody after you?"

Joe caught his sister's hand and pressed it to his lips. "I ran for miles," he said wonderingly.

"Who from, Joe?"

"White men, Hildy. A whole passel of 'em." He chuckled. "White and bright like the noonday sun."

"What're you doing here, Joe?"

"I came home."

"It's the first place they'll come. You've got to leave, Joe."

"I came to see Tyler."

"Damnit, Joe, you've got to get up."

"I need to see Tyler."

"There isn't time. Get up, Joe. Run." She tried dragging him down the stairs.

"Hildy, let go—"

"White men lynch Negroes. You've gotta run, Joe. You can't stop running." Hildy tugged desperately. She pounded him with her fists. "Damn you, Joe. You think I took care of you all these years so you could get hung. You gotta run, Joe."

"Hildy, no, you don't understand—"

"You gotta run."

"I love you, Hildy."

Hildy stopped. "Joe," she asked, insistent, "why won't you run?"

"I've got to see Tyler."

"They'll catch you."

"They won't."

"Who won't?" asked Emmaline, leaning over the banister, her hair twisted around curling rags.

"Lord," muttered Hildy. "Mother's not far behind."

His mother appeared, elegant, at the top of the stairs. "What's going on here? Aren't you supposed to be working, Joe?"

"Somebody's chasing him," hollered Emmaline, leaning over the banister.

"What did you do, Joe?"

"Mother—" warned Hildy.

"Gambling? If you think your father will pay your gambling debts, you're mistaken."

"I don't owe anybody."

"What did you do?"

"Nothing."

Her lips scrunched into a pout. "You must've done something."

"If Joe says he's done nothing, he's done nothing," said Hildy. "There's some misunderstanding, Mother."

"A woman then," she countered.

"It doesn't matter. Joe's got to get out of here."

Joe watched his mother descend the stairs, her nose tilting upward with distaste. "You're just like your father," she said scathingly. "Your brother, too, gone to hell."

In the entryway, the chandelier swayed slightly. Joe swallowed. *Someone passed him on the stairs.* "I've got to see Tyler," he murmured.

"Not until you explain yourself," Mother said, digging her nails into his forearm. "Not until you explain the shame you've brought to us."

"Wasn't your magic any good, Joe?" mocked Emmaline from above.

"You have no respect for privilege," Mother berated him. "No respect for history. You've learned barbarous behavior from your father's people. Dirty, illiterate slaves. My family was always respectable. Always free coloreds. New Orleans Creoles."

"Mother!" shouted Hildy.

"You. Henry. Your father. Every one of you a disappointment. Each of you bringing this family shame."

"Stop it, Mother!"

Joe staggered back against the wall. He'd never seen his mother's face so ugly. "I'm sorry, Mother. I never meant to hurt anyone." A yellow rose appeared in his hand.

She crossed her arms. "Emmaline, get your father. Tell him I want him home. Tell him Joe's gone wild. Tell him Joe's disgraced us."

Joe dropped the rose. He climbed the steep stairs, moving beyond his silk-robed mother.

Emmaline stared at him curiously as he reached the second floor landing.

"Joe—" She caught his arm. "What's wrong? Can I help?"

Joe studied his sister's pinched face. She looked like Mother. Shadows lay beneath her eyes; fine lines tugged at her mouth.

"Get Father, Emmy," murmured Joe. "Tell him to bring roses for you and Mother."

"You're a fool, Joe."

"Do you believe in ghosts, Emmy?"

"Emmaline, if you love him at all—" Hildy pleaded. "Tell him—tell him he's got to run. White men are chasing him."

Joe chuckled, "Nigger run faster."

"I'll get Father."

"Hurry, Emmaline," his mother ordered. "Your father will stop this nonsense."

Joe laughed. "That's right," he shouted down the stairs. "Father doesn't own a bank for nothing. He's a big man. The biggest Negro in Tulsa."

"Joe, don't you care about anything?" wept Hildy. "Don't you care about your life?"

Joe raised a finger. "Sssh. Don't worry, Hildy. I've outrun the pater-rollers."

He opened Tyler's door and stepped into a dim world, smelling of dust, menthol, and urine. Drawn curtains kept the ruby furniture from fading, kept out the fresh air.

"Tyler—" Tyler's bed dominated the room: white sheets, white pillow cases, white ruffles on the base. Sheets thrown back, wearing white pajamas, Tyler looked dried and twisted like a blackened stump. His eyelids twitched with dreams.

Joe's confidence had fled. He was wearied by the run, his mother's bitterness, wearied by trying to escape a nightmare. "Tyler," he whispered.

He searched the room. The walls were covered with dozens of paintings of the same landscape—rows upon rows, acres of wheat captured at sunrise, sunset, high noon. Joe shook his head.

He looked at Tyler. He needed to ask him something, but couldn't remember what. He couldn't remember what he was doing, why he was here. He'd run the distance.

Tyler was incapable of running. Incapable of leaving his bed except with the help of a son who carried him downstairs for meals and a daughter-in-law who pushed him onto the porch, locking his chair's wheels, for an hour's sun.

When Joe was born, Tyler had already been too old to play marbles, give him piggy rides, or eat sweet corn. Except for one Juneteenth when he'd marched with his grandson, before his stroke, Tyler had spent his days painting the same lush fields.

"Tyler." Joe sat on the four-poster bed. He straightened Tyler's brittle legs. Joe tapped his hands on his lap, softly chanting, "Run, nigger, run. The paterrollers come."

Tyler grunted.

"Run, nigger, run. The paterrollers come."

Tyler's mouth crooked into a smile. A Bible, a glass, and pitcher were on the bed stand.

Joe bent, staring into cloudy brown eyes. "I did good today. You would've been proud. I escaped the slave man."

Tyler shook his head, his mouth salivating.

"I did good."

Tyler's clawed fist hit the mattress. "Tyler?" Joe gripped his hand, feeling the toughened skin, the gnarled bones. "Tyler?" He laid his head on his grandfather's chest. Feeling the frail ribs, listening to an erratic heart, Joe murmured, "Tyler? Did you ever feel as free as when you ran? When you escaped?"

"He can't talk."

"I *know*, Hildy." Joe watched Tyler's face—his lashes fluttering, his lips stretching paper-thin skin. "You don't have to tell me what I already know."

"Then why bother, Joe?"

"You see him, don't you?" he asked irritably. "He's not dead yet. He understands. If it hadn't been for Tyler escaping slavery, we wouldn't be here."

"He was freed, Joe." Hildy moved to the bedpost.

"What are you talking about?"

"Emmaline's right. You're a complete fool. Men chasing you and all you can do is sit."

"He outwitted them all."

"What are you talking about?"

"Tyler. He escaped."

"Tyler was freed," Hildy snapped back. "The only running he did was in the land rush to get the acres."

"What acres? What are you talking about?"

"Here's a canteen, Joe. It's Henry's. You need to run. I figure you've got minutes. Five to ten at most, somebody's going to be here. White folks aren't all slow."

"What land?"

Tyler worked his jaw, trying to speak.

"Sooners, Joe!" Hildy said exasperated. "Ex-slaves coming to Tulsa. Every thief, every poor white man racing to stake a claim. 'Like rabbits,' Mother always says. You *know* this, Joe. That's the history Mother can't stand. Said it was disgraceful to be running after God's land. Squatting on dirt. Said it wasn't respectable."

"But Juneteenth. His song about running from the paterrollers."

"It's a song, Joe."

"Joe—the sheriff is here!" Back stiff, Mother trembled just inside the door. "He's driving up. Run, Joe. I don't want a son of mine in jail."

"I need some things."

"No time, Joe," said Hildy, shoving the canteen at him. "Get to the riverbed. Lena's. I'll bring food tonight."

"I'll delay him," Mother murmured, hurrying down the stairs.

"De . . . de . . . de—" Tyler was trying to sit up. Veins rose in his neck and forehead.

"What is it, Tyler?"

"Joe, there's no time."

"De . . . de . . . dee—"

"Joe! Leave through the kitchen."

Joe squeezed Tyler's hand. "I'll make it, Tyler. I'll beat the paterrollers." He rushed past Hildy, but instead of turning down the stairs, he turned up, toward the attic.

"Joe! They're here," Hildy shouted, flying after him.

Joe moved two, three steps at a time. The rush was inside him: quick bursts of air, his body filled with adrenaline.

His bedroom seemed foreign. Small. The ceiling angled too steeply. Cloudless sky filled the window. His sheets were still tangled from his dreaming. Opening his trunk, he grabbed his lock pick, another set of handcuffs, cards, and his two hundred dollars.

He smiled, hearing his mother shrill, "Do you know whose house this is?" He heard a low, answering murmur.

Hildy stood in the doorway, hairpins loose, hair falling to her waist, her apron awry. "You've waited too long, Joe."

"I need to find it."

"What, Joe? What do you need?"

He was searching rapidly through his photos.

"Joe, please."

"Here it is." Houdini, manacled, leaping from the Golden Gate Bridge. Joe folded the photo, slipped it inside his pants pocket.

He looked at Hildy. "Aren't you going to ask me if I'm guilty?"

"I don't need to, Joe."

"Thanks, Hildy."

The footsteps on the stairs came closer. Because he'd stopped running, dread trapped him. He licked his lips, caught a glance of himself in the mirror. A wild-eyed man. Joe couldn't figure out who he needed to be. He was so tired, so thirsty. He raised his brother's canteen, swearing he heard, "*Water.*"

"Come along, son."

He heard his brother, "Run, Joe!"

There was nowhere to go. Sheriff Clay fell upon him. He slammed Joe's face into the floor, jerked his arms back, and locked handcuffs, good and tight, about his wrists. The canteen skittered under his bed.

Joe heard Hildy weeping. He heard his mother shouting below stairs; he heard a keening which he thought was Tyler. *He heard a sigh as soft as rain.* Sheriff Clay dragged him to his feet. *Through the window, Joe saw Henry escaping, leaping, roof to roof, across Deep Greenwood.*

"Let's go." Sheriff Clay pulled him upright. Ashamed, Joe stared inside his trunk. Atop his magic props, photos of a grim faced Houdini, fluttered, shifting in the breeze.

12

Gabe made himself walk. White folks already had one nigger running. If he ran, he'd be a dead man. War was like hunting squirrels. It was more fun to shoot the ones running.

Tulsa, like France, had plenty of white men wanting to shoot him. He'd played possum in the Ambrose and except for a trampling, a few kicks to his ribs and groin, he'd escaped. Now he needed to get to Greenwood fast. He made for Courthouse Square, then cut diagonally across the well-tended park. He was behind enemy lines. If he stayed visible, he'd be less suspicious.

Gabe shook his head. Beneath twin oaks, a platform was being built for tomorrow's speeches. Greenwood men—Sam, Coolie, Wydell—were doing the hammering and sawing, setting up hundreds of wood chairs. He recognized toothless Gus planting rows of red and white carnations. A young woman with ribbons in her blonde hair was sticking tiny American flags into the bluegrass. Every few inches of flags, she'd stand up, hands shading her eyes, and shout orders at the men. "Sam, those chairs aren't straight. A little to the left, please. Gus, the pattern is red then white . . . red then white. Coolie, please, will you hurry up. I cannot do everything myself."

"Control, Private. If you want to survive, exercise control. Focus under fire, that's the thing."

Gabe had punched his smirking, pasty-faced lieutenant in the mouth. Man didn't think Negroes knew anything. Negroes were *born* behind enemy lines. A segregated unit with an inexperienced, white officer had only proved it. Anyone dumb enough to lecture while his men dug trenches, deserved to be hit. Gabe had spent a week in the brig.

He spat on the sidewalk. The sun was heavy, streaking the trees orange-red. Mosquitoes were hustling blood. Gabe sensed the strain in the Square. Palpable like the humidity. Joe must've passed through the park. Folks, sitting on benches, watched him warily. Brown girls hustled white babies home. When he passed, Coolie's saw lost its rhythm, Sam's hammer fell silent. White men were gathering in front of the city jail. By nightfall, all the Greenwood workers would be home, doors locked, having heard about Joe and a white woman.

Lumbering, his trench coat flapping, Gabe hoped he looked too crazy for anyone to bother him. But if some fool wanted to call his bluff, he'd pull his service revolver and it would be all over. For him and the fool.

"Control, Private. Yes, sir." He knew the routine. Eyes on the ground. Jaw loose, act stupid. Sometimes black skin worked like a charm. Germans seeing their first Negro would hesitate for a second, stupefied. A second was enough time to pierce a heart, rip intestines, or slice through an eye. He'd even got a citation for saving his lieutenant's skin.

Decoration Day. Shit, he hadn't even been invited. But that was all right. He hadn't fought for Tulsa. America. World peace. Not even Deep Greenwood. Henry hadn't wanted to go alone; so, Gabe had enlisted too.

He should've stayed in Greenwood. Married Emmaline. Fathered fat babies. Then, he never would have met Francine. Now each day he didn't blow his brains out surprised him. Henry's baby brother was giving him another chance. Payback. One brother's life for another.

Gabe quickened his pace as he turned onto Elgin. At least Joe had sense enough to run. Poof! Disappear.

He'd seen plenty of soldiers who'd quit, laid down and moaned about Jesus. But Gabe knew as long as your legs would carry you—*run*. He'd seen a man, his hand shot off, running like a streak of fire. It wasn't about cowardice, it was about cutting your losses and surviving.

Keep running, Joe. Make yourself invisible. But given time, Gabe believed, every man was found.

Gabe crossed into Greenwood, up the hill, past the tall spires of Mt. Zion into a colored world. Young boys pitched coins against the curb, a matron carried a squawking chicken to the butcher's. In front of the hardware shop, Step, the numbers runner, took penny bets. No white Tulsans here, no enemies. But it wasn't home anymore. The war had made him realize Deep Greenwood was simply where Tulsans had fenced coloreds in.

America's boys hadn't wanted to fight with coloreds. French troops had been glad of their Negro friends—"*Compères.*" Glad to eat, sleep, and fight with Negro men. When French women called, "*Bonjour, homme brave,*" they weren't seeing monkeys, coons, niggers—just men. The French reminded him every day, there was nothing wrong with loving his black skin.

March on 369th, heads high.

He would've stayed in France if it hadn't been for Henry's haunting.

He'd lied to Joe. Dead did come back. Henry's ghost had followed him home, peering inside his parents' windows. So Gabe built his shack by the riverbed with thick pine and boarded windows. He pretended he'd dreamed Henry's face, just like late at night, sucking whiskey out of a bottle, he pretended it was only the wind, howling, kicking up dust, tossing branches at his door. Shit.

Gabe saw black script written on a gold background: *Samuels & Son.* Striding purposefully, he entered the bank. It was one place Gabe figured he wouldn't find Henry's ghost.

The glassy-eyed clerk rose quickly as Gabe walked past his desk. "Sir, can I help you? Can I help you, sir?"

"I'm going to see Samuels."

"I'll see if he's free."

"Get out of my way." Without knocking, Gabe opened the door.

Samuels looked up from his desk, "Gabe?"

"Should I call the sheriff?" the clerk asked.

"Should he, Gabe?"

Gabe hated Samuels' arrogant smirk. He'd always been too dark, too poor for the Samuels' family. Too illiterate. Emmaline, as much as she tried, could never make her father believe otherwise.

"Sheriff's already busy chasing your son."

"What the hell do you mean?"

Gabe smiled, pleased he'd unsettled Samuels. With a curt nod, Samuels dismissed his clerk.

Gabe slumped into a leather chair, rested his feet atop the mahogany desk. "Henry used to tell me about your office. Said the bank wasn't much to look at but your private office was as luxurious as any oil man's. I'd agree. Maybe too fine to let your nickel and dime customers see. Hunh, Mister Samuels?"

"What about my son?"

"The one dead? Or the one alive?"

"Nigger, if you've got something to say, say it." He pushed Gabe's boots off the desk.

"Henry always said you were a tough bird. Said you were the meanest man alive. I guess I came to find out if it's so."

"What's this got to do with Joe?"

Gabe shrugged. "I wasn't sure you'd care. Joe's in trouble. I need cash. At least five hundred. Else Joe'll be coming home in a pine box."

"I'll not pay ransom." Samuels lifted an ivory-handled pistol from his drawer. "I'll not be held up in my own bank. You've got one second to tell me about Joe." He aimed. "One."

Gabe relaxed into the chair. Samuels cocked the gun.

Gabe laughed. "You do not play."

"No. I do not play."

"Henry was right, you're one tough bird." He leaned forward, elbows on his knees. "You're going to need to be," he said, serious. "The sheriff's chasing Joe 'cause he was alone with a woman. The woman screamed. The *white woman* screamed."

Samuels shut his eyes.

"It was in the Ambrose. The lobby was filled with white men who heard their flower scream. When the doors opened, the woman was on the floor and Joe was off running.

"If Joe's going to escape Tulsa, he's going to need cash. You're his father and the man with the money. I'll see that he gets it. I think I know where he'll head. But we've got to be quick."

Samuels studied him then leaned back in his chair, the gun resting on his lap. "I don't need your help. Joe'll be fine. I'll have a word with Ambrose. He'll settle this, I'm sure. Joe needs to turn himself in."

"Are you a damn fool?"

Emmaline burst in the room. "Father! Father, Joe—"

"He knows already," Gabe said.

Breathless, shoulders heaving, Emmaline looked at Gabe, then her father. "Sheriff's hauled Joe to jail."

Gabe's spirits sank. "Then we're too late to save him."

"You did this, Gabe. I know it," Samuels said bitterly. "The war didn't change you. You destroyed one son with your niggerish behavior. Drunkenness. Gambling." He pointed the pistol at Gabe's heart. "I should shoot you like a dog."

"Pull the trigger. Go on and pull it." Gabe faced him across the desk.

"Father, don't," Emmaline pleaded.

"Do it, man. Come on and shoot me."

Samuels slowly lowered his gun.

"Not so easy, is it?" taunted Gabe. "Especially when you and I both know you're telling lies. You destroyed Henry before he went to France. Something you said or did—I don't know what."

"You should've come home dead. Not my son."

"You think that's right, Emmaline?" Gabe asked, searching her face. He found himself wishing he could turn back time, love her better. At Henry's funeral, Emmaline had stared, her eyes never leaving him, making him feel guilty and lost.

"I just wish the Gabe I knew came back."

"You don't understand—"

"You never gave me a chance," she said.

"That's enough Emmaline," Samuels interrupted. "Clear out, Gabe. This is a family matter. Family business."

"Even a man with your wealth can't change things now. Once a white woman screams and a Negro gets caught, they'll hang him. No way around it."

"No," Samuels rasped. "I'll speak to Ambrose."

"It's too late for words. It's time for doing. I'm going to bust Joe out of jail"

"Ambrose and I will settle this," Samuels shouted, his fist pounding the desk. "An agreement will be reached."

"An agreement?" snarled Gabe. "This isn't a business deal. We're talking about your son, not a piece of land."

"You're just an ignorant nigger. Ambrose owes me. He owes me I tell you." He looked at Gabe and his daughter. "He'll see that Joe's safe."

"You just can't stand that you need my help, can you?"

"What I need is for you to stay away from my family. Stay away from Emmaline, stay away from Joe."

"Father, maybe Gabe can help."

"Emmaline," Samuels barked. "Gabe will get Joe killed. Another son murdered while he stands by."

Gabe rocked back on his heels. "You fight dirty, Samuels. Henry always said you did. But I'll save Joe anyway. At least one of us is man enough to fight for him."

"An ignorant nigger, like I said."

Gabe turned. Emmaline grabbed his arm. "Can I help, Gabe? Maybe I could distract—"

"Not another word, Emmaline. Not another word," Samuels bellowed. "We're going home now."

"Please Gabe, let me help."

Pulling free of her grasp, Gabe stuffed his hands in his pockets. "You're lovely, Emmaline," he said softly. "Always was, always will be. You can't come. I won't get you killed trying to save Joe."

She looked desolate.

Unable to help himself, Gabe's fingers touched her lips. "Fill a pack with food. Leave it at my shack."

"I'll not allow it," Samuels said.

Emmaline smiled and the sight gave Gabe strength. He'd need it. Breaking Joe out of jail had to be the stupidest thing he'd ever done.

Gabe turned to Samuels. "You're a fool and a coward, Samuels. Next time you wave a gun at me, I'll kill you." Without a backward glance, he marched out.

13

Mary awoke, feeling safe and warm, lying on a cot in Allen Thornton's back room. A thin blanket had been draped over her. Light seeped through curtains, which served as a doorway to the shop. Discarded clocks—all dusty, some broken, some upright, some lying on their sides—crowded the shelves. Most of the faces read 8:30. A cuckoo door opened: a birdless wire jutted out. Another clock chimed softly.

"Mary." She tasted her name. "Mary, Mary, Mary." As her voice grew louder, rising above the ticking clocks, her fear and pain dissolved. It was as if Dell had never touched her. Pa had never cast her out. *Mary*—her name was her charm.

She curled on her side, legs tucked, her head cradled by her arms. All those years she'd swallowed her feelings. She'd been a "good girl." She'd been "hush."

She could still hear her own screams—good, long howls, spiraling in the elevator. She was probably fired, but it didn't matter. She'd scared Bates, the old, fat-bellied idiot, always yelling at her and Louise. Trying to rub against them whenever he had the chance.

"Ma," she murmured, "you were wrong. There's no sense in being quiet." No sense at all. She should've yelled when her mother was dying.

Mary remembered how she'd turned away to stare at the stained stove, the blackened pot, the blackberry stems in the trash. She'd been trying to keep from crying. Trying to take her mind off her Ma's splayed legs, the sluggish stream of blood trailing to the screen door. When she'd turned back, her mother was dead. One minute Ma had been behind the blue irises; the next, she was gone, her eyes still open, framed by gold lashes.

"Ma," she said loudly, holding the pillow against her body, stroking it. "Ma."

She wept. *Blood didn't cloak the scent of berries.* "Ma." *Didn't cloak her mother's beauty.* "Ma," she cried.

She heard her mother calling, "Mary. Mary Elizabeth. My sweet Mary."

She cried, feeling her mother was near, feeling it was all right to shout, scream, and holler. "Ma." She needn't be silent again.

"Mary, are you all right?" Allen pushed through the curtains.

"Yes, yes, I'm fine." Embarrassed, she sat up, clutching her hands. The room now seemed smaller, dim; the cot hard. She could see a shelf where Allen had a two-burner hot plate, a kettle, and leftover pie.

"You're crying. Let me get you some water."

"No, I'm fine."

Allen cocked his head. "I'll get you some water."

"No, Al," she wiped her face. "I'm crying but I'm fine. I feel better."

Settling her feet on the floor, Mary reached for him. Allen clasped her hand. "It means something to cry out, don't you think?"

"Yes." Allen pulled a chair next to the cot.

"Makes some of the pain go away."

"Yes, Mary."

"You're making fun of me."

"I'm not." He stroked her hair. "I—I sing. I sing all the time. When I'm happy. Sad. Either way it makes me feel good."

"Like my crying."

"Yes," he said.

"I'm happy. Though I wanted to die earlier."

"I understand."

"Do you?" Weary, she lay back, her head on the pillow. "You're a strange man, Al Thornton."

"I suppose I am." He grimaced, touching his colorless face.

"I didn't mean—"

"It's all right."

"No—" she scrambled onto her knees. "It's not all right. I didn't mean to hurt you."

Hands on his belly, Allen stretched his legs, tipping the chair backward. Mary didn't doubt he lived here—sleeping on the cot, rising to wash in the basin before passing through blue curtains into his larger shop where there were hundreds of clocks, watches for sale, and a work bench with scattered parts.

"You've rescued me twice." She propped her head in her hand. "I guess it's my day for having fits. Why, Al? Why'd you keep doing it?"

Allen flexed his fingers. Repair oil stained the skin beneath his nails. "Sometimes a man is helpless. Makes sense that he—I—should do what I can, when I can. It's my pleasure to help you, Mary. You've helped me too."

"How?"

Allen flushed. "If I hadn't met you, it would've been an ordinary day. I wish the circumstances were different. But I don't regret meeting you, Mary. Not at all."

Her throat constricted. She could see caring in his eyes. Something she'd not seen in Dell. Feeling afraid again, she started to cry.

"I'd like to be your friend, Mary. I think you need a friend." Bending forward, Allen looked at her unflinchingly, "You're safe here. I want you to know that. You'll always be safe here."

"He wouldn't stop," she said, rocking, her voice strained. "I told him to stop."

"Mary, I can take you home—"

"I don't have a home."

"Or to Mrs. Cutter. She rents rooms to young women."

"Damn him. He wouldn't stop."

"Or you can stay here, Mary. I'll sleep in the front. Or I could rent a room if it'll make you more comfortable." He touched her arm. "But you needn't do anything you don't want."

"Never?" she whispered, suddenly still.

"Never."

Mary clasped her ankles. Her tongue thick, she murmured, "Do you know what it's like to be touched, when you don't want to be?"

"No. I can't guess."

Mary shuddered, pressing her mouth to her knees.

Allen tugged his beard. "The sheriff's handling it."

"How'd he find out? Did Pa tell him? No, it must've been Jody."

"Jody who?" Allen asked. The clocks rang 8:45, a disorderly series of chimes and bells. "Who are you talking about?"

"My brother," she scooted forward on the cot. "He must've told the sheriff about Dell."

"Dell?"

"Our farm hand. He raped me. This morning."

"But the young man, the Negro boy—"

Mary blinked. What was Al talking about?

"The sheriff went after the Negro boy."

"What boy?"

"The one in the elevator with you. Today. This afternoon. Joe Samuels."

"Joe?" she said dully.

"Don't you remember? My God, Mary." Allen stumbled up, began pacing, kneading his forehead, repeating, "My God."

"Stop it, Al. You're scaring me."

Allen staggered through the curtains into his shop. Mary ran after him.

"Mary, did the Negro, Joe Samuels, hurt you? Touch you? Tell me the truth, Mary."

"No."

"God damn," he yelled.

Mary flinched.

"Sheriff's got him in the jail." Allen collapsed on his stool. "I didn't mean to yell, Mary. But a man's life—" He licked his lips. "I yelled at him. Called him nigger. I never say that word. But I was afraid—" He paused, looking up, "Maybe you can't remember. What happened in the elevator, I mean. People do that. They forget horrible things all the time."

"No, I remember. He frightened me. But he didn't touch me. Didn't hurt me at all."

"Are you sure?"

"No colored has ever touched me."

"Only—Dell?—touched you?"

"Yes."

Allen rose, his arms wide, offering comfort. Mary hesitated, then awkwardly leaned into his embrace. She couldn't remember the last time anyone had just held her. Faces pressed side to side, she could see Al's work bench. Her broken shoe lay amid a pile of brass wire and gold chains.

"Then what happened in the elevator?"

Mary closed her eyes.

Allen held tight. "They'll ask."

"He asked me about magic. Ghosts. Asked me if I knew what it felt like to die."

"He threatened you?" Allen pulled back, searching her face.

"No. He was asking me." She bit her lip, puzzling. "I think he thought I might help."

"I don't understand."

"Neither do I."

"You were screaming, Mary."

"Not about Joe. Not about him. I don't believe he'd harm me any more than you would."

"Mary," he whispered. "Mary."

Trembling, she buried her face in her hands. "Please hold me again." He did.

She remembered Joe standing like a shadow behind her. She remembered pushing the levers to make them go up, seeing them both reflected in the mirrors, thinking it strange a colored was riding the elevator, that he seemed as sad as her.

"They'll kill him, won't they?"

"If they haven't already," said Allen.

Chimes sounded. Clock doors opened—red-crested, blue-bellied, brown birds jutted out, crying "cuckoo." Nine times. The day was almost gone. The rhythmic ticking grew louder; Mary thought of all the time lost in her life. "Let's go see the sheriff," she said, putting on her broken shoe.

She should've screamed when Dell had raped her.

14

◈◈◈

Like he knew Houdini would, Joe measured out his cell three times. Three times he walked heel to toe. Three times, ceiling to floor, he ran his hands over bumpy concrete walls, slid them down cool metal bars. There was no mirror to see himself in, only a sink and a porcelain bowl filled with somebody's urine. He took apart his bunk, lifted the mattress, scraped his fingers across the metal slats. Joe shook the sheets until they billowed like waves. Three times he glanced out the window at the seventy-foot drop to Courthouse Square. Tugging the window bars, he tested each for weakness. Three times he did everything. Three times he took calming breaths.

They had dressed him in overalls. No pockets. No belt. Only buttons down his chest and on his fly. They'd taken away his socks, but left him his shoes (no laces), his deck of cards.

The cell across from his was empty. He listened for other men—but heard no one.

Joe went back to the window. The half moon was rising. He studied the square below; white folding chairs encircled a speaker's platform.

Lamplights glowed yellow; fireflies hovered among oaks; lovers strolled. A woman laughed. He heard a piano, clear tones rising beyond the park. Chopin. His mother loved the passionate, frenzied measures. Would she miss him at dinner? Row after row of tiny American flags were stuck in the earth. Greenwood folk would be home from work. Curfew was ten o'clock. He wondered if he was the only Negro left in Tulsa.

White men were going to burn him alive.

To the left, across the park, stood the Ambrose Building. He was nearly right back where he'd started running.

Joe felt helpless. He wanted to howl, bray at the moon. He wanted to be at his attic window, staring across rooftops, knowing Miss Lu was mixing cinnamon and apples for her pies, and Charlie T. was rocking tirelessly on his porch, studying Orion. He wanted to see the fenced-in plots of lawn and backyard gardens of tomatoes, snap beans, and yams. He wanted to hear mothers calling for their children, see circles of light appear then disappear in houses, as families bedded down until morning. When blue-black darkness blanketed the town, he sometimes heard Lying Man's harmonica wailing from his back room. Or he heard Hildy fixing tea in the kitchen, knowing she was up late reading about Moses leading his people to the River Jordan.

Longing pierced Joe. He suddenly feared Greenwood no longer existed, that it wasn't just three miles down the road. He'd conjured it up. He closed his eyes, feeling a rattling in his bones.

There'd never be enough water to save him.

He thought of all the tricks Houdini had done in water: chained upside down in a water tank; jumping handcuffed off bridges; being lowered into the depths in a locked box.

Maybe his brother's ghost had come to watch him die. He wouldn't die a soldier. He wouldn't be anybody's hero.

Joe swallowed his fear and, with his tongue, pushed out the thin metal pick he'd concealed in his mouth, gripping it between his teeth.

Sheriff Clay rounded the corner, carrying a tray. "Hungry?"

Joe waved his hand in front of his face. Lodging the lock pick between his two middle fingers, he slid it onto the window ledge.

"Chicken and biscuits."

"I'm not hungry."

Clay shrugged and turned away, heading back to the front office.

"Aren't you going to interrogate me?" called Joe. "Ask questions?"

"Should I?" Clay stuffed his hands in his pockets.

Joe shrugged. He lifted his cards from the bed, shuffling them rapidly before cutting the deck. "Pick a card."

Clay set the dinner tray on the floor. "I know this trick."

Joe stuck his hands, holding the fan of cards, between the bars.

Clay took one. "Now you're going to tell me what I've picked. That's the trick. Guess my card."

"No. Put it back in the deck," said Joe.

Clay slid the card into the middle of the pack.

Joe handed him the deck. "Shuffle." Clay did.

Joe smiled. "Find your card."

Clay flipped through the cards. "Queen of diamonds. Two of diamonds. Joker. Ace of spades, seven clubs, three of hearts, eight of hearts." On and on, he kept searching, his fingers shifting through the deck. "It's gone. Flown the coop. How'd you do that?"

Joe smiled grimly. Another trick he'd pulled off, but, so what? Here he was, caught. His dream seemed more and more likely to come true.

Joe, suddenly tired, laid on the bunk. Sweat beaded his forehead.

"Are you sure you're not hungry?"

Joe didn't answer.

"You can't be more than—what? Eighteen?"

"Come Wednesday." Joe wondered if the sheriff ever had nightmares.

"Pretty young to be jailed for a capital offense." Clay leaned into the bars, "You're the only one on this row. Thieves, brawlers, drunks are jailed around the corner. You know what a capital offense is, don't you?"

Joe thought the sheriff looked like a prisoner: sad-eyed, his fists wrapped tightly about the bars.

"Has my father telephoned?"

Clay nodded. "I expect he'll be here soon. He said he'd talk with Ambrose first."

Joe flipped onto his stomach, hugging the bed's railing. "I'm in trouble," he said dully.

"Did you do it?"

Joe looked up, guileless. "Can I have the chicken, sheriff? Thigh with gravy?"

Clay cocked his head. He stuffed the cards in his shirt pocket, picked up the tray, and unlocked the cell. Joe watched him move forward slowly. Watched him balance the tray with his left hand, drop the key into his pants pocket with his right.

Joe sat up. Wasn't the sheriff worried he'd knock him down? Dash past him? Fly through the door, clear out of Tulsa?

"I've got leg. Thigh. Gravy on the potatoes. Corn. Black coffee." Clay placed the tray on the edge of the bed. He lifted his baton from beside the spoon. He slapped it into his palm, before slipping it inside his belt. "Precautions never hurt."

Joe folded his hands in his lap.

Clay walked to the cell door. "The handcuffs in the elevator?" He slammed the door shut, locked it. "Were they a magic trick?"

Joe didn't answer. The sheriff was just another white man looking to hang him.

"Why'd you frighten her?"

"Did she say I did?"

"Mary Keane will speak in court."

"That's her name? Mary Keane? It's a pretty name." Joe sipped the coffee, his eyes glanced at the window ledge, hoping the sheriff couldn't see his lock pick.

Clay cleared his throat. "If you have something to say, you should say it now. I might not be able to help you later."

Joe stared at the sheriff. "Were you ever a paterroller?"

"A what?"

"Slave catcher."

"There haven't been slaves in fifty years."

"Nigger catcher, then?"

"Only if they've done something wrong."

"Ever make mistakes?"

"I try not to."

Joe nodded. "One of your deputies—the one with the straw hair—said he knew what to do with the baton. Said he knew exactly where to put it."

"Lucas." Clay rubbed his eyes. "He means what he says too. He hates coloreds. Or unionizers. Drunks. Anyone who looks at him too long. Or doesn't look at him long enough. Lucas came with the job. He's been deputy longer than anybody's been sheriff." Clay studied the motionless Joe. He started to speak, then shook his head, saying instead, "Someone will be back for your tray later."

"Sheriff," Joe called. "Can I have my cards back?"

"Sure," said Clay, waving the deck through the bars. As Joe reached for them, Clay jerked the cards out of reach. "Remember the joke you told me? Last week, was it?"

"I remember. You laughed hard. I remember you like Markam's Black Paste too. Light. Not too heavy."

Clay flushed and said sharply, "You understand the handcuffs, your clothes, money are evidence. A white woman's word counts for a great deal. You understand?"

"I understand."

"Good. I thought you might." Clay let go of the cards.

"Good-bye, sheriff."

Clay paused. "You mean good night. We'll both be here in the morning."

"Sure, sheriff." Joe blew across the top of his deck. An ace of spades lifted, fluttering in mid-air.

"Well, well, well. You have finally exceeded all my expectations."

Joe turned to see his father, dressed in a three-piece suit, shoes waxed to a bright glaze, standing hat in hand like a rich John Henry capable of plowing through a mountainside.

"I can let you inside." Sully, pimple-faced and thin, swung his keys. "Might be more comfortable."

"I'll not be placed inside a cell for any reason."

"Yes, sir," Sully said, then bristled, realizing he'd said "sir" to a colored. He walked quickly down the hall.

Joe tried to appear relaxed as his father glared.

"Did you think white pussy was going to make you manly?"

"That's crude, Father."

"This is crude business. I've spoken with Ambrose. It was most inconvenient. For him and for me."

"That cost you, didn't it?"

"I never guessed I'd have to beg for my son's life."

"At least not this one."

"No. I never thought you'd do anything out of the ordinary."

Joe inched toward his father.

"Your brother, for all his faults, was the better man. He kept his randiness at home. When there were mistakes—"

"What mistakes?"

"A few dollars always took care of it—"

"What are you talking about? Henry's been dead four years and you're talking about mistakes. What mistakes?" Joe gripped the bars.

"Sometimes Henry slipped in the back door when a husband left by the front. Sometimes he drank too much. Hit a man too hard. But he was never fool enough to take a white woman."

"You believe I did?"

"That's what Gabe told me."

"Gabe would never say that." Joe turned from his father. "And I don't believe Henry hurt anybody."

"You don't have to believe it. It didn't cost you anything. I paid for Henry's troubles. But I don't have enough money to undo what you have done today."

"That bothers you, doesn't it?" he said angrily.

"You were always dreaming. Ignoring what I had to offer. A throwback to Tyler. Illiterate, dreaming Tyler. Painting pictures when there's gold to be made in land."

"He's your father. You talk like he's nothing."

"He was—*is*—a man without vision."

"What was Henry's vision?"

"He was coming round to it," his father responded warily.

"So he went to war."

"To serve his country."

"To get away from you," Joe hollered.

"I will not be disrespected, Joe."

Joe stared at his father's well-shined shoes. "You should've taken me fishing."

"Fishing?"

"Other fathers took their sons fishing."

"I was hoping you could buy the damn pond. I was building a

future for you and your brother that most whites would envy. A business. A house. Education."

Joe shook his head.

"I was dreaming of having a son in business with me. If your magic could've made gold, I might've taken you fishing. You might've been useful."

Joe slumped against the bars. "So hard, Father. Why've you got to be so hard?"

"It's a hard world. If you want to be a man, I'll treat you like one. But I will not hide my feelings. I will not hide the truth. We are one generation from slavery. The only thing the white man respects is money. Money and property. Tyler would've turned his land into wheat. I made gold. I provided for the family. And whether you admit it or not, everything you have, wear, eat—I paid for. Even your feelings. You want to rebel by shining shoes? Fine." He paused to catch his breath. "But without the food and bed I give you, you'd have a miserable existence. Me and my money make all things possible for you. You've never had to survive on your own. Never had to scrape two dimes together while someone called you 'nigger.'"

"You could've pretended you loved me. At least when I was a boy, couldn't you, Father?"

Joe watched his father clench his hands, shut his eyes.

"You might not realize this, but I did try. There's no rule that says a father has to like his son."

"Or a son his father."

His father opened his eyes. "No. I might not be the best father. But I provide. I take care of my own."

"You went to Ambrose."

"Yes. I begged for his mercy." He massaged his chest. "Damn these lungs. You are my son. There were no promises. But it's possible you may be moved. To another jail. Another county. Ambrose plans to announce for governor tomorrow. So the issue is," he searched for the word, "sensitive. But I do not think you will be hanged." He wheezed. "I do not think I can bear two sons dead." He turned.

"Father," Joe called, trying to squeeze his face through bars, trying to see him as he moved around the corner. "Don't you want to ask if I'm innocent?"

"It wouldn't matter if you were. Either way, I'm still going to pay."

Joe stumbled to his cot and lay down. The cell seemed smaller. He concentrated on feeling his ribcage expand and contract. His father had never believed in him. Never would.

Someone turned off the lights in the hall; moonlight bounced off the pale walls. He felt so tired. If he went to sleep, would he dream? Maybe it didn't matter. He was going to die. His father had never loved him. The darkness lulled, Joe closed his eyes. He slept without dreaming.

The sound of breathing woke him.

Henry's face, thick-browed, dark as loam, was inches above his. He was splendid in his uniform, healthy and strong.

Crying out, Joe jerked away.

"*Easy, little brother.*" *Henry sat on the cot's edge, his arms crossed over his chest.*

Joe knew Henry wasn't there, yet he *was* there. He ached with loneliness.

"You left me."

Henry nodded.

"I don't need you anymore."

"*I wouldn't be here if you didn't need me.*"

"Don't you say anything. Just shut up." Inexplicably, Joe wanted to hurt Henry. Plow a fist into his face.

"*Joe.*" *Henry gripped him. His touch felt cool. Then, Henry opened his palm; blood trickled from his thumb. He wiped it on Joe's brow. "Brothers. Always.*"

Tears blinded him. "Why'd you come back? You're supposed to stay gone."

"*You wanted me back.*"

"That's a lie."

"*I'm here to tell you what you already know.*"

"I don't want to hear anything from you. You're *not* here. You're not even real." Then, lurching forward, Joe swung, howling, "Damn you. You're not real."

Henry disappeared.

"Henry!" Joe dashed, searching the corners of his cell. All his anxieties, his boyhood fears welled. He'd never played with other children. They weren't rich enough, genteel enough. "Play with Henry," Father had insisted. Loneliness had crushed him when Henry no longer wanted to play with him. Wandering Greenwood, he'd been grateful for the kindnesses of adults, the warmth of Lying Man's shop. But none of it made up for Henry being gone. "Henry! Don't leave me," he called, desperate.

Henry reappeared by the window. "I'm here, little brother. I'm still here."

Joe collapsed onto his knees. "You left me. You left me by the riverbed. You left me knowing I didn't have anybody else, knowing Father didn't care about me. I thought I'd done something wrong. Thought you didn't love me."

"You're a man now, Joe. You've got to face a man's problems."

Joe stumbled forward. "You never faced anything. The war was an excuse. You were tired of Tulsa, tired of me."

"No, not of you."

"I don't believe you."

"Think. Think hard, Joe."

Joe stared. He wanted to touch his brother's face. Press his fingers against his cheekbones, his brow, the arched bridge of his nose.

"I was old enough to enlist when I found out. But I'd known beforehand, had always known. Think hard, Joe. You remember. You know the secret. All of us knew. What's the secret, Joe?"

"I don't know what you're talking about."

"We never crossed to the other side. Never went to the west side of Lena's River. How come, Joe?"

"I don't know what you're talking about." In his mind's eye, he saw derricks lined up like sentinels across the river.

"How come Father, a Negro man, speaks to Ambrose? Gets favors? Gets seed money for a bank? Guess the secret, Joe. Why'd you run home to Tyler?"

"You're talking nonsense. You're making excuses for leaving me."

"I couldn't stay anymore. I'm sorry, Joe. I wasn't much of a man at twenty-two." Henry paced. *"Father showed me the deed. Said he wanted me to know my history. Wanted me to understand what he'd accom-*

plished." He stopped. "Look at me, Joe. Tyler never ran from paterrollers. He wasn't running away. He was running to get something."

"He was a Sooner."

"Yes, that's it. You remember Tyler's land."

"De . . . de . . . dee . . . " Deed. Tyler had been stuttering about the deed.

Joe remembered himself as a child, trying to heave sticks across the river, trying to sail a toy ship to the rocky shore. But he was on the wrong side, the side of endless green. Not the side where Ambrose's derricks rose and fell, day and night, pumping a steady stream of black gold above the ground.

"Tyler won that land. He raced faster than hundreds of men—black skinned and white. He staked his claim. Staked out two hundred acres around Lena's River where the Ambrose fields are now."

"I remember," Joe murmured. When Tyler could still hold a brush, he painted the same landscape: plains of tall wheat. When a painting was finished, Tyler wept through the night.

"Father stole the land from Tyler."

"Sold it to Ambrose," said Joe, realizing he'd always known it. "But why, Henry? Why?"

"Said a Negro man was allowed only so much power. He sold the land, started his bank, bought pieces of Greenwood. But that land—its oil, Joe, acres of it—fueled Ambrose's wealth. Built Tulsa." Henry sat on the cot, his cheeks and eyes wet. "Father seemed so proud of what he'd done. That's what tore me up. Father knew there was oil. Tyler never said a mumbling word. Never.

"Father just wanted to believe I was a little wild. Wanted to believe I'd settle down and become a banker. Just like him." His face contorted. "Then Tyler had his stroke. The war came; I was glad it came. I ran. I wasn't man enough to stay in Greenwood."

A train whistled.

Joe realized it was a ghostly echo. Henry's train.

"I can't stay now."

"Henry, don't leave me.

"Henry! I'm scared." Joe fell to his knees, trying to catch the air where his brother had been.

Henry quivered; light shone through his form. "Fear's all right. But only if it's useful. Fear made us keep Father's secret. Mother, Hildy, Emmaline, me. We buried the truth, good and gone. And if Tyler's pictures reminded us of the truth, we said it was an illusion. Father was the great one, the provider. I think he was more scared than any of us."

"You weren't scared. You were a war hero."

"*Is that what you believe? You're a fool, Joe. I was always scared. So scared, I hid from myself. So scared, I didn't give a damn for anybody."*

The train squealed again. Joe heard a babble of voices, hollering for Henry. Steam filled the cell.

"Joe, when you going to start thinking of yourself as Joe Samuels? Not Father's son. Not Hildy's baby. Not even Henry's little brother."

"Who should I be, Henry?"

"*This is your dream. You figure it out."*

"I don't understand."

"*Dreams mean something, Joe."*

"That's what Hildy said."

"*What do you want, Joe? You can't spend your life pretending you're a black-faced Houdini."*

"Damn you."

Henry laughed softly. "I am, Joe. Good and damned." The train whistle grew louder. "You know all you need to. Your magic is in your bones, Joe."

"Henry!"

The cell wall had disappeared. Henry stood on the train's platform, his lips moving.

"Henry, what?" Joe felt himself a boy again, stumbling, running after his brother.

The train gushed steam. He heard Henry shouting, "Stay! Stay —" Is that what Henry wanted? For him to stay? In Greenwood?

"Hen—ry!" Joe shouted. "Henry."

"Quiet in there. Who you talking to?" The light snapped on.

"Henry?" He beat against the wall. "Wait! How'd you die? Henry!"

Lucas clanged his baton across the bars. "Crazy nigger. Shut the hell up."

"How'd you die?"

"Acting crazy won't keep you from hanging," Lucas sneered.

Shivering, Joe felt the cell wall. No ghost train. The wall was solid.

He heard a whistle screech and ran to the window. "It's the 9:45," he murmured. "To Frisco."

"Bet you wish you were on it, don't you, boy?"

"You could buy me a ticket."

Lucas chortled, "Crazy nigger." He rattled the baton on the bars.

Frisco sounds fine, Joe thought. He wouldn't make the same mistake twice. He'd hop a train. Never look back. Henry was dead. Joe looked at his lock pick tucked on the window's ledge, glittering in the moonlight.

15

"Are you sure you're up to this?" asked Allen.

Mary nodded, her hand on the door knob. Inhaling, she pushed open the door and stepped inside a shallow office. The room was stark, flooded with artificial light. Metal file cabinets, chairs, and desks were arranged haphazardly. Bars covered the windows. Holsters, handcuffs, and leather batons lined the back wall. Framed, on the left wall, was the front page from *The Tulsan,* April 22, 1915—"*German Gas Attack.*" The photograph showed puffs of smoke hanging over a field. A platoon of soldiers lay dead.

"You needed to see me, Miss Keane?"

Mary was terrified. Sheriff Clay sat behind his desk. He'd been eating pie. Blueberry. Beside the pie lay a baton and gun. Two deputies were in the office. One—his feet on the desk, his hands folded on his lap—seemed to be laughing at her. He seemed aware of her discomfort, aware of how flushed her body felt. She patted her wrinkled dress, wishing she had undergarments. The other deputy was younger, plain-faced like her. Sympathetic.

"Miss Keane?"

Sheriff Clay's face was bland; his eyes, noncommittal. But Mary knew he was studying her too. She guessed he knew her exact height, weight, how her left foot was placed slightly in front of her right, how calluses covered her palms. She felt like she was back in the kitchen. Outnumbered by men. Placed in the wrong. She wanted to run from the room, but a man might die because of her. And if he died, she'd want to kill herself, like Lena did. She'd float face down in the river. Her feelings surprised her. Joe Samuels had nothing to do with her. Yet he had everything to do with her.

"Miss Keane?"

"He—" Her tongue thickened; tears pricked her eyes. Fool, she thought. Fool.

"It's all right, Mary." Allen patted her back.

She crossed her arms over her belly. Al wanted something too. Gratitude? She owed him that. Affection? She didn't know. She only knew she felt both trapped and exposed. The men's stares were unnerving. It wasn't fair. She wanted a woman with her.

"Perhaps you'd like some water, Miss Keane. Sully, get Miss Keane some water."

She shook her head. "No, I'm all right." She clasped her hands. "Sheriff, he didn't . . . I mean he didn't—"

"*Got to be a woman sometime, Mary.*"

Nausea swept through her. She swayed. Clay reached out to steady her; she grasped his hand, thinking his eyes were bluer than Dell's. *Her womb contracted; she remembered Dell plunging inside her.* The deputies leaned forward like crows.

"He didn't do anything," she said fiercely. "Not anything. He didn't touch me. The young colored man. Joe."

Lucas' boots hit the floor. Mary dropped the sheriff's hand. Lucas moved toward her, deliberate and frightening. "You needn't be embarrassed, ma'am," he said softly. "Even if you encouraged him."

"I didn't encourage anyone."

"Boy deserves a lynching. He had no business in that elevator."

"You don't understand."

"I understand plenty." Lucas grinned, shifting his weight into his hips. "There's misunderstandings at times. A woman might say no when she means yes. Now isn't that right? You might encourage a man without realizing it."

"I didn't encourage anyone."

"No need to be embarrassed, ma'am. Most women marry the man, misunderstanding or not. You know what I mean?"

"I didn't encourage him."

"But no respectable woman," Lucas paused, "ever has such a misunderstanding with a colored."

"What do you mean?" demanded Allen.

"She knows what I mean, look at her."

Allen lunged. Lucas gripped his arm, pulling him face down onto the floor, his arm bent behind his back. "I can arrest you for assaulting an officer."

"Let him go, Lucas," ordered Clay.

Reluctantly, Lucas released his hold.

"He's got to answer for his lies," Allen raged.

"That's enough, Thornton," Clay snapped. "Lucas, do your rounds. Sully and I will handle this."

"Suits me fine," said Lucas. "But I know my duty. Niggers need to be kept in their place." He belted his gun about his waist. "And ma'am," he looked pointedly at her breasts and crotch, "whatever you did, still don't excuse a nigger from looking at you." He sauntered out, closing the door softly.

"He's gonna see the Knights," murmured Sully.

"I know." Clay tossed his pie in the trash.

"Can't you stop him?" demanded Allen.

"He hasn't broken the law."

"You mean you *won't* stop him."

"I mean I can't," said Clay.

"Fine logic. A sheriff can't uphold the law. Is that why you let a mob lynch David Reubens?"

"That's enough, Thornton."

"You're going to let them take Joe, aren't you? Take him and lynch him."

"That's enough."

"Planning another fishing trip?"

"Damn you, Thornton." Enraged, Clay stood, his chair toppling.

"Joe Samuels is safe in this jail. There's only one entrance and exit. Guards are posted on each level. So, I'm telling you, Mr. Thornton, Joe Samuels is safe. I know how to do my job. I intend to do it."

"Then you should release Joe," said Mary. "He's innocent."

Clay sighed, "Miss Keane, Miss Keane. The circumstances are suspicious."

"Dirty minds make it so."

"I uphold the law."

"There's been no crime."

"Miss Keane, this is a delicate situation."

"Nothing's delicate about it."

"Sit down, Miss Keane."

"I will not," she shouted. "I will not sit down. You're holding an innocent man. Joe Samuels and I, we work in the same building. He's never been less than a gentleman. No, that's not quite right," she exhaled. "He's never been anything to me. Those coloreds, those shoeshine boys never stared at me. The truth is, sheriff, not too many men pay me any mind. I am not a pretty woman."

"Mary—" Allen reached out, protective.

"It's true. I do know what I look like." She looked at the three men—Al, Sully, the sheriff, daring them to contradict.

Clay cleared his throat.

"Sheriff, I have no reason to lie. I am not half-witted. Or overcome by imagination. I am a woman, with a woman's feelings. I know how to recognize advances." She paused. "Sexual advances. Joe Samuels never—" Mary closed her eyes, trembling coursed through her.

She remembered Joe's hands: dark, slim, and strong like a piano player's.

"He never touched me." She opened her eyes, repeating, "He never touched me."

The room was still. Mary looked at Allen; he was slouched against the wall. Sully, head bent, still held the glass of water. Sheriff Clay was the only one looking directly at her. Mary thought he looked sorrowful, like Jody.

"I believe you, Miss Keane. But there's something you're not telling. Why'd you scream, Miss Keane? Something made you scream."

"Is this an interrogation?"

"Stay out of this, Thornton. I'm trying to help her. That colored boy too. I can't let him go without a credible explanation for her scream. Everyone heard it. By now, everybody in Tulsa knows about your screaming."

"He's innocent," Mary said stubbornly.

"I know that. Only a complete fool would rape a woman on an elevator, then ride the elevator down to a crowded lobby. Any other floor would've had a fire escape. Samuels could've been off and running by the time your elevator reached the lobby."

"So you think he's innocent."

"What I think won't matter. I need proof. I need to know why you screamed."

Mary compressed her lips.

Al nodded sympathetically. Mary appreciated his silence. It'd felt right to tell Al about Dell. But did that mean she had to tell the sheriff, his deputy? Would the sheriff even understand she'd screamed because hours ago a man had raped her, years ago her mother had died, and, in a moment, she'd realized she'd let life slip through her fingers?

Except for the afternoons with her mother, she'd never been happy.

"Do you believe in ghosts?" Joe had asked. "Yes," she'd replied. She believed in ghosts.

"He didn't touch me," she said to the sheriff. "Why can't you believe me? Why isn't my word good enough?"

"Oh, it's good enough. But it isn't satisfying. A mob is likely organizing as we speak. We need a story. A good one. One that quenches their need for blood. It's like war, Miss Keane. Once the adrenaline gets going, you want to kill something.

"If I'm to keep Joe alive, I'm going to need a better story, Miss Keane. Something that explains why you screamed, something that makes these men not want to," Clay looked at Allen, "burn him alive. Can you give me such a story? A better explanation for your screams?"

Mary said nothing.

"She's given you her answer," said Allen.

Clay stepped toward Mary. "Why don't we go see the boy, maybe that will jog your memory?" He grabbed a ring of keys.

"You don't have to, Mary."

"I want to." Allen took her arm and they followed the sheriff down the hall. Sully unlocked a gate that let them into a passageway of cells.

Eyes darting, Mary saw young men, old men lying on cots. Coloreds were on the left; whites, on the right. Some were sprawled, drunk. Others slept, their mouths hanging open. A rheumy-eyed man reached through the bars. Mary cringed. A man, bleeding on one side of his face, stared. Someone whispered, "Is she the one?" Whisperings circled her like bees. "Is she the one?"

They turned a corner. Clay stopped short in front of an empty cell.

"Goddamn," hollered Clay. "Shit." He quickly inserted his key.

"I don't believe it," muttered Sully. "I don't believe it. The nigger's gone."

Allen whistled, "It's a miracle."

"Miracle, hell," said Clay, struggling with the lock.

"He's gone," breathed Mary.

Clay unlocked the door. Enraged, Clay kicked the cot, overturned the frame, the thin mattress belly-flopped on the floor. Cards—aces, kings, numbered hearts, diamonds, and spades—flew.

"I'm glad he's gone," sighed Mary. "He's free now."

Clay slammed his hand against the wall. "Don't you understand? He hasn't a chance now. Not a goddamned chance. They'll kill him."

Mary stumbled backward.

"If they find him, they'll hang him." Clay stooped, grasping the eight of spades. "Shit." He ripped the card. "Who'd a thought? A goddamned Houdini."

"I'll tell folks Joe's innocent. To leave him alone. Let him go."

"Too late, Miss Keane. A jailbreak? Colored man on the run?" Clay kicked the cell door, shutting himself in. "It doesn't matter if you say anything now, Miss Keane," he said savagely. "Doesn't even matter you exist. Nothing matters now. In Tulsa, Joe's guilty."

Mary started weeping. Al held her.

"Damn." Clay examined the lock mechanism; he rattled the door. "Sully, get Eddie, anybody else you can find. Have them search the building."

"Yes, boss," said Sully, running off.

Clay tugged the window bars.

"You shouldn't have screamed, Miss Keane. If nothing happened, you shouldn't have screamed."

"You don't understand."

"I understand plenty. We're here because you screamed. Joe's on the run because you screamed. What else is there to understand?" Clay unlocked the cell door with his keys.

Mary clamped her hands over her mouth.

Sitting on a bench in the center of Courthouse Square, Mary searched the darkness for Joe. She remembered his gold-flecked eyes, how they'd looked as if they were floating in a pool of tears. Though a man and colored, he'd seemed as vulnerable as she.

Mary peered into the shadows. She imagined Joe jumping from the arms of an oak tree, pressing against its trunk before darting across the lawn, weaving among forsythia bushes, daisies, and maple seedlings. She caught her breath; in the shifting light, she saw a man hurrying across the lawn, a coat flapping at his knees. *Joe?* On a clear patch of bluegrass, she thought she saw Joe stop to wave. *Thought she saw him spinning, his feet lifting before he flew straight toward the moon.*

She asked, "Do you think Joe'll make it?"

"No," Allen sighed, his head bent, his arms dangling. "A man only has so much luck."

"I never had any luck," Mary said. "If I was lucky, Ma never would've have died; Pa would've struck oil. Would've loved me better." She edged sideways on the bench. "Are you lucky, Al?"

He laughed softly, his shoulders shaking. "Would you believe this is the luckiest I've ever been?" He laughed again, letting his head tilt upward toward the stars. "I used to dream of nights like these. Sitting in the square with a woman, feeling the summer breeze, the day's heat fading." His fingertips lightly touched her hair. "I used to dream of kissing a girl here. Having fireworks explode, a band strike up. I'm a romantic, Mary. Nothing sadder than a middle-aged romantic." He dropped his hand.

Except for the white Decoration Day chairs, the park was cloaked in comforting black. If it weren't for daybreak, Mary thought, she and Allen could hide themselves forever. There didn't seem to be any town beyond the square park.

"Were you born in Tulsa?" Mary asked.

"Yes, to my dismay. Though I like to lie and say I was born in New

York. Only problem is that I know the difference between reality and fantasy well enough.

"Every train trip to New York, I think I'll never come back. But I do. I told myself I was too old to fight Germans—I had responsibilities here, as though no one but me could fix the clocks of Tulsa. Five years ago, perhaps, I could've left. But I waited too long. I'm too old." He paused. "Maybe I was waiting for you, Mary. I could leave with you."

Mary stared into the shifting shadows.

"They're going to kill Joe Samuels," he said softly. "We won't be able to stop them. Can you live here, after that?"

Mary could already hear whispers blowing through the trees, tickling strands of grass. "She's the one . . . she's the one he touched." If she stayed, Pa would force her to marry Dell. Dell would expect her to be grateful for the rest of her days.

"Leave with me, Mary. I wouldn't touch you, unless you wanted me too. But I would hope you would—that you'd want me to love you." He slid closer. "I'm nobody special. I know that, Mary. But I did something special today. Didn't I, Mary?"

"Yes," she squeezed his hand.

"I helped you, didn't I? Brought you into my shop. And I helped again at the Ambrose. I brought you home. Covered you with a blanket. Let you sleep.

"I've felt magic today, Mary. I'm not making good sense. All my days I've wanted to be happy. I've never been. I've never reached out to anybody, even when I wanted to—in theaters, I imagine I'm the tap-dancing hero winning the girl." He shrugged. "I'm a foolish man, Mary. An ugly and foolish man. Yet I believe I can be happy with you. I want to be happy. I think I can make you happy. We just have to leave Tulsa."

"Al, don't—"

"If we stay, I'm afraid I'll do what I've always done—hide. Not really live in this world. It's been an extraordinary day. I'm not myself. Yet I'm more myself than I've ever been. I could do it with you. I think I could be happy with you."

"Please, Al."

"You can't stand to look at me, can you?"

"That's not it."

"Then you'll come with me?"

Mary tried to imagine what it would be like to go with Al, journeying to Chicago or New York, leaving Pa and Jody behind. Try as she might, she couldn't quite see herself anyplace but Tulsa. And then there was Joe. His trouble was her fault. She had to do something.

"You're telling me no, aren't you?"

"For now," she said softly, then blurted, words tumbling, "I need you to help me one more time. Please, Al. Drive me to the Samuels' house."

"They're not going to want to see you, Mary."

"I know." She felt small again. Joe's folks would hate her for sure. But she had to do something. She'd tell them he was innocent. But they knew that, didn't they? He was their son. So, why was she doing it? To make herself feel better? To ease her guilt?

Allen closed his eyes, letting the emotion drain from his face. "It's late. Almost eleven o'clock."

"I don't think they'll mind."

"Sure, middle of the night, white girl goes calling in Greenwood. They'll strike up a band, welcome you with open arms. Sing ditties for you. Dance a cakewalk."

"Stop it, Al." She plucked at threads on her dress. Back-handed, she wiped her tears.

"I'm sorry, Mary."

"I'm sorry too. Sometimes I think it's not right I was even born."

"Mary," he breathed, rocking, "Mary, Mary."

"My Ma taught me to say 'sorry.' Maybe my sorry won't do the Samuels any good. Maybe it's just about my heartache. But I tried the sheriff. That didn't work. I'm scared the Samuels might throw me out, curse me. But I'm trying to do right. If I shut up now, Al, I might never open my mouth again. Might never say another word."

The train moaned again; a gust of wind shuddered through the trees; several chairs tipped over.

"Mary," said Allen, his voice bleak, "this is real, isn't it? The sun will rise and I won't be a prince. Nobody's hero. Just Allen Thornton, repairer of clocks. I don't even carry a watch. Did you know that, Mary? People should tell time from the sky, from the positions of sun, moon, and stars."

"I never paid time any mind," said Mary. "But time matters now. Particularly for Joe and his people. He's out there lost."

"And you, Mary?"

"I'm lost too."

"This is it. At least I think it is." Allen applied the brake. "It must be the biggest house in Greenwood." A street lamp illuminated the gingerbread porch, white shutters, and gabled roof. "It's beautiful," murmured Mary.

Allen pointed to the side. "A light's on in the kitchen. A maid, most like."

"I didn't know coloreds had maids."

"Samuels' father owns a bank."

"Why'd Joe shine shoes?"

"None of this is his. Leastwise not until his father dies. The boy probably wanted to make it on his own." Allen opened the car door. "Let's get this over with."

Mary stopped him. "I'll do this alone."

"I'll wait for you then."

"No. You've done plenty."

"Mary, it's dangerous."

She studied the empty street, the row of pastel-colored houses, the abandoned rockers on porches, the gardens packed with peonies, berries, and marigolds. The Samuels' house was less welcoming, more formal than the others, but the light from the kitchen gave her hope.

"You can't do this, Mary."

"Good-bye, Al." She opened the car door, her feet touched gravel.

"Mary, please—"

Smiling, she poked her head through the car window. "You can leave, Al. You've got a fine courage. You don't need me to leave Tulsa."

"Mary—"

"Sssh. It's late. Go home, Al."

"Mary, let me wait. I won't go up to the house with you. I'll stay here in the car."

"White men are hunting the Samuels' son. They won't appreciate you sitting out here."

"But I want you to be safe."

"Joe's the one in danger. And it's my fault. The sheriff was right. Go home, Al. I've got to see if I can help."

She walked toward the house, and didn't look back when the engine hummed into gear, and the Packard, reversing, caught her in a flood of light before screeching down the road.

Her shoulders slumped; her steps slowed. She couldn't turn back now. No Allen to use as a safe haven. She'd been brave enough to make him go, now she needed to be brave enough to do as she'd promised herself. She smelled roses. She stared, studying the vines clinging to the porch rail and threading upward to the second-floor windows, heavily curtained and dark.

She'd never been close to coloreds, never been close to where they lived. They lived better than her. She ducked her head, feeling as self-conscious as when she saw rich, oil wives' homes.

She glanced up again at the dark windows, wondering if anyone was watching her. Wondering if there were ghosts in the Samuels' house. Wondering what it would have been like to grow up here, on a street with other families, instead of on a farm with Jody and Pa.

She inhaled, focusing on the kitchen light. She murmured, "Joe." His name gave her courage. His people had feelings too.

She ought to be woman enough to honor that.

16

Hildy kept seeing Joe, caged and hurting. A jailer wouldn't feed him proper. Wouldn't care if he was cold and heartsick. Father refused to let her visit, saying, "One Samuels inside a jail is enough." She should've gone anyway, disobeyed his commandment. Now Hildy imagined Joe beaten and downtrodden, with nobody to comfort him. She fidgeted about the kitchen, restacked the dishes in the drying rack. She knew she wouldn't sleep. First thing in the morning, she'd see Joe, take him cornbread and pie. Read scripture to calm his spirit.

Hildy sat at the table, her tea beside her, trying to focus on the Bible passage she'd just read—Shadrack thrown into the fiery furnace. An angel had protected him. Hildy prayed the Lord would send an angel to guide Joe.

She'd known something was wrong with Joe. He'd been out of kilter—like a child's spinning top. She should've found out what was wrong. It nagged her that she'd somehow failed him. When Joe was newborn, she'd been charmed by his down-covered body, his sleepy eyes, and she'd sworn to love him better than she'd been loved. But she hadn't loved him well enough to find out what was wrong.

She'd seen Joe's haunted look, the circles under his eyes. He'd said he was all right, but she'd known he wasn't. He'd become a man and she didn't understand him. She didn't know his dreams anymore, didn't know why he defied Father. She'd let him slip away. Lord forgive her.

She didn't know what she'd do without Joe. He was in the fire now and she feared she couldn't get him out. She feared she'd never see him again. Joe knew she loved him. But did he know caring for him had kept her alive, kept her from being bitter?

Hildy bowed her head. She tried to feel the Lord's song in her heart. Tried to feel His grace and charity. A noise startled her.

"Who is it? Who's out there?" She turned on the porch light.

Behind the screen, Hildy saw a sorry-looking white woman. Low class, Hildy knew, because the woman didn't wear a hat. She looked pitiful, hair tangled like a bird's nest. Her shoes and legs were scratched; her arms, dirty. Hildy wanted to slam the door. It didn't make sense for a white woman to be in Greenwood. Days, salesmen with cheap goods knocked door-to-door; nights, Klansmen splintered mailboxes with baseball bats. White women stayed across the tracks. Always.

"Miss Mary, I think you'd better go on home."

"You know who I am?"

"It says so on the dress."

Mary clutched her breast pocket.

"You sick?"

"No, I just thought you knew all about me. I thought it'd started."

"What started?"

"The rumors."

Hildy stepped closer, studying the face pockmarked by shadows. "What should I know about you?"

Mary flattened her palms on the screen. "Please, I'd like to see Mrs. Samuels." A moth swooped, attracted by the light. "I need to talk with her."

Hildy hissed. It was her, thought Hildy, the woman who caused Joe's trouble. She slapped the screen; the door rattled. Mary jerked back.

"You've got no business coming here, the trouble you've made. If your business was honest, you'd be coming to the front door. Coming during daylight. There's no need for you to see Mrs. Samuels."

"Please, you don't understand."

"I understand plenty."

"I'd like to see Mrs. Samuels. Call her. I'll wait right here."

"I'm not calling anybody."

"You've got to. Mrs. Samuels can decide if she wants to see me. Not you." Mary flushed. "I'll wait on the porch."

Hildy didn't move. She'd never wanted to hurt anybody in her life. But she wanted to hurt this scraggly woman. Joe in jail and Miss Mary wanting to pay respects. Like he was dead, like she hadn't any blame. "You must be stupid. Thinking I'm a maid."

"I only want to see Mrs. Samuels. Mr. Samuels, if he's in."

"I'm Joe's sister." Hildy glared, wanting to scare this woman, drive her away from the house. Hildy noted how Mary didn't flinch. How she pressed against the screen, insisting, "Let me in. I need to talk to you."

"You'll be sorry if you do."

"Not any sorrier than I already am. Please," she said. "I need to say I'm sorry about Joe."

"You've said it," said Hildy. "Now, go on home." She started to close the door.

"Forgive me," Mary said desperately. "Please forgive me."

Hildy stopped short. "Forgiveness." Psalms 145. *The Lord is gracious and merciful, slow to anger and abounding in steadfast love.*

"Please, let me in."

Hildy closed her eyes. Surprising herself, she opened the door. Mary needed a bath, a clean dress. And she needed a keeper if she felt talk could ease Joe's troubles. Yet, Mary stepped bravely into the kitchen, arms wrapped around her waist, holding in her fear. "You can sit," Hildy said gruffly.

Mary nodded, moving toward the Blue Willow tea service. Beside a porcelain cup was a Bible with gold trim. Lovingly, Mary touched the tissue-thin pages.

"You read the Bible, Miss Mary?"

"I can't read." Mary ducked her head like a baby bird. "Pa reads. Parts about daughters obeying their fathers. Lot's wife."

"There's lots better parts than that."

"Pa doesn't know them then. Sometimes I think all he knows is how to make good things bad and bad things worse." Mary flushed again.

"If I didn't read my Bible, you wouldn't be here. I figure I can be charitable for five minutes. Then you've got to leave."

Mary nodded.

Hildy surprised herself again by offering tea. Mary sat.

"Sugar?"

Mary lifted the sterling spoon, dipped it in the sugar then twirled it in the tea, creating puffs of steam. "I've never seen such a lovely service." Carefully, she laid the spoon on the saucer.

Hildy blinked. If she disremembered who this woman was, disremembered the whiteness of her skin, she'd appreciate the moment more. She'd offer shortbread, berries, and cream. Mother and Emmaline never sat in her kitchen. Church women sometimes visited. Nevertheless, her evenings were lonely. Hildy tapped her Bible. Colossians 3:13. *As the Lord has forgiven you, you also must forgive.*

Hildy wouldn't let herself sit. Christian or not, she wanted to hurt this woman. She wanted to rage at her for hurting Joe.

Hands unsteady, Mary lowered her cup. "Thank you. You don't owe me any kindness."

"No, I don't."

Mary shook her head, wonderingly. "I should be ending my day in my own kitchen, Pa's kitchen. On the farm. Instead I'm here. Drinking the best tea of my life. In a colored person's house."

"Are you trying to be funny, Miss Mary?"

"No, no, I'm not." Tea spilled onto the saucer. "I'm trying to understand how I got to this place. How I began the day milking and ended here. How I hurt Joe when I didn't mean to hurt anybody."

"What happened?"

"Nothing that folks say."

"I know that. What did happen?" asked Hildy, her lips thin and dry.

"Sheriff says it doesn't matter what I say. Joe's escaping changed everything."

Hildy felt as if she'd been struck. "Escaped? When?"

"An hour ago."

"You waited this long to tell me? You come strutting in here worried 'bout sorry, knowing Joe's running—and you don't tell me? You don't tell me 'bout my brother? You're truly a fool, Miss Mary."

"I'm sorry. I didn't think. You don't know what I've been through today."

"My brother might be lynched and you're talking about you." Hildy knocked aside Mary's cup. "Get out. You think being white makes it okay for you to be here. Saying 'sorry.' Saying 'Oh, I forgot, your brother's on the run.'"

"You don't understand."

"I understand plenty. Fool white woman."

"I'm sorry. I want to help Joe. Let me help."

Hildy fought back tears. "There's nothing you can do." She collapsed in the chair. The thought of losing Joe overwhelmed her.

"Sorry I didn't tell you right away about Joe." Mary's voice raised in pitch. "I'm sorry." She leaned forward. "Today happened to me too."

Hildy dug her nails into the wood. She didn't want this white woman to see her cry.

"He might make it," Mary whispered.

Hildy's head lifted. Yes, if Joe was free, he'd head for Lena's River. "He'll need food," she said, rising, tugging a canvas bag off its peg. She opened the ice box, gathering leftovers—chicken, chunks of Colby, powder biscuits, pie.

"Let me help."

"Don't need your help."

"You know where he's gone, don't you?"

"It's time for you to clear out. Go home. You've had your say. Your say doesn't help Joe."

"That's not fair. I can help."

"Fair? You think you can walk in here and make everything better for yourself. Well, you can't. Joe means more to me than the world—I raised him."

"I understand."

"No, you don't."

"I do," Mary shouted back. "I raised a brother too. Jody. He lost a leg in the war."

Chest heaving, the bag heavy in her arms, Hildy stared at Mary. Face to face, she could see they were the same height, about the same age given their gray hair, the lines tugging at their eyes and mouths. "You're an old maid," she said disgustedly. "Same as me. A useless old maid."

Mary sighed. Taking the heavy bag from Hildy, she laid it on the table. "I can work. Same as you. You've got a jug for water? You'll need to take him water."

Hildy relented. It was easier to let this white girl help her than waste time arguing. She motioned to the cabinet beneath the sink.

"Ice box? You got ice box water?"

"Yes," said Hildy, watching Mary fill the jug.

"I'm sorry. For hurting Joe. For hurting you and your family." Mary rearranged the bag, with the water at the bottom. "Seems like folks decided to walk right over me to hurt Joe. I don't know why I'm surprised. Nothing I say means anything. Not even the sheriff believes me. My words count for nothing."

"You have to be somebody before they listen to you in Tulsa." Hildy wrapped matches in waxed paper.

"You know Joe never touched me."

"I know. If a black man's a mile down the road and a white woman hollers, it's rape. But if a white man tears off a Negro woman's dress, no one believes her. It isn't rape." Hildy moved closer. "Why you think that's so, Miss Mary?"

Hildy needed to hear this white woman's answer. She needed to hear her say something stupid, so she could hate her outright. Not care about Christian charity. Not care about Mary's pain. If she said something stupid, she could slap her, push her out of the kitchen door, down the porch steps.

"Truth is I never paid colored folk any mind." Mary spoke slowly, cautiously. "I've worked at the Ambrose for six years. I couldn't tell you when Joe started. I couldn't tell you a damn thing about him. Hair, height. Being colored just made him disappear for me. But after today I could tell you there's gold in his eyes."

Hildy nodded.

"Joe let me see him. Let me see myself shining in a pool of tears. We were both of us drowning. Both of us trying to come up for air."

"But you screamed. You must've screamed."

"Yes." Her shoulders drooped. "The one time I should've stayed hush. But I couldn't. I hurt so bad."

"Miss Mary," Hildy said, vehement. "You're still talking about you. You haven't done nothing for Joe."

"I tried."

"Maybe you didn't try hard enough, Miss Mary. You're free—Joe's on the run. Saying sorry is one thing, making good on 'sorry' is another."

"I'm doing it. I'm helping you, aren't I?" Mary dug inside her dress. "Here." She pulled her rumpled dollars from her pocket. "Take this to Joe. It's all I have. Take it."

Hildy clutched the bills. "I'll take it. But now leave my father's house. Leave my kitchen, Miss Mary. You're not welcome here." Hildy turned away, disgusted. She didn't hear footsteps. All right. Well and good. Miss Mary could take a minute to gather herself.

Hildy went into the pantry and digging behind a flour pail, she pulled out a small pouch. She counted bills and coins. She had nineteen dollars, twenty-seven with Miss Mary's eight. She turned off the pantry light, expecting Miss Mary to be gone from her kitchen. But the crazy woman was still standing there pale as a ghost. Hildy could feel her fury rising again. One more minute and, Lord forgive her, she'd beat this woman out her kitchen. Christian charity or not.

"I'm Mary. Just plain Mary." Mary's face was dull. Her hands hung limp at her sides.

Hildy shivered. She heard such hurt in Mary's voice.

"I was raped this morning. By a white man. Pa's hired hand. I told Sheriff Clay Joe didn't touch me but I didn't tell him who did. I was a coward. I didn't want folks talking about me any more than they already were. I didn't want to tell the sheriff something so," she looked down at her shoes, then up again, "personal."

Mary limped forward. "But I promise you—if it will help Joe, I'll tell the entire city, the whole world, if necessary, that a white man raped me, not Joe."

"Why should I trust you?"

"Maybe you shouldn't. But I never accused Joe. Never. No one will ever make me say any different."

Hildy felt the Lord taking her by the hand, leading her to a greater light.

"I want to help Joe escape. Besides," Mary stated grimly, "if you're stopped by the Klan, my whiteness might be useful to you. To Joe's safety."

Maybe the woman would be useful. It wouldn't be easy to get Joe out of Tulsa. Father wouldn't help Joe escape, that was sure, thought Hildy. She could ask Emmaline, but Emmaline might tell Father. Hildy looked closely at this strange woman in her kitchen.

"You understand I love my brother?"

"Yes," Mary answered simply. "I do."

Hildy stretched out her hand. "My name is Hildy."

Hildy felt Mary's matching calluses, the matching strength in the white hand cupping her own. Slowly, she exhaled, thinking the Lord was putting her in the fire as well. If she made a mistake trusting this woman, she might fail Joe again.

Mary's eyes never wavered.

Hildy nodded.

"We can carry the supplies to Lena's River," said Hildy. "Joe'll go there, if anywhere."

17

Clay couldn't quite remember the joke. It bothered him—something about a rabbit and a lion. It wasn't really a joke. More like a joke on the lion. Some trick, just like Joe's trick. He'd underestimated the boy.

Almost midnight and Clay still hadn't found Joe. He'd sent deputies fanning out across the roads between Tulsa and Greenwood. Sully was in charge of door-to-door searches. Coloreds would be riled, but Clay didn't have much choice. He didn't doubt he was racing against Klansmen hunting for Joe.

Clay searched alone. For reasons he couldn't explain, he wanted to find Joe himself.

He'd parked his car at the station and now he moved through the railroad yard, stepping quietly over steel ties and rods, breathing through his mouth. He wished he were hunting squirrel or, better yet, fishing bass outside of town. He'd wanted to escape the war, but he was right back in it. His first few years as sheriff hadn't been bad—drunks, belligerent gamblers, the occasional prostitute batterer. But progress had come to Tulsa as streams of oil gurgled from the ground. Now murder was on the rise: shootings, lynchings, brutal beatings. He couldn't figure it. Everybody was better off. Coloreds had their own town. No white people were starving. Yet night riders, like Lucas and Bates, lynched coloreds and Jews.

Ambrose had a clear purpose—to make Tulsa the rival of Chicago. "Hell, better than Chicago." The Klan was his tool to make Tulsa the most admired, the most civilized, the most patriotic city west of the Mississippi. No wonder Ambrose was announcing for governor. Tulsa was the cow town transformed: a city of Christian schools, a new Convention Center, and an expanding railroad to haul oil and cattle out, silks and good whiskey in.

Clay stooped, his fingers touching a clean print in the dirt. He'd been lured to Tulsa because he'd heard it was a hunter's paradise. In his mind, Tulsa had risen like a dream: rolling hills, musk and cedar scents, woods with free-roaming deer, rabbit, clear streams stocked with crappie and trout, and a horizon clouded only by startled ducks in flight. He thought he'd forget Pittsburgh's molten steel, its soot-clouded sky, brick-paved hills, tenements overrun with Poles, Italians, and the coloreds' shanties by its dirty rivers. Tulsa was "the West"—the land of cowboys, open spaces. In Tulsa, his innocence would be reclaimed; a sheriff always kept the peace. How simple he'd been.

Ambrose had hired him because he was a decorated veteran. Clay didn't tell him his medals were at the bottom of the Monagahela. Clay wasn't proud of surviving a gas attack, machine-gunning ragged soldiers who thought they were advancing on an unmanned trench.

Clay believed Mary Keane. He wanted justice done. He just wasn't sure how to do it.

Sweat was dripping into his shoes. He wanted a drink badly, but the flask in his back pocket was empty.

His revolver was loaded. He had cuffs, even cord to hog tie Joe. Clay stopped, his head turned into the wind. Smoke rose from a campfire; hobos were arguing. The train was a stinking, easy rambler of thirty cars hauling cattle and pigs, due to leave at 12:18. The engineer was building pressure in the valves and the crew was loading gear in the caboose. Clay was betting Joe would hop the train. It wouldn't be easy. But Joe had already done the unbelievable. Clay looked at the train.

Where would he hide? There were no passenger cars, not even flat cars carrying wood.

The train gushed steam. Cows lowed like they were in pain. Pigs grunted and squealed. Hooves scraped boxcar floors.

Clay didn't want to be seen. He ducked behind the rear cars, running low past the couplers, pressing himself flat against the last cattle car. Horns poked through the slat rails; the steers were hungry, restless. No sense feeding animals on their way to slaughter. When he peered into the car, all he saw were thick shapes, the glint of horns, and moonlight catching the frightened glitter of a cow's brown eye. Splinters dug into his skin.

Clay heard something like a moan. He released the safety on his gun. He was scared, just like in the war. He didn't want to kill Joe. Steam hissed. Clay stared inside the car; a cow was down, slowly being trampled.

The whistle shrilled. Five minutes. The train would leave. Clay started trekking toward the engine. He stumbled over loose rock, dodged, darted between cars, feeling the rush of air in his lungs as he passed a seemingly endless line of cars, searching for Joe. Clay thought he should be the one leaving. He should hop the train and go.

He'd gone to David Reubens' funeral knowing he wasn't welcome. Thornton had gotten a colored mortuary to bury him. Some barber had played a harmonica while a woman wailed: "*This train's bound for freedom. Children, get on board. There's room for many a-more.*"

Clay moved rapidly from car to car. The woman's song had switched to a blues: "*How long, how long, tell me how long the train's been gone? Baby, how long?*" Emotion had rocked him and he'd nearly fallen to his knees, despairing opportunities missed, how corrupt he'd become.

He was twelve cars back from the engine. He'd made a mistake. Joe wasn't on board. He slowed. Animals caterwauled; the station master yelled, "Twelve-fifteen. Last call." The engine pulsed with power, metal wheels strained to turn.

Clay squinted at a cattle car. "Gaines' Tobacco" was in red at the top. Shadows moved behind slats. It was quiet in the car, hushed like animals after feed.

He drew closer, peering at the steers pressed too tight, hides slicked with sweat. Their heads bunting toward the slats for air.

Out of the corner of his eye, to the far right, he saw an open space, not blunted by any form, any shape. With so little space, so little air, it didn't make sense for the steers to avoid a corner of the jammed car.

"Joe," Clay called softly. "Joe?" He inched forward, focusing on the blank space. He lowered his gaze. "Joe?" He could see the boy sitting, cross-legged, on straw. Joe was barefoot and soaked. He must've hidden in the water trough until the train was ready to leave.

"Are you all right?" he asked. He thought he saw the boy nod.

Joe had astonished him: disappearing from jail, calming cattle as if by magic. Whoever heard of slaughterhouse cows standing still? Unlike him, Joe seemed unafraid.

Clay stooped. Joe scooted forward, leaning his brow against the wood. The boy was shivering, his arms curled about himself.

"Did you remember the joke, sheriff?"

"No."

"Too bad. It was a good one."

"You have to come with me, Joe."

"Do I?"

Clay cursed.

"I want to see the ocean. Ride the train to Frisco. Have you ever been to Frisco, sheriff?"

"No, Joe."

"You should go."

Clay reached inside his jacket. "I found this in your personal effects."

Joe reached for the square. "Did you look at it?"

"Yes." Clay remembered the brutal, lovely picture of Houdini leaping from the Golden Gate Bridge, crashing, handcuffed and chained, into the water.

Reverently, Joe unfolded the picture. "I tore this from *Magical Arts*. Houdini surfaced in fifty-seven seconds and swam to shore. I've never seen the ocean. Have you?"

"The Atlantic," said Clay. "I threw up the whole trip to France. I couldn't keep water down."

The whistle shrilled again. The train was ready. Cows lowed; pigs whined.

"Sheriff, maybe you never saw me here? Maybe it was too dark?"

Shadow and light streaked across Joe's face, his expression hopeful. Joe was young enough, Clay thought, to believe in miracles. Clay considered following the boy's lead. Getting the hell out of town. Clay envied the boy. Now he understood—he'd been hoping to witness Joe's escape, not capture him.

Joe handed him the picture. It was damp, the paper curling where Joe's fingers had touched. Houdini risked everything to prove he was invincible. Clay hadn't risked anything and felt vulnerable every day of his life.

"All right," he murmured. "Send me a postcard. Let me know when you're safe."

Joe grinned. There was a steady clanging. A green light lit the track. Clay nearly laughed outright. The two of them had bested Tulsa.

Horn blaring, a truck swerved onto the lot, its sharp stop kicking up gravel and dust. "Shit." Nearly a dozen men jumped from the truck's flatbed. Clay watched Ambrose get out of the cab, stop at Clay's car. "Damn."

Ambrose shouted, "Hold that train."

"What is it, sheriff?" asked Joe.

The men fanned out, flashlights focused and glaring. Waving Joe quiet, Clay drew his gun, flattened his back against the cattle car. "I've got to think." Panic was rising. "Shit." He should've known better. Ambrose was starting his election run.

The men began searching the train, starting from the back and moving systematically forward. Ambrose had moved out of sight, but Clay knew he would be in the thick of it. Joe swinging from a tree would make Ambrose a hero.

"Joe, trust me. You've got to let me take you in." Clay cursed; Joe looked dull-eyed, defeated. "Ambrose and his men are here. You've got to let me take you. It's your only chance."

Clay undid the latch, slid back the cattle door. Brown noses pushed forward. "Come on, Joe."

Joe waded forward, pushing against the steers to keep from being crushed.

"Come on, Joe. Come on."

"Hey, who's there? That you, sheriff?"

"Hurry, Joe," Clay whispered, extending his hand. Joe clutched it.

"They'll burn me."

"Not if I can help it." Clay unlatched his cuffs. "Hands behind your back, Joe."

Animals survived by admitting defeat, going belly up. War had taught Clay men weren't so reliable. But it was worth a try. He snapped the clasps shut and pulled Joe into the open, away from the train.

"I've got him," Clay shouted, firing his gun in the air.

Other shots rang out; men hollered, "We got him. We've caught the nigger." Men were running, bearing down upon them.

"Steady, Joe," said Clay.

Joe, head bowed, wet and stinking from the trough, didn't move.

Men formed a circle around them, some darting forward to sneer, poke a stick at Joe. Clay, gun still drawn, felt like firing into the middle of them.

"Lynch him," a voice started the chant. Then they were all yelling, foul mouthed and insistent, "Kill the nigger."

"Get the rope!" someone shouted. "Here." A heavy rope appeared.

Ambrose stepped into the circle, his bow tie askew, still wearing tails from the evening's fund-raiser. Though his hair was thinning, his flesh loose at the neck, he still exuded charm. Charming and ruthless, Clay thought.

"So. You found him, boys!" crowed Ambrose, flushed and excited.

"I found him," said Clay, holding tight onto Joe's arm.

"Of course." Ambrose stepped closer. He lifted Joe's chin.

Joe shuddered, tried to look away.

Ambrose gripped his jaw. "Look me in the eye, boy. Who do you think you are? You think being Douglass Samuels' son makes you special?"

Ambrose struck Joe square in the mouth.

Joe staggered back.

"You're nothing. Nobody."

Someone tripped Joe, hit the back of his knees. Clay lost his grip. Several men swarmed, kicking Joe as he writhed on the ground. The rest kept the circle, cheering, encouraging the beating. Clay recognized Bates, his jowly face alight with glee.

The men's fury needed some outlet. Clay hoped Joe would stop struggling, fall unconscious. Moving next to Ambrose, he said smoothly, "I can haul him into custody. This boy won't be any problem."

"Damn right," said Ambrose. "He'll be dead tonight." As if on cue, a blunt, bull-headed man slipped the rope about Joe's neck.

Clay leveled his gun at the nearest man and, facing Ambrose, shouted, "Leave him alone. I'm taking him to jail."

Ambrose looked hard at Clay and said quietly, "You're interfering with justice."

"No, just upholding the law." Clay moved toward Joe, using his gun to wave the surly men back. "You'll hang him all right. After the judge says so. And he will. Nigger's guilty. No doubt about it."

"We can hang him now, he's only a nigger."

"A lynching might make a stir, Ambrose. With a quick trial, you can hang him. Same result. But you'll be a statesman. Tulsa is civilized after all, this isn't the Wild West."

Ambrose didn't say anything, his face a blank slate. Clay couldn't read him. He stooped, patting Joe for broken bones.

"Heard you let this nigger get away the first time. Ought to let us finish the job," one of the men called.

Clay pulled cord from his pocket. "He won't escape a hog tie."

The men laughed as Clay tied Joe's feet and lifted him, blood draining from his mouth, bruises swelling on his face, like a sack. "Besides, tomorrow, he'll be too sore to move." Clay hefted Joe on his shoulder. "Judge can arraign him in the morning."

The men hadn't moved from their tight circle. Ambrose still hadn't said anything and Clay knew the men were waiting for his word. Clay struggled under Joe's weight and locked eyes with Ambrose. "Hang him tomorrow. Decoration Day. A nice touch, don't you think, governor?"

Ambrose smiled. "I'll see you lynched, too, if you lose him again."

Bates stood in Clay's way. Clay's shirt was damp, absorbing water and blood from Joe's clothes. Still, Bates didn't move. Clay could feel the other men's hatred, disappointment. They'd tear him apart if they had the chance. They were hoping Bates would give it to them. Bates glanced questioningly at Ambrose.

"Ambrose," said Clay. "Do not make the wrong decision here."

Ambrose must've nodded, for Bates stepped aside and the men behind him did the same.

Breathing hard but trying not to show it, Clay walked.

Ambrose called wryly, "Need some help? One of my boys could help keep an eye on him."

"This nigger ain't going to wake any time soon," Clay hollered back.

Men hooted and guffawed. Clay stepped across ties, past the still locomotive and slaughterhouse animals. He walked to his car, knowing Ambrose's mob was watching every step. Joe, unconscious, was awkward to carry. Suddenly, he remembered Joe's joke.

The well. That was it. It was a story really. Lion was a vain, lazy bossman who demanded the other animals bring him meals. No one dared threaten his power. Except Young Rabbit. Rabbit tricked Boss Lion into diving into a well, attacking his own reflection.

Clay trudged the last few steps and then slung Joe like a bag of feed into the back seat. He wiped his forehead and drew out his flask. He had it to his lips before he remembered it was empty. Then he laughed. Yes, in Tulsa, he was surely Boss Lion deep at the bottom of the well.

18

Mary heard it first, an engine cutting abruptly, wheels rolling on gravel. She'd just finished wrapping slices of jerky, washing her hands at the sink when she heard the soft whir abruptly die, and she looked up, out the kitchen window. Headlights drew close, parallel, lighting tangled ivy, startling a cat at the base of a fence. Fear settled in her chest and chased away the contentment she'd felt working in the kitchen with Hildy. It wasn't the same sweetness she'd felt with her mother, but she felt a hint of belonging, of being, if not precisely wanted, at least useful.

Hildy was humming, securing the sacks they were taking to Joe. "Hildy," Mary called. Then, with more urgency, "Hildy!" as the car stopped in front of the Samuels' house.

"What's wrong?"

Mary didn't answer. Hildy drew beside her and the two of them stood at the sink, staring into the darkness at the police car and the three men getting out. Lucas, a holster and pistol draped on his hips, stepped quickly; Dell, slower, had a revolver sticking in his belt; Jody used a shotgun to steady himself on the path.

Hildy moved first. "I've got to warn Father." Mary nodded dumbly as Hildy left, the kitchen door swinging furiously. She watched Jody and Dell climb the steps behind Lucas until they were all caught by the porch's yellow cast. Moths fluttered around their heads.

Mary stepped outside the kitchen door, turning left, until she had a clear view of the three men at the front door. "What are you doing here, Jody?"

Lucas turned, drawing his gun.

Jody stayed him. "I could ask the same of you, Mary."

She walked toward them.

"The lady who got raped." Lucas stared, his fingers locked into his belt above his crotch.

Mary felt unclean again, felt as if he were undressing her. She held her ground. Dell didn't look at her at all.

"There's going to be trouble," said Lucas. "You should go home."

Jody leaned on his gun. "None of this would've happened, Mary, if you'd stayed put."

"Nothing did happen. Joe's not here. Leave these people alone, Jody."

"A man's got to protect his sister."

"Is that you talking? Or him?" She cocked her head at Lucas.

Lucas stepped close. Behind him, the porch lamp made an odd halo. "The nigger's free. We're going to catch him."

"Nothing happened. He never touched me."

Lucas smiled. "A running nigger is always guilty of something. Maybe you're too ashamed to admit it."

Mary reached back to slap him. Lucas caught her hand, twisting it behind her back.

"Let me go."

The front door opened and Mary glimpsed a tall man, sturdier than Joe. He was dressed in a wrinkled suit, his vest half-buttoned, his shirt collar undone. Yet he seemed more elegant than most white men she ferried in her elevator.

"What's going on here?"

Lucas shoved Mary backward. She reached for Jody. "If you love me, if you ever loved me, don't do this. Leave these people alone, Jody." Her brother turned away.

"This is private property," stated Samuels. "You have no right disturbing my house. No right coming here in the middle of the night."

"We're searching for Joe Samuels."

"He's in jail. You'll find him there."

"He escaped."

"I spoke to my son myself. In jail. A few hours ago. He's to be moved to Oklahoma City in the morning."

"Your son had other plans."

Samuels raised his brow. "Are you telling me you lost him?"

Lucas raised his gun. "I'm telling you we're going to search this house."

"Do you have a warrant?"

"No, but a bullet ought to do fine."

Mary watched as the men glared, wary like two cocks. From the house, she heard a woman crying. Joe's father snapped, "Be quiet, Ruth." Then, with deliberate dignity, he opened the door.

Lucas sauntered into the house, aiming his gun at the cluster of women—Hildy and, Mary guessed, her mother and sister. Jody stepped into the vestibule, his eyes taking in the splendor: the winding staircase, the chandelier hanging above, the glimpse of a dining table, a crystal bowl cradling fruit.

Mary clasped Dell from behind, her arms circling his waist, her cheek pressed against his spine. "I'll do anything you want. Anything. I won't tell anyone what you did. Don't harm these people, Dell. They don't deserve it."

"They're niggers, Mary." He looked over his shoulder. "Besides you'll do what I want anyway. Damaged goods, Mary. No one else will have you." He pulled free of her arms.

Mary began locking away feeling, swallowing screams as she watched the three men's backs. Jody held the shotgun on the family as Lucas ran up the stairs and Dell explored the first floor. Upstairs and below, there were jarring sounds, overturned furniture, breaking glass. Samuels stared at Jody like he was filth. Ruth whimpered, "My house.

My house." Mary heard a shout from above stairs. Lucas was leaning over the banister. "There's a nigger up here in bed."

"That's Tyler," Hildy called. "My grandfather. He's paralyzed."

"He doesn't know anything," said Samuels.

"If I'd known he couldn't get up, I wouldn't have hit him," said Lucas.

"Barbarians," said Samuels, starting forward.

"You're the jungle bunny," countered Jody, his shotgun raised.

Dell entered from the side, red striped wings splayed in his palm. "Butterflies," he said disbelievingly. "Dead. Pinned in velvet cases. Never seen such a thing. Seems like a woman's hobby, don't you think, Samuels?" Dell blew and the dead butterfly fluttered into Samuels' face.

Mary watched Samuels clench his fist, saw him straining not to knock Dell down. Hildy soothed, "Let them finish their business, Father. Let them finish. They'll see Joe's not here."

Hildy looked at Mary—a look that blamed her for everything. Mary wanted to cry.

Lucas slid down the banister, feet first like a boy. He leaped lightly onto the floor, strutting forward. Mary realized he enjoyed this, enjoyed flailing his gun in Samuels' face, belligerent, demanding, "Where is he? Where'd Joe go?"

"I don't know and, if I did, I wouldn't tell you."

Lucas pressed the gun to Samuels' temple.

Samuels flinched. Hildy moved to her father's side; he waved her away. "You're just another Klansman," he spat, "dressed in a deputy's uniform."

Lucas depressed the gun's hammer. "I'd like to blow your brains out. Splatter them onto your polished floor."

"Stop it," whispered Mary.

"I'd like to see you and your runt, Joe, dead. Like to see you both hanging, dancing on thin air."

"I've always known white men were spineless. Cowards. It takes three of you to terrorize helpless women, a sick man, and myself."

Lucas hit him with the gun.

Samuels collapsed onto his knees. Blood ran from his mouth.

"Father!" Hildy pressed her apron to his lip. "That's enough," she screamed at Lucas. "Why don't you leave us alone?" Her mother wailed; her sister called on God.

"Should I hurt him, Jody, or let you do it?" asked Lucas. "She's your sister."

Jody trembled, his fake calf and foot angled awkwardly.

"Is this what you learned in the war, Jody?" Mary asked. "How to hurt unarmed men?"

"Shut up," he turned on her. "This is your fault. None of this would've happened, if it weren't for you."

"Then punish me."

"They're niggers, Mary," said Dell.

"You think you're better?" she demanded angrily. "You're the one who ought to be running, Dell. Not Joe. But Jody, you've never hurt anybody." Tears filled her eyes. "You used to cry when I burned my fingers. You don't mean this, Jody."

"What do you know about me?"

"I spent my life raising you," Mary snapped. "If it hadn't been for you, I would've left the farm long ago. But I stayed."

Jody turned away.

"Jody! Dell raped me! This morning, in the barn."

Jody looked at Dell.

"Ask him. It's true. Part of his plan to steal the farm. Come with me. We can tell the sheriff, maybe make some difference."

"The hell with this," growled Lucas. "Nigger's on the run. These folks know where he is."

"They don't know anything," argued Mary.

"Somebody's been packing supplies in the kitchen." Dell grinned. "Ain't that so."

Jody's Adam's apple bobbed. Sweat beaded on his forehead.

"Jody—"

"Leave me alone, Mary."

"I know you won't hurt these people."

"You don't know anything about me."

"Who raised you? Who loved you, if not me?"

Samuels, staggering upright, said, "Scum. Worthless, white scum."

"Watch your mouth, nigger," threatened Lucas.

"Jody, you didn't come back from the war for this."

Jody's face distorted. "You don't know anything about the war," he said bitterly. "You're a woman. You don't know anything about war."

Swinging round, he smashed the butt of the shotgun into Samuels' shoulder. Hildy dashed forward, her fists jabbing—Jody knocked her aside. He hit Samuels again. Then again.

"Jody, no," Mary begged. Dell grabbed Mary, pinning her arms to her sides.

Swift, brutal swings with the butt forced Samuels, hands flailing, to his knees.

"Now you're talking," said Lucas. "Now you're talking." He kicked Samuels in the back and when he fell, he kicked again. Mary heard Samuels' arm crack, a piece of bone tore through his skin.

The women screamed. Mary twisted helplessly in Dell's grasp.

"Where's Joe?" asked Lucas, gripping the back of Samuels' neck. "Where is he?"

Samuels made incoherent sounds; the rage in his eyes was clear.

"Father doesn't know anything. Leave him alone," cried Hildy.

"Where's Joe?" asked Lucas again. He bounced Samuels' head against the wood.

"Stop it," cried Mary. "He can't tell you anything. He didn't even know Joe'd escaped."

"Maybe he can shine my shoes then. Isn't that what his son did?" Lucas stood. "Dell, get this nigger a rag."

Dell released Mary's arms. She watched Hildy creeping forward. Lucas aimed his gun at her. "Move again and I'll kill you."

Dell tore Hildy's bloodied apron and stooped, stuffing it into Samuels' limp hand. "Shine my shoes, nigger," said Dell. Samuels didn't move. "Shine them."

Lucas was furious. "Move, damn you. Move." His boot pressed Samuels' side.

Samuels stirred, his head lifting a bit. He spat, bloody saliva speckling Lucas' shoes. Lucas kicked him, the force rolling him over. Samuels groaned, blood flowed from his arm. Lucas kicked him again.

Mary's stomach heaved. "You're killing him, you're killing him."

A shot was fired from the stairs.

"Tyler," Hildy yelled. "No, Tyler, no."

Mary saw an old man at the top of the stairs, belly down, poking a rifle through the banister rails.

"Shoot him, Jody," crowed Lucas.

"Jody, no," Mary screamed.

Jody aimed. His shotgun blast ripped through the rails. Brains and bone splattered. Tyler, nearly headless, rolled down the stairs.

Lucas called, "Fine shot, Jody. Damn fine!"

Hildy, weeping, started to sing, "*Go down, Moses, way down—*"

"Shut up," said Lucas.

"*In Egyptland. Tell Pharaoh—*"

"Shut up!"

"*Let my people go.*"

Mary realized it was only a matter of time before Lucas killed Hildy, before the crazy men killed them all. She took her chance and flew out the door, down the stairs. She ran, screaming, thrown off-balance by her shoe, Jody cursing, "God damn, Mary. Get back here. Get the hell on back."

She screamed into the night's stillness, "Help. Help. They're killing them." She stumbled up steps, banged on doors, moved from house to house, repeating, "They're killing them."

Porch lights flicked on; faces pressed against windows; people stared through locked screen doors. Mary knew she looked crazy, a witch of a white woman. She went right up to doors, stared into suspicious eyes and said calmly, "The Samuels need help. My brother is killing them."

When nobody believed her, she grew hysterical. She tried pulling an old man out of his house. "Please. Listen to me. You've got to believe me." Babies were crying. A woman shouted, "Grady, you stay in here." "It's a trick," said another, "a Klan trick." Dogs barked and growled. Mary whimpered. Why wouldn't they listen? She imagined Hildy already dead, crumpled on the floor.

She saw a tall man stepping into the street carrying a large revolver. She ran to meet him. "You're going to help them?"

Mary looked into the man's unforgiving eyes. The moon hung low over his shoulders. "Joe never hurt anybody," she breathed. "Please. Save his family."

Slowly, he nodded. Shouting orders, he moved in a fast trot toward the Samuels' house. "Bill, get Lying Man. Tell 'im what's going on."

A voice hollered back, "Sure, Nate."

"Chalmers, bring your .38."

"Okay, Nate."

"Find where the hell Gabe is." The tall man, Nate, ran faster, and Mary saw dozens more men coming down from porches, flowing into the street. Some had guns, most had broomsticks, fireplace pokers, baseball bats.

"Come on, men," Nate shouted.

"Hold on, Hildy," Mary prayed to herself. A woman in a green housecoat was beside her.

"You need help? You all right?"

"I'm fine." Mary wiped away tears.

The Samuels' screen door slammed open. Lucas charged out, firing into the crowd.

Mary yelled, "No—" There was a scream; someone fell. The crowd scattered.

Nate kneeled on the lawn, firing.

Lucas sprinted to the car with Dell close behind. Jody hobbled down the steps and shot at Nate. The shot missed. Dell fired wildly, keeping the men at bay. "Hurry up, Jody. Shit." He revved the engine.

Jody was almost to the car when from the other side of the lawn, Mary saw a man in a coat run up, gun in hand, and take aim.

"Jody," Mary couldn't help crying out. Jody looked toward her. The man fired and Jody clutched his gut, blood spilling through his hand.

"Dammit, man," hollered Dell. Mary saw Dell grab Jody and drag him, face down, into the back seat. The car swerved down the street, the door wide open, Jody's legs dangling, his artificial foot flying off.

"Jody," Mary moaned. She searched but the man in the coat had disappeared.

A small crowd surged into the Samuels' house. Standing on tiptoe, Mary could barely see inside. Tyler was dead on the stairs. Joe's father was still on the floor, his head cradled in his wife's lap. She couldn't find Hildy. A doctor pushed past her. The crowd parted then closed again, and Mary found herself alone on the porch. The yellow light was still attracting bugs. Mary walked around to the kitchen. Opening the screen door, she saw Hildy, her head resting on the table.

"You all right?"

Hildy looked up. Woeful, she shook her head.

Mary put her arms around Hildy. Chest heaving, Hildy was swallowing her grief. Mary rocked her, murmuring, "It's all right to cry. Cry it out."

The scent of gunpowder lingered in the house. Mary thought how quiet the kitchen seemed against the gunshots still ringing in her ears.

19

Tuesday, May 31, 1921

Joe moaned, slowly pulling out of darkness, a dreamless sleep. He was back in jail, clothes torn, stale blood in his mouth. He tried to move, but his hands were cuffed, roped, and tied to his feet. Someone—the sheriff?—had tossed him onto the cot. His body ached. He could feel where boots had scarred his ribs, clubs had battered his spine. He remembered being outnumbered, helpless, hands trapped behind him, trying to dodge blows, unable to shield his face and abdomen.

It was all a matter of will.

Houdini had lied. Twice he'd failed to escape. When Ambrose's fist slammed into his mouth, he'd tried to disappear. Displace himself outside his body. *Poof. Puff of smoke.* Instead, his beating and nightmare had intertwined.

"*Who do you think you are?*" He'd been startled by Ambrose's eyes—fierce like Houdini's, like the man in his nightmare, daring him to show any defiance. He'd thought: here was the man who'd stolen Tyler's land, the man Father had begged for his life. Hatred had swelled in Joe and he'd answered Ambrose's glare. Ambrose swung with such force, Joe saw stars. He remembered shoes—polished wing tips, dulled work boots scraping the ground, rearing backward before battering his legs, back, and arms. "*Who do you think you are, boy?*" He'd managed not to cry out, not to groan. He'd dodged as a metal-rimmed boot rushed toward his face; the blow glanced off his head; and, then, he hadn't felt or dreamed anything.

"*I'm nobody.*"

Tied like a heifer, wet, sticky in a cold cell, Joe felt doubly betrayed—by himself and by Houdini.

Houdini had never been hunted, beaten. He didn't know anything about being called a nigger. Joe felt he should've just crawled into his brother's grave. Accepted he was ordinary. Plain Joe. The banker's son. He should've spent his life counting dollars, making his father happy.

Houdini was a poor hero for a Negro.

Joe flailed; rope cut into his ankles and wrists. Pain was the only real thing about him.

"*Who do you think you are, boy?*" His nightmare mocked, letting him know beyond a doubt, he was going to die. He wasn't anyone special. It didn't matter that he'd promised to quit dreaming. Ambrose would kill him.

Despairing, Joe remembered he'd lost his lock pick. When he'd dived into the railroad's trough, gulping for air, the pick had floated out his mouth, sinking to the murky bottom.

Joe arched his fingers, trying what he'd never tried before. He concentrated on his left hand, clasped in steel, resting on the small of his back. He tugged, steady and hard. Sweat covered his forehead. He shifted his forefinger and thumb, dislocated bones until he could slip his hand, trembling, through the loop of the cuff. He unclenched his teeth, swallowed blood. He inhaled, trying to control his pain.

Joe shuddered. The sky was lightening. Mist streamed through the window. It was Decoration Day. They'd parade the veterans home from France. Maybe Henry would parade with them, haunting the white soldiers.

Tomorrow was his birthday. He thought of Myra, his "easy girl"—how last week as he'd kissed her hair, the slope between her breasts, she'd refused his dollars, claiming her loving was his birthday gift. He'd been thrown off-balance by her generosity, by the notion that maybe, just maybe, he was worth loving.

Damn Houdini. Damn his brother's ghost.

Grunting, he slid out of the hog tie, unwinding the dirty cord from between his legs. He swung his feet to the floor. Joe tried to stand—dizzy, blood rushing through his limbs, he fell to the floor. "Goddamn." They'd beat him good. He wouldn't be able to run anywhere. He couldn't even stand. "Well, fine. Goddamn fine." He'd lay here then until the sun rose, until they came for him. Until they took him to a field, beat him again, and burned him alive.

His eyes rolled back in his head; darkness taunted him. Joe cradled his hand; it was monstrous, swelling, just like in his nightmare. He was helpless. Gently rocking, he focused on the dust, the rough cracks in the floor. He knew he'd never see his family, never see the rooftops of Greenwood again.

He saw shoes. He flinched, his hand flying upward to protect his head. *Black, polished leather. Brass couplings for the laces.*

"Sheriff?"

No answer.

Joe blinked. He hadn't heard the cell door open or the shuffle of steps. *Henry?* No, Henry wore service boots. These were rich man's shoes—calves' leather—something his father might wear. *The pants cuffed, pleated, and shiny like a dime. The stance solid.*

Joe was scared. He felt like a child, afraid to look up, afraid to be, afraid to do anything other than shiver in his wet clothes, gasping at the pain in his bones.

A soft swish and the shoes stepped inches from his face, smelling of sweet wax. Joe was thirsty, bone weary.

Legs bent. Buffed nails, lean fingers snaked around a cup brimming with water.

Trembling, Joe swatted the cup. *It disappeared. He looked upward into Houdini's eyes. Eyes which had haunted him; eyes which had always dared him to be better than he was.* Joe scuttled backward. Houdini squatted, smiling, without a care, in his cell.

"Hello, Joe."

"You can't be here."

"Why not?"

"You're a picture. From a magazine. The pictures in my trunk."

"As you say, Joe," Houdini whispered dryly. "As you say."

"Shit. How'd you get here?"

"You invited me. Don't you remember?"

Furious, feeling mocked, Joe dragged himself forward and, with a shove, toppled Houdini.

Hair ruffled, feet splayed, Houdini stared at Joe, angry, imperious. Light cut across his blunt face, deepening shadows. Then, he smiled. "You shouldn't waste your strength, Joe."

Joe stared at his hand, startled he could touch Houdini. His fingers tingled from sensing skin beneath wool, from feeling bone, sinew, and the tremor of a heart.

"I've gone crazy. That's what Emmaline said. Crazy nigger." *Houdini's luminous eyes pierced him, seeming to press him against the cot's rail.*

Wildly, Joe thought Houdini had come to kill him. Like the man in his dream tossing the match, like Ambrose hitting him—the same unnerving look, the same arrogance daring him to be better than he was. But the underbelly of the glare also said he was nothing. Nobody. Joe moaned; his head lolled to the side. He howled, a low rattle tearing up through his gut.

"Quiet, Joe." Houdini was beside him. "No one must hear. I'm here to get you out."

"I don't believe you."

"There are three rules of survival, Joe. The first is dream what you need."

"Is that what this is—a dream?"

"Perhaps." He cocked his head. "Didn't Hildy say dreams are important, Joe?"

"How do you know that?"

"I know everything about you, Joe."

"You're the devil then." Joe hooded his eyes. "Not a dream. Not a ghost. You're too solid to be either."

"Sleight of hand then. Mysticism. Wonder. You, better than anyone else, should know such things. I'm your magic, Joe."

"I don't believe you."

"Magic is survival, escape. Moses' magic turned a rod into a snake,

transformed the Nile into blood, and freed the Israelites. The greatest magic of all time, Joe."

"I know you're the devil now."

"You think I blaspheme?" Houdini glared.

Joe felt a churning in his gut.

"The second rule of survival is will."

He smelled ash, an acrid burning. Bile rose his throat.

"Who are you, Joe?" Houdini gripped his shoulder. Joe felt fingers digging into his skin. It was a mystery. All of it. Houdini here. A photograph come to life. *Broad brow, angular nose, jutting chin. But it was the eyes—always the eyes—which challenged him.*

"Who are you, Joe? You've got to be somebody."

Joe felt hypnotized; flecks of light shifted within Houdini's eyes. He trembled, believing suddenly that it was really he. *Houdini.* This was the man who escaped from coffins floating underwater; who escaped from straitjackets while hanging, upside down, from skyscrapers; who escaped boxes, locked and chained, and lowered into the muddy Charles River.

"You have to be a man sometime. It's not how the world sees you, but how you see yourself." Houdini produced a small mirror. "It's not my eyes or your father's that matter, but yours. Who are you, Joe?"

Joe cringed, seeing his swollen face, blood crusted above his eye, lips split and bleeding. He didn't know who he was. He only knew he was a disappointment as a son and a failure as a brother.

If he knew who he was, he'd want something. But all he wanted now was to stop struggling. He pushed the mirror away. He was crazy. Everything that had happened served him right. He let his head fall backward onto the cot.

"I can't abide quitters, Joe. Quitters or liars. You're lying to yourself, Joe. Night before last you wanted something."

"Get out of here." His head ached; he closed his eyes.

"What did you want, Joe?"

He'd wanted to hop a train to the Pacific, dive into the waves, to be as brave and as willful as Houdini.

"There's only one Great Houdini."

"Yeah. That's right. One Houdini. And he's white," Joe said bitterly. "I might as well give up now. No hope for a black man here."

"Joe, Joe." Houdini shook his head. "A whole people escaped from Egypt's bondage, surely you can escape from this tiny cell?"

"I did," he said stubbornly. "They just caught me again."

"Don't be caught. Disappear. Outwit them all."

"Shit. I'm dreaming."

"You're conjuring, Joe. I'm your magic telling you what you need to know, what you've always known. The first thing you can do is believe in your own power. The only thing keeping you from freedom is will. Tyler, David, Henry—they never found theirs. 'Let my people go.' Some make it. Some don't."

"You telling me I'm going to make it?"

Houdini's eyes glittered. "It's not decided yet. You haven't decided yet. Who are you, Joe?"

Joe shivered. *He could see himself in Houdini's eyes. The image changed. He saw Tyler trapped in his bed, gripping his arm, trying to tell him about his lost acres. Then, Henry, in a coffin, buried, coming back as a spirit, unable, either living or dead, to stay in Greenwood. A ghost train taking him away.*

"And David," Houdini whispered. "Don't forget David."

Houdini's breath touched his face. Light flickered inside his irises. Joe heard Lying Man's grave murmur: "Same age as you, Joe. Same age as you."

Then he saw David's battered body—handcuffed and chained, hanging from a tree, awash with fire. "He wanted to build houses and schools. Same age as you, Joe."

Shaken, Joe turned away. "You said it was a matter of will." Even to himself, he sounded petulant, childish.

"Survival is will. Escape artists survive. You're doing that, Joe. You could've crawled in a grave like your brother. Instead you chose me. David waited to be captured. You ran. Tyler trapped himself, letting his son decide his fate. Choose, Joe. Stay or escape."

"Escape? I can't do anything without a pick."

"You're out of your cuffs."

Joe cradled his mangled hand. "I dislocated my thumb and finger. Read that's how you did it—so I did it too."

"A lie, Joe. I never did. Smoke and mirrors. I said that so no one would ever look for my pick. I always had my pick." He touched Joe's blood-

swollen palm. Joe winced. "I didn't think it was possible to slip a cuff like that." Houdini slid a pick from his vest; he unlocked the metal cuff dangling from Joe's right wrist.

"You said you were trying to reach the dead. Is that a lie too?"

"No. I consider spiritualism the real art. Proving resurrection beyond the grave. Yet, except for you, I haven't met a spiritualist who hasn't cheated. I've debunked them all. Charlatans. I hate chicanery, Joe.

"I've never known anyone who could reach the dead. But, you, Joe, you've done it. You reached Henry. I am in awe. I think your will, your magic is far greater than you know."

Sunlight streamed through the window. "You're not dead," Joe said, awestruck.

"No, Joe, I'm not of the spirit. The first two rules of survival: Dream what you need, and will yourself free. Come. We must get ready for your next escape."

"I'm not going to die?"

"Only if you want to. Fix your hand, Joe."

Joe looked at his crumpled index finger and thumb.

"It's all in the hands. Flexible. Strong. Isn't that right? Fix your hand, Joe. You'll need it. Two swift, steady pulls."

"I can't."

"I dare you." Houdini's lips quirked into a smile.

Joe inhaled. He gripped his thumb, swallowing his cries as he pulled, waiting for the bone to slip back into the joint. Beyond the pain, he heard Houdini's low murmur.

"Magic is in the hands, but also in the head, in the heart. It's all a matter of will—wanting to live. Believing in yourself."

"Yes," Joe gasped, nearly speechless.

"The index finger, Joe."

His hands pressing hard against his abdomen, Joe pulled.

"And, then, sometimes it's just luck you survive. I was buried in a coffin. The panel behind my head was a trap door. The plan was once I'd freed myself from chains, opened the panel, I'd dig myself out. I tested the trick at two feet, three feet, five. But, for the challenge, I insisted upon six. A mistake that almost killed me."

It was done. Joe's hand hurt horribly, but it was whole again. He collapsed on the cot, overcome by the effort.

"My second mistake: I panicked inside the coffin. Being buried alive unmanned me. Once I controlled my breathing, my anxiety subsided. I freed myself. But the soil was too hard, the weight of the earth too much. Digging upward, dirt caking my eyes, nose, I realized I wouldn't make it. I screamed for help. Dirt flooded my mouth. I was going to die."

Houdini, elegant in his black suit, stood over Joe.

"I nearly gave up. Then I found a shard of pottery—my luck—nondescript, red clay. But it was enough. I could dig faster with it. I nearly died anyway. Suffocated. I'll never climb in a grave again, not while there's life in me."

"Are you really Houdini?"

"I'm yours, Joe. Your magic, not mine. Tell Henry you're not a black-faced Houdini; that's vaudeville. A minstrel show. This is something else. Finer. When the Egyptian magicians failed to match Moses' wonders, they told Pharaoh, 'He's touched by the finger of God.'" He handed Joe the lock pick.

"Trust your skills, Joe. Escape.

"It's about creating the magic, the miracle. It's about picking a lock, slipping past sleeping, stupid guards, crawling through tunnels, air ducts, scurrying across rooftops."

Joe felt hopeful. Yes, he could do it again. He'd survive.

"But what are you escaping to, Joe? Who are you?"

Other than a vague dream of traveling West, mimicking Houdini, Joe didn't know who he'd be once he got there. He'd just known he'd wanted to leave Tulsa, leave his father's house.

"You've got to be a man sometime."

"Yes," Joe breathed.

Houdini started to lose substance.

"What's the third rule? You only told me the first two."

"I told you. Luck. Chance. Fate." Houdini was vanishing. "Divine intervention. Call it what you will." He pointed at the barred window. "Daybreak—you haven't much time, Joe. Best be about it."

Joe stood. The circulation in his legs was better. He limped toward the window. The horizon glowed orange; the sun and moon shared the sky. He felt hungry. He guessed he wanted to live.

Turning around, he saw his plain cell. Bare walls. Cot. Urinal. *Houdini was gone.*

He opened his palm. The pick was solid, real. Joe smiled, feeling lightheaded. In a matter of minutes, he'd be out the door, tiptoeing down hallways.

Joe inhaled. He felt strong again.

"Relax, Joe."

Yes, the trick was to remain calm.

Pick ready, he leaned against the door and it swung open. Joe chuckled softly. The sheriff had forgotten to lock his cell. Probably thought a man, hog tied and beaten, had run out of luck. Grace.

"Who are you, Joe?"

For now, he was Joe Samuels—Escape Artist, running for his life.

Joe felt invincible. He'd never be captured again.

20

Clay was cold. He arched his back, trying to ease his stiffening spine. The chair was damnably uncomfortable. He buttoned his jacket, stuffed his hands in his pocket, and tried to dream. To imagine himself gutting fish beside an open fire, tasting burned trout and smoke beneath a blackened sky. His dream was simple: land for hunting, a job that offered self-respect. He'd enlisted eager for glory, eager to escape a lifetime of driving iron into a forge, heat blistering his hands and face. He'd gone from defending democracy to enforcing Ambrose's civic pride. Tulsa—no better than Pittsburgh.

Disgusted, he slammed his feet down from the desk, swiveled in his chair. His chin was stubby; he needed a shave. He poured himself another bourbon. He'd sent five deputies to guard the jail's perimeter and patrol the park. Except for the buzz of his dim lamp, it was quiet in his office. He was all alone in the near dark. Drinking himself into a light stupor.

He was sorry Joe had to take a beating. Not once had the boy cried out. Or begged for mercy. Everything about the boy was a puzzle. He didn't rely on his father's wealth. He told stories while shining shoes. Whoever heard of a colored dreaming of Houdini? Doing magic, illusions?

One winter, before his troop shipped out, Clay watched Houdini, chained and bound in a box, being lowered into the Hudson. Clay had thought him stupid, risking his life. When he'd emerged, Houdini, wet, had ignored the crowd and looked upward, shaking his fist at the sky.

Clay's feet hit the floor. He didn't understand any of it.

Clay guessed dreaming of Houdini was better than not dreaming, believing in nothing. Useful too. Clay still couldn't figure how Joe had escaped. The kid so startled him, Clay could scarcely credit he was colored. But even dumb, lowing cows had known Joe was touched by grace. Clay wanted Joe gone. To San Francisco. Wherever. He didn't belong in Tulsa.

Clay wasn't certain he could keep Joe alive. Joe's bruised, bloody body was an affront; that's why he'd laid the boy on the cot and left the cell fast.

But who was he kidding? He'd given a few orders, had a few drinks, and fallen asleep. In a goddamned metal chair. No grand plans. No standing guard at the window. No dreams of substance. The key to life—sleep it off. Wake up. Another day. The problem might be gone. Shit. Clay hurled his bottle. Glass and brown amber stained the white walls.

He rested his head on his desk. He'd traveled west to nowhere. No wife. No friends. Maybe it was time to pack up and move on. They were going to hang Joe, just like Reubens. He was fooling himself if he thought he could stop it. Mary Keane or not.

Clay straightened, staring at the shadow of the barred windows on his wall. He lit a cigarette. Okay. Some game got away. Some battles weren't won. Mistakes, foul-ups happened.

God, he was a son-of-a-bitch. He'd just grown old, not wise. He had to save Joe. Or drown in the well.

He got up, drawn to the window. Lace-edged leaves arched toward the sky. Courthouse Square was supposed to be an oasis. A garden flanked by the city's best—the best hotel, the newest high-rise, the most modern jail, and a courthouse with the finest, swiftest justice. Citizens strolled in the park enamored of their city's pleasures. Today they'd sit on white chairs, hands folded, eager to be instructed in Ambrose's version of the truth. Civic pride, boosterism of the worst kind. Full employment for whites. Any job whites didn't want offered to coloreds.

Spiraling beyond the park's center were smaller communities. Towns within the city. Black Greenwood. Brink and 24th—dirt alleys snaking between Tulsa and Greenwood—where the races secretly mixed, where Prohibition didn't exist, and women were bartered for gaming chips. The other neighborhoods—all white, some rich, some poor, righteous and unrighteous—expected Clay to keep coloreds in their place.

Clay pressed his forehead against the window, trying to see if his sentries were still on duty, whether they'd decided to give up the ghost. Whoever heard of white men protecting a nigger?

The sky was going to be goddamned blue. Night was just fading, but he could tell already it would be a cloudless, blue day. Ambrose was probably rousing the judge out of bed, expecting Clay to bring the prisoner to the court for a special arraignment. He wouldn't be surprised if Joe was convicted with spare time for a final meal. Then the town could hang him in good conscience. He doubted if Mary Keane would be called to testify.

He'd better untie Joe, get the blood flowing in his arms and legs so he could at least stand for judgment.

"Sheriff."

"Hey, Sully." Clay crushed his cigarette in the tray.

"You should see this."

Clay stared stupidly at the paper. Black lines and dots blurred, meaningless.

"Read it, sheriff."

His eyes focused. "'NIGGER RAPES WHITE WOMAN.' Who wrote this?"

"Greenly's been complaining about circulation."

Clay stared at Sully. He looked like a dumb, pimple-faced kid. He was twenty-nine. His family was poor, but Sully had made good.

"Says, '*Brute tore her clothes.*' Says Miss Keane wasn't even working. Says she was '*visiting her dead father's lawyer.*' Said she was '*mercifully*—'"

"'*Mercifully unconscious,*'" read Clay, "'*when the nigger had his way.*' I'll be damned."

Sully pointed, "Read the last line."

"'*Lynching is the only justice.*'" Clay tore the paper. "Sully, I want you and the deputies to collect these papers. We'll destroy them. Impound Greenly's press."

"Sheriff—"

"Ambrose will help. He won't want a mob stealing his thunder."

"Sheriff—"

"Goddamnit, Sully," Clay pounded the table. "There must be at least the semblance of justice. A semblance, mind you. Joe is owed at least that." Breathing heavily, Clay collapsed in his chair; he stared dully at his desk, then disgustedly swept his cigarettes, ashes, papers onto the floor.

"Sheriff," Sully said patiently, "it's past dawn. Papers already delivered. Newsstands ain't open. But all it takes is one man or woman padding to the porch, picking up the paper, reading the headline. Not even dressed yet. No coffee. No breakfast. One person and the calls start getting made. You know that."

"I know that," Clay muttered into the wood, his head resting on his crisscrossed arms.

"You also know phones have been ringing for hours."

"Yes."

"Probably some colored who sweeps the *Tribune*'s floors, cleans the toilets, told folks before the printer started rolling. Everybody in Greenwood knows. Probably known it for hours."

"Yes." Clay squeezed his eyes, he could see it all happening: folks staggering awake, whispered voices, muttered curses. Phones ringing. Maybe the harmonica man calling folks together. In a church. On the streets. Harmonizing his blues. Greenwood awake while Tulsa slept.

"Yes. Coloreds would know. Samuels would know. They're probably on their way here."

"The Klan will follow soon enough."

"Extra! Extra! Read all about it." Clay looked up at Sully's thin, scarred face. "You're a good man, Sully."

He shrugged. "Don't be counting Lucas out. Ambrose can't control him any better than you can."

"What about the deputies?"

Sully studied the floor, stuffed his hands in his pockets. "They'll stay."

Clay sensed another failure. "Thanks, Sully."

He retrieved his gun from its peg on the wall.

Sully moved to the window.

Clay unlocked a cabinet racked with rifles, ammunition. "Call in the off-duty officers. We'll walk the streets. Use patrol cars, bull horns. Tell everyone to stay calm." He stacked Winchesters on the desk. "Sully, you supply folks from here. I'll ask Ambrose to get Greenly to print a retraction. Notify folks the law will run its course."

"Too late, Sheriff."

"What do you mean?"

Sully angled his head.

Clay brushed Sully aside and peered out the window. "Shit." Coloreds were marching across the park, right in front of Ambrose's Decoration Day platform. "Goddamn. Shit." Clay wanted to retreat. Lead with his feet and run.

Some of the men wore Army green. Service caps. A few had Army rifles with bayonets. They weren't a rag-tailed mob. They moved with grim purpose, marching in lock-step like an advancing army. "Goddamn." Bringing up the rear was a midnight man in an ankle-length service coat. Clay remembered seeing him in the Ambrose. The man's head was high—if Clay didn't know better, he'd have sworn the man was a general.

"Let's go, Sully. We'll stop them at the steps."

Clay's heart was pumping. He was in the war again, struggling to make do, to survive. He dashed down the stairwell, almost tumbling down the flight of stairs. He could hear the approaching men, feet pounding, moving forward. He was glad Sully was at his back.

"Damn," Clay swung open the doors and shouted, "Don't fire," to the deputies on duty. "Sully," he said breathlessly, "there should be seven. Who's not here?"

"Eddie. John. Peter."

"Find them. Tell them to be calm. Don't do anything."

Sully hesitated.

"For God's sake, Sully, do it. One shot and we're lost."

Sully nodded, skirting the building's side.

The coloreds chanted: "Free Joe. Free Joe." Clay could hear other voices, words floating up, syncopating the chant: "Joe's innocent," "Let him go," "Let our people go."

Sucking in his gut, trying to appear calm, Clay studied the band. At least three dozen men. He recognized some of them: meat cutters, chauffeurs, clerks who swept grocery aisles. Faces mottled, they waved the *Tribune*, cursing, shouting, "Free Joe." The men angled through the trees, heading directly toward the street, the jail.

Clay recognized the veterans—expressionless, trained to be deadly, they were focused on him. Even the ones who'd never fought, who'd served in latrines, commissaries, had the warrior's face. Dispassionate, steel-edged. Fear and pain would come later. But nothing was lost yet. The war hadn't begun.

War.

As soon as he thought it, he knew it was true. War was coming. Clay couldn't help feeling he was to blame. He'd let injustice hide within justice, tried to ignore the twin-edged terrors of Ambrose and the Klan. The lines here would be drawn colored and white as they'd been in Europe. But there wouldn't be a common enemy. Just common hatred.

The coloreds spread out below him, blocking the jail's entrance. Their voices and steps diminished, softened to an uncanny stillness. To the left of him, Clay heard a gun being cocked. "Easy, Pete."

Clay exhaled, wondering where Sully was. Joe's words came back to him: "*Were you ever a slave catcher?*" He felt like one now. The coloreds looked at him, waiting for a signal, but Clay knew it wasn't his signal to give. All of the men held themselves in check. Clay felt the tension. The crowd parted. The man in the Army coat stepped forward.

Wiping his palms on his pants, Clay moved downward to greet him. He offered his hand and caught the man off guard. He didn't take his hand, but Clay hadn't expected he would. He'd hoped to buy time, a few seconds of peace.

"You've got Joe Samuels in your jail. We've come for him before he's lynched."

"Nobody's going to be lynched." Clay was surprised he'd said it.

"Hung then. Same difference. Same white justice. Same way one of your deputies killed Joe's grandfather, beat his father last night."

"Terrorized the women," shouted someone else.

"I didn't send any deputies."

"Tell 'em, Gabe, how Deputy Lucas tore the house apart."

"I'll have his job."

"Too late now."

Clay turned to the sandy-colored man.

"Damage is done," sneered Sandy. "Tyler's dead. Mr. Samuels' blind in one eye."

Clay turned back to Gabe. "Corporal. You were a corporal, weren't you?" It was a calculated risk. Clay saw pride, disdain ripple across the veteran's face. "I have to consider tactics. If I let you take Joe, hundreds might get hurt."

"So you'll sacrifice Joe. What's one less nigger?" a taller man exploded. "Isn't that what white folks want—one less nigger?

"Quiet, Nate."

"Gabe, he's mocking you, man."

"I'm not mocking anyone," said Clay. "I don't want folks hurt."

"What about this?" Someone shoved the *Tribune* at Clay.

Clay focused on Gabe. "I intend to impound the paper. Joe's innocent until proven guilty. Miss Keane swears Joe didn't touch her. I believe her."

"Did you believe Joe?"

"Yes." Clay shouted in the direction of the voice. There were murmurs in the crowd.

"He's lying out of his mouth," said Nate.

"I don't think he's lying."

Clay recognized the harmonica man.

"Lying Man, go on now," said Nate. "White men lie. Hated us since we got home from the war. Angry 'cause we want our rights. You read the Chicago papers, New York. They had their hot summers."

"We agreed, Nate," insisted Lying Man. "No harm to anyone."

"That's right," Gabe murmured. "I don't want a riot. I want to save Joe."

"This way," said Clay, looking at the armed men, "will surely get him killed."

"Lieutenant," sneered Gabe, "you must've been a lieutenant, right? If we let you keep Joe, can you swear he won't be dead in a day?"

"No lynch mob will get him. I promise you. I represent the law."

"Lieutenant, that's not enough. Will your law do right by Joe?"

Clay should've bluffed. His body betrayed him. He glanced at the cracked pavement, away from Gabe's piercing stare.

Gabe responded grimly, "I'll guess we'll take him, sheriff. Be man enough to step aside. No harm will come to you or your men."

"If you do this, if you take Joe, there'll be no holding back the town."

"They're not going to be held back anyway," answered Gabe. "Never have been. Never will be. How many Negroes you got in your jail? That's what it was built for—to hold Negroes, keep us in place.

"I'm going to climb these steps, sheriff, and collect Joe. I'm asking you to help me. Asking you kindly. Step aside."

Clay pondered. His honor had shrunken to a small, piddling thing. If he let the men take Joe, it might be the best thing he'd done in years. But there'd be hell to pay. Come nightfall, there might not be a Greenwood. He looked at the small band. Soldiers. Prepared to do what was necessary. They were asking him to surrender. He looked at Gabe: eyes sunken, cheekbones prominent.

"I wasn't a lieutenant," Clay answered slowly. "A sergeant. Steel hicks from Pennsylvania were mostly grunts. You were 369th? Right?"

"What about it?" asked Nate, jostling forward. "Lots of Greenwood men served."

Clay didn't take his eyes from Gabe. Cynical, that was it. Gabe looked even more cynical than him. Clay wondered if the war still haunted Gabe, if he drank deep and heavy.

"Deal, sheriff?" Gabe spoke so softly, Clay wasn't sure he'd heard or just imagined his words.

Tulsa was supposed to be the magic city. City of possibilities. Potential. Clay stared across at the park, at the grand trees, tendrils arching from branches, marigolds edging the blue grass. Oasis, hell. There was no refuge here. He had to choose.

Horns blared. A flatbed truck, loaded with white men, turned onto the street in front of the jail. Lucas stood on the running board, waving. He held a rope, already tied into a noose. There were farm boys, some off-duty deputies. Klansmen in white, flowing robes. Bates' fat face was thrust out of the truck's window.

The Greenwood men stood taut, heads turned toward the motley caravan. Clay saw Lying Man place a hand on Nate's shoulder.

Lucas hopped down as the truck pulled to the curb. "What's this—a nigger rally?" As Lucas pushed through the Greenwood men, Clay realized Lucas didn't have any fear, any sense that the colored men might be dangerous. Lucas and his crew expected servility, expected the coloreds wouldn't challenge a lynching. Wouldn't dare. Hell, Lucas probably thought he could hang them all. They'd line up for him—one by one.

Lying Man sang out, "Easy, men. Losing our heads won't save Joe. The battle against Pharaoh can be won. But easy now. Y'all, hear? Easy now." Lying Man hummed a refrain. Clay felt an answering tremor. There were murmurs, "Yeah," "All right," "Unhuh," and, like magic, Clay saw the men's shoulders relax.

Lucas stepped even with Clay. "We've come for Joe."

Bates, who'd lumbered behind Lucas, chortled, "Got no choice, sheriff. Justice demands its due." Four other men fell in beside Bates.

Clay's deputies moved behind him. Sully and Eddie appeared on Clay's right. The battle lines were falling into place. All he needed now was an archduke.

"You're fired, Lucas."

"I figure I'll have your job when this is through."

"Not killing innocent men, you won't."

"The niggers been whining, have they? Did you hear the cripple shot at me, killed Miss Keane's brother? Even the *Tribune* doesn't know that. Ambrose doesn't know. But me and my men do."

"Your Klansmen."

"What does it matter?" Lucas asked fiercely. "Jody died before dawn, bleeding like a gored pig. Man gave his leg for his country. Once any self-respecting American hears about Jody Keane, they'll thank us. Can't have niggers assaulting our women, killing men defending their sister's honor. So, sheriff," he spat the word, "and any other nigger-lovers . . ." Lucas pulled his gun. "Step aside." He looked at Sully, the nervous, awkward deputies on the steps, then back at Clay. "Sorry, sheriff. Might've been different if you'd been Tulsan."

"You can't have Joe," Clay said grimly. "Sully, you and the others, take Lucas into custody."

No one moved.

Clay cursed. He swung around, arms outstretched. "What about the law? Sully—"

Sully shook his head, muttering, "Sorry, sheriff. The town will be turning against us, not Lucas."

"Sully, I thought you knew right from wrong," raged Clay.

"White man's justice," chanted Nate. "White man's justice." The words were heralded, taken up by the crowd.

"Shut up," said Lucas, firing his gun into the air. "Shut up."

"If you want Joe Samuels," Gabe stepped forward, "you need to go through me."

"I don't deal with niggers," said Lucas.

"This is a police matter," said Clay.

"Joe's innocent," said Lying Man. "Boy wouldn't hurt a soul."

"He had no business near a white woman." Lucas glared.

"Men," shouted Gabe. "Close ranks."

The Greenwood men formed a solid circle around Clay, Lucas, and their men, trapping them against the steps, their backs toward the jailhouse door, cutting them off from the carloads of whites.

"Niggers are dumber than mules. I'll shoot each one of you." Lucas aimed at Lying Man's heart. "Ten seconds. All of you, get the hell out. Go on home."

"Don't do this, deputy," warned Gabe.

"Lucas. This is a police matter," insisted Clay.

Clay heard Lying Man murmur, "I'm a witness, y'all hear. A witness. My people will be free."

"No nigger's worth a white man. Ought to have barred niggers from Oklahoma Territory. Are you with me, men?" shouted Lucas. "Are you with me?"

"We're with you," answered Bates, and there were other assents. Explosive curses, snarling at the colored men.

"Ten . . . nine . . . eight," counted Lucas. "Niggers, get. If you know what's good. Go on home."

"We only want Samuels," seconded Bates.

Clay lunged at Lucas, but Sully grabbed him and hung on. "Lucas!" Clay shouted.

"Six. Five. Move, niggers. Move."

"I will be redeemed," hollered Lying Man.

The Greenwood men—some, linking arms, some clutching bats, rifle handles—rocked with emotion. "Tell it, Lying Man." "Preach."

"We are all witnesses."

"Shut up," shouted Lucas. "All of you. Move or this man is dead."

"Treated us like dirt in the war," shouted Nate. "Always treated us like dirt," echoed Sandy. "Never respected us for nothing," said another.

"I'll be redeemed."

Gabe stepped in front of Lying Man, so Lucas' gun pointed right at his chest.

"Three . . . two—"

Clay watched, helpless, as Nate, like quicksilver, darted forward, aimed his pistol, and shot Lucas.

The blast ripped through Lucas' lungs. Mouth puckering, his eyes rolled backward in his head. He toppled sideways onto Clay. Clay heard more gunfire. Bursts of smoke dotted the air. Clay shoved Lucas off.

"Now it's war," said Clay, mournful.

"Always was," answered Gabe.

Clay looked toward the park—the Greenwood troops scattered, some taking cover behind trees and parked cars, the truck cab. Those with guns fired wildly. One colored man and two whites lay crumpled, bleeding on the steps. Clay wondered if Ambrose would be able to get the blood cleaned off before his celebration. Sorrowfully, he shook his head. His deputies and Lucas' stragglers were running and firing, scattering across the park, down the street, behind the jail.

"Lying Man, I'm going after Joe," said Gabe.

"No, I'll get Joe for you," said Clay. "Get your men in formation, corporal. Klan reinforcements will be here soon."

Gabe hesitated, then nodded. "All right, sergeant."

Clay opened the jail door, his hands sticky with Lucas' blood. He couldn't help smiling. This was his chance to climb out of Lion's deep, murky well. Clay pictured how astonished Joe would be when he set him free, put him on a train to Frisco, away from trouble, away from Tulsa.

21

A breeze touched Joe's hair as he stepped onto the roof. Tar clung to the soles of his feet. He shivered; his clothes felt cold and stiff. He smelled musty—every part of his body ached. He could see the dirty rooftops of Tulsa edging the park. Northeast was Greenwood. He wished he was at his attic window. But there was no going home now. He'd head for the train, ride west toward water.

Joe wanted to shout. Thank the sun for rising. But he didn't—he was free, but not safe.

He'd unlocked two doors to reach the roof. Now he had to get down. Seven stories. He tugged the flat bands of a fire hose through the steel door. Another bit of luck. But also will; Houdini had dared him not to quit.

Gunshots cracked, echoing across the roof. Joe ducked, then realized the sound came from the street. There was a volley of shots. He crawled to the ledge. A crowd below surged and broke apart like marbles. Two bodies lay in the street; three more on the jail steps. Joe could see Gabe, Nate, and Lying Man. Ernie and Chalmers. Old Sandy, crouched behind a tree, a Lucky dangling from his mouth.

Greenwood had come to Tulsa. *Had they come for him?* Joe felt elated, then fearful; he didn't want anybody hurt.

Whites were fleeing. Gabe, gun in hand, lead the Negro retreat north. Sporadic fire continued.

"Gabe!" he shouted. "Lying Man. Wait for me!"

Nate swung around. Gabe, crouching, stared left and right.

"Here. I'm up here."

Lying Man pointed skyward and Joe, hands sore, waved mightily.

"Joe." "I don't believe it." "Joe." "Hot damn," shouted Ernie. "Joe!"

Joe wished he could fly off the rooftop, right into the men's arms. Stunned, mouths open, his friends looked comical. Their disbelief became awe and amazement.

Lying Man ran, loping, toward the jailhouse. The others followed: sallow-faced Billy, Chalmers, Bertie, and Pete from Booker T., Clarence, one of Zion's deacons, and James, a lawyer graduated from Howard. Joe waved them to the side, the alleyway.

He looped the hose through the drain bordering the roof, tied it off, and cast the end over the building's side. The hose fell short but Joe didn't have time to spare. He had to get away, climb down. He clutched the hose; his body felt awkward and stiff. His feet pushed off brick and he started downward. His left hand gripped poorly. One floor. Another. At the third floor, Joe dangled by his right hand. The pavement seemed miles away. He exhaled. His friends were looking up, breathless, expectant. Everyone silent.

Joe's left hand was useless. He held on with his legs, scraping his knees against the brick wall. With his right hand, he lowered himself, inch by inch. His hand rubbed raw against the hose.

"Got to hurry, Joe. Troops coming back," called Gabe.

Joe nodded. He focused on moving past each row of bricks, thin bands of mortar. He counted himself down—one row, two, three rows.

Strength was leaking out of him. He came to the end of the hose, thirty feet from the ground, wondering how to make it down. Wondering how to grip the ledges between brick.

"Let go, Joe," Lying Man called. "We've got you."

He looked down at the upraised brown and black faces.

"We've got you, Joe," echoed Gabe. "We've got you."

Back arching, arms outstretched, Joe let go. He fell through the air, for a moment, floating, feeling free, even of gravity—before landing in the arms of Lying Man, Gabe, and Nate. They lowered him to the ground; Gabe pulled him to his feet.

He was the center of a crowd. Palms reached, patting, turning him around. All the men wanted a look. Joe saw himself reflected in their eyes; he was one of them. Just Joe—but special.

"A miracle," said Lying Man.

"Magic," called Chalmers. Sandy crowed. Nate thumped his back, "Who'd have thought." "Let my people go." "Yes, Lord," said Ernie. "Didn't know you had it in you."

Joe could feel their wonder. He'd done it. Escaped the prison. Slipped the cuffs. He felt as comfortable as he did in the barbershop. The same expansiveness, the same enveloping love. Joe smiled. He hugged Lying Man. "Our Houdini!" whooped Nate.

Gabe hadn't said anything. Joe turned to him, waiting. The other men fell hush as Gabe reached out, clasping Joe's shoulder. "I'm proud of you, little brother. Henry would be too."

Staccato chants of "Joe. Joe," rent the air.

"Quiet!" Gabe shouted. "We've got to get to Greenwood. They'll be coming now."

"Joe can magic us back," exclaimed Sandy.

"Those whites won't be in any hurry to see us again," boasted Nate. "Did you see the way they ran? Scared out of their wits."

"That's right," said Gabe. "Scared. But they'll be back with an army. We'll make our stand in Greenwood. Come on."

Joe hesitated. How could he tell Gabe he wanted to hop a train, ride the rails out of Tulsa? "Sure. Greenwood. Let's get back safe." The train wasn't leaving 'til nightfall. He'd help his friends, then go.

"We'll cut back across the park," said Gabe. "Tulsa's waking up." He led the charge, the dash from the alley, across the street, and onto cushioned grass. Through the trees, they saw vendors opening shops on Main. A custodian washed the Ambrose's revolving door; an old man was walking his dog.

Someone gave a shout: "Hey!"

Gabe urged the men to run faster. Sandy held a hand to his chest. Herb was sweating heavily. The younger men ran swiftly, strong. Eager to prove themselves.

At the park's edge, Gabe raised his hand. The men crouched in a circle. "Chalmers, give Joe your .38."

"But—"

"Do it."

Joe took the gun; it was heavier than he expected.

"The next two miles," said Gabe, "will be the toughest. Not much cover."

"Look." Lying Man pointed.

A flat-bed screeched to a halt in front of the jail. "They're coming," said Joe. On the park's west side, men, heads and weapons poking out car windows, cruised Main.

"Nate, get everybody safe to Greenwood. To Mt. Zion. Me and Joe will slow these folks down. Hole up in the church. Make a stand there if you have to."

Nate nodded grimly, called, "Come on," before darting, half-stooped into the alley behind Pearson's Clothing, leading his troops. "This way."

"Lyman," hollered Joe. "Be careful."

"Will do. Owe you a birthday shave." Lying Man took off, supporting Sandy.

"Come on, Joe," said Gabe. "We're the decoy."

Joe grinned, for now, content to dodge behind Gabe, zigzagging, following his lead.

Joe and Gabe moved to the center of the street, facing an oncoming truck. Joe heard men cursing, calling them coons. Niggers. He saw the tips of firearms. Heard voices shout, "Run 'em down." The truck's horn blared. Then another truck from the east side, near the jail, headed toward them. Others were running across the park.

"When I yell, follow me across Main," said Gabe, calmly.

Joe's heart started to race. The truck sped up; men held on like a wild, carny ride. Joe recognized the driver was Noland, a law clerk from the Ambrose. He'd shined his thin-soled leathers many a time.

The truck was almost upon them. Gabe took aim, fired at the front wheel. Rubber exploded; brakes squealed as the truck swerved, tilted, then rammed into a post.

"Now!" shouted Gabe. "Now!"

Joe sprinted after Gabe, his feet slapping on the dusty street. *Run, nigger, run.* He heard shots behind them. Gabe turned the corner onto Ash, pulling them up short, tight against the building. He held his gun steady, gut level.

A man with a rifle raced into view; Gabe fired point blank, hitting him in the chest. The man fell, rifle clattering, rolling into Joe's legs and nearly knocking him down. Joe stared as the man's mouth filled with blood.

Gabe turned and ran. Joe followed, unable to shake the feel of the man's weight slapping his legs. He kept his eyes focused on the pavement, on Gabe's heels. Tried to ignore his blood-streaked footprints. Stay alive.

Gabe skirted northwest then doubled back, coming full circle into an alley behind Main, not far from the dead man. He leaped down a stairwell, tugging at a padlocked door. He hammered it with the hilt of his gun.

Joe pushed him aside and pulled out Houdini's pick. His hands shook. He steadied his breathing.

"Which way?" someone called from the street. Gabe readied to fire.

Joe probed the lock. The tumblers were stiff, but eased into place. He pulled the lock free; the door swung open. He and Gabe tumbled into darkness, closing the door, shutting out the stairwell's gray light.

Neither man breathed, listening. The darkness stank of grain, machine oil, and dry rot. Gabe struck a match. A small glow. They were in the basement of Ailey's Hardware. Picks, shovels, rakes were stacked against one wall. Another wall had two-by-fours, boxes marked: nails, sheet metal, tools. Pipes for plumbing, digging wells lined the far side. A maze of crates stacked two, three, four high, covered the floor.

The light blew out.

"We'll rest here," said Gabe, his breathing shallow. Joe heard Gabe crawling on his knees, before resting his back against crates.

Shouts came from above. Joe heard the heavy slap of boots against the pavement. Someone fired a rifle. "Over here, over here." Then another shot. A fresh patter of feet. Scurrying like rats. "They found the body," murmured Gabe.

Joe couldn't move. The darkness had its own pressures, possibilities. Joe felt panic rising, unable to step right, left, forward or back.

"Sit, Joe. Straight down. Straight on down."

It was all in how you relaxed.

A horn blared. Footsteps. Cleats tap-tapping. "Check here." Outside, the railing rattled. Gabe and Joe didn't move.

"Naw. Waste of time. They're gone." There was another shout. The sound of men running.

Joe sat, cross-legged, sweat rimming his neck, his body sore.

"Underground Railroad," Gabe rasped. "Best hiding place was right before the slave catcher's eyes."

Joe arched his back, shivering from his still-damp clothes, the exhilaration of being safe.

"*This train's bound for glory.*" Gabe struck a match. His eyes were velvet brown; his shadow stretched across the ceiling. "Brother man. An hour's wait and we're out of here. Moving on. Got that, Joe?"

"Yes."

"Take my coat."

The streets above fell silent. Gabe dipped a cigarette into the flame; a circle glowed. The match blew out.

Joe wrapped the coat about him. Rough, heady with Gabe's scent. Not the pomades men got in Lying Man's shop. More like loam, sweet and sour. Like the soil beside Lena's River. Brother man. Inhale, exhale.

The cigarette flared. Smoke streamed from Gabe's mouth.

Joe buried his face in the Army wool. He'd done it: sprung the trap, outrun the slave catcher, vanished like Houdini. Joe chuckled softly. He hoped the sheriff laughed when he'd found his cell empty.

22

The kitchen was in mourning. Sunlight poked through the screen door and a honeysuckle breeze stirred the curtains. Linoleum sparkled and the metal rim on the cold stove reflected rainbows. There weren't cooking smells: no sweet yeast and rising biscuits, no berries, pungent, ripening to syrup, no smoked bacon frying. The pantry door was closed. Despite the sun, there was a wounded pall to the day.

If Mary held her breath, she could hear muffled voices, footsteps tiptoeing, shuffling through the Samuels' house. Undertaker, preacher, doctor. Solemn men at work since dawn—the undertaker transforming the study into a viewing room for Tyler's casket; the preacher ministering to a weeping Mrs. Samuels and Emmaline; and the doctor, trying to convince Mr. Samuels—arm broken, blind in one eye—his bank didn't need him for one day.

Hildy was slumped over the kitchen table, her head cradled on crisscrossed arms, her lids fluttering with dreams.

Mary peeked out the screen door. A hearse was parked at the curb; behind it was another car with a white cross painted on its hood. The preacher had walked, his long-tailed coat flapping like blackbirds' wings. Mary had watched him stop and bless the house—eyes closed, his mouth muttering prayers, then he'd strode forward and blessed the grass stained with Jody's blood; the steps littered with shotgun casings; and the porch, its yellow light still on, insects flattened and dried on the glass.

Mary could go to Jody but, somehow, just before sunrise, she'd sensed he'd died—bitter, doubled over his wound, reaching for his missing leg.

Mary exhaled, digging her nails into wire mesh. She needed to help Hildy. Like a sentry, Mary watched the street, hoping she'd serve Hildy better than she'd served her mother. Everyone needed some time not to be strong. Some time to be safe.

Mary knew better than anyone that folks forgot the strong ones. If a woman didn't cry, folks didn't think you needed. If you kept your mouth shut and endured, folks forgot about helping. Forgot all about you, if you tried too hard to keep your dignity.

Since the evening's terror, she'd watched Hildy moving gracefully among father, mother, sister. Kissing dead Tyler. Calling the doctor, the preacher. It was Hildy who soothed her mother, tucked her in bed. Hildy who calmed her sister by telling her how strong and helpful she'd been. Hildy who cleaned her father's wounds while he cursed, complained just like Pa.

Feeling useless, Mary had shadowed Hildy, then left to do what she could—restore Hildy's kitchen. She'd gathered the broken porcelain, mopped tea, swept dried beans and shattered jars of peaches, wiped the counters, placed the Bible on the table, and waited.

When Hildy stole away to the kitchen, Mary had seen the struggle she'd endured—hooded eyes, rigid mouth, knees locked to hold her upright, nails digging deeply into her own skin.

Hildy had looked across at Mary and whispered, "Joe?"

Mary'd wanted to cry. Joe was still on the run. Had to be. If he wasn't. . . . She'd imagined Joe hanging from a tree, his tongue thick, his chin on his chest.

Mary'd said, "Rest. Rest, Hildy." She'd helped her to the chair. Hildy laid her head down on the table and sighed. Mary understood the comfort of cool wood and warm arms.

Before she drifted to sleep, Hildy had murmured, "Let me know when the women come. Wake me when the women come."

Such a strange idea. *Wake me when the women come.* Mary remembered the years she'd been waiting for women, a woman to come. Always just Pa and Jody came. Later Dell.

Mary turned and saw her mother sprawled on the floor. The linoleum spotted red. "Oh, Ma." Tears welled. Dying without any women. Just a terrified daughter who hadn't any power in her hands. *Ma's body was bathed in light.* Mary reached out to touch her, tried to sweep the loneliness from her heart. *Her mother faded.* "Ma."

Three short raps, like firecrackers, rattled the door. "What?" Mary turned and saw a woman on the porch, apron-askew, holding a platter of sliced ham and biscuits.

Mary unlatched the screen. The woman, brows raised, pointed at Hildy: "She all right?"

"Yes, I think so."

"The rest of the family?" A gravelly whisper.

Mary cocked her head, uncertain about what to say, whether she'd a right to say it. "Struggling," she said.

The woman nodded. "To be expected. To be expected." She extended the platter. "I'm Mrs. Jackson from across the street. Others are on their way."

Mary carried the platter to the counter. Mrs. Jackson sat across from Hildy, murmuring, "Sleep can be a mercy." Then, she turned, "Biscuits be better warmed in the oven."

"Yes, ma'am." Mary smiled, found a match to light the stove.

Another knock and three women, crosses stitched on brown cloaks, stepped into the kitchen, carrying baskets with gingham linings. "We've brought the pies," said the leader, a woman with saucer eyes, a calming voice. Mary recognized her from the night before. She'd worn a green housecoat and asked if she was all right. Beneath the cloaks, Mary saw all the women wore white dresses, white stockings and shoes.

"I'm Nadine Franklin, president, Zion's Sanctified Women." The woman smiled sweetly. "We help the Lord's business." "Amen," the two women chimed. "I believe Eugenia will bring the salad." Nadine held out her basket.

"Oh, yes." Flustered, Mary took the basket, carried it to the counter, then turned back for the other two. *Wake me when the women come.* All four women were looking at her. Not unkindly, but curious. "I'll wake Hildy," she said.

"A few minutes rest would be better," complained Mrs. Jackson. "The Lord appreciates rest."

Mary plucked nervously at her skirt. "Hildy would want me to wake her. She told me to wake her."

"Hildy knows it's time for doing," piped Nadine, her hand upraised. "Never shirks her duty."

Gliding past the church women, Mary gently shook Hildy. "Hildy. Hildy," she breathed.

Yawning, struggling awake, Hildy smiled. Mary smiled back. Then Hildy looked at the women. "I knew you'd come."

Mrs. Jackson patted Hildy's hand. "They should've let you rest."

Rising, Hildy hugged the sanctified women. "Martha. Nadine. Gloria." "Amen," said each woman in turn. "Praise the Lord." She pressed her cheek against Mrs. Jackson's.

Mary felt a lightening of spirit.

"Is anybody going to open this door?" A tall, stout woman with a younger, cherry-lipped version of herself, hollered from the porch. "Cheese. I brought my macaroni and cheese. Here," she handed the casserole to Mary. "Don't let me forget paprika. Just before serving. A teaspoon sprinkle. Just a teaspoon."

"Yes, ma'am." Mary nodded shyly.

"Eugenia, please. My daughter, Lilianne. You're Mary, aren't you?"

"Mama, she's the one—"

"Hush, Lilianne." Her mother pinched her. "Good is as good does. We are all guests in this house."

"Eugenia, I thought you were bringing salad," said Nadine.

"Macaroni is salad."

"No, I mean green."

"I felt like macaroni."

Another knock. Heart fluttering, Mary turned, careful not to upset the casserole, opening the door to two gloved women wearing double-strand pearls. They were lovely, elegant like oil men's wives.

"Claire!" said Eugenia. "Bertha! Coming to the back door. Wonders never cease."

"Don't tease, Eugenia." Hildy embraced the fashionable women, saying, "Mother will be so glad you've come. That you've all come."

Hildy was radiant, standing in the room's center, surrounded by women.

"The Samuels are our first family," said Claire.

"You and your first family stuff," snapped Eugenia. "Samuels ain't better. Just colored folks with money. That's so, isn't it, Lilianne?" Her daughter nodded.

"You don't appreciate—" said Claire.

"I appreciate plenty. Unlike you, I don't need pearls to appreciate the sunrise."

"Ladies, ladies," said Hildy, comforting an offended Claire.

"Family," said Mrs. Jackson. "We're here as family."

"Family," echoed Nadine. "Amen," chorused her two companions.

Mary ducked her head, suppressing a smile.

There was another knock. Two new women were at the door.

"Miss Wright. Miss Wright, you came." Hildy guided the frail, elderly woman.

"Of course, I came. Is that you, Lilianne? I can always tell you by your flower water. How's the library? Did you order those books I told you about?"

"I did, Miss Wright."

Miss Wright's eyes were glassy blue, her wrinkled hand grasped a cane. Behind her, a woman, nearly as tiny and old, was poised to steady her. "My sister, Leda, brought me."

Hildy, stooped, embracing Miss Wright and the buzzing women fell silent.

Mary felt blessed. Wind rattled the door. Sunlight streamed in. Rainbows extended up the wall.

Mary turned to the cabinets, selecting, for the viewing, the rose-trimmed plates and cups. The women had come. Men had come through the front. But these good women had come through the kitchen, the house's heart, and restored Hildy. It amazed Mary to know Hildy hadn't doubted. She hadn't even needed to shout. Mary had thought she and Hildy were kin in their loneliness; but there'd been a difference. Hildy's loneliness had a limit; when the worst happened, she'd known—always must've known, the women would come.

"Where is she? This white woman. Show her to me."

"Here, Miss Wright. . . . Here." Hands gently passed, guided Miss Wright across the room.

"Her name's Mary," said Hildy.

Trembling, Mary set down the stack of dishes. She didn't want to be thrown out; she didn't want to be asked to leave.

Hildy stood beside her. "Feel her hands, Miss Wright. Feel her hands."

Mary's hands were squeezed in a powerful grip. The blue eyes, reflecting her own, were unnerving. The roomful of women were expectant, waiting for judgment. Scowling, Lilianne stood apart.

"Working hands."

"Yes, ma'am," answered Mary.

"You were schooled?"

"Not much."

"Miss Wright taught school," said Hildy proudly.

"Third grade. I taught Hildy's Daddy. Then Hildy. Emmaline. I taught Joe. Joe was . . . is my favorite." Dry lips smacked. "Isn't that right, sister?"

The tiny woman behind her nodded. "You taught the town."

"And you kept house. Thank you, sister," replied Miss Wright. Leda smiled. Mary envied the sisters, imagining them growing old together.

Miss Wright handed her cane to Hildy. She stepped closer. Mary smelled lavender. Ma's scent. Miss Wright's face was golden, her skin, tissue-thin, her hands strong. Callused fingertips traced Mary's brows, her nose, chin, and lips. Mary wanted to tilt her head, bury her face in the sweet-smelling hand.

"You caused Joe trouble."

"Yes, ma'am. I didn't mean to."

"White women never mean to," muttered Lilianne. "Trouble follows just the same."

"Lilianne!" her mother answered sharply.

"She's tried to set things right," offered Hildy.

Miss Wright lowered her hands.

Mary ducked her head. She understood being disliked. She'd learned to weather Pa's indifference. Yet, how could she explain she needed to be here? Hildy might not need her—she knew that now. None of the Greenwood women *needed* her. Being useful was not the same as being needed. But she needed to see these women loving Hildy. They confirmed her belief that things might've been different if her mother had lived; she, too, could've been surrounded by women.

"I heard you yelling," said Miss Wright. "From my bed, I heard you yelling. Yelling to save the Samuels."

"She *did* save us, Miss Wright," said Hildy, fiercely. "I would've been dead. The entire family would've been with Tyler."

"A good man, Tyler."

"Praise be," said Eugenia.

There was breathless silence again.

Clasping her cane's hilt, Miss Wright spoke. "No sense holding a grudge against someone who's tried to set things right. If I know anything, I know all the fault for Joe's troubles doesn't lie at your door. There's a story, history behind everything."

"Amen."

"Greenwood's always been the fly in Tulsa's milk."

"Truly, Miss Wright," nodded Claire.

"That was your brother shot?"

"Yes, ma'am."

"I'm sorry for it."

"Thank you, Miss Wright," Mary said, unsteadily. Then, she began crying, mourning her only brother; mourning Tyler. Joe on the run. This household in sorrow. She wailed louder and the women's hands reached for her.

She could feel Miss Wright's bony body pressing against her, Hildy's hand embracing round her back, and the other women circling closer. Lilianne stared beyond the screen door.

"Nobody deserves dying," said Eugenia.

"The Lord protects the righteous."

Mary shuddered, feeling the sanctified women's passion.

"Mercy," said Miss Wright. "Lord have mercy upon your brother's soul."

"Upon Tyler," said Hildy.

"Me," said Mary. "Upon me."

"Us all," replied Hildy.

Mary looked at Miss Wright's upturned face. The angle of her head, the pressure from her fingers made Mary feel she could see.

"Time to be doing," said Mrs. Jackson, breaking the spell. "Men might be needing us later."

"What do you mean?" asked Hildy. "What's wrong?"

No one answered.

The group broke apart. Eugenia looked at the curtains. Claire at her suede pumps. Nadine closed her eyes, her hands crossed over her breasts.

"It's Joe, isn't it?" Mary whispered.

"Sheriff caught him," said Eugenia.

"No," breathed Hildy. Mary reached out to her.

"The papers said they'd lynch him," said Claire.

"So Gabe gathered the men," said Eugenia.

"They're planning to stop it, if they can."

Hildy rocked back on her heels. "They're going to lynch him. Negro's name in the paper means he's dead or soon will be. Lord, have mercy," Hildy raged, rushing toward the door. The women reached out. "Let me go," shouted Hildy. "Let me go." She squirmed; taut arms held her back.

"Hildy, listen to us."

"Let go."

"Trust the men to handle this."

"I need to see Joe."

"Hildy Samuels, be still this instant," snapped Miss Wright.

"Miss Wright," Hildy moaned. Eugenia and Claire each held an arm. Hildy hung limp between them, her knees scraping the floor. "I've got to go—" The *o* trailed into a moan, making the women shudder and sigh, "Mercy."

Miss Wright clutched Hildy's shoulders. "Hildy, listen to me. Life ain't fair by half. But you're needed here. There's work to do here. In this house. Or have you forgotten?"

"They're going to lynch him."

"I'll go, Hildy."

"No you won't, Mary," said Miss Wright sternly, "no one's going anywhere. Our men are handling this."

"Bennie went," said Mrs. Jackson softly. "My Ray," said Eugenia. "Daddy," said Lilianne. "Clarence," said Nadine. "James," said Claire.

"Most of the men went to save Joe," said Lilianne.

Hildy exhaled. "I'm being a fool."

"Sure are," said Eugenia, signaling the other women to let her go.

"I didn't think."

"You should know better, Hildy," said Claire.

"Though," Eugenia declared snidely, "if Joe hadn't been 'first family,' James might not have gone."

"Don't be rude, Eugenia," answered Claire.

Nadine fluttered, "Ladies, ladies. There's God's work to do."

"Amen," said Miss Wright.

Nadine pressed open the swing door. She looked back at Hildy. "Time to cleanse Tyler. Prepare for his service. Prepare ourselves for meeting the Lord."

Hildy clasped her hands. "Through faith, we will rise."

The women started to file through the door. Awed, Mary realized their passion and strength would fill the house, lift the Samuels' spirits. As they emptied out of the kitchen, she heard calls of "Good morning" to the undertaker, blessings from the preacher. Mary realized the men, too, had been waiting for the women to come.

She turned back to the empty kitchen. There were more baskets to open, food to be heated. She'd set the dining room table for guests so everybody could help themselves. The men would return hungry—looking for their wives, daughters.

Lilianne's head poked round the door. "I need cloth. Water bowls."

Mary looked at her blankly.

"For the cleansing." Lilianne stepped inside the kitchen, her arms clasped across her breasts, glaring. "Hildy said you'd help. Said you knew where things were."

Mary nodded, selected two large, china bowls and filled them with water. From a drawer, she drew linen edged with lace. *Ma went to the grave not quite clean. At seven, her hands hadn't been quite big enough to do what needed doing. Her rags stained red.* Guiltily, she wondered who would care for Jody. Overwhelmed, she buried her face in her hands.

"You feel 'shamed?"

Mary shook her head.

"You ought to. Feel ashamed for the trouble you've caused. The trouble you've brought to Joe. This town."

"No, not shame—"

"My daddy's carrying a gun because of you."

"Sorrow," sighed Mary. "Deep sorrow."

"That's not enough."

"I didn't expect it would be." Mary lifted one of the bowls. "Let me help you carry these upstairs. Please."

Lilianne stood stiffly.

She was proud. Lovely. Not more than twenty. Mary couldn't remember being that young. Gently, she handed Lilianne the bowl, then lifted the second bowl, the towels. Careful not to spill the water, Mary followed Lilianne through the dining room, up the curved stairs. Water slapped inside the bowl. The undertaker tipped his hat as she and Lilianne entered Tyler's room. The burgundy curtains and windows were thrown open. Breezes stirred the curtains. Sunshine lit the walls, the paintings of endless wheat.

The women circled a four-poster bed: Nadine, Hildy, and Eugenia near the head. They were all focused on Tyler. Murmuring prayers. Mary set the bowl and linen down, feeling grief swell.

Tyler was naked except for the sheet draped across his abdomen and the towel wrapped around his crushed skull. Thin legs, a plump belly, skin dry and wrinkled like walnut skin. Brave Tyler. Hildy and Eugenia began washing his body. Mary backed toward the door. But the vision of the women held her. Bodies swayed. Serene, Miss Wright clasped her sister. Claire touched a cross to her lips. Nadine's fingertips reached toward the heavens. She saw snatches of Hildy's, Eugenia's hands. Loving hands cleaning, caressing Tyler's body.

Nadine nodded to Hildy. Then, in turn, she looked at all the women, and her alto voice soared:

Lay down body, lay down
Lay your burdens down.

Lilianne's soprano matched, melded with Nadine's alto. Martha started up the song again. Claire's voice was the sweetest: the vowels elongating—laaaayyy dooowwn booodeeee. Voices overlapped like a round. Gloria stomped her feet; Mrs. Jackson clapped staccato; Miss Wright tapped her cane. They all sang: "Lay your burdens down," their voices growing stronger. Hildy and Eugenia washed, humming, punctuating the song with "Jesus." "Praise be." They gently wiped Tyler's legs and toes as the sounds vibrated, rattled the walls:

Lay down body,
Lay your burdens down
Lay down body,
Lay your burdens down

Nadine raised her hands toward the Holy Spirit. Leda clutched her sister's arm. Lilianne cried. The song quickened: "laydownbody, laydownyourburdens down, layyourbody down." The women rocked faster. They rocked and wailed and Mary felt love flowing in and around her. Louder. Louder. A clapping, stomping, singing roar. Voices layering, shouts counterpointing the melody, the spiritual rose in pitch. When the sound couldn't expand anymore, the women, in unison, stopped.

Unable to help herself, Mary cried out into the stunning silence: "Rise."

The women nodded.

Hildy breathed, "Amen."

23

Their breathing was in sync. Joe watched Gabe crush another cigarette beneath his shoe. The red circle burst into a shower of embers that flared and died on the floor.

"Hardware store be opening soon," said Gabe.

Joe heard him sliding boxes, treading gently through the dark basement.

"Before the war, I worked for Ailey. There's a kerosene lamp here somewhere. It'll give just enough light. Not too much. Shit." Gabe had stumbled. "After work, we'd come down here and play poker. Ailey never liked losing." Gabe struck a match. "Got so Ailey was winning all the colored boys' salaries back. It was let him win or lose our jobs." He pushed stacked crates aside with his knees, exposing a small card table and four chairs. He struck another match. Joe slid into a chair.

Gabe lifted a lantern from beneath the table. He lit the wick, his face iridescent, slick with sweat. "My word, Joe. You look like shit."

"Feel like it." Joe cradled his sore hand.

"Jailbreaks. Much better than your tricks with quarters. I tried rescuing you twice."

Joe chuckled. "I would've waited if I'd known you were coming."

Gabe reached out; Joe stretched his good arm.

"Black magic, Joe. The finest black magic. I'll be damned."

Forearms entwined, they clasped at the elbows. Joe was amazed at Gabe's strength. Amazed at his own swelling pride.

"You're a man now, aren't you? Baby brother has grown up."

Joe ducked his head. "If it means being scared, I'm a man."

"Fear's all right. As long as it's useful."

"Henry told me that."

Gabe released Joe's arm. "Henry was a fine man too. Scared all the time. Maybe too scared. Don't get too scared, Joe. Not scared enough, you're a fool. Too much, you lose control. You hear?"

"I hear," Joe murmured, transfixed by Gabe's face. *He saw bone beneath black skin, ghostly white curving beneath his jaw line, a splash of bone across the forehead, brittle sockets circling warm eyes.* The lantern glared yellow.

"Did you know Tyler died?"

"No," Joe flinched, wondering if Tyler would haunt him too. Come back from the grave, angry and preaching.

"One reason to get the dynamite. Blow the—"

"Who killed him?"

Gabe took another draw on his cigarette. "Mary Keane's brother. A deputy named Lucas. Busted into your house looking for you. The brother—I shot him on your front lawn."

"Hildy," he asked softly. "Is she all right?"

"Yeah. Emmaline, your mother too. All fine. Father messed up some."

Joe couldn't still his trembling. He stared at the fire trapped in the glass. He couldn't have borne it if Hildy was hurt.

"War can be scary. Make no mistake, Joe. This is war. We got to get on to Greenwood."

Joe looked at Gabe's shuttered face. He murmured, "How'd we get here, Gabe? How'd it come to this? I swear I didn't do anything. I didn't touch that girl."

"You're an excuse. It's always been like this. We've always been here—at war in Tulsa."

Joe kept shaking his head, thinking of the train, the rumble out of town. He'd make it this time—*"dream what you need"*—he'd spirit himself to a new world. A man might be afraid; the trick was not to get trapped by it.

"Joe," Gabe said urgently. "Joe."

Joe looked up, thinking Gabe looked younger, vulnerable. *Like a trick of the light, he saw glistening bone—Gabe was a bones man.* Dread settled in his gut. Joe remembered a rail-thin Gabe coming to the porch, asking for Henry, waiting in the front yard because he knew Mother didn't appreciate him in her clean house. Father didn't appreciate him at all. Gabe had been—what? seventeen? eighteen? As young as Joe was now.

"Joe."

"No, Gabe—" The air was heavy; Joe felt disoriented.

Gabe straddled the chair, rattling the table, nearly upsetting the lamp. "Joe, I've got to tell you something. I haven't told any man."

"Don't."

"In case anything happens. Something might happen today—might not have another chance."

"Nothing's going to happen." Joe averted his eyes. First Henry. Now Tyler. Soon Gabe. Joe wanted to scream. He buried his face in his hands. "Dynamite," he whispered. "Let's get the dynamite, Gabe."

Gabe slid his hands along the table's edges. Back and forth. Back and forth. He swiped the dusty surface with his palm. "Sometimes Henry joined me, Ailey, and the rest playing poker down here. Sometimes I'd fold if I thought Henry had a chance at winning. Ailey didn't get so angry when Henry won a few."

"I don't need to know, Gabe. I don't want to know anymore."

Gabe gazed at the flickering light. "Henry thought he knew all about me. Knew all the cards I was holding. Figured I'd fold when he had a winning hand. Do what needed to be doing for him.

"I could've stayed in Greenwood, married Emmaline. Figured how to get around your father. Instead I went to France with Henry. Brother man." He looked up. "I should've stayed."

"Gabe, you don't have to tell me."

"I've got to tell it." Joe heard the pleading in his voice.

Gabe slumped in the chair, chest concave, his Army-issue shirt sticking to his skin. "'How'd my brother die?' isn't that what you asked? 'How'd he die?'" Angrily, he slapped his chest.

Joe caught his breath. "Henry—" *Just beyond the lamp's glow, stood Henry.*

"Was a good man," drawled Gabe.

Gabe's fingers, shaped as a steeple, pressed against his lips. More softly, he said, "Henry died like anyone. Stopped breathing. Body just stopped. Like the man who rolled into you. Blood spurting out of his mouth. Just," Gabe swallowed, "stopped. Legs give way. Fall to the ground. Stopped."

Joe felt trapped, back inside his nightmare. "We need to get to Greenwood, Gabe. We need to get to Greenwood."

"Deal straight up," said Gabe. "I'm going to deal straight up, Joe. You ready?"

Joe peered into the darkness: at the soft shapes, shadows of boxes, oil and farm gear.

Gabe slipped his gun out of his pocket, laying it on the table, giving it a slight push toward Joe. "I'm doing what I have to do. You do what you have to."

Joe lifted his hands up in the air. "I don't mean to do anything, Gabe."

Gabe shrugged. "We all do things we don't mean. 'I'm sorry,' isn't that right? That's what we say, 'I'm sorry.' Henry could be one 'sorry,' son-of-a bitch."

Joe heard Gabe's bitterness, knew Gabe's words would undo what little victory he'd earned.

"Henry'd say 'Sorry I got you into this, Gabe.' 'Sorry I got angry.' 'Sorry I took your money. Cut in on the dance. Drank your liquor. Cheated you at cards.' Sorry didn't stop him from taking."

"Shut up, Gabe."

Gabe arched his brow. "Henry could be a complete son-of-a-bitch. You know I don't lie. You ever known me to lie, Joe?"

"No." He rocked his body. Father said Henry'd cost. Maybe everybody paid. Joe wanted Gabe to shut up; he wanted to disappear. He wanted to plow a fist into Gabe's mouth. "Why?" he asked.

"Why'd I stand by him?" Gabe leaned into the table. "Why'd you? He was your brother, sure. But why'd you love him?"

Henry drew close behind him. Joe could feel his brother's breath on his neck.

Joe added it up: there were more summers when his brother ignored him, than played with him at Lena's River. More days he spent drunk, sprawled in bed. More times silent than talking. Months of Henry's indifference. More times when Joe thought he'd die from loneliness.

"Blood brothers," said Gabe.

"Not enough," said Joe. Saying it, he knew it was true. He'd spent his life making not enough into something more. It wasn't enough to feel loving in the blood. He'd failed his brother; his brother had failed him.

"You were young, Joe. Henry was an arrogant son-of-a-bitch. Wanted everybody to love him. And we did. Henry was an expert at sorry.

"I admired how he didn't make excuses. Just said sorry and took the blame. No excuse. No explanation. Take it on the chin. Later I realized Henry didn't have an explanation. He never thought about why he did anything. He did," Gabe's face twisted, "what felt good.

"Afterwards he was good at sorry. So good you'd start saying 'sorry' for being angry at what he'd done." Gabe clenched his hands.

"Maybe we should just let it go, Gabe. Henry's dead. Let it go."

"That's what I'm doing, Joe. Letting it go.

"Service treated us like dumb animals. When we were given a chance to fight, we had no recon, broken radios, defective masks. Seen men die from gas? Negro men turning purple? I think the Army begrudged feeding us.

"But the French were generous. The women were especially nice, grateful for the Americans. Don't get me wrong. They weren't anybody's whores. They were clawing for life, just like we were. Didn't care about Negro or white.

"The women didn't cringe, didn't slant their eyes, didn't turn from Negro men. Kind, open-hearted women. Knowing we could—they could soon be dead.

"The 369th gave all they had. But it was hard knowing your own officers didn't mind you dying. A woman could restore you. That's what Francine did for me. Despite myself, despite Emmaline, I started to love Francine. Had nothing to do with color. All to do with her being there, wanting to be there. With me." Gabe paused. "Ever been in love, Joe?"

Joe shook his head.

"Better than any magic you can dream. So powerful a man might lie to himself to keep feeling good. Maybe the war blinded us. Blinded me. Spent every minute I could with Francine. After the war, I figured I'd stay.

"Maybe for some it was white pussy. For me, it was Francine. The world was Francine. I could be with Francine and *feel*, feel grateful to be alive. Like water in a desert."

Gabe let his head fall backward. To Joe, he looked headless. A shudder rattled Gabe's body.

"I think that was what bothered Henry. It was about me and someone else, not him. You see him strutting?"

"I see him," mumbled Joe.

"Always the lady's man. Always charming. Always with money for champagne, silk, flowers.

"Henry was the world to me. First, I thought it was about Emmaline. He was worried about his sister being hurt. Now I think it was about him. Couldn't stand me being happy. Couldn't understand, couldn't stand me loving. If I'd married Emmaline, I think he would've been in our mess too. Henry fucked hundreds of women, but never loved one of them. I wouldn't have minded if he'd loved her.

"Every woman I ever met preferred Henry. Better looking, more fun than me. Henry could charm the dead. Henry probably charmed God to let him into heaven."

"What're you saying, Gabe?"

"Don't you know?"

Joe groaned. "No, Gabe. I don't want to hear this."

"You don't have a choice. 'Sides you already know what I'm going to say. You know Henry. You've always known him. Now ain't that right?"

"Why didn't you tell me before?"

"You weren't man enough to carry it. You've been wagging your tail behind Henry so long, you couldn't stop once he was a ghost. You've known all along what kind of man Henry was. But, today, you've shown yourself what kind of man you are. You don't need to be Henry."

"Shut up, Gabe."

"You don't need to be me either."

"I'm not anybody." Joe laid his head on the table.

"You don't mean that," answered Gabe. "Moment ago, you were proud of yourself. Keep that feeling." He stroked Joe's head. "You're strong enough to carry the truth. I know you are."

Joe felt sorry when the gentle weight lifted from the back of his skull. Felt sorry he was here. Sorry Henry was a son-of-a-bitch. Sorry the tale wasn't done.

Gabe rasped: "I found them both sprawled on the kitchen floor. Hadn't even made it to the bed. Clothes everywhere. Francine flat on her back, mouth open, ugly in sleep. Henry, on his stomach, his hand on her breast."

"I'm getting the hell out of here, Gabe. Out of Tulsa."

Gabe went on, relentless. "I started kicking Henry telling him to get the fuck up. Francine clawed at me, cursing. Liquored up, the both of them. I got some good punches in. Henry never once hit me. I just stopped. Francine tried to cover herself with her slip. Henry was still on the floor, cross-legged, his balls hanging, his face swelling up.

"I asked 'Do you love her? Do you love her, goddamnit?' Henry said: 'Thought you wouldn't mind.' I kicked him in his side. Henry fell over, his legs curled up like a baby. He lay there laughing. At me? Himself? I don't know.

"'Do you love her?' I demanded. Henry stared right through Francine: 'I don't love anybody.' Francine cursed, started battering Henry. I reached to catch her. But she righted herself: face pinched, hands flailing, screaming: 'You said you loved me—*amour—t'aime moi.*' Called us both niggers. Didn't sound right with her accent. Such fury. At Henry. At me. *Niggers.*"

Joe stood. "I don't want to hear anymore, Gabe. Greenwood needs defending, then I'm gone." He clutched the lamp, turning side to side, the light swaying, arcing across the walls, the stacked boxes. "Where's the dynamite? Let's get what you want, then get the hell out of here."

"Gotta tell you how I killed Henry."

Joe spun around, the light sliced across Gabe's face.

"I killed Henry."

Joe lurched forward. "Don't joke, Gabe."

"Everybody knew what good friends we were," Gabe said dully. "Nobody questioned things might've changed. Duty sergeant put us in the same trench."

"No, Gabe."

"We'd been under fire three days. Sweating our brains out during the day; water flowing out of our damn helmets. Our feet, sticky in thick boots. Nights cold. Shivering, teeth chattering cold." Gabe was breathing heavily.

"I told Henry 'Don't say nothin'. Not a damn thing. Don't say nothin'.' Three days we managed to get along. Three days firing at Germans. Ducking snipers. Hearing the boom of artillery. Shells showering dirt. The trench: miles long, deep and as wide as a grave. All of us told to be silent. Lay low. On the lookout for the enemy trying to breach the line." Gabe was crying. Fat tears rolling, dropping off his face.

"Night came. There'd been a lull. A few hours of quiet: no shelling, no fire. Henry and I standing side by side in our helmets, peering over our rifle scopes. Couldn't see shit. Then, Henry turned to me and said: 'Sorry.' Nothing else. Just 'sorry.'

"I climbed all over him. We fought, grunting. Had to keep quiet. Enemy just over the line. We're scuffling hard. My lip burst. Henry's nose bleeding. We fought sloppy. Sloppy and tired. Hadn't slept. Not doing any real damage. And all I could hear was 'sorry' and see brother man fucking Francine.

"I pulled my knife. Henry knew I was going to kill him. Knew by my eyes. Knew there was no room to reason. I sliced at him. He dived, jerked back. Not much room to go. Pushing him into the corner, end of the trench, end of the line. He couldn't get around me. I lunged and Henry scrambled out of the trench like a rat. He spun around. 'Goddamnit, Gabe.' He was standing straight up when the shell landed. Shrapnel tore through him.

"He didn't moan, didn't cry out. Just kept calling, 'Gabriel, Gabriel.' I crawled on my belly. Another artillery shell went off, a piece of steel ripped into my side. I grabbed Henry's hand and slid him, inch by inch. When I pulled him into the trench, he fell hard, no hands to break his fall. His guts spilled out, blood draining out his mouth, his eyes, nose, ears."

Gabe shook his head. He wiped his wet face. "Then he stopped."

Joe gripped the table's edge, to keep from falling. "You said he told you he loved Mother. Told you to help me find Lena's bones. You lied to me, Gabe."

Gabe didn't answer.

Joe thought about smashing the lamp, burning them alive. Thought about shooting Gabe in the eye. Thought about falling, laying on the floor until Ailey found him and carted him away, like a good nigger, to be lynched.

And there, across from him, sat Henry. Handsome, charming Henry looking ready to play poker. Deal the cards. Joe laughed, hysterical, thinking he'd play poker with all his dead relatives. Tyler. Tyler's father. A whole line of Samuels. Joe groaned.

"I'm sorry," muttered Gabe.

Joe almost punched him. Gabe looked worn, pathetic in his old uniform. Four years, Gabe had been holed up in his shack with nothing. No family, no love. Henry was just as pitiful. A damn ghost wandering Tulsa. Trying to get Joe to stand in his place.

Both men were asking forgiveness. Trying to help him now. Both men were his brothers.

"Come on, Gabe," he said softly. "Got to get to Greenwood. Folks needing us."

"That's it?"

"Yeah. That's it." Joe extended his good hand. "Samuels men have always been selfish. Time we stop. All the pain in the world isn't ours."

"I believe that," Gabe smiled grimly, clutching his hand.

Henry nodded.

"You see him?"

Gabe turned, looking at the empty chairs. "I don't see anybody."

"Must mean he's forgiven you. 'Cause I see him. He's there."

"Henry?" asked Gabe.

"He's smiling. A big smile. Like a cat that ate a mouse." Joe handed Gabe back his coat. "Come on, let's get the dynamite." *The lamp glowed brighter.*

Gabe sighed. "I figure we can blow the Ambrose building. Destroy a good part of Main."

Joe imagined the hotel, revolving door, the elevator cage, and the shine boxes, all collapsing down in dust and smoke. "No, Gabe. We'll defend Greenwood, not attack Tulsa."

"Okay, lieutenant." Almost joyful, Gabe slapped Joe's back. "A few sticks for defense. Is that all right?"

"Yeah, that's all right."

Gabe rummaged among the boxes.

Melancholy gripped Joe. In his mind's eye, he kept seeing his dream. Greenwood burning. Him cuffed. *Will*, he needed to remember that. *Will.*

Joe looked at his brother. *He could see Henry, glowing almost, outlined against the jumbled boxes of hardware.* Joe felt angry, furious he hadn't known his brother. Betrayed because what he now knew was so ugly.

"Isn't it time you left?" *Henry didn't say a word.* Joe stepped forward. "Go on, Henry," he whispered. "I don't need you any more. I know where I'm headed." *His brother shrugged. A train whistled.*

Joe reached out, touching the space where his brother had been.

24

Joe jerked awake, lifting his head off his chest, and remembered where he was: Mt. Zion.

He peered out the church window down the slope of Greenwood Avenue where Gabe said the men would come. "They'll have to charge uphill, head on. One advantage we've got." The street lay silent, empty of children playing stickball, women hanging laundry. Halfway up the hill, two overturned cars served as a barricade.

They'd been waiting for hours. For a sound, a tremor. A movement just beyond the trees. Joe couldn't see anybody yet, but they'd be coming. Gabe said so. He checked for the tenth time that the .38 was still loaded, that he had the safety off, that he was ready to shoot it. He'd never shot anything before—not even squirrel or rabbit. He kept seeing the man Gabe had shot—collapsing, rolling into his legs, eyes open, blood gurgling from his mouth.

Joe realized he'd slept without dreaming. No nightmare. No haunting. Maybe he'd outrun his dread. Maybe saying good-bye to Henry, he'd laid his fear to rest.

Joe looked around the church at the men—some rested on pews, some cleaned, recleaned their hunting rifles, some paced before the altar. Maybe thirty men in all. A dozen were perched in the balcony and choir loft, aiming at the roadway below. Others, like him, were on the ground floor staring through the church windows—stained glass pictures of Christ wrestling with the devil, Christ riding a donkey over palms, Christ hanging from the cross, Christ rising into the heavens. Sunlight streamed through the glass, wrapping the men in fractured hues of red, blue, and yellow.

Bill Johnson fussed, "Preacher won't like us busting his glass."

"Preacher won't mind, long as we save Greenwood," said Lying Man. "Everybody knows you bought these windows so Preacher wouldn't preach against your cinema show."

"I was being Christian," said Bill, indignant.

"Complaining about your pocket," smirked Ernie.

"I'm not complaining," said Bill, tapping his finger on Christ's robe. "I'm just saying Preacher won't 'preciate us ruining his church. Each window cost ten dollars. Eighty total."

"You charge ten cents for the movies. Last movie I saw—what's it called? *Queen of Arabia*—was awful," answered Chalmers.

"I like Chaplin. Man's funny," said Sandy.

"When you going to get movies with Negroes?" asked Chalmers.

"I don't make movies. I just show 'em," said Bill, slinging himself into a pew.

"I'll pay fifty cents if I can see a Negro," piped rheumy-eyed Herb. "A dollar for a Negro woman."

"Where you going to get a dollar?" barked Chalmers.

"You can barely see," muttered Ernie. "Shotguns no good for a half-blind fool. You expect to hit something? No, that's out of the movies."

"Naw, it ain't," said Bill. "My movies are realistic."

"Realistic, hell," said Chalmers. "Movies are filled with fools. I'll bet you—"

"Nothing. Absolutely nothing," hollered Nate, disgusted. "Everybody loses."

The men hushed.

"Talking about movies with the Klan rising. Johnson's worried about breaking glass. Go on out the door, Bill. Shoot a rifle in full view.

Get yourself killed. But if you want to shoot from inside, you've gotta shoot through stained glass."

Bill Johnson squirmed. Ernie stuck out his lip. Tater swept the aisles. Joe felt sorry Nate had stopped the men's talk. For a moment, it'd felt like the barbershop. He'd felt almost peaceful.

Nate stood sentry at the door.

Lying Man patted Bill's shoulder. "We'll save what we can, rebuild later."

For hours, the men watched Greenwood Avenue, barely saying a word. Clarence had brought his medic kit and sheets from Nadine's closet. Herb and Sandy helped cut bandages. Chalmers filled canteens of water, distributed ammunition. Ernie practiced aiming at a candle. Lying Man blew softly on his harmonica. From time to time, somebody would ask, "Why aren't they here? If they want to fight, why aren't they here?" The sky was cloudless, blue. Waiting pricked and frayed at their nerves.

"White men must be chicken-hearted," clucked Herb.

Nate exclaimed bitterly, "White man's playing with us. Wants us humbled. Fighting on his time."

Lying Man snapped at slow-witted Tater.

Joe checked his gun a dozen more times.

Hildy had sent her love, dry clothes, and baskets of food. Seeing the church fill with Greenwood men, Joe knew, for now at least, he couldn't be anywhere but where he was. Gabe, like the best general, had stationed lookouts and snipers throughout Greenwood. A band of men were at Booker T.; others, at Standpipe Hill. But Zion was the main battlefield. "Strategic," said Gabe. "They have to take Zion to take Greenwood."

On the far left, Sandy was perched in front of Christ walking on air; old Mr. Jackson rested on the stairs; Tater, who'd set aside his broom, passed out sandwiches. Chase, his belly resting on the sill, peered beneath the glass donkey. Last month, his wife had a baby girl. Joe smiled. Chase had gained more weight than his wife.

Joe felt guilty he'd put the town at risk. He shouldn't have rode the elevator. Never mind that that woman had seemed as lost, as hurting and needy as him. He'd only thought about wanting to be treated like a man, about wanting to ride because he'd been told not to. Regardless of what happened today, he couldn't help thinking he caused it. Risked fine men, each one of them somebody's father, brother, son.

Shuffling backward, unrolling a coil fuse, Gabe entered the church. "There'll be some surprise for 'em, hey, Nate?"

"Won't be nothing compared to me shootin' 'em from the roof," countered Nate. "Those white men'll be ducks in a pond."

Price hollered over the balcony. "I can outshoot you ten to one, Nate. Got the sniper's pin to prove it."

"Nothing beats hitting squirrel," said rheumy-eyed Herb. "A man's a big target. Now a little bitty squirrel—"

"There you go again, Herb," said Ernie. "Last time you killed a squirrel was ten years ago."

"A man can't help getting old," nodded Herb from his pew.

"Some of us were born old," said Lying Man, blowing a mournful chord. "Been old all our lives."

"Old is better than dead, don't you think, Gabe?" asked Sandy. "Old is better than dead."

Heads lifting, the men stared. Something about Sandy's tone challenged.

"Guess so, Sandy," said Gabe calmly. "But I wish I'd grabbed more dynamite." He walked toward Joe. "Dynamite works better than bullets."

Joe watched Sandy approach, hands deep in his pockets, shoulders slumped forward. "I still don't know about this, Gabe. Maybe we'd best go on home."

"We already decided," snapped Nate.

"I know. But I've been thinking some more, standing here waiting—"

"Oh, Lord," said Nate.

"Don't take His name in vain," said Clarence, looking over his wire rims. "This is His house."

"Maybe they won't be coming," Sandy hurried, his voice high. "Maybe they don't know who was at the jail. Maybe they'll just let it be."

"You ever known a white man to let it be?" asked Nate, smacking his fist into his palm. "'Sides, we already argued this out."

"That's right," said Gabe, gazing at the men. "We all decided this was the best course. The best way to defend Greenwood."

"But what good are we doing here?" asked Sandy. "Mt. Zion ain't going to save us. They'll send more and more men."

"You're a coward," said Nate.

Sandy made a fist. Gabe stepped between them. Joe couldn't help thinking it'd be an uneven fight: Nate, big enough to bust through a door; Sandy, small-boned, aging.

"Ain't fair, Nate," said Ernie. "Ain't fair. Sandy's a Buffalo soldier. Fought cavalry. Spanish-American War."

"Negroes didn't just learn how to fight in the 369th," added Herb. "There was the 24th. My Daddy joined after the Civil War."

"I'm not a coward, Nate," said Sandy, softly, shoulders squared. "Nothing wrong with wanting to live."

Lying Man slipped behind him. "That's right, Sandy. Nothing wrong with wanting to live."

Sandy flushed with relief. "Thanks, Lyman."

The men gathered around, faces calm. Yet Joe knew by their eyes, there was something at stake. Another battle being decided right here.

"I mean I haven't done anything," said Sandy. "Minding my own business. Sleeping in my own bed. Chalmers running over to my house saying Joe's in jail."

Joe stiffened.

"And here I am thinking, today I'm going to die in this church." Sandy looked up at the balcony, at the men on his right and left. "If I go home, I might be left alone. But if I stay here—" A few men behind him nodded.

"Get the hell out, Sandy." Nate lunged for Sandy's collar. Gabe restrained him, twisting his arms in their sockets.

Nate raged, "In the war, they called us cowards. You're a coward, Sandy. Never thought I'd be ashamed of a Greenwood man."

"It's fair perspective, Nate," said James, stepping forward. "Fair for a man to consider how he uses his life. None of us did anything wrong."

"I hear that," mumbled Ernie.

"It's my fault," said Joe, moving center. "You're right, Sandy. No sense dying 'cause of me. It's my fault."

"No, it's not," said Lying Man.

"Joe!" cautioned Gabe.

"No, I mean it, Gabe. It's my fault. I'll give myself up."

"It's no more your fault for breathing," argued Lying Man. "For living. *Being.* Just is," he raised his voice so every man could hear. "It could've been any one of us. Sandy," his voice soothed, "nothing wrong with wanting to live. But you've been living long enough to know a white man only has to look at you, to have an excuse to kill you. Now, ain't that right?"

Sandy studied his shoes.

"Ain't that right?" Lying Man asked the gathering men. Some men murmured assent, some stared ahead, baleful. Clarence said, "Amen."

Herb complained, "Fifty-eight. Been a nigger all my life."

"That's my point," bellowed Lying Man. "How many white men see us without thinking nigger? Even a Negro soldier can't get treated equal."

"I can't see you, Lying Man," a voice called.

Lying Man stood upon a pew. "Since soldiers came home, things haven't been right."

"Truth is they never were right," said Price, leaning over the choir railing.

"Only been getting worse," said Nate.

A ceiling fan whizzed above Lying Man's head. He was splashed with color. The altar cross towered behind him. Joe knew Lying Man was comforting them.

"Hasn't it always been that way?" asked Lying Man. "Blink an eye and another colored man's been picked up. Run out of town."

"They tarred Bobbie's boy," said Ernie.

"Has anybody seen young Jim?" asked Clarence. "Every Christmas his momma cries. He's been missing for two years. Went out to chop a pine."

"Killed my dog," said Tater, who rarely spoke. "Shot Dempsey. Said he was on Ambrose land. Shot him six times." Eyes wet, he went back to sweeping.

"Burned a cross in front of my store," said Reye, "'cause I didn't want to buy overpriced feed from Ailey. Now I buy anything Ailey wants to sell."

Men nodded. Some fingered their guns; some crossed their arms over their chests.

"Greenwood's been safer than most places," said Lying Man. "Safer than Chicago. Huntsville. Baton Rouge. We've been lucky. Tulsans're content 'cause folk's making money. Oil bubbling out of the ground like magic. Plenty of work for Negroes: hauling, lifting, cleaning. Samuels has more money in his bank. Folks can afford Bill's picture show. I got folks wanting styling, instead of just a shave and a cut."

Joe thought Lying Man was working his own magic. Words, like hands, were gathering the men's souls. Joe swayed, feeling Lying Man's power.

"Being Negro is serious business in America. Make no mistake—this is payback because us Negroes," Lying Man slapped his chest, "we built a community. Thrived. We didn't gamble or liquor our money away.

"This is payback because we sent our men to war—"

"And some came back," interjected Nate.

"I hear that," said Ernie.

Lying Man looked upward, then at the men pressing forward. His voice quieted. "Greenwood has to choose. Maybe we could give them Joe. Maybe they'd be happy with six, a dozen of us. Burn our houses. Businesses. Isn't that their way? The Klan has its own seasons. The law is deaf, dumb, and blind when the Klan lynches another crop."

"That's the truth," said Ernie.

"I might keep my shop. Bill, his theater. Reye, his merchandise. Chalmers might keep his home. Things'll go on. Going from bad to worse. Or we can stand. Stick together. Not let them take us one by one. Sandy, you believe Joe's guilty?" demanded Lying Man.

Joe inhaled, waiting for Sandy's verdict.

Head bowed, Sandy reluctantly answered, "Guilty of being colored."

Lying Man smiled grimly. "You know the answer then, don't you, Sandy? All of you," he scanned the room, "know the answer."

"The best sermon never has to be preached," said Herb.

"'Cause it's lived," said Lying Man, his voice arcing high. "That's what we're doing right now. Living it."

"Maybe dying for it," challenged Sandy.

"Maybe," said Lying Man.

"Everybody's got to die sometime," said Nate.

"Been dying," said Ernie.

"There's heaven after," said Clarence.

"You want to know the colored man's heaven?" shouted Gabe, climbing onto the bench beside Lying Man. "It's standing. Standing, right here. Nobody expects anything of a Negro. But I need each and every one of you. Here. Right now."

Men edged closer; others leaned over the balcony.

"I need Greenwood men. Not the boys the white men say we are. Braving war, we're 'boys.' Providing for our families, we're 'boys.' Playing checkers as old men, wise from living, we're 'boys.' I don't see anybody's boy here." Gabe looked straight at Joe. "I see men. Trying to do right. Standing."

"Got to stand," shouted Mr. Jackson, tossing his hat high.

"I didn't stand for Reubens," shouted Lying Man, "but I'm standing now."

"I didn't stand for Henry," said Gabe. "I—" his words trailed. For a moment, Gabe's heartache was exposed, then he said fiercely, "I'll stand for Joe."

"Might as well call me Joe," said Lying Man. "Same difference."

"I'll stand," said Sandy, solemnly.

Gabe stooped, clasped his hand.

"Count me in."

"Me too," said Bill.

"All together."

"I don't mind dying," said Nate.

"Greenwood," Chalmers shouted.

"Greenwood," murmured Joe, caught by the whirlwind, feeling pride swell his heart. The men in the balcony were stomping, the sound deafening; those on the ground floor were whooping, clapping hands. Chalmers grabbed Ernie and spun him around. Lying Man played a lively tune.

"Okay. Okay, okay," Gabe shouted, settling the men. "It's been six hours. Not a good sign. The Klan—maybe the whole damn town—is marshaling some offense. I haven't been to church in a long while. But, today, we can't afford to turn the other cheek."

"God didn't always turn."

"He sent Moses," said Lying Man.

"Well, we got Joe," said Gabe, cracking a smile. "Anymore magic left, Joe?"

Joe looked around at all the brave men. "I've got a few tricks left." He pulled a lit match out of Sandy's ear. "So does Sandy." Sandy scowled. Laughter shook the church. Chalmers slapped Joe on the back. Gabe jumped from the pew and hugged Joe. "Brother man." Joe saw himself reflected deep in Gabe's eyes.

"Here! They're here," yelled Mr. Jackson. "They're here!" He broke the stained glass with the butt of his rifle. Others followed suit. Chunks of colored glass fell onto the floor.

"Hold up. Don't shoot," shouted Gabe. "Don't shoot."

"Damn," whispered Bill Johnson, awed.

Joe gripped the window ledge. Behind him stood Gabe, Nate, and Lying Man.

Gabe whispered, "War's here."

Nate sighed, "They surely hate us."

Lying Man said, "Stand."

Sandy replied, sarcastic, "Nothing like good odds. Don't you think, Gabe? Nothing beats good odds."

Gabe ignored him, ordering, "Wait 'til I give the signal, men. Wait for the signal."

Joe's mouth was dry. Three truckloads of men with guns. "Ambrose Oil" was written on the cabs' sides.

"Damn that's a lot of 'em," said Chalmers.

"Just more ducks for me," called Nate, slinging his rifle over his shoulder. "I'm going to the roof, Gabe."

"Don't shoot 'til they're past the barricade," Gabe hollered as Nate scrambled out the back door.

Joe held his breath as the flatbed trucks began lumbering up the hill. The men looked like they were on a hunting trip. Some were swigging beer. Others were hooting "nigger," jagging bayonets, rifles into the air, calling to friends across trucks. Some wore infantry uniforms, others were still in their Sunday best. Just like this was part of the Decoration Day celebration. Bates, gleeful, in the first truck, waved a confederate flag.

"Come on, come on. A little further," Gabe urged the drivers. "Come on." When the trucks halted in front of the barricade, Gabe lit the fuse. Crackling smoke snaked out of the church.

"Get down." Lying Man tugged Joe.

"Heads up," shouted Gabe, before diving, covering his head.

The church windows shattered. "Goddamn, eighty dollars," cursed Bill.

The blast had lifted the two overturned cars and the first truck clear off the ground. The Greenwood men cheered. Joe heard Nate banging on the roof, screaming, "Go on, Gabe. Go on!"

"That showed them. Goddamn."

The second truck careened wildly, backward, down the hill, bouncing over the curb, slamming into an elm, spilling men about onto the lawn, street, and sidewalk.

The third truck swerved and stopped on the roadside. Men leaped out, charging past the barricade, crumpled metal, and bodies.

"Ready," said Gabe.

Joe checked his gun.

"Aim."

Joe smelled gasoline. Then he heard a whoosh as the truck's tank ignited. Flames shot twenty feet high. Joe ducked his head. Then, looked again. Moans rent the air. Men were on fire: rolling on the ground or else still, unconscious or dead. Bates' flag was a blackened stick. A torched man zigzagged then spun in lazy circles; orange-red flames streaked; he dropped to his knees with arms outstretched; he fell flat forward. Black smoke billowed from the truck. Flesh stunk like grilled meat.

Nauseous, Joe swallowed bile. Mr. Jackson threw up. Chalmers closed his eyes. Lyman called for "Mercy." Gabe watched the flames, unflinching.

"Ready, men."

A dozen white men broke the spell and charged. Screaming, rifles flailing side to side, they ran mightily. Joe marveled.

"Fire," ordered Gabe.

The Greenwood men opened fire.

"For the heart. Aim for the heart."

Joe aimed at the figures, not certain he was hitting anyone. Was this what war had been like for Henry? No time to think or aim, just shooting. Confusion and smoke. He realized his gun was empty. He looked at the Greenwood men, intent, shooting down the enemy, striking back for lynchings, old grudges, and lost honor. Pieces of Christ were on the floor. Tater, tears on his cheeks, fired methodically. Gabe was shooting with two barrels. Lying Man squinted, aimed, repeating, "Mercy." Joe started reloading.

Suddenly, the men gave a great cry. The charging white men turned, running back down the hill toward Tulsa. Greenwood was still theirs.

Except for the bodies, Greenwood Avenue was deserted again. Inside, they whooped and hollered. Tater beat his broom against a pew like a victory drum. "That did it!" "You saw them!" "I got two of them."

Only Gabe failed to celebrate. Joe watched Gabe peer anxiously out the front of the church, then dodge around to glance out the back.

Outside they heard the whine and popping of the truck burning itself out.

Gabe called, "It's not done. Get on back to your windows. They'll come again."

It seemed to Joe the waiting was even longer. The victory was disorienting. Joe wished he was gone. He could see the dead lying in the street. He didn't want to shoot anymore men.

Then he heard the sound of a plane flying low. The sound was irritating as a mosquito. "Reconnaissance," said Gabe. The Greenwood men held still, listening as the plane circled above the church. After a while the plane went away and the men went back to waiting.

Joe was wondering whether Tulsans were so startled by colored men returning fire, they'd decided to give it up, lose the battle, when a rifle shot cracked and Sandy jerked backward, bleeding from his gut, spilling his blood in a hot arc across Joe, the pews, the floor, before falling.

"Sniper!"

"Where is he?"

Lying Man crawled, reaching out to hold Sandy's hand.

"I knew I was going to die," Sandy whispered.

Lying Man murmured, "You'll be fine. You'll be fine, Sandy." Even Joe knew Lying Man was lying. First time ever. Blood drained from Sandy's gut. Joe thought of Henry torn by shrapnel. Another shot. Joe didn't see where it hit. Peering over the window, he didn't see anybody. No one in the street, no one hiding on rooftops.

A third shot and Gabe yelled, "There! In the trees!"

Joe aimed but missed. Nate was still firing from the roof.

"Second wave," called Gabe. "Second wave."

Three carloads of men toting rifles roared up the street. Two were police cars and Joe wondered whether the sheriff had come. They halted at the barricade, the men taking cover behind their cars, truck debris, behind trees. They didn't move. "What the hell are they waiting for?" yelled Ernie. A straining truck shifted into third gear, climbing the hill. "National Guard," said Gabe. The Greenwood men were stunned. "Bastards called the National Guard."

Men in beige uniforms, round helmets, leaped from the truck, fanning out, scattering themselves, belly down in the dirt, rifles aimed at Zion. Some moved from the line of vision, skirting toward the back.

Gabe shouted, "Reye, Herb. Barricade the back door."

"Outnumbered. Isn't that what movies say? We're fucking outnumbered," moaned Chalmers.

Overwhelming odds. Nobody said a word.

Joe swallowed. Time slowed. The Greenwood men seemed to be moving beneath water. Gabe lowered his head to his chest. Chalmers edged slightly forward through the window. Even panicky Ernie seemed to shake his head in slow motion. Joe looked back, Sandy had stopped breathing. Lying Man, slowly, ever so slowly, closed his lids.

The sniper fired again. Nate tumbled from the roof. Joe gasped. Nate landed on the church lawn, flat on his back, arms outstretched, blood pooling around his chest.

Tater was crying aloud. Joe drifted beyond feeling.

The plane buzzed again. The sound was further away, to the west of the church. They heard short pows. Explosions.

"Dynamite," said Gabe. "They're throwing dynamite out of the plane. Barricades mean nothing to a plane."

"We've got to get out."

"Nadine," hollered Clarence.

"Eugenia," called Ray.

Hildy, thought Joe. He thought of his mother, father, Emmaline, but it was Hildy whom he saw and heard, "*We all need loving, Joe.*"

Before the Greenwood men could escape from the church, Tulsans opened fire.

"Shoot, men," commanded Gabe. "Don't fall apart. We've got to stand."

Grimly, the Greenwood men returned fire.

"Be calm. No way we can stop a plane. But we can stop these men," Gabe exhorted. "We've got to stop them if we want to leave Zion, see our families. We've got to stop them if we want to survive."

Smoke rose like fog, outside and inside the church. Some of the whites fell, but more were always coming, marching forward, closer to the church. Joe kept firing at an oak until a man fell, cracking through green branches. For a moment, Joe felt exhilarated, then he saw Mr. Jackson clutch his stomach and sit quietly against a wall; he heard Chalmers screaming, his leg shot apart at the thigh. Ernie collapsed beside him.

"Reload. Shoot," insisted Gabe.

Reload. Shoot. Joe thought he was dreaming; on the periphery, he saw flames. Wind was skipping fire across rooftops. Greenwood was burning and he was helpless, trapped, tied down in Zion.

Gabe clutched his arm. Blood dripped from his fingers.

"Clarence," Joe shrieked.

"I'm all right," said Gabe, dismissing Clarence, pacing behind the line, yelling, "Stand. Reload. Shoot."

Another truck rumbled up the street, past the barricade, loaded with burning straw. The driver aimed it at the church and leaped clear. The truck bounced over the curb, crashing into the corner of the church, crushing Bill Johnson against the wall.

More shots were exchanged. The church got smokier. Men coughed, gasping; eyes stung. Almost a third of the Greenwood men had fallen. But the rest still shouldered rifles, aimed pistols, and fired. Joe realized they were all heroes. Crouching, Gabe pulled Joe and Lying Man toward the back of the church. "Gotta start getting some of us out here."

"No." Joe halted, pushing away Gabe's hands.

"Retreat and regroup, Joe. Someone's got to survive, help the town. You and Lying Man go first."

"I won't run," said Lying Man.

"You've got to. You need to testify." Blood draining down his arm, Gabe tore aside the wood planks stacked against the back door. "Slim. Help me with cover." He looked at Lying Man and Joe. "Do as I say now."

"Let me stay, Gabe," murmured Joe.

Gabe shook his head. "Henry wouldn't want me to."

"Please," Joe begged.

"Your life ain't over yet. Ain't meant to be. You need to care for Lying Man, Joe. Both of you need to care for each other." Gabe pointed his gun at Joe's abdomen. "I want you to go. You hear? I'll shoot you if you don't."

Lying Man clutched Joe's arm. "Come on, Joe."

Gabe angled his head. "Thanks, Lying Man. You understand?"

"If we all go, they'll overwhelm us, shoot us like dogs."

"That's right. Two can squeak by. I'll send us out two by two."

"What about you, Gabe?"

"I've got two sticks of dynamite left. When I open the door, I'll throw one left, one right. Run like hell." Gabe clasped Joe's shoulder. "Slim and I will provide cover. Just run. Don't look back. Ready?"

Reluctantly, Joe nodded.

"Find my wife," said Slim. "Make sure she's all right."

"We will," said Lyman.

"Joe. Tell Emmy I loved her." Gabe lit the fuses, flew open the door, and threw. One, two explosions.

Joe stumbled.

"Run!" shouted Gabe, firing his pistol. "Run."

They ran—Joe behind Lying Man, ducking and dodging. Running like wild men. Running down the slope toward home.

Joe couldn't help looking back. Slim was down, sprawled in the dirt. Gabe was still firing, moving backward into the church.

Flames climbed the church roof. "Don't, Gabe!" wailed Joe.

Gabe waved—Joe couldn't see well—but he thought Gabe was smiling, striding into the burning church, like an angel wrapped in smoke. Overhead, Joe heard the sound of the plane again, like a spirit far off, going someplace he couldn't imagine.

25

Mary felt a kind of happiness, solace. Hearing the women's song, she'd felt her mother's presence stirring. For the first time, she felt her Ma, like Tyler, was properly mourned. Loved. She'd dispelled the memory of her mother going cold, unremarked to her grave. She was a good daughter.

Now she hoped to be a good friend to Hildy Samuels. She sipped warm tea, lulled by the sun as Hildy collected a bowl, flour, lard, and water.

They'd received news that Joe was free. The men were preparing to defend Greenwood: some posted at Mt. Zion, others scattered throughout the town. Mr. Samuels had insisted on driving to his bank. The women had left at mid-morning.

"I should be going," she'd said to Hildy, staring at the black-speckled linoleum.

"Dangerous," Hildy had replied. "Wait 'til folks settle down."

Mary sighed. She'd found grace. She'd never felt the Holy Spirit like she had in Tyler's room, in Hildy's kitchen. Not in Pa's dreary sermons, his grating, "Repent." It lived in the women, in Hildy.

She'd helped Hildy pack food for Joe, for the men at the church. They'd washed dishes, cleaned the kitchen. They'd gotten on their knees and prayed. Mary couldn't help thinking God would listen to Hildy. There'd be deliverance. He'd protect Greenwood. There'd be a new, shining day.

Mary sipped as Hildy hummed, preparing bread for dinner. Brown hands kneading, twisting, turning dough on cool marble. How many times had she done the same thing? And seen no beauty, no grace?

How strange. How luxurious, taking tea and dreaming about building herself a future. Tomorrow, she'd celebrate Joe being safe. She'd look for work selling perfume and rouge. Or maybe dresses, soft and beautiful. No gray uniforms. Or else she'd cook meringues and sell pies. Nothing ordinary like apple or cherry. Rhubarb. Lime. Chocolate cream. She'd take care of herself just fine. No running home to Pa.

Mary licked her lips, feeling the mid-morning sun splashing her lap. Hearing the slap of Hildy's loaves. Smelling pungent yeast. She thought about Allen. He didn't mind a tall, not-so-pretty girl. Maybe she'd get a chance to know him better. She wanted to know him better. He wasn't like Dell. Mary clutched her abdomen, remembering Dell's rutting, repeating softly, "Allen isn't Dell."

She wanted to be caressed. Admired. She wanted, as she'd always wanted, a sweet respite. Someone's touch to ease loneliness. Was that love? Had Ma loved? Mary felt her smile slipping. Maybe she was asking too much, being greedy—expecting love when she'd just started to feel a measure of happiness.

"Hildy, you ever been in love?"

Hildy stopped kneading biscuit dough. "Love?" Hildy wiped her brow with her forearm. "Have you?"

"No."

"I thought I was in love once." Hildy plunged her hands into the flour.

"What happened?"

"Found out my sister loved him."

"Did he love her?"

"I don't know," said Hildy, smacking the dough. "He went to war. Left without asking Emmaline to marry him. He was one of my brother's friends."

"Joe's?"

"No. My brother Henry's. Henry died in the war."

"I'm sorry, Hildy."

Hildy shook her head. "Some men are born restless. If Henry hadn't died in the war, he would've been killed here. Henry told every woman he ever knew he loved her."

"Did you tell the man—"

"Gabriel?"

"You loved him?"

"No. He never looked at me." Sprinkling flour, she patted the dough into a bowl and covered it with a towel. "Gabriel only knew me as Henry's maiden sister. Sometimes I wonder if it would've mattered if I was younger. Baby-face pretty like Emmaline."

"Life's hard on a woman."

"That's the truth. I decided no sense in being soft then. No pretending you can't do, when you can. So it's been a while since I've been kissed." Hildy sat, wiping dough from her nails with a kitchen cloth.

"Did you ever want babies?"

"Joe's my baby. No, I shouldn't be telling that lie. Joe's a man now. That is, if he survives. Eighteen tomorrow."

Mary stared at the leaves in her cup, wishing she could tell the future. But it had to be all right. Everything had to be all right. She peered at Hildy. "Do you think you could find someone else?"

"I might start looking," said Hildy, suddenly deciding. "When I know Joe's safe." She stared at her hands. "But he's got to be a kind man."

"I met someone kind."

"The secret is out," Hildy teased.

Flustered, Mary pushed through the screen door. She inhaled. Last night she'd smelled the roses. She wished she could smell each peony, each marigold bordering the Greenwood fences. Birds glided along the horizon. The street was unnaturally quiet, empty. Mary knew women were inside their kitchens, parlors, trying to remain calm. She thought maybe she was foolish, thinking about love.

"I didn't mean to embarrass you," said Hildy, following her onto the porch.

"You didn't. It just feels funny," said Mary, squinting in the sunlight.

"Saying I met a kind man. I never said that before in my life. Not meaning it the way I did."

"I've never met a kind, white man," said Hildy, staring at the deserted street.

"I've never met a kind, colored man. Except Joe."

"Negro," corrected Hildy.

"Negro." Mary clutched the rail. Tension settled lightly, like Hildy's flour on dough.

Hildy looked at Mary. "How do you know he's kind?"

"He found me, wandering, hurting. He looked out for me, treated me with respect."

"Respect's important."

"Pa never learned the trick of it."

"Neither did my father."

Mary rested her head on the post.

Hildy sighed. "A woman sometimes makes do. That's been my life's surprise. Making do." Hildy shrugged.

"Better than not making do," answered Mary.

Hildy nodded. "See that spire? That's Mt. Zion Church. It'd be a glorious day, if the men weren't at Zion. These streets would be filled with children. Mrs. Jackson be gossiping about who loved whom. Nadine be murmuring about her visions. Eugenia be teasing her. Telling her to play the numbers. Saying eighty-three signified heaven. Sure to win—ten dollars on a quarter bet. You know," Hildy looked at her curiously. "I'm not supposed to know you."

"Yes," said Mary, "I'm not supposed to know you either."

"But knowing you, and if the men weren't at Zion, I'd fix us a lunch and have us sit on the moss by Lena's River. Relaxing, worrying about nothing. Not a damn thing." Hildy closed her eyes. "You ever hear how Lena drowned herself?"

"Yes."

"Over some man?"

"Yes. She wasn't pretty enough."

"I don't believe it. I believe she was beautiful. Don't believe she killed herself over a man. One day I hope to prove it." Hildy stretched her arms high behind her head. Red highlights streaked through her hair; her skin was burnished copper. "One day, I'll prove it.

"Don't anybody know anything about Lena 'cept what had to do with some man. But Lena did things—had to have done things. Cooking, cleaning. Maybe she had the best potato pie. Maybe she sang like an angel. Or danced like one. I know she had a last name. But nobody remembers it.

"Don't know if she was Negro or Indian. Don't even know the year she died. But I know she was a woman—somebody's daughter, sister, mother, maybe. Somebody's friend. Someday, I'll find out. That's my dream."

Sitting on the porch rail, the sun shining behind her, Mary thought Hildy was beautiful. At ease with herself. Mary had a glimmer of how to save herself.

"You got a dream, Mary?"

She swallowed. "I dream about somebody loving me. Arms holding me through the night."

"Not a bad dream."

"I'm spoiled now."

"You believe that?"

"How could Allen ever want me? After Dell?"

"Not too long ago you were smiling. Drinking tea and smiling. Thinking of Allen."

Mary blushed.

"You got another dream, Mary? Another way to be happy?"

"I could be happy with a small house," her voice was soft, tentative. "A kitchen facing east. A porch to shell peas. A friend—a woman friend, to keep me company."

Hildy cocked her head. "You making an offer?"

"I don't know," Mary replied, blue eyes staring into brown.

"You couldn't do it," said Hildy. "'Sides Tulsans wouldn't let either of us."

Mary felt Hildy's withdrawal, how her eyes shuttered, undoing expression.

"If Joe's killed, I'll hate you for the rest of my life."

"I know." Foreboding overwhelmed her; grace wasn't going to be enough. Mary felt like she was being schooled again. Hard lessons were coming. Like oil beneath the soil, she understood she wasn't just Pa's daughter, but Tulsa's.

She'd done the same living as Hildy—wiped a sink dry, washed greens, cooked with fatback boiling in the water. She'd dusted, hung out wash, folded linens, and nights, exhausted, she'd stared at the same moon. She'd known Greenwood existed, but it had been nothing to her. Like Joe, the other colored—Negro—men. Now she knew Greenwood was flowers, pastel homes with sweeping porches, and Hildy.

How naive to think she could be Hildy's friend. Tulsa had drawn the line. Crossing it brought hatred and violence. She'd learned that. She'd always be a danger to Hildy. Just like she'd been to Joe.

Tulsa had drawn a line against her too. Different, but carrying its own pain. She hadn't minded quitting school to care for Jody. No crude fed Pa's crop, and she'd sat, friendless, in the back row, transfixed by giggling heads, hair plaited with ribbons, clean collars, and imitation pearl buttons. "No 'count," girls would snicker, shoving her in the corner, pulling on her gingham dress. "No 'count." Those girls became prosperous men's wives. Poor girls, like her, worked.

Mary straightened, her gaze caught by a man running down the avenue. She leaned over the rail.

"What is it?" asked Hildy, turning to see what Mary saw. A white man, perspiring heavily, mud on his shoes and coat, was running toward the house. "I'll get help," Hildy said.

"No. I know who it is."

"I'm going in the kitchen." Hildy looked back, her face shadowed by the wire screen. "Tell him it's not safe. Not today. Not for a white man."

Mary watched Allen, slow, lumbering like a tired soul. His hair streaked with sweat and dirt, his skin almost translucent, he wove a bit on the sidewalk. Stumbled on cracks in the uneven pavement. Her heart raced a little. She knew if Allen had risked coming to Greenwood, he'd done it on her account. To help her. She felt thankful, sweetly cared about.

She stepped off the porch, her arms outstretched, offering comfort.

"Mary, Mary, Mary." Allen burrowed his face against her neck. "Mary."

"I'm here," she whispered as she would've once to Jody.

He trembled. She could smell his fear, a deep, musky sweat pouring from his body. Tightly, she held on to him, feeling his lungs straining for air. Over his shoulder, she saw the red-stained grass. Across the street, Nadine peeked from behind a curtain.

"It's all right," murmured Mary, fearing his words, relishing the comfort she knew how to give. She wanted to stop time, delay bad news.

"The roadways are blocked. I had—I had to walk. I thought I wouldn't make it in time. I almost didn't make it." He shifted uneasily within her embrace.

"Rest, Allen." She steered him toward the steps.

"I can't. They're everywhere."

"You can."

"It's not safe, Mary."

"Rest."

"You don't understand." Frustrated, he hit the rail. "I can't rest. It's not safe. Courthouse Square looks like a massacre. Mary, Mary. Goddamnit, Mary." He jerked the rail.

She watched him trying to gain control.

He exhaled, tucked in his shirt. He brushed back his sweep of hair. "They busted Joe Samuels out of jail."

"I know." Mary kept still, watching Allen pace. His pocket watch glinted. Sweat creased his collar.

"They found Sheriff Clay handcuffed. Locked inside Joe's cell. Deputies accused him of helping Negroes. Clay laughed like a hyena. Said he was overcome by magic. Ambrose is pissed as hell. Lucas and four others, dead. I saw the bodies myself. Not a single Negro found dead. Ambrose says it's suspicious. 'Nigger mumbo-jumbo. Hoodoo.'"

Mary looked up. Hildy was on the porch.

Allen stopped pacing, his expression bleak. "Ambrose got authorization to call the National Guard."

Mary couldn't breathe, couldn't look at Hildy.

"Mary."

She flinched, feeling guilty. She was the cause of this.

Allen's fingers dug into her arms. "I came to get you out. Couldn't get here any faster. I ran. Had to duck and hide. Travel back roads. I'm sorry, Mary. I'm sorry."

She stroked his brow. "It'll be all right, Allen," she said, trying to convince him and herself. "It'll be all right. Joe's all right. Greenwood's got men defending it."

"Won't work." Allen looked up, but Mary knew he didn't see Hildy. Allen had his own visions. "You should've seen what they did to Reubens. You should've seen."

"Who's Reubens?" Hildy asked, stepping down.

"Reubens. A poor, sweet kid." Allen, arms flung wide, slowly spun. "Crucified him like Jesus. I carried him off the cross."

"What are you talking about, Al?" whispered Mary.

Allen blinked. "*Evil lies close at hand.*"

"Romans 7:21," murmured Hildy.

"Yes ma'am," said Allen. "Romans." He slumped onto the stoop, his spirit drained. "I don't know what they're going to do. But they'll do whatever is necessary. Not just to catch Joe, but to teach Negro people, all of Greenwood, a lesson."

Mary swayed, gripping the rail.

Allen's voice cracked with emotion. "Come with me, Mary. We can start over somewhere else."

"I can't leave yet," said Mary.

He gripped the hem of her skirt. "Kiss me, Mary. Just once. I was so frightened. I'm so frightened, Mary."

Mary kissed his brow. She wasn't certain what she felt about Allen. He'd been very kind. She was grateful.

"Thank you, Mary. Promise you'll leave. Promise—"

An explosion sounded near the church. Tremors shook beneath their feet.

"It's started," said Allen.

Neighbors rushed outside onto their porches. "What's happened? What's happened?" Startled, hollow voices. "Hildy, what's happened?" A cacophony of sound. Children were crying.

Hildy's mother ran out of the house, screaming, "What's wrong? What's wrong?"

Mary pointed at the smoke rising over Zion. The wind swirled dark streams around the steeple. Shotgun fire carried faintly through the air.

Folks congregated in the street, their gaze fixed on the rising slope of the hill. Nadine began prayers. A woman with a green scarf wailed, "Bill." Lilianne, proud and strong like her mother, nonetheless whimpered, "Daddy." Eugenia held her.

Mary felt a fool. She'd thought of Greenwood triumphing, but hadn't weighed the costs. She could see ash falling from the sky, taste the smoky bite blooming in the air.

Silence. Ten seconds, ten minutes, ten hours. Mary didn't know. But there was a lapse in the gunfire, an unnatural silence settling like a shroud. She thought the world had stopped. The Greenwood women were rigid, painfully quiet, even the babies ceased crying. The sky above Zion was red, but overhead, it was still blue. Cloudless and blue. Birds had disappeared; wind didn't stir. Songs, rustling leaves didn't drift from the trees. Even the flowers' scents had dulled.

Mary looked at Allen on the stoop, his elbows on his knees, his hands covering his eyes. Hildy, spine curved, stood before her, near the fence.

Mary murmured, "Let it be over. Let it be over."

From the west, there was a light buzzing, like an army of wasps. Mary shaded her eyes and stared. A dark speck, like a target, appeared on the sun. At first, it seemed suspended. Then, it grew larger; its irritating hum, louder. Flying straight out of the sun came an airplane, glinting silver, soaring effortlessly.

"Mama, look," cried a boy in brown knickers. "Look."

Everyone looked heavenward, watching the progress of the prop plane, swooping, circling over Greenwood. The plane righted itself and flew low to the ground, directly on course to the Samuels' house. Mary could see two goggle-eyed men. Saw one grin clownishly, waving out the window, mouthing "niggers" as the nose of the plane tilted up, up over the Samuels' attic window.

Mary was more frightened than she'd ever been in her life. Shots, faint but distinct, started again at the church. Allen was whispering in her ear. "We've got to get out. Take the train. To Chicago. On to New York."

Mary closed her eyes and leaned against him. His arms closed around her waist. "Come with me."

She didn't think she could go with him. She couldn't imagine herself in Chicago. She saw the plane doubling back. She craned her neck, watching it dip and sway.

The plane was several blocks away when one of the goggled men dropped a stick. It spun like a red baton. Mary was still struggling to find words when Hildy screamed, "No." Allen shouted, "Dynamite." A shattering of earth, wood, and glass flew skyward. Flames leaped. Cries echoed from the neighboring street.

"They hit a house," raged Mrs. Jackson. Nadine called on God. Otherwise nobody moved. They were transfixed by the plane's route, curving right, then flying a straight, smoke-filled line. Two more sticks fell in quick succession.

Mary thought of running beneath the plane's wing, snatching dynamite as it fell. Or else rising like an angel to battle the demon. She imagined Pa flying the plane; Pa insisting there was no place for niggers. Mary ached. She'd caused all this—spread her hurt through Greenwood.

"There's no accounting for evil." Hildy squeezed Mary's arm as she passed. "I'm going to call the firemen."

"They won't come."

Stricken, Hildy and Mary turned toward Allen.

"Look. The plane's bombing a square. Flying the four corners. The fire will move inward, burn Greenwood."

"The whole town will be destroyed," murmured Mary.

"That's their plan," said Allen.

"I've got to try and stop it," said Hildy, racing to the phone.

"The plane's turning," someone cried. "Turning again. Heading straight way. Heading here."

"Run," screamed Mary. "Run."

The crowd burst apart, running crazed. Babies wailed in their mothers' arms. Children tripped, bloodying their hands and knees. Women searched for a place to hide, torn between possibly dying at home or in the street.

The plane's roar was deafening. Mary dashed toward the street. "Dirty bastards. Bastards. Rot in hell." Allen caught her. "Do something," she yelled, struggling, battering Allen. "Do something."

"You can't stop dynamite, Mary. You can't stop men in a plane. I would if I could. But I can't. No one can."

Mary whimpered. She slumped against Allen's chest, thinking she'd stepped inside a nightmare. Pa's hell. Fire and damnation.

The plane terrorized the runners. Some huddled under cars, on porches. Lilianne and her mother ran home. Mrs. Jackson slammed the door on her yellow house. Miss Wright, staring blindly, Leda weeping beside her, insisted her neighbors "Stay calm. Everybody stay calm." Most ran crazed. Two young girls, running like headless chickens, dashed back and forth, up and down the street, trying to outrun the plane. Relentless, the plane dove, lifted, turned, soared back, swooping like a monstrous bird. It dove again. Three times. Each dive, screams pitched higher. Three times, the plane toyed with families. An old man threw his cane at the silver bird.

Dynamite fell on two houses, one painted green, the other yellow.

Mary fell, Allen atop her, as shards of glass and wood shattered over them.

"Mrs. Jackson, Mrs. Jackson," a girl with braids yelled at the burning house.

The fire was dazzling. It bloomed—a hot, roaring flower, Mary thought. The man who'd thrown his cane clutched his chest and sat in the dirt. Hildy hurried to the burning house. A woman pulled her hair, crying, "My home. My home." Nadine, dust-covered, pulled glass from her breasts.

The plane flew on toward Tulsa.

"Water," others shouted. Allen helped form a bucket brigade. Women, their skirts hitched, carried water in buckets, pots, and pans and tossed it on the flames. Hildy sprayed water from a hose. It was useless. The homes burned. A small woman with black curls and an infant suckling, kept repeating, "Who's going to tell Mr. Jackson? Who's gonna tell him his wife died?" She cooed to the baby. "Who's going to tell Mr. Jackson?"

Mary tasted grit in her mouth. She looked at the skyline: Smoke lay heavy over Greenwood now. Gunfire had intensified at Zion. She couldn't hear the plane any longer. Only neighbors struggling, praying to hear the fire trucks' siren and bell.

There was weak breeze, but it was enough. Flames skipped from Mrs. Jackson's roof to another, then skipped again. If the fire trucks didn't come, the entire street, the whole community would be ablaze. Mary's eyes watered. She felt responsible for this evil. She wanted to believe in miracles. But God hadn't listened to Hildy. Mrs. Jackson was burned to nothing.

Smoke billowed, harsh and black, gagging Mary. She saw a man running mightily down the street's center. Like a mirage, he disappeared in another burst of smoke. A roof caved in; a porch collapsed. The flames were traveling. The makeshift brigade was trying in vain to save the intact homes. Allen, face smudged black, used his coat to stamp out fires starting in the bushes. Hildy cried and cursed, raining water on a third house burning from the roof and awning.

Mary peered down the avenue again. A man was running, a gun in his hand, running as if his life depended upon it. The man drew closer. He was barefoot. His shirt was pale blue. She trembled. Through the haze, she concentrated on his face—bruised, swollen along the jaw and side. He was running toward her. Coming closer. Closer.

Mary felt a profound joy. She recognized the look in his eyes—the sweet, direct gaze, the yearning. She lifted her hand and waved. Miracles happened.

"Joe!" she called. "Joe Samuels."

She laughed, wanting to share the glory she felt. She called, loud and clear, "Hildy. Hildy. Look who's here."

Hildy dropped the hose and ran. Embracing, Joe lifted her, spinning, off the ground. Hildy shouted, "Praise be." They rocked, holding one another in the street.

Mary couldn't stop her tears.

Allen came and stood beside her.

She turned, looked at him—his cheeks and ears pink like a baby rabbit. She dusted ash from his hair. His jacket was singed. Her fingertips touched his bottom lip. His eyes, almost colorless, fixed on hers. Allen saw her. Really saw her. Maybe it was enough that he was kind. She didn't have to be alone.

She leaned forward and kissed him. "Al, I'll go. Wherever you want, I'll go."

26

Belly down, Joe and Lying Man hid in the dirt. Zion's steeple was afire and flames swarmed over the truck that had crashed into the east wall.

"What's taking them so long?" asked Joe.

"Don't know," murmured Lying Man.

"They're supposed to come out two by two. Gabe said, 'two by two.'" Joe swallowed, trying to still his anxiety, thinking it must be hell inside the church—thick smoke, burning lungs, the dead mingled with the living.

Joe understood survival. He'd wanted to run when Gabe said "go." He wanted the hell out. But now he felt guilty because he couldn't answer, "Why me?" He hadn't survived because of skill—he'd been spared by Gabe. Told to turn tail like a boy.

But others weren't so lucky. Slim lay sprawled in the dirt. Sandy shot in the gut. Petey slumped dead. Bill Johnson crushed by a truck. But others were still alive—Ernie, Clarence, Herb. Joe couldn't run until he knew they were running too. Gabe had promised they'd be coming. "Two can squeak by."

He heard firing from the church's north side—unsettling, echoing volleys. "Gabe said, 'Two by two.' Gabe promised to send the men out—'two by two.'" *His nightmare was twisting, coming alive in a new way.*

The sky overhead was silent, no roaring engine, no shrill explosions. Joe nervously glanced at the church door, then at the crashed truck, wondering when its gas tank would catch fire.

"Look. It's Tater." Lying Man slapped the dirt. "Tater and Herb." Tater was loping like a scared bear. Herb shot frantically into the trees, running backward, protecting slow-witted Tater.

Joe exhaled, grinned foolishly, "They'll make it. Won't they, Lying Man?"

Tater fell, but picked himself up. Joe cheered, watching Tater stumble-run down the hill, a foot behind Herb. He'd buy Tater a dozen cherry pops. Play checkers all day with Herb, if he wanted.

"Look," called Lying Man. "Price and Jay."

Price's right arm dangled, draining blood. Jay clutched his waist, tugging him like a bale of cotton. Price wouldn't win another sniper's pin. Still, he was alive. *Two by two.*

"Look."

"Clarence and Ernie." Gabe had kept his word. *Brother man.* Joe now knew Gabe was, had always been, a better man than Henry.

"Look," Lying Man repeated, his voice strained.

White men—some robed, some not—were ducking, dodging behind azaleas, juniper bushes, circling like cowboys in a picture show. They carried shotguns, ax handles. Clarence and Ernie were a few feet from the door. "Round 'em up," a hoodless Klansman ordered with fierce pride. "Run," Joe murmured, "Run." There was a barrage of fire.

"Got to help them."

Lying Man clutched his arm. Joe was surprised at his strength.

"No good going back. Got to go forward. Can't go back. Look." Lying Man pointed.

Soldiers with rifles, bayonets flowed from the church's sides. Thin, strutting boys dressed in fatigues, helmets. Moon-faced ghosts. Joe heard Ernie scream as soldiers flung him down, as bayonets threatened his back.

"No retreat," muttered Joe. "No retreat." Tulsa had sent its army, invaded Deep Greenwood. Didn't matter if Joe was innocent. Didn't matter if Greenwood men were defending their homes.

"National Guard," Lying Man cursed. "Uncle Sam appreciates his niggers. Appreciates their valiant dedication to the war. Decoration Day, shit."

Soldiers and Klansmen: some, Joe guessed, were just following orders; some just hated coloreds, some did and felt both. Some were ordinary Tulsans protecting their womenfolk. Joe felt himself stiffening. Felt his skin turning brittle. Felt as though parts of him would fall away, be buried in the dirt.

Clarence almost made it—a man dressed in suit and tie slipped out from a hedge and (like he was hitting a homer) slammed a wood plank into Clarence's face. Joe shuddered, watching Clarence go down like a felled steer. No, like a good nigger.

The church door remained closed. How many were inside? Twenty? wondered Joe. Nonetheless, their choice was no choice—be burned alive, killed escaping, or surrender.

Joe cocked his gun, veered the barrel right, then left. The range was too great. As he thought about firing, guardsmen drew closer to the church. Fire raged, consuming air, both inside and outside the church. Sandy was right—Tulsa had numbers on its side; they'd always win the war. What was Greenwood? A small town where Negroes lived.

The church door opened and black men filed out—weaponless, faces streaked with soot, hands upraised. He saw Guardsmen grab, shove them 'til everyone lay face down in the dust. *No more two by two.* "Gabe?" Joe called, woeful.

Lying Man squatted, drawing a square in the dirt. "I remember when we built Zion. Just enough wood for the frame."

Joe stared at the thick church door. It swung open again. Harry, Ray, Ed, hands up, heads down, ducked under arching flames. Ray was coughing. Smoke rose from Harry's jacket. Ed squinted like a newborn.

"We had a picnic—cobbler, potato bread, corn relish."

Gabe was a bones man.

"Remember we didn't have a town without a church. I can remember sawing wood, nailing, tugging on the rope with a dozen men, Sandy, your grandfather, Tyler, to raise the frame."

"He's not coming out," said Joe, softly. The church's east wall collapsed onto the scorched truck. Greenwood men were hauled to their feet, cuffed and chained.

Lying Man stood. "We've got to go, Joe. Time to be moving on."

Joe stared at the door. Flames peeled the door's varnish, the mahogany stain. He heard troops marching, officers shouting orders, Tulsans taunting as soldiers herded Greenwood men—his friends—into two thin lines. Except for the whine of burning wood, yielding plaster, breaking glass, and the roaring fire itself, no human sound rose from the church. No sound from Ernie, Ray, from the men standing tall, prisoners of war.

"Come on, Joe."

He jerked from Lying Man's reach. Gabe was the hero, he was the coward.

"Got to run."

Joe stared at the closed door; Lying Man tugged. "Come on, Joe. Got to run."

Almost every man he'd loved was dead, dying, or a prisoner. He imagined Gabe in the fiery furnace, deciding to die instead of being taken alive.

"Gabe," he whispered, lifting a hand. "Gabe."

The soil rocked. His knees buckled. The truck in the church wall had exploded. Zion collapsed inwards like cards—roof crashing, sides falling—wood and oxygen fueling a fireball.

Joe swore he smelled burning flesh. No more Gabe, no more Zion.

He hadn't the strength to get up. He wanted to lay quietly in the dirt until the sun bleached his bones. He would have—except Lying Man was raging, cursing, his hands digging into his arms, lifting, pulling him up. "Don't you quit on me. Don't you quit."

He could hear the smaller man's fury; miraculously, it felt like a balm. Gave him something to reach for, to steady his legs and walk. To keep moving until nightfall, when he'd take the train west.

Lying Man led Joe deeper into Greenwood. Around a corner, down First Street and Missouri, down Elm. Homes, gardens, cars burned, smoldering or layered with smoke. Guardsmen hadn't yet infiltrated

Greenwood. But they would. Air attack, then land. They'd march down from Zion.

He'd thought his nightmare had been only about him. But it was Greenwood's nightmare.

A breeze rocked a porch chair. An oak he'd climbed as a boy swayed, inviting. Below it, ripening tomatoes hung ready for picking. But Greenwood would never be the same. Joe knew Lying Man was headed for his shop.

The business district staggered him. On either side of the street, for the length of three blocks, buildings were burning or bombed into rubble and ash. The Dream Time Cinema blazed, its marquee and ticket booth destroyed. A singed Mary Pickford smiled behind glass. The Confectioner's fountain stools tilted at odd angles; the tiled, black-and-white counter had been blown to bits. Reye's Grocers was simply gone. Amazingly, Samuels & Son was unharmed. The barbershop still stood.

Joe looked skyward. No rain clouds, no water to quench the fires. He felt helpless beyond imagining. Felt a sheen of sweat on his skin. The heat was intense. His eyes stung. Air stunk of melting tar, scorched brick. Shards from the barbershop window layered the sidewalk.

Lying Man opened the door and the bell rang clear.

Pomades and sweet aftershave had spilled. Towels, straight razors, red and black checkers littered the floor. Tater's stale pop had dripped red from the counter. Glass speckled the leather chairs.

Lying Man didn't cross the threshold.

Joe got scared, thinking Lying Man had turned to stone, wasn't real any more.

"I'll help clean, Lying Man. Like new. We'll have this place like new."

Lying Man shut the door, the bell tingling. "Best to get home, Joe."

"What about your shop? We can save it."

"No need."

"I don't understand."

"The men from the church are my shop. God willing, they'll survive. Let's go, Joe."

"I dreamed this—"

"Best get home to your family, Joe. We've got to save who we can, where we can."

"No, you don't understand. I dreamed this, Lying Man," he whispered. "All of it. Dreamed it three days running. Greenwood burning. Up in smoke."

"Part of your magic, Joe."

"I don't want it."

The Confectioner's roof caved, showering sparks and embers.

"We've got to get on," said Lying Man. "I'll see about Slim's family. You see about yours."

"Hildy," Joe murmured.

"That's right."

Joe blinked. Lying Man's skin was ashen, covered with wrinkles. His eyes a bit dulled. He wasn't big at all; he barely reached Joe's shoulders. As a boy, Joe'd thought Lying Man was the biggest man in Greenwood.

"When'd you get old, Lying Man?" he asked mournfully. "You've gone and gotten old on me."

"I could say the same about you, Joe."

"Gabe let himself die."

"Gabe's been dying ever since he came home from the war. He chose it, Joe. Don't you choose it." He started walking.

"Why me, Lying Man?" Joe asked, insistent. "Why'd you look out for me?"

"I don't answer fool questions. Need to get to Slim's family," he answered, his pace quickening.

Joe ran after him. "Why me?" He needed some other magic, some missing piece to make him strong.

Lying Man kept walking. "You should know what you're worth, Joe," he lashed out angrily. Joe staggered beside him. "A man should know his own worth. Otherwise, he's not a man. That's why I let you sit up in my window. Hoping you'd find it. Hear it in the echo of the men."

"I don't understand."

Lying Man stopped. "Your dream, Joe. What did your dream tell you?"

Joe closed his eyes, remembering: *himself, charred and screaming. Sparks leaping from his skin, clinging to porch steps, the rooftops of Greenwood. Bursting into showering flames.*

"You've got to figure this out for yourself, Joe. Your dream told you Greenwood's going to burn? Well, it's burning. Zion's gone. By nightfall, none of these buildings will be left. Maybe nothing will be left. And I tell you, Joe, it's never been more alive."

"I don't understand."

"Then I can't teach you."

For the first time, Joe felt as if he'd disappointed Lying Man. He stared at the ash blanketing the road.

"Break the news gently to Hildy that Gabe died."

He looked up. "You mean Emmaline?"

"I mean Hildy." Lying Man shook his head, disgusted. "Just 'cause your eyes are open, don't mean you can see. 'Cause you dream, don't mean it's all coming true. Don't even mean you understood what you dreamed."

Turning his back, Lying Man walked off, blowing his harmonica. Joe knew the tune:

This train's bound for glory.
This train's bound for glory.
This train's bound for glory.
Children get on board.
There's room for many a more.

For the first time, Joe thought Lying Man was mocking him. Maybe he guessed Joe was leaving at nightfall. Else he was playing a truth Joe couldn't understand.

Looking around at the devastation, Joe felt shame welling again. He needed to help. Joe set off running—running, heading back from where he started. Home.

Joe thought he was dreaming. A white woman, shoulders rounded, arms limp, stood in the middle of his street, watching him run. Maybe she was Francine, Gabe's girl. Another ghost come to haunt him. He wanted to run, plow right through her. Knock her down.

He ran faster. Closing in on the woman. Fifty feet. Forty. Thirty. Her features sharpened, her hair darkened against the backdrop of thick smoke rolling over Greenwood. It was the woman from the elevator, watching as fire dried gardens, destroyed what generations of ex-slaves and their children had built. Tyler had run for this land. He wanted to scream, "Look what you've done."

That wasn't fair.

In the elevator, she'd looked so forlorn: eyes and nose rimmed red, her hands shaking as she closed the doors. "What floor?" she'd asked, not looking at him, her chin on her chest. In the tight space, the mirrors duplicated them endlessly. She'd pressed fourteen. Bathroom. Where else would a nigger be going?

"That all right?" she'd asked, looking across at him. The thinnest thread of . . . what? Concern, compassion? Seeing the pain in her eyes, he couldn't help showing his. For a brief moment, they were at the bottom of the well together, trapped in the same cage, needing comfort. A healing touch.

The white woman—what was her name?—was smiling now. The woman pointed, calling his sister's name, "Hildy! Hildy!" Joe looked to the left; his sister ran to meet him. He embraced Hildy, swinging her off the ground. His sister breathed, "Joe, Joe, Joe." He felt Hildy's tears, the strength in her fingers, her faith in him.

"Where's the fire trucks?" Joe murmured, his arm still about his sister.

The Jacksons', Nedicks', Williams', and Bakers' homes were all black and burning.

"Not coming."

Joe turned. It was the albino man from the elevator. The one who'd called him "nigger." What an odd couple he and Mary made. Odder still they'd both be in Greenwood, but Joe was too tired to challenge them. Hildy accepted them; for now, that was good enough. Besides he knew the man was right. Greenwood would be leveled.

Women and children, a few old men stared, demanding something from him. He could feel light hands touching, stroking his sleeves. He shifted nervously. Some had already lost husbands, cousins, friends. He couldn't tell them about the men being chained.

Joe shouted at his neighbors, "Load up. Take food, clothes, money, whatever you need. We're going to caravan out of here. We can't put these fires out."

Dirty, tired women surged, clambered round him. "We'll lose everything, Joe." "Help will come." "We can't give up." His mother was irate: "I won't go." Voices rose steadily; Joe could hear the panic. No one wanted to yield their faith that their homes would be all right.

"Do you think that's wise?" asked Miss Wright, her sister leading her forward.

Joe sighed. "Yes, Miss Wright. If help was on its way, it'd be here."

Clarence's wife, Ernestine, had her new baby wrapped in a shawl. Her son, Dovell, who loved marbles, looked about to cry. Eugenia, her dress singed, looked furious. His mother was thin-lipped and proud.

Joe wanted to gather the women in his arms. Especially the older ones whose skin and hair had thinned, whose spines had gently curved, making them small again, like children. They'd watched over him when he played kickball, chastised him when he'd been headstrong. They'd passed him pieces of pie, candy, jars of iced tea, put iodine on his knees.

"It's safer to go than stay. Few more hours the air won't be fit to breathe."

"Mrs. Jackson died, Joe," said Pauline, pulling on his shirt, her pigtails unwrapping. "Her house fell on her."

"I'm sorry." Joe bent and hugged the small girl.

"Are the men coming?" asked Eugenia.

"Mr. Jackson didn't make it," he offered.

"Mr. and Mrs. Jackson are angels," said Pauline.

"That's right, honey," said Hildy.

"Bless the Lord," answered Martha.

"Are the rest of the men coming? My Ray?" asked Eugenia.

"Was Clarence all right when you left him?"

"Did the men send you here?" asked Leda.

Looking at the taut, strained faces, Joe decided to lie. He didn't want the women to despair. Didn't want to hurt already mourning children. "The men sent me ahead to get you ready. To make sure you're all safe, if they're delayed. But they're coming. They'll all be here." He rubbed his hand over his heart, feeling he'd missed something. Some grace in the women. Some resiliency in their children.

Hildy said, "You have to tell the truth, Joe. You mustn't lie."

Joe looked again at the women. Weary. Afraid. But not brittle. He met Eugenia's gaze.

"Ray was captured. National Guard charged Zion and captured all but four men. Ray was standing when I left."

"Bent but not broken."

"Not broken."

"Clarence?"

"I'm not sure. I saw him go down. He was hit in the face with a board."

Ernestine stooped, hugging her baby and son to her chest.

"Gabe?" asked Hildy.

Joe shook his head. Mary touched Hildy's arm. Joe was amazed Mary knew what he hadn't known.

"Reckless?" asked Hildy.

"Brave," said Joe, averting his eyes, looking at the flames burning beyond the small group. "Gabe burned inside Zion."

"Lord, have mercy," said Miss Wright.

Hildy touched her hand to her throat; he could see her pulse fluttering. Gabe had missed smelling gardenias. Missed knowing Hildy's loyalty.

"He refused to surrender."

"I'll tell Emmaline he died a hero."

Joe nodded.

"Hurry," he urged the grieving women. "Grab what you need. Guardsmen will have us all surrendering. Chained. Go on, now. Load up your cars. Hurry!"

Women who'd lost their homes and belongings helped others—scooping up fat-legged toddlers, guiding frail Miss Wright and Leda. Eugenia aided Ernestine. Lilianne held brave Dovell's hand.

"You need to get your father and Emmaline, Joe," said his mother pointedly. "You need to get them."

"Aren't they here?"

"Father wouldn't stop worrying about the bank," said Hildy. "He was in no condition to go. When he didn't come home for lunch, Emmaline went after him."

"Damn. I'll drive by the bank."

"He took the car," Hildy said, urgently. "Joe, most these women can't drive. How are we going to get them out of here?"

"Help might come soon. Maybe Lying Man, some of the other men."

"What if it doesn't?"

Joe shook his head. "I don't know, Hildy. I don't know."

"I'll help." The albino man stepped forward. "There's some men, cars left here. We can caravan the people first, come back for possessions later."

"Don't trust this man," said Ruth, vehemently. "This woman either. They want us to leave our homes so they can steal everything. A man protects what belongs to him, Joe. That's what your father is doing. That's what Henry would be doing, if he were here."

"Mother, please," Joe tried to explain. "You need to be safe."

"I trust them," said Hildy. "Allen and Mary."

"You're all fools," said Ruth, quietly. "I will be in my house. I will not leave my house." Spine erect, moving as languidly as if she were hosting tea, Joe watched his mother leave.

"Don't worry, Joe," said Hildy. "She'll leave if Father says leave."

Joe looked blankly at Allen, not quite able to focus. But he could feel his own fear rising, taste bitter smoke in his mouth.

"We won't hurt anybody," Allen said. "We only want to help."

Joe felt overwhelmed. He watched his mother enter "the tallest black man's house," freshly painted each year and lavished with his mother's love.

"Joe, I have to tell you—in the elevator, I got scared—that's why I screamed. I'm sorry." Mary's voice was almost inaudible. "I was hurt real bad. Seeing the cuffs reminded me of when I couldn't get away. When I was tied down. By a belt. Bright silver buckle." She turned her wrists over, her skin inflamed and bruised. "A man raped me yesterday. You understand?"

He hadn't had any more roses, his pockets were empty of coins, but Joe'd thought he could make her smile, himself too. Houdini's basic trick—escape from handcuffs. It was all in how you relaxed. The cuffs had caught the light, glinting brightly, reflecting rainbows in the mirrors. She'd started screaming, flailing, fighting ghosts, slapping the cuffs to the floor. Their nightmares had intertwined.

"You understand? How I felt? I thought I wasn't ever going to get free."

He realized how insignificant he and Mary were. For those needing to hate, her screams and his running were all the excuse necessary.

He could decide not to hate Mary. Or Allen. Neither had chased him, jailed him, beaten him. But trusting white people was hard. With the sheriff, he hadn't had any choice. How did he know that by rescuing Father and Emmaline, he wasn't risking Mother and Hildy?

Knowing Greenwood was dying, men *had* died at the church, how could he trust any Tulsan?

"Did you think I was going to hurt you?" he asked. Mary had such sad eyes. Not accusing. Just sad.

"No. I never did, Joe. I never thought you were going to hurt me."

Joe stepped closer. He could see damp, sweaty hair clinging to her brow and throat. "Mary." Gently, he reached out—watching to see if she cringed, felt disgust—giving her time to pull back, giving Allen time to protect this woman, this white woman, Mary, from a Negro man's touch.

Joe laid his palm on her shoulder, feeling the curve of her bones.

Mary smiled.

"Do you still believe in ghosts?"

"Yes, Joe, I do."

Joe wasn't certain his world was real anymore. Wasn't certain he was awake, instead of dreaming. Wasn't certain Mary wouldn't disappear. Everything was an illusion, including trusting these white people. "Help Hildy and Mother. Help Greenwood."

"We will," said Mary.

Joe turned toward his sister. "Can you drive?"

Hildy laughed. "Don't tell Father. I made Henry teach me."

Joe hugged his sister, taking solace from her quiet, "We'll be all right." Breath swept past his ear. "Gabe should've lived. No matter what happens, you live, Joe. Live. Hear me?"

"Get folks to safety. You haven't much time. Get yourself to safety."

Joe walked backward, watching the trio: Allen holding Mary's hand; Hildy standing comfortably beside them. Behind them, smoke and flames. Magic.

"*Brother man.*"

"*Hurry, Joe.*"

He turned and started running.

27

◈◈◈

Joe zigzagged down Archer, leaping from shadow to shadow—hot on Henry's heels, his brother's ghost leading him into war. White men—guardsmen, Klansmen, looters—roamed Greenwood. His home was being conquered. What was built could be unbuilt. Razed by dynamite, by scavengers, by frolicking men torching homes and cars, hunting Negroes.

He saw Jay beaten in his yard. Saw Herb handcuffed and manacled. Didn't matter they'd made it back from Zion's battle. Didn't matter they were defending their homes. The National Guard was rounding up Negroes, prodding them onto trucks like cattle. He swallowed his grief, concentrating on each step, his lengthening shadow, thinking of Emmaline and Father. Hoping they'd already left the bank, escaped Greenwood altogether.

He ducked behind Claire Greene's porch, pressing flat against her ivy trellis, as a pair of white men emerged from her door. They each had rifles: one had a whiskey bottle and a gilt mirror under his arm; the other carried a woman's purse and a handful of pearls. Joe wanted to shoot them. He could do it. Easy. Aim Chalmers' old .38 and fire.

He studied them: one was trying to light a cigarette without dropping his whisky; the other fished out a small roll of bills and threw the purse on the ground. They couldn't have been more than sixteen, standing beneath Mrs. Greene's cascade of flowering azaleas, in their hats and bulky overalls.

What would it matter if he shot them? Squeezed the trigger and watched them fall? There were always more men. He knew that now. Just as he knew he couldn't ambush anyone, shoot them in the back. He knew he wouldn't have made a good soldier.

Cautious, he slipped in the back door, calling, "Mrs. Greene. Mrs. Greene." He smelled lemon wax and ammonia. Claire Greene sat at the table, like a queen, as properly dressed as he'd ever seen his mother. Tendrils had fallen out of her bun; her pearls were gone, but her lace collar lay starched and prim.

"James?" Her eyes flickered.

"Joe Samuels."

"I've heard they've taken James."

"Yes, Mrs. Greene."

"I'll wait here for James. We never had any children. I'll wait here." Her voice slowed like a wind-up toy, running down.

"Folks are leaving. You should go. Mother and Hildy can help you."

"You're a good boy. Raised proper." She folded gloved hands in her lap. "I'll wait here."

Joe stumbled out the parlor, out the back door. He still had to find Father. Heart aching, he knew he would've had to drag Mrs. Greene from her house.

On the steps, he saw another set of footsteps running beside him. Even. Matching him gait for gait.

Joe slipped behind Mrs. Greene's shed and ran down the alley toward his father's bank. Thick smoke cloaked the entire district, rolling in brash waves; he ducked low, eyes stinging, his sleeve covering his mouth, trying not to cough as he ran.

His father's car was parked in front of the bank. Joe's heart sank, he'd hoped for a little luck. The cinema was almost entirely ash. The heat was furious; there seemed little left to steal. But flames had skipped haphazardly. Lying Man's shop was gone now, the barber chairs molten; yet the mortuary down the street and the bank were still sound. Soon looters would brave the smoke and heat. Joe feared they'd all be caught—him, Father, Emmaline—and carted away. Or simply shot and left in the street.

He burst into the bank. "Father! Emmaline!" His words echoed. His feet tapped noisily on marble; the teller's cages were vacant. It was tomblike. No sight or smell of the fire raging outside; nobody depositing their hard-earned two, five, or ten dollars in the bank.

It'd been years since Joe'd been inside the bank, ever since he realized Samuels & Son had meant Henry.

"Father. Emmaline." His father's office was empty; the desk askew, the leather chair toppled. "Father!" There was only one other place to search. He darted down the hall, stopping at the vault's entrance. The door and walls were reinforced metal. Joe banged against the door. He pressed his ear against it. He didn't know what he expected to hear. But he wanted some sign that his father and sister were safe.

"A two thousand dollar door," Father had bragged. "Strong enough to withstand burglary, fire."

The locking mechanism was embedded in a five-inch steel frame. Joe started picking the lock, sighing when the tumblers quickly settled in place. Poor Father. The lock was the simplest mechanism. His vault was only for show.

He shoved open the door. "Father? Emmaline?" Deposit boxes lined the walls and the small safe, which held, Joe knew, over twenty thousand dollars, stood in the far corner. He pushed the door wider.

Father sprawled on the floor, his arm in a sling, his left eye bandaged. He didn't have a jacket. His shirt was unbuttoned; his vest torn. Blood stained his pants leg. He cradled a thin deposit box. Near his head was a pint of whiskey, half-gone. He looked dead, but Joe could hear the whistling, the low rattle in his chest.

"Father?"

An eye opened. "Joe, the prodigal son. I thought you were in jail."

"I've come to take you and Emmaline home."

"I am home. Everything I need is right here." Father lurched, sat up.

"Where's Emmaline?"

"Home with your mother."

"She came to fetch you. She left home headed for here."

Father's eye watered, blinked like a weary Cyclops.

"Guardsmen are catching Negroes. Emmaline might be trapped. Caught."

Father tried to stand. "I'll speak with Ambrose. I have to speak with Ambrose." He stumbled. Joe caught him. "Father." Joe buckled under the weight. He and his father edged toward the floor.

"I'll make this right, Joe. Don't worry. I'll make this right with Ambrose."

His father smelled of alcohol, dried blood.

"Samuels are honorable men. We expect, demand honorable consideration."

"We've got to find Emmaline."

"We've got to take the long view."

"The long view?" Joe asked, astonished. "The long view is that Ambrose hates Negroes. Greenwood's burning. Emmaline's gone. They're burning us out, Father."

Father looked at Joe as if he was crazed. "This is the Negroes' Wall Street. Industry. Progress. No other colored town has our resources. Me and my money. My bank built this street, this community. Negro Wall Street."

"Have you been outside? Your street is burning," said Joe, ruthlessly. "By nightfall, looters will be coming to pick the leavings. Your money will be gone."

"It's secure."

"You think so? That explains why it was so hard for me to break into your vault."

Father pointed. "That safe came from Germany. The finest money can buy."

"If you're dead, folks can take the whole damn safe."

"You don't know anything about how the world works."

"I know you're more worried about money than the lives of your wife and daughters."

"This money *is* their life. You think a man can survive empty handed? Build a family without money?"

"Father, we've got to leave now," said Joe, exasperated. "While we still can."

His father looked at him coldly. "If it hadn't been for you, none of this would be happening. If Emmaline's lost, it's your fault. If Greenwood burns, it's your fault. This destruction hangs over your head. Not mine."

Joe flinched. "Then maybe I should quit, like you. Lie here stinking drunk in the vault while Greenwood burns." Joe picked up the flask.

"Henry wouldn't have caused me this. Now Tyler's dead too."

The whiskey went down hard. "You believe in ghosts, Father? Magic? Miracles?"

"No such thing as ghosts. Magic is how well a man grows his money. Though I might've believed in miracles if Henry had come home living. I am, if anything, a practical man."

"Except that you loved him."

"He was my first son. When he was born, I wanted to build an empire for him. Pass on what rich white men did for their sons. Color is color; a Negro is always disadvantaged. But I wanted a jump start. Something to keep generations of Samuels ahead of the game."

"How could you give away Tyler's land? How could you do that to your own father?"

"Ambrose was going to take it." His voice was pained, rough. "You think white people were any kinder thirty years ago? Ambrose wanted Tyler's land. Over two hundred acres—the land west of Lena's River. Tyler was only interested in wheat. Farming. There was oil on the land. Ambrose knew it. Thought I didn't. One way or another, Ambrose was going to get that land.

"I persuaded Ambrose to buy us out. You want to talk about miracles?" He slapped his knee, started coughing. "That was one. Persuading a white man to pay me for what he'd take anyway. Fifty dollars an acre. Ten thousand dollars with land to spare to build Greenwood, my bank. In exchange for land worth hundreds of thousands.

"It was a good deal. I still had a chance to build a fortune, a future for my son. When the oil struck, I acted so surprised, Ambrose gifted the bank with two thousand dollars." Father laughed, proud of outwitting his enemy. "Ambrose thought me slow. But I tricked him twice." He opened the deposit box.

Joe recognized Tyler's scrawl.

"I came here for the deed." He shook the paper, the silver territory seal. "Ambrose and I shook hands, but I never gave up the deed."

Joe despised his father's laughter. Inside the vault, Joe could almost forget the burning outside. But his father's world was just as ugly. Joe could still see Tyler paralyzed in the bed, calling for his deed.

"How'd you get the deed from Tyler?"

"Ambrose was cocky. Thought he didn't need paper when, any day, the Klan could kill me. Twenty years, I didn't press for any rights. But I spoke to Ambrose about you. I can speak to Ambrose about Emmaline. This paper," he shook the deed at Joe, "is my insurance that the Samuels will always be all right. A man running for governor can't afford scandal."

"How'd you get the deed from Tyler?"

"Tyler?"

"Your father? What'd you do to betray him?"

"I didn't betray him," he scowled. "That's the whole point. I always had the deed right here in the bank. Safe." Father swallowed from the flask.

"How'd you get the deed, Father? What'd you do to get it?"

Father looked perplexed. "I took it, Joe. Tyler didn't understand what needed doing. So, I took it. There wasn't anything he could do about it." He glared at Joe, his one eye red.

Joe was disgusted. He'd been awed by this man. He'd always thought his father powerful, competent. Willful. It certainly took will to steal from your own father.

"We're leaving, Father." Joe stood up. "We've got to find Emmaline. Take care of Hildy and Mother."

"Didn't you hear what I said?"

"I heard. We need the car. Come on now."

"Aren't you going to thank me? Aren't you grateful for what I did?" Holding onto the wall, Father pulled himself up. "When will you realize that Emmaline, Hildy, the whole family's safe? Thanks to my forethought and planning. I just need to get to Ambrose."

"I'll leave without you if I have to."

Father shouted. "Aren't you going to thank me?" He was wheezing hard. "All my life I've worked hard."

Joe thought his father was a sorry drunk. Sorrier still because Joe could see how hard he was trying to stay in control. Trying not to slur, to stay upright and dignified.

"My father died not forgiving me. Henry didn't understand my plan. It would mean something," Father slapped his chest, "if you understood, Joe." He doubled over, trying to catch his breath.

How strange—his father asking for comfort from the son he'd loved least. "I understand, Father," said Joe, "but you've done nothing to keep us safe. You didn't have the power. Ambrose can still kill you any second; he *is* killing you. Everything you've accomplished has been because Ambrose allowed it."

"That isn't true."

"Sleight-of-hand, Father. Men like Ambrose let you think Greenwood existed. A magic word, a stick of dynamite, and *poof*. All gone, Father. Look outside."

"You're lying."

"We've got to help Hildy, Emmaline, Mother."

"You of all people can't help them." His father turned away.

"You're drunk, damn you."

His father looked where Joe had grabbed his arm.

Joe let go, saying quietly, "Come with me. Stay. I don't care. But I need to leave now."

"I'm the one who knows what's best for the family."

"Damnit, Father." Joe could barely contain his fury. He wanted to hit him. He cried out in frustration.

His father tried another drink; the flask was empty. "I'm going to go and see Ambrose. In a minute, I'm going to walk out of here and see Ambrose. At his house, mind you," he said, punctuating the air with the bottle. "I'll be walking in through the front door." He looked back at Joe.

Joe had never seen his father look so unbearably sad. Not even when Henry died.

Lucidly, clearly, Father said, "I would've been a great man, if I was white. Might even have been governor." He slowly slid onto the floor again, his back curved, head bowed, the pint bottle still in his hand.

Joe found himself crying. If *he'd* been white, he wouldn't be running from the law. Greenwood wouldn't be burning. Yet it saddened him to think his father blamed his failures on his color. Joe looked at his hands—a "bit too brown" for his parent's taste. But he'd always felt comfortable in his skin. Just uncomfortable with his parent's hopes.

He'd wanted to be like Houdini, create his own destiny, overcome challenges. *Your magic is far greater than you know.* Joe exhaled, wondering whether his father had ever liked himself.

Perhaps Father was just stating a fact—if he'd been white, he *would've* kept the oil. But building Greenwood meant something too. Maybe meant even more because it hadn't been easy. Father had done wrong, but he'd been chasing his own dream. Joe had to admit Father was due some credit.

Seeing his battered body, the drunken bobbing of his head, Joe felt his father had lost his balance. Surviving had taken its toll. But being down didn't mean he couldn't get up. Joe tried a different tack.

Stooping, Joe gently shook his father. "Thank you, Father. Thank you for saving the family."

"You mean it?"

"Yes. Now we've got to get out of here," he said slowly, deliberately as if talking to a child. "Check on the family. Get to Ambrose."

"Yes, that's right," Father nodded. "The money. We'll need money, Joe." He crawled to the safe.

"Hurry, Father."

"This is the finest safe money can buy." He spun the combination one last time to the right. "Here," said Father, grinning, offering Joe a small money box. "I've got the deed in my vest."

"Good, Father." His father was on his knees, transformed. A happy drunk.

"You've finally got some sense, Joe. Tomorrow, you can help out at the bank."

"I'll help in the bank. Let's move on, Father."

Father reared back. Joe saw himself reflected in Father's eyes. A young man with a gun. Dirty-faced, bruises discoloring his skin. Smoke in his hair and clothes. His father smiled.

"Joseph David Samuels. You're kinder than Henry."

His father's face contorted with bitterness. He threw his bottle, didn't flinch when glass exploded. "I've lost everything." His words were dry, all the emotion squeezed out of them.

"No you haven't, Father. We've got to get home."

Father patted Joe's leg, then his eye blinked, his mouth slackened as he said, wonderingly, "I don't think I can walk. I don't think I can get up."

"Then I'll carry you." Awkwardly, Joe lifted his father, balancing him on his shoulder.

Father was a big man. Joe didn't know where he got the strength; his footfall was heavy on the marble. He concentrated on placing one step in front of another, left then right. Father would end up like Tyler. Bitter because his dreams had been stolen. What would Father think when his bank burned down?

Joe opened the door, letting in a shaft of sunlight. The Dusell was ten feet away. "We're almost there, Father." He stepped onto the pavement. To his left, he sensed movement. He couldn't reach his gun. Shots fired. He lurched forward. He slung his father off his back, into the car's rear seat. Joe climbed in and pulled his gun. Another shot. Joe fired back.

"I winged him. I think I winged him." Joe swung around to his father. Mouth open, fingers splayed wide, blood drained from a small hole in Father's temple. Joe moaned.

A shadow fell across the back seat. A second man. He didn't have time to grieve. Joe grabbed the money box, kicked open the back door, fired twice, and fled.

28

The world was ending.

Hildy scooted behind the wheel, ready to drive Miss Wright and Leda, Ernestine with her baby and son Dovell to safety. Mary sat in the car behind her, Allen in the car behind that. Old Mr. Thompson would drive Lilianne, Eugenia, Pauline and her family. His young grandson, not yet fifteen, manned a truckful of mothers and children. A caravan to freedom. A train to some new promised land.

There weren't enough cars. Folks squeezed tight. Babies fretted. Belongings were left on the sidewalk: a favorite umbrella, a box of baby toys, a prized, stained glass lamp.

Hildy wanted to cry. Homes were collapsing; gardens, wilting. She remembered the Johnsons painting their home a new pastel each spring. The Browns had just replaced shutters. Last week, Ernestine had planted impatiens, in honor of her new baby girl who'd arrived a week early. All gone. All the hard work. All the care. All the memories of making home.

Mother, sullen, outraged by her "traitorous daughter," sat in Mr.

Williams' car with Nadine and Gloria. Hildy knew she'd done right, forcing her mother to go. Forcing her to leave behind crystal, sterling, and clothes. "Only your jewelry, Mother." Already flames licked the porch, climbing the trellis to Joe's attic room. Mother's and Father's pride, "the tallest black man's house," was as doomed as Greenwood.

The air was almost unbreathable. But worse, her family was scattered. Father, Emmie, Joe, out of reach.

Greenwood had become Armageddon. On the hilltop, Mt. Zion had disappeared and the horizon sparkled with cinders, below a blue, dusky sky.

Hildy looked into the rearview mirror and waved. Mary started her engine. Other engines followed and they all began their drive out of Greenwood. She couldn't shake her dread, thinking of white-robed ghosts, of Henry buried in the cemetery, of Tyler, not buried, maybe burning in the mortuary, of Gabe burning at Zion, of Revelations: "*Woe, woe, woe to those who dwell on the earth.*"

Miss Wright comforted Dovell. Beside her, Ernestine cooed, rocked the baby. Hildy said a prayer for her missing family. She pressed harder on the gas. The plan was to get twenty miles outside the city. Twenty miles and a few days for Tulsans to regain their senses. Beyond that, there was no plan.

Ahead of her, she saw another caravan: four trucks looming with lumbering, thick wheels. Behind them police cars and private autos. Dust flew; gear shifts whined. "Jesus," moaned Ernestine, squeezing the baby against her chest. The baby started crying. Miss Wright demanded, "What's wrong?"

As the lead car, her choice was to stop or crash into the oncoming trucks.

Her vision blurred. The car floated, without an engine. She wasn't steering it, wasn't seeing trucks, soldiers framed in the windshield, bayonets piercing the sky. Wasn't seeing Greenwood men manacled like slaves. Fragments of color, shape became solid, more real. She knew not to scream, nonetheless, she did scream, in a place so deep, no one could hear.

A soldier pulled her out of the car. She yelled, "Miss Wright is blind." Miss Wright and Leda were shoved forward, herded with a sobbing Ernestine, and a kicking, screaming Dovell. The men—some guardsmen, some Tulsans—urged the old men and women forward with guns.

Spiritless, Mother leaned heavily on her arm. Hildy stroked her brow, whispering, "Love you." She realized she'd not said it for many years.

She heard someone—*Mary?*—shrieking, "It isn't fair. It isn't fair." When she looked back, Mary and Allen, their cars abandoned, argued with a guardsman.

The men—Mr. Williams, Mr. Thompson, and his grandson—went onto the first truck. She saw Doc Grey and Preacher Martin. She didn't see Joe or Father. On the second truck stood men who'd fought at Zion. She wanted to touch each man's careworn face, comfort the wounded. The men's eyes were shuttered; they held their bodies stiffly, embarrassed their families should see them defeated.

Grief rattled Hildy's bones. Her world was over. She'd never sit in her kitchen at sunset, feet up, with her Bible and tea. Never see the sunrise while she swept down the porch as her kettle hummed.

"Mother! Hildy! Here!" Emmaline stooped, reaching through the slats of the third truck, which overflowed with the press of women.

Mother moaned, shouted, "Emmaline."

Hildy knew she and mother would be in the last truck. She wanted to ask Emmaline about Father—had she seen Joe?—instead, she clasped her hand, said hurriedly, "Gabe's dead," and watched her sister's face crumble, her eyes rush with tears. She hadn't believed Emmaline had truly cared. She'd never understood why Emmaline, if she loved Gabe, had obeyed Father. If Hildy'd been given the choice, she would've flown to him. Would've loved, worked beside him, matching strength to strength. Now she knew Emmaline had loved Gabe after all. Gabe would be well mourned.

The crowd pushed her onward to the next truck. She hollered back, "He loved you, Emmaline. He loved you." But she couldn't see Emmaline's face, couldn't tell if her words had soothed her sister's pain or made it worse.

"Gabe was no 'count."

"You knew nothing about him, Mother."

"I knew enough."

"Not nearly." Nothing about his grace, his loyalty. About the jokes he told waiting in her kitchen for Henry. Or the stories he told about B'rer Rabbit, a child outwitting the wolf, the fox, the sly crocodile. How once, in church, she'd heard him sing with the tenor of an angel.

"Get aboard. Get your butt up." The guardsmen poked her arm with his rifle. She helped Mother, climbed up behind her, then reached back to help Miss Wright, Leda, and all the other neighbor women, until they stood, jostling against each other, steadying themselves on the flatbed.

"Where're we going?" she asked the soldier latching them in.

"You'll know when you get there."

She didn't trust herself to know anything anymore. Just as she'd misunderstood Joe's fears, she'd missed the signs her world was ending.

Had she missed robins gathering on the roof? Missed yeast souring in the pantry? Missed mixed-up breezes, quickly shifting east then west?

She knew she was supposed to trust in the Lord and sing. Yet she couldn't sing her sorrow. A plague had visited Greenwood; God was readying to stand in judgment. She was terrified, not just for others but for herself as well. *The world was ending.* Would she be found wanting? Had she lived well enough?

The impossibility of her love for Gabe lay heavy in her heart. And Joe, whom she loved more than anyone—she could only hope he was on the run out of Tulsa, never to return.

The truck lurched. Hildy braced herself. Mother buried her face in her hands. Miss Wright stared at what she couldn't see. Eugenia slipped her arm about Lilianne.

The truck backed up, reversed its direction. Hildy stared at Greenwood. Perched high, she had a sense of the fire's scale, of shimmering flames moving energetically beyond the power of any amount of water. She saw great smoke to the west: the business district leveled (Father's bank probably gone); another thick cloud where Zion used to be. Flames scoured the east side—in her mind, she saw Booker T. and the nearby row homes where newlyweds first bought, scorched and gutted. By nightfall, in all directions, there'd be orange flames, nasty air, and few, if any, buildings left. Two generations' work undone.

"Let them go. You have no right. Let them go." Mary flung herself at the guardsman on the running board. "Let them go." Her fists barely reached his shins. The truck still in reverse made Mary skip backward to avoid being pulled beneath wheels. The truck turned, righting itself due south. Mary cursed the driver. She ran after the truck, fists flying, battering the soldier's legs, trying to climb aboard or else pull him down.

Hair undone, dress and face filthy, she looked like a witch, screaming, crying, "Let them go." The truck picked up speed. Mary couldn't keep up.

Mary fell to her knees. Behind her a truck screeched to a halt, horn blaring, causing a chain reaction in the other two. No guardsmen would run over a white woman.

"I'm sorry, I'm sorry," shrilled Mary. "This is not right."

Two guardsmen dragged her.

Mary kept screaming, twisting, bucking with her body. "This is not right."

Mary pounded the ground, hollering, "Take me too."

Hildy clasped her arms about herself. The truck rumbled on; wind whipped her hair; she gripped the rail to keep her balance.

Mary, like Greenwood, faded from view. Hildy focused on the sun, squinting, trying to stare directly at it. Her eyes watered. "*I am . . . the bright morning star.*" Revelations 22:16.

Hildy felt a song stirring in her throat, she swallowed it—knowing later she would savor the sound when she could savor the memory of Mary doing right. A white woman saying what Negroes knew, "This is not right."

Hildy sighed. She was traveling down a different road. It scared her. Yet, wherever the truck took her, she knew she'd survive.

The bright morning star.

"Joe," she called and the wind snatched the sound, carrying it back to Greenwood.

29

Joe was on the run again. *Run, nigger, run. The slave catcher come.* No refuge—no home. He'd seen Emmaline, Mother, Hildy hauled away on a truck. Father was dead.

Sun going down. Slave catcher come. Nigger run faster.

No place to go but Lena's. No place to be except the riverbed. He'd bury his grief, his mourning. Bury his memories of Greenwood afire. Bury the money box. Bury himself until the looters and guardsmen were gone. Thought gone. Feeling gone. Bury himself until the moon glowed yellow and it was time to board the train to glory.

Breathing hard, Joe slipped down the embankment. He knew just where to go. Beyond Gabe's shack, under the willow where the river curved, there was a depression where silt gave way and the bottom dropped. Not deep, but deep enough to hide the money and himself. The sun was half in, half out the earth. He ignored Ambrose's fields across the river, the seesawing knell of oil rigs, and focused on stones, the dry earth, memories of him and Henry searching for Lena's bones.

He heard shouts in the distance. Fear pricked at him again. He pushed on, ignoring his tired legs. Until he was out of Tulsa, he feared his dream of being set afire could come true. He slid on his backside into the water. Mud sucked at him. Reeds, dead twigs, and surface algae covered his lower body. He heard shouts, the faint barking of dogs. *Every Negro rounded up.*

His hands tugged at the tree's stiff roots, silt and earth shifted. He used the money box to claw a hole, then shoved the box inside, behind tangled roots. He was satisfied the box would hold even if it stormed or the water receded.

"Over here. Someone's over here."

Joe leaned backward, submerging himself in the pitch black water, anchoring himself with his hands. Algae blanketed him. He heard nothing above the surface. When his lungs ached, he pressed his lips to the surface, sucking in air, then drifted toward the bottom.

Relax. Inhale. His mouth gasped air.

"Over here, I tell you. A nigger's over here."

He stayed under, quelling pain. He felt lightheaded, trapped. Mud soaked his clothes, every crevice of his skin.

He surfaced again, heard footfalls, and quickly dived. Voices faded. Dogs quieted. It was calming inside the muddy water. He rose. Algae trapped the last sheen of sunlight. *Inhale, then sink.* Surface and sink. He heard thrashing in the water. Cursing then gunfire.

Inhale. Exhale. Inhale. Lulled by silence, the firm hold of earth mixed with water, he seemed to stay submerged longer. At each breath, he caught glimpses of the world above—willow branches hanging over the bank; the sky shifting to red dusk; an owl flying overhead.

Surfacing was rhythmic, automatic. He felt weightless, comforted by the riverbed. *Time slowed.* It was quiet inside the water. He reminded himself to breathe.

His pursuers could be anywhere.

"*I have such dreams, Hildy. Terrible dreams.*" Tadpoles wriggled against his legs. *He felt buried alive like Houdini had been.* But he couldn't escape now. Couldn't panic.

In his mind's eye, he saw Tyler's bony body, shriveled and dying. Saw Henry rotting, cushioned inside a steel coffin; saw Gabe, waving, before falling under the weight of flames; finally, saw Father, the hole in his head, eye open, jaw slack.

He started to believe he was nothing but water and mud. There wasn't any Joe Samuels.

Mud filled his ears, nose, pressed against his mouth. Taste, smell, sounds disappeared. Eyes shut, he lay blind, seeing only with his touch. Fingers dug into the muddy silt. He felt snake scales, fish skeletons, dead leaves, and, he was sure, Lena's bones. Letting himself float, he imagined Lena rocking him. She lived inside the riverbed, inside him. Dead, not dead. The sluggish water teemed with life: reeds, fish, minnows, river snakes. Creatures pierced his skin, floated in his blood, stirring his heart.

"You've done it, Joe. Your magic is far greater than you know." He'd reached the dead. Lena's ghost. Yet, not a ghost. Bones cradled him. There was something he was meant to know. Understand. Yearning flooded his soul.

Breathe.

He plunged deeper into the watery soil. Grabbed fistfuls of mud, rock. Tiny insects bit his hands; he concentrated on feeling. His lungs complained, telling him to rise. He burrowed deeper into the muddy cavern. His chest ached. There was something just beyond his reach, elusive. Something in the soil. He grabbed a fistful of muck. Something. Had to breathe. Breathe. Unable to restrain himself, he burst upward through the water.

Other sensations returned. He was cold, hip deep in water. The split moon hung low on the horizon. Pulling on the tree's roots, he dragged himself out of the water. Mud plastered his clothes, weighing him down. He smelled the decaying tang of a river at night, heard its incessant rippling.

To the east, over the rise, Greenwood was gone. He looked west across the river Father had warned him and Henry never to cross. He blinked. *For a moment, he thought he saw glowing, moonlit stalks of wheat. Tyler's acres. His painted fields. Fields painted in oils.*

Oil fields.

Joe grabbed a handful of rocks and threw them across the river. Handful after handful of stones, pebbles, dirt, he threw across the river while he raged, not certain at whom. Father? Ambrose? Himself.

The derricks moved as rhythmic as breathing, up and down. Rhythmic as breathing.

At least the money was safe. He'd get a message to Hildy. She could come get it, take care of Emmaline and Mother.

He began washing himself at the river's edge. He'd look for clothes in Gabe's shack. The 9:45 would be leaving. One last disappearing act—his grand escape from Tulsa.

Joe opened the door to the shack wide, letting in as much moonlight as possible. He moved cautiously; remembering the oil lamp on the desk. The fireplace was empty, the windows still boarded. He lit the lamp and saw a sack, a canteen, and a note. *"Gabe, here's food and clothes for Joe. Keep him safe. Come back to me. Love, Emmaline."*

Joe ate a piece of cornbread, drank clear water.

Underneath the cot were a pair of dress boots and an Army duffel. Joe emptied the bag: a corporal's and a private's insignia (one Gabe's, the other, Henry's); six letters from Emmaline; a box of .45 ammo; and two grenades, their safety clips fixed. The grenades came all the way from France. Joe held the grenades gingerly, thinking Gabe must've had some purpose for keeping them.

Joe slipped the insignias into his pocket. "Henry was a good soldier," Gabe had said. Henry had said the same about Gabe. He slipped the grenades into his pockets too, stuffed Gabe's boots, the canteen, clothes, and food in the duffel.

Joe wasn't certain of the time, but before catching the westbound train there was one last thing he needed to do.

Picking up the oil lamp, he marched out of the shack, down the embankment. Ambrose's drills pumped Tyler's earth, reaching through topsoil to black gold. He set the duffel on the shore, then waded halfway across the river, the lamp swinging in his hand. For Gabe, thought Joe. He pulled the clip, aimed, then let the grenade soar. It sailed over Lena's River, exploding a rig. Metal, dirt, and oil flew skyward; oil streamed out of the ground. For Henry. He threw the second grenade; oil pooled in the new crater.

"Damn." He'd wanted a fiery explosion. He'd wanted it to be easy.

Joe finished wading across the river. Oil gurgled around the twisted rig. Joe hurled the lamp. *Whoosh*—the land was aflame; the plume of orange fire rising into the sky would last for weeks, months.

Joe thought Tyler might be proud.

He sloshed back across the river, like he was crossing the River Jordan. He grabbed the duffel of dry clothes and marched on, liking the music of burning Ambrose oil and knowing all the water in Lena's River couldn't quench it.

30

Looking out Allen's shop window, it amazed Mary that Main looked so normal and calm while a short car ride away, Greenwood burned. Glorious red, yellow, and orange streaked the darkening sky. The Emporium's windows glittered with sequined combs, feathers, elegant dresses. Harper's Grocery advertised lettuce, two cents a head; come morning, there'd be trays outside with peaches, berries, and tomatoes. The street was quiet, deserted as if it were the end of an ordinary business day.

Allen busied himself in the back room; without asking, he'd left her alone. Except for the ticking of clocks, Allen's shop lay hush.

Hush. Such a fine, horrible word. So nice, whispering across the tongue.

Mary had decided to be hush again, to clamp her mouth shut, clasp her knees to her chest, and will the world away. It'd been simpler, less painful being Pa's quiet, good girl.

Hush. Her head lolled. She felt tremors moving through her body.

Her words hadn't mattered to anyone: not the looters she'd shouted at, trying to drive them away; not the guardsmen she begged to put her on the truck with Hildy. A soldier with eyes as blue as Dell's thought she was crazy, proclaiming Joe's innocence. He'd never heard of Joe Samuels, didn't care how the rioting started. She hadn't found Sheriff Clay. But she'd seen plenty of his deputies terrorizing.

She and Allen had taken a car into Tulsa. She'd wept as the Guards imprisoned Greenwood families in the Convention Center. Arms flailing, she'd railed at the men who leveled guns at children, poking, urging them along, railed at the deputies tagging, numbering Negroes, and railed at the sentries who had orders to keep "whites out, coloreds in." An officer had lightly touched her arm. "Ma'am." Tall, earnest, he removed his hat. "They're just niggers."

His words had unnerved her. She'd stopped. Stopped speaking, moving. Just stopped as a new loneliness stole over her.

"Mary. Please, Mary."

Allen had led her away—past trucks unloading dispirited families, past bloodied flatbeds of wounded, past a truck stuffed with dozens of dead Negroes, eyes glazed, jaws slack, headed for mass burial out of town.

She let Allen bring her to his shop because, finally, there seemed no place else to go, nothing else to do.

Lord, she was tired. Clocks measured the seconds, minutes, hours she'd sat before Allen's window. Relentless, the rhythm inspired quiet. *Hush.* She couldn't help thinking she'd failed herself, failed Hildy and Joe.

"Mary? You should eat." Allen set down a tray.

Walking to his workbench, she looked down at the platter. "Never had a man fix me food before."

"I'm not very good at it." Shyly, he ducked his head.

"It's nice." There was cold chicken, biscuits, and peas. A glass of milk. "I wonder if anyone milked the jersey."

"What?"

"I'd finished milking when Dell," she swallowed, "when Dell caught me. I wonder if Pa milked the jersey." Their jersey didn't know about a son dying, a daughter leaving.

"Eat, Mary. It'll do you good."

She tasted the biscuit. "Here. You eat too." She offered Allen half.

They sat beside one another on metal stools. Mary stared beyond brass, gears, canisters, springs, wondering if Hildy's kitchen had finished burning.

"There was nothing you could do."

She shrugged. "I'll always wonder." She set down her biscuit. "I was scared."

"I thought you were brave."

She looked up, thinking Allen sounded like Jody. She'd been thirteen and they'd gone honey gathering. Impatient for the bees to be smoked out, she'd stuck her hand in the honeycomb too soon. She'd been stung good. All the way home, Jody kept marveling at how brave she was.

"I've been a fool," she said to Allen. "All my life I've been a fool."

"Don't say that."

"It's true."

Brows furrowing, Allen clasped her hand. "Marry me, Mary."

She laughed bitterly. "Dell asked me. A dream come true."

"I'm not Dell," he said fiercely.

"No, you're not. I'm sorry."

"You said you'd come with me. Chicago. New York."

Allen reminded Mary of a ghost. His skin was clean again, translucent. She could see blue-red veins beneath his eyes, the jutting of white cheekbone. Smoke lingered in his clothes. "I can't go now. I'm not sure I can do anything anymore."

"You don't have to be sure. Sometimes a little faith helps."

"I don't have any faith."

"I'll care for you."

"I don't want your care," she snapped, digging her nails into wood. Two days ago, she'd thought a man's touch would end her loneliness. Now she knew wishing didn't make it so.

"We don't have to go," he said abruptly, lifting the tray. "You don't have to do anything you don't want."

She listened to Allen moving in the back room, behind the curtain. A little too noisily. She could hear him scraping away food, the fork rattling on the plate, the rush of water. How many times had she done the same? Busy hands hiding rage, sorrow. Her fingers glided across his workbench. The magnifying lamp glowed: such thin wire, tiny springs, small tweezers to pluck the insides of a pocket watch. Sheer cotton to wipe invisible dust. Tedious, delicate work.

She flexed her hands—rough and blunt, made to manage a farm. Allen's lean hands stopped and started time. Busy hands kept a person hush.

"Al?" She didn't hear any sounds behind the curtain. "Al?"

She got up slowly, thinking Allen had seen her for who she was—a plain and lonely woman—but she hadn't seen him.

She ducked through blue curtains. The lamp was off. She saw and heard nothing. She knew the cot was to the right and she imagined Allen there, motionless, mouth turned toward the pillow, breathing lightly, shallowly. *Silently mourning, as if he had no right to breathe, to be alive.* Mary knew that pain—its intensity, desperation. Trying to be hush.

"Al."

Using her hands to guide her, she found Allen, face down. She sat on the cot's edge, laying her hand gently upon his shoulder.

Allen half-moaned, sighed.

"I called Joe a nigger," he said, dejected. "Never even said sorry."

"You never called him that."

"I did. You were unconscious. I never said sorry."

"He must've forgiven you. He let you help his family."

"But I never should've called him 'nigger'. I know better. '*Albino Allen*' knows better." His fist rammed the wall. "'Ugly Allen.' 'Monster Allen.' I know better. Just like I know better than to expect you could care for me. A freak. Goddamned freak." Pulling his legs into his body, he shifted away from her. Mary let her hands fall into her lap.

"You're tired, Allen."

"I'm tired."

"Life's hard."

"Life's cruel."

Darkness enveloped them. Mary guessed she and Allen could shelter in shadows forever, pinching their lives into small rooms, small ways. *Hadn't she learned anything?*

She concentrated on Allen's ragged breathing, the rhythm of her own heart.

She remembered Joe's eyes: his yearning, confusion matching her own.

Hildy said nobody knew anything about Lena. A mystery. All her life Mary'd been a mystery to herself. She'd never envisioned the kind of woman she wanted to be. She'd dreamed a man would find her, tell her who she was.

"Al," she whispered, feeling herself gaining strength. "My voice wasn't enough. I've got to find a way to make a difference. To Greenwood. Tulsa. Something I can do."

In a burst of sound, clocks chimed the quarter hour. Allen remained still.

Mary left, went into the shop where the light was brighter. She blinked. Birdhouses hung upon the wall, pendulums swung. Outside the window, she saw street lamps lit. Evening. She'd leave, find lodging. Tomorrow, she'd find a way to help the Samuels.

"Mary?"

Allen's face was white as alabaster. His eyes were iridescent; his pupils, piercing. His hands hung limp at his sides.

"We should call the Red Cross," he said. "I don't know if anybody's done that. Greenwood folk are going to need food, medicine, supplies."

"Yes." She felt hopeful—Allen wanted her to have her chance. "What about tonight? Do you have blankets for the children?"

"Not more than two or three."

Mary thought of Zion's Sanctified Women. "Is there a church nearby?"

"The First Baptist. Tulsa might not take kindly—"

"I'll convince the women." She smoothed his hair. "Some will be good-hearted."

"Yes." He cupped her face within his palms. "Like you. Some will be like you."

She exhaled. "I—we can stay right here. In Tulsa. Be useful."

"All right."

"Are you sure? I thought you needed to leave."

"There'll be folks sorry for what's happened. They'll want to help Greenwood. Maybe Tulsa will change."

"I'd like that."

"What else would you like?"

Mary heard the question hiding within the question. She looked at him forthrightly, speaking her heart. "Not to be alone in the world."

"Together, we'll promise not to be so alone. Sunday afternoons. On Sundays, we'll get ice cream sodas. What else would you like?"

"I'd like to be friends with Hildy."

Allen nodded solemnly. "And?"

Mary paused, afraid she was asking for too much. "One day, I'd like a parlor for women to call and sit pleasantly."

"I'm not rich but I have a little money set by. We can have a small house." Allen's hand slipped round her waist. "You're trembling."

"Yes. This scares me."

Allen removed his hand. "I can wait, Mary. We've got our whole lives."

Mary's fingers curled around his. "We almost did good, didn't we, Allen? We almost got some families out of Tulsa."

"Almost."

She laid her head on his chest. "I think Joe's safe. In Courthouse Square, I dreamed him flying free." She placed Allen's hand upon her waist. "I still believe in ghosts," she murmured.

"Ghosts. Miracles. Anything can happen. I believe we're going to be happy. I'll make you happy. Look, Mary."

She turned and saw their reflection in the window: her hair dark, his white, their arms entwined.

"I'm taller," she said.

"That you are, Mary. Lovely Mary."

She matched his smile. *Outside, beneath the street lamp, she saw a winged angel.* "Look, Al. Do you see?"

Allen didn't shift his gaze from Mary.

Mary pressed her palms against the pane. "Ma," she murmured into the glass. *The figure twirled, wings outstretched, ascending into the night air.*

"Did you see?"

Allen lightly kissed her nose. "Did I ever tell you about time?"

"Yes," she answered, looking skyward, "you can tell it by the stars."

31

Clay had burned every goddamned bridge there was. He'd called Ambrose the asshole that he was, punched Sully, and thrown his badge into the river. But he didn't feel any better.

He patted the ticket in his jacket pocket. He was getting the hell out of Tulsa.

Staring about the train's platform, it surprised him not many Tulsans were leaving. As though rioting were an everyday occurrence. But then, Tulsa was undamaged. In a few hours, Greenwood's destruction would be total. Controlled burn. Newly virgin land.

He wouldn't be surprised if Ambrose claimed the acres, making coloreds pay to rebuild. And they'd pay over and over again. Every hammer, every nail, every piece of lumber would have to be bought in Tulsa. Trust Ambrose to take care of his self-interest. He'd issue work passes so coloreds could leave the Convention Center. Being locked up wasn't an excuse for being lazy. Tulsans would be outraged if coloreds didn't sweep the ballpark, clean the city's sewer, wash a fat baby's bottom, smile "Yes, sir" to visitors, shine expensive leather, and keep the Henly Hotel's linen service up to par.

Ambrose would be touted a hero, the best choice for governor. A man who cleverly kept niggers in their place.

Clay would be remembered as a nigger lover, a coward.

He didn't care about that. But he should've gotten charges dismissed against Joe Samuels, kept Ambrose in check, prevented Greenwood from burning. He was supposed to enforce the law, keep the populace safe. He'd turned a blind eye to Greenwood just as he had to the murder of Reubens. Now he understood the events were connected. Waver on the law and the stink never faded. Clay didn't think he'd ever shake Lucas' smell of musk, gunpowder, and entrails as he died.

Maybe it would've been different if he could've stopped Lucas. Clay hadn't wanted Lucas to die. Nor Bates or any other man. And for each white killed, a dozen Greenwood men had died.

Clay had seen a truckload of bodies hustled out of town, probably headed for a common pit. Ambrose would want things covered over. Most likely, he'd succeed. Folks might never know how many colored men died.

Clay paced the length of the train, carrying his small suitcase. On board, he'd order bourbons (as many as it took) until the sleeper car rocked him to sleep.

He checked his watch—in ten minutes, the conductor would call, "All aboard." He'd heard there were redwood forests just beyond Frisco. Maybe he'd go walking and let himself get lost. Try to forget about Joe Samuels.

"Don't move, sheriff."

Clay reached for his gun.

"Please."

Clay couldn't stop smiling. "You're a fool to be here, Joe."

"I want on the train." Joe crouched between two coach cars.

"You're likely to be lynched."

"I thought you could help me."

"You helping me climb out of the well, Joe?"

"I don't know about that. Just thought you could give me a helping hand, sheriff." Joe leaned forward out of the shadows.

Clay winced at Joe's swollen face. "I quit being sheriff."

"I guess that means you can't arrest me."

"Tell me, how'd you escape your cell?"

"You left it unlocked."

Clay hooted. "Either you are a remarkable man or I am a complete fool." Clay stooped, opening his bag. "You'll have to let me cuff you. These are yours. I found them in the elevator." The handcuffs opened easily.

"Didn't we try this before?"

"You got a better plan?"

Joe shook his head and Clay felt sorry for him. Joe looked desolate, changed from the boy he'd first picked up in Greenwood. "Is it your birthday yet?"

Joe was surprised. "Yeah, it is."

"An omen then. You made it this far." Clay snapped on the cuffs and scooped up Joe's duffel. Clay was at least thirty pounds heavier than this wiry young man. Yet he thought Joe was more solid, more real than him.

"How do you know I won't turn you in? How do you know you can trust me?" Joe stepped back, suspicious. "I'm sorry, Joe. You can trust me. I was just curious—how you knew it."

Joe lifted his shoulders. "I know you, sheriff."

"Did you know I was going to give you to the Greenwood men? I was coming to your cell to let you go."

Joe stuck out his cuffed hands. "Take me on board, sheriff."

The train gushed steam. The conductor called. Businessmen, couples, traveling salesmen with huge cases surged onto the coaches. "Come on." He pulled Joe by his elbow. Beneath the lamps, Joe sagged, looked defeated. Clay dragged him straight ahead, ignoring the stares, the harsh whispers of other passengers. The conductor was almost running toward him, complaining, "Sheriff, I wasn't informed. I wasn't informed."

"I've been busy. A riot's going on." He jerked Joe closer to him. "This boy's going to Oklahoma City for trial. It's a federal charge now."

The conductor looked bug-eyed behind his spectacles. "I need to call for authorization."

"Sure. Call. You want a riot here at the station? You want to advertise I've got Joe Samuels? Dozens of folks anxious to kill him. Call. You can leave for Frisco tomorrow. Or the next day. After you've cleaned up the mess. After my deputies collect evidence and take statements from every passenger."

The conductor frowned and Clay realized his dilemma. The conductor couldn't put Clay on the colored car without violating segregation. And white passengers would complain about being near a colored, cuffed or not.

"The caboose. I can let you have it as far as Oklahoma City."

"Fine. No need to go farther."

"You got a ticket for that nigger?"

"I don't need one," said Clay. "Neither do you. This is official business." Clay stared hard. Then he swung Joe around and sauntered toward the back of the train. "I can find my way."

Clay was startled by the train's wail. Three short bursts, one long. He exhaled. "I could use a drink, Joe. A drink and a smoke. You?"

"I just want to be gone."

"You will, Joe. Good and gone. After Oklahoma City, we can relax."

Clay laughed to himself—he sounded so positive, so sure of himself. Well, why not? He had done good.

"We're almost home free, Joe."

"Thanks, sheriff."

Clay held back, watching Joe climb the short stairs. "Thanks, sheriff." Joe's words were a balm. Imagine that. Clay felt a great peace. Riding in the back of the train, not certain where he was going, without a job, without much money, he felt lighthearted. He hadn't felt this way since he'd left the service and headed west. Maybe that was still the answer, head west. Maybe he just hadn't gone far enough, hadn't found yet what he needed. He was older, but he wasn't dead.

Clay laughed out loud—he'd escaped Tulsa.

He looked down the track, toward the engine. Two thousand miles to Frisco. Nothing but steel rails embedded in the earth. But, beyond rails, beyond cities and towns, there were still forests, lakes, and open land. Enough for a man to breathe, to walk among cedars, to drink water from a stream.

32

When Henry and Gabe left for war, there'd been a cheering crowd at the station, a band playing marches. Perfumed women handed out cake. Children ran shrieking along the platform, waving flags. The station was quiet now, somber. The air was heavy, humid, stinking of fired coal, mechanic's oil. Smoke drifting from Greenwood. But Joe wasn't complaining. He was breathing and Sheriff Clay was getting him out. A few more minutes, the train would be on its way. He'd figure a way to ride it to Frisco. Hide on the roof or in the baggage car, if need be; pretend he was Clay's prisoner all the way to the Pacific. So far, his luck had lasted.

Clay stepped in front of him, slid open the caboose door. "You ought to leave the cuffs on, Joe. In case anyone comes in."

Joe didn't move. He smelled urine and tobacco juice. The interior was dim, littered with dirty clothes, stale food. There were four unmade bunks. Under the window stood a table full of cards and empty whiskey bottles.

Clay slid a stack of ticket books from a chair. "Sit, Joe." He tried to turn up the lamp. The small flame wouldn't budge.

"Maybe I can find some more whiskey," said Clay. "We can have a drink. To success. To glory. How about that?" Clay was triumphant. Joe couldn't shake a sense of failure though, of something he'd missed. He felt cheated: His nightmare had stopped. He was alive. That should be his triumph. There was a low rattle in the engine, a slight give, a tiny momentum in the wheels.

"I found it." Clay held up a quart of rye. "Railroad crews drink. Riding the rails, going nowhere, back and forth, point to point. Same stations. Almost as bad as being sheriff." He laughed, pouring Joe a glass.

Hands clasped, Joe swallowed. His throat hurt. He knew he was hungry, but he didn't feel like eating. Maybe if he drank more whiskey, he'd be lulled to sleep. He couldn't imagine there were any more nightmares left to dream. The train lurched. *Joe saw movement in the shadows.*

Clay's whiskey spilled. "Shit."

Joe couldn't figure where he'd gone wrong. Steam hissed, billowing outside his window. He felt as lost as before.

"Got another story, Joe?"

"Not the kind you mean." Joe knew stories—Tyler's, Henry's, Gabe's, Father's. *In the shadows, he saw the men's faces, heartbreaking and sorrowful.* The train moved slowly. Clackity-clack. Joe broke into a sweat.

Henry sat on the lower bunk, to the left of Clay.

"I've been decent to you. Haven't I, Joe?"

Joe was startled by Clay's question. He realized for Clay the struggle was over. His own would be forever postponed. As long as he was colored, he'd be running. The unfairness of it gripped him. He wanted to lash out at Clay, have Clay carry some pain.

Clay stretched out his legs, hands behind his head.

Joe was innocent, but he was the one still chained. No justice. Would it be any better in Frisco?

He was tired of running.

Clay hadn't waited for an answer. Joe wished his answer counted for something.

"You count for something, Joe."

Ignoring Henry, Joe took another drink and stared out the window. The station had disappeared, he could see the outskirts of the city passing. The rhythm was steady, the slap-slap of wheels upon the rails. Loneliness haunted him again. Henry was wrong, he counted for nothing. He was no one. Clackity-clack.

Henry was singing, "This train's bound for glory, bound for glory."

"Shut up, Henry, just shut up."

"Are you all right, Joe?"

Joe said nothing. He swayed with the train, vibrations rattling him, making him feel out of kilter. He should be happy, he kept repeating to himself—happy.

"It's harder for you than me," said Clay. "I know that."

"Let it go, sheriff."

"Greenwood destroyed."

"Greenwood ain't dead." As soon as Joe said it, he knew it was true. *"It's never been more alive," said Henry.*

Joe felt himself back in the river—lying in muck, barely breathing, feeling life inside the earth and water.

Folks told about Lena's dying, but, Joe'd discovered, from inside the river, the story was also about living. Searching for Lena's bones was about being, feeling, memory. Just like Greenwood. Just like his memories of Henry. But with Henry, he'd felt only loss and forgotten pleasure. He'd forgotten he'd a choice to grieve and go on. Not run from, but run—arms wide—toward life. Just like he had a choice now. Just like Lena, when she let herself drown, had a choice to get up.

Henry. Tyler. Father. Gabe. They all had choices. Choosing was hard. He understood that. A matter of will. Inhale, exhale. Surviving. Living.

He'd survived and Joe couldn't help feeling a stirring of pride.

"Magic is in the hands, in the head and heart. Wanting to live. Believing in yourself."

Joe stared at his hands, working at the cuffs. He could see bones and veins. His cuffs dropped to the wood floor.

"I don't think that's wise," said Clay.

"I do," said Joe. How could he explain he didn't want to be bound? Not for pretend, not as a magic trick, not ever again.

Clay shrugged. "You ever see Houdini? I did."

Joe saw Houdini now. Sitting in Henry's space. Houdini in button-top boots, black vest, and jacket.

"Houdini leapt into the Hudson. Straitjacket, handcuffs, chains, the works." Clay poured another drink. "It made me feel mortal. He was a fool to take such chances. Like I was a fool for going to war."

Clay cradled his glass against his stomach. Joe could tell Clay was a sad drunk. He felt sorry for him. "Got any friends, family?"

Clay shook his head. "None that care to remember me."

Joe cleared his throat. "I've only read about Houdini in magazines."

"*That's not quite right, is it, Joe?*"

"Ain't that something," said Clay, starting to slur words.

The train rumbled steadily.

"You'll have to tell me how you did those tricks. Amazing." Head bobbing, Clay stared at his glass like it held precious gold.

The ghost changed form—sometimes Henry, sometimes Houdini. Sometimes Nate, Sandy, or Chalmers. In the rattling darkness, nothing was certain. *Gazing at the bunk, Joe saw Henry smile, heard him sigh, "Little brother."* The train curved, heading further from Tulsa. *Houdini stared back at him, eyes focused, challenging.* There was some trick here, some artistry, he'd missed. "*Dream what you need.*" Maybe they weren't ghosts at all—just a dream to counter his nightmare.

"I need another drink," said Clay, reaching for the bottle.

What did he need? Him, Joe Samuels. He needed magic. The impossible, extraordinary. He needed to prove Greenwood wasn't dead.

Deep Greenwood—deep in strife and triumph, deep in suffering and redemption. Greenwood couldn't be dead, not unless every Negro was dead. He remembered his crow's-eye view of the town; how, as a boy, it'd been his glorious kingdom. Pennies from Mr. Jackson. Schooling from Miss Wright. Peach pies from Miss Lu. Lying Man spinning him in the barber's chair. The town gave him love, even, Joe realized, respect.

Joe smiled, feeling his spirit rising. He needed to help Greenwood—and himself—rise from smoke and ash. He understood will and magic.

Deep Greenwood had been created from Negroes' lives. Fine, black magic woven for generations, long before he'd ever read about Houdini.

Tyler had run for the land; his father had built his bank. But they hadn't realized Greenwood was more. It wasn't land or Samuels & Son. Greenwood was the men in the church standing strong. Greenwood was the women singing glory. And Greenwood was still standing.

Joe stood, his legs steady on the swaying floor. "I'm going back."

"Are you crazy? You'll be lynched."

"A Negro can be lynched anywhere. Isn't that what this is about, sheriff? Isn't that why they burned Greenwood?"

"I won't let you go," said Clay, rising.

"You're not the sheriff anymore. You're not even my friend."

"I've been a friend to you Joe," he said, indignant.

"My real friends are back in Greenwood."

Clay blocked him. "I thought you wanted a chance to see Frisco, the ocean."

"I do."

Clay looked pained. "I don't understand."

"Surviving Tulsa is a harder trick than escaping Murderer's Row."

Clay slapped Joe on the back. "Have a last drink."

"I don't need it."

"You're walking into the fire. I don't expect you'll live 'til tomorrow."

"I'll live. I have the will for it."

Clay shook his head. "How come I feel I'm wrong getting the hell out, and you're right? Hunh, Joe?"

"I'm not going back because it's right. It's because of who I want to be. Joseph David Samuels."

"You'd give up San Francisco for Tulsa?"

"No, for Greenwood." Joe slung Gabe's duffel over his shoulder. "Bye, sheriff."

He slid the door open, braced his legs. The train was moving at a good speed. He could see dirt, scrub brush, a velvety darkness. The moon shone on the rails, a silver path back toward home.

"Are you going to be Moses?" asked Houdini.

"No, just Joe Samuels," Joe laughed. The rushing wind snatched his words.

"It's too dangerous," yelled Clay. "Stay, Joe."

"That's right, stay," said Henry. "Stay in Greenwood."

Joe gripped the door frame. He'd use his father's money for wood, nails, and glass. He'd organize the men. Starting with the church—they'd work side by side hammering, sawing, building. One by one, they'd raise the school, homes, businesses.

Greenwood rose before him, shimmering right there on the rails. Lying Man, in front of his bay window, blew his harmonica. Joe smiled, knowing, with certainty, Lying Man wasn't dead. *Spiraling beyond him were dozens of new houses, gardens, shops. Street lamps and porch lights sparkled like gems. Hildy waved from her kitchen. He heard voices calling, "Evening Joe. Fine evening, isn't it?"*

He knew who he was—a Greenwood man.

"Blood brothers, always," said Joe, leaping from the train, soaring, hearing in the thundering wheels, Henry's answer.

"Always."

Author's Note

In a 1983 *Parade Magazine,* I read the headline: "The Only U.S. City Bombed from the Air."

A black-and-white photo, taken in 1921, showed a community burned to ash. The story, no more than a few paragraphs, cited these basic "facts": Dick Rowland, a shoeshine, was accused of assaulting a white female elevator operator. A riot ensued and the National Guard bombed Deep Greenwood, a thriving black community known as the Negro Wall Street. More than 4,000 blacks were interned in tents for nearly a year and given green cards.

The subject haunted me emotionally and intellectually. How and why did blacks migrate to Oklahoma? Why did whites have enough tolerance to allow the black community to establish itself, but not enough tolerance to allow its success? How was it that I'd never heard of the Tulsa Riot? Why was this history suppressed? During my research, I found that both Rowland and Sarah Page, the white woman, were victimized by yellow journalism that inflamed racial tensions. Ultimately, charges against Dick Rowland were dropped—Sarah Page refused to testify.

My novel is an imaginative rendering of the Tulsa Riot. Dick Rowland bears no relation to my character, Joe, just as Sarah Page bears no resemblance to my Mary. As a novelist, I invented characters struggling to define themselves and their responsibilities to their communities. I envisioned a spiritual awakening that sustained the human spirit in a time of crisis. Mary and Joe's humanity is as important in my novel as Tulsa's riot.

When I discovered Tulsa was called the "magic city" during the 1920s, I thought of America's spiritualism movement, Houdini, and the linking of African-American and Jewish traditions in the spiritual "Go Down, Moses." Tulsa, during the '20s, was a stronghold of KKK activism, which included the persecution and lynching of Jews, suspected communists, and pro-labor leaders. The character David Reubens was created as another bridge between Jewish and African-American struggles to escape bondage, and as an illustration that prejudice blunts growth, literally and spiritually.

I hope my novel inspires people to reaffirm that hatred for any reason—race, religion, gender, class—diminishes us all.

For those interested in reading a nonfiction accounting of the Tulsa Race Riot, I highly recommend Scott Ellsworth's *Death in a Promised Land.* In addition, the PBS video "Going Back to T-Town" vividly documents how Deep Greenwood rebuilt itself after the riot.

Acknowledgments

With profound gratitude to Jane Dystel and Miriam Goderich of the Jane Dystel Literary Agency. Thank you for believing. Heartfelt thanks to Peternelle van Arsdale, my brilliant editor.

Thanks also to Claudia Nogueira and Elizabeth McNeil for their research assistance, and to Bert Bender and Judith Darknall for their gracious support.

Love to Jan Cohn for her continuing guidance and wisdom.

Extra special love to Brad, my husband and first reader—*vous et nul autre.*